SEASONS OF AN APOCALYPSE

Apocalypse Summer
Apocalypse Fall
Apocalypse Winter
Apocalypse Spring

Tyler H. Jolley, Mary H. Geis
David J. West, Holli Anderson

SEASONS OF AN APOCALYPSE

APOCALYPSE SUMMER

Tyler H. Jolley
Mary H. Geis

For Keaton, thank you for being my sounding board and for all the brainstorming
sessions that you let me put you through.
And thank you to the 80's for being so rad.

CHAPTER 1

A frantic hand slapped a round portal window, jarring Matt Voorhees awake for the first time in many years. He wiped crusty gunk from his eyes and blinked wildly. His surroundings should have been familiar, though he had no idea how much time had passed. Gray padding lined his oval cryopod and was supposed to give it a calming tone. He tried sitting up, but he only succeeded in tearing the feeding tube out of his belly button.

"Ah!"

Blood pooled in the fresh wound. He shook his head, trying to get his bearings, hand pressed hard against his stomach, his heart beating in his ears. Now unencumbered, he peered out the small viewport. A muscular boy with blond hair and striking deep-gray eyes stared back at him, yelling something and pawing at the lid to Matt's cryopod. Matt pressed his ear against the window.

"What?" Matt yelled. "I can't hear you!"

The boy's jaw slacked; his shoulders rolled forward, then a thin, yellow substance forcefully hurled out of his mouth, covering the window.

Matt jerked back as if he was in the splash zone. His free hand landed on something plastic.

A VHS tape.

His face twisted in confusion. Even in the dim light he could make out at least half a dozen black tapes littering his pod. He tried to suck in a breath, but the air felt thick and old.

"I can't breathe!" Matt banged on the roof, hoping it'd budge. "Get me out of here! Hurry!" He scratched at his neck.

Not even his forceful kicks could jar the lid's seal. His chest heaved with struggling breaths. Sweat dotted his brow.

Thud!

Thud!

Thunk!

Matt peered through the vomit-covered viewport once more. The blond boy held a heavy tree branch like a baseball bat and swung, rattling the entire pod. His tan tank top—official uniform of the Save the Population Project—clung to him. Muscles bulged each time he swung the weapon. Bits of bark and splinters flew off, landing on the view window.

"Yes!" Matt yelled at him. He angled himself to get the most leverage and pressed against the top with his knees. His gut seared with pain.

Matt doubled over, clenching his stomach. Crimson liquid erupted like a volcano. The last time he'd felt that kind of pain, a girl had kneed him in the family jewels.

Saliva gathered under his tongue. His stomach lurched, but Matt swallowed hard. Bile burned his throat like he was drinking fire.

He rubbed a frustrated hand over his buzz cut, smearing his head with blood.

Then the idea clicked.

There had to be a latch somewhere inside the pod.

His hands reached blindly onto the smooth edges. He pulled back the fabric, desperate to find a seam or handle, his only source of light now stained and cracked. Shadows danced across the viewport. Matt shook his head.

"Come on, figure it out!" he said to himself.

The air felt thin, tasted empty, and his vision clouded.

He fell back into his seat and waited for darkness to take him.

A burst of light stunned him, two hands grabbed the front of his skintight uniform, and the blond boy dragged him onto the cool ground.

Before thanking him, Matt asked, "Did we make it? Did we survive the apocalypse?"

CHAPTER 2

"I ain't got a clue," the boy replied. "Get up, you gotta help! There are others."

"Where are we?" Matt yelled.

"Your guess is as good as mine." He held out his hand and pulled Matt to his feet. "Name's Cody."

"Matt." He scanned the area. "What the—what happened?"

In front of him, a green army-issued cargo truck sat cockeyed. Burnt rubber still lingered in the air. Strips of the blown-out tire and shattered pieces of solar panels lay on top of leaves. In the back of the truck was carnage. Like a toppled pile of stones, scratched and dented egg-shaped plastic cryopods spilled out of the canvas-covered bed.

Matt shook his head, taking in the scene. Fully grown, large trees shadowed the heavy layer of pine needles covering the ground.

"Forest?" Matt questioned. "Where are we?"

No answer. Cody was busy arming himself with the thick tree branch he'd used to crack open Matt's cryopod.

"Grab a stick, help me. Could you breathe in there?"

"No, not really," Matt said, still trying to make sense of all of it. "I mean, I guess I don't know. I felt like I was suffocating, but I think I was panicked."

"I don't know how much time we have," Cody said.

"Wait, how'd you get out?" Matt's stomach fluttered.

"Him." Cody pointed. A pair of crushed legs peeked out from under a smattering of pods behind the truck. Just like the Wicked Witch of the East under Dorothy's house. Blood slowly saturated the ground around him. "He got me out and said to help. Then he went to get another pod off the vehicle and then . . . I don't know. I guess they all tumbled. Crushed him. I tried to pull them off, but I couldn't do it by myself. So I opened yours. We gotta save him!"

Before Matt could react, the bile he'd forced down came up without warning.

"There ain't no time for that!" Cody yelled. He waved Matt toward him.

Lightheaded, Matt stood on the opposite side of a pod. "On three!" Matt yelled. "One, two, three." His voice strained on three.

Inside, a girl desperately pounded on the round window. Her muffled screams and tear-stained face begged for a way out.

"Hang on." Matt placed his hand on the viewport and turned to Cody. "We need to get her out. It's too heavy with her in it."

Matt again searched the edge for a latch or handle.

"Back up," Cody said, wielding a branch.

A dirt road next to the truck was lined with large rocks. Matt had seen similar paths for hiking when he was in the Scouts. He ran over and picked up a heavy, smooth rock. When he returned, Cody had busted a hole in the seam and had shoved in two thinner branches to pry it open. It was large enough for Matt to get a proper grip and lift. The plastic groaned under his weight and finally snapped open.

"Thank you," the girl gasped.

"Be still," Cody said. "We need to take out your feeding tube."

Although her hair was matted with sweat, the long black curls reminded Matt of a singer from *before*. *What was her name? She only had one name. Why can't I think of it?*

"Cher," he blurted out.

"Catherine." She wrinkled her nose at him. "Did you just call me Cher?"

"No. I mean yes. Are you okay?" Matt asked.

"I'm so confused. I feel sick. Are *you* okay?" She pointed to his stomach and blood-smeared face.

"Fine. It's fine. Look, you'll probably puke. We both did. Here." He offered her a hand, then slipped on the crushed man's blood.

She screamed. "What is that?"

"We'll fill you in later, but we need to get all of these open," Cody said.

Matt grabbed one side of the empty pod, and Cody did the same and nodded at him. They heaved it like a sack of potatoes and threw it aside, revealing a smashed arm beneath.

"We have to get the rest off him," Matt said. "We have to save him!"

Catherine returned with a bundle of sticks. Her uniform had the number *17* on the left breast of her tank top, same as her pod.

"Okay," Matt said. "Cody, hit that side; I'll use my rock on the other. Catherine, when one of us breaks the seam, put the sticks in and pry it open."

"No," she said. "There has to be a better way."

"Unless you got a better plan, we're gonna do this," Cody said.

Every smack of the rock sent shock waves up Matt's arms and into his spine. He pounded and pounded on the same spot until a hole formed. "Bring me some sticks," he yelled.

Catherine pushed a thick branch into the void and pressed down on the end like it was a teeter-totter. "I've got this. Go to the next one," she said.

Matt looked down at his own bloody wound and said, "Don't forget about the feeding tube."

"I need some help, y'all," Cody called out.

A boy, over six feet tall, stumbled out of the pod. Matt helped Cody slide the final pod off the old man. Long, wiry gray hair a shade darker than his equally long, frizzy beard was matted in the coagulated pool of blood. Coke-bottle lenses had been smashed into his face and were embedded in the skin over his orbital bones. His body looked flat, too flat under his white lab coat. Blood seeped out of every orifice. There was no saving him.

They were on their own.

CHAPTER 3

"He's dead," Cody said.

"Who the heck is he?" Matt asked, putting hands on his hips.

Catherine pointed to the pods. Faces filled the portholes, banging and screaming against them. "There's no time to waste. They're running out of air! Let's figure out who he is later."

"She's right," Matt said. He picked up a new rock.

"There must be a more efficient way to do this," Catherine said.

"If you find a way, let me know." Cody abruptly turned and continued his assault on the cryopods.

Somehow, in all the chaos, Matt hadn't noticed Cody's heavy southern accent until now. A memory of meeting him *before* flashed through his mind. He pressed his palms into his eyes. *No, not now.*

Between people hitting the inside of their pods and the three teenagers breaking into them, Matt was sure they'd draw some attention and, more importantly, help. Next to him, the tall boy Cody had freed stood shell-shocked, holding his gut.

"Grab a rock or a branch," Matt said. "Help us get them out."

"My name is Justin," he replied. He stared forward, unmoving.

Matt pointed to the pile of cryopods in the back of the truck and the ones scattered on the ground. "Fine, whatever, just get something to wedge these open."

Justin's sandy-blond hair stuck to his sweaty forehead. He blinked but said nothing.

"What's your damage?" Matt shook Justin's shoulders, immediately regretting it. Up close, he realized that Justin not only towered over him but was also strong, more muscular than Matt had initially realized. "Snap out of it!"

Justin brushed Matt's hands off him. He dropped to his knees and held his head. "Sorry, I—I'm just a little dizzy."

This time, Matt ignored him and returned to his task at hand. Justin was either going to help or not. But babysitting him wasn't an option. Matt lifted the heavy, smooth rock overhead and brought it down as hard as he could. The humid air didn't satisfy his thirsty lungs as he worked. His fingers bled, but he hardly noticed.

"I got one," Cody yelled.

"Over here! Me too," Catherine said.

"That fast?" Matt turned. "How? Oh man, Catherine, are you okay?"

Blood covered Catherine's hands and feet. It was smeared up to her arms, and splatters dotted her thighs and tan-colored shorts.

"I found a key," she said, "on the dead guy. I knew there was an easier way. Every problem has a solution. I'll unlock, you pull them open."

"Rad," Matt said.

The old man was now facedown. His belt had been pulled free of his body and lay next to him like a dead snake. A small coin purse had been carelessly emptied onto the soft, bloody dirt. Chapstick, a Swatch with a colorful band, and a utility knife were strewn about.

Catherine stepped from pod to pod, locating the inconspicuous lock flush with the plastic. Matt wondered how she had even found it in the first place.

The airtight lid hissed as Matt lifted it. A beautiful girl with blond hair sobbed.

"Get it out! Get it out! Get it out!" She pointed at her stomach.

"Okay, just stay still. Justin," Matt yelled at him, "we need your help, now!"

Matt carefully held the feeding tube. The girl grabbed his arm. "No, not you. Look at your stomach. I can't have a scar!"

"Your belly button is already a scar."

"Don't touch me!" she hissed.

"Then stay still until someone can unhook you!" Matt yelled more forcefully than he'd intended.

By now Catherine had unlocked all but one pod. Justin and Cody had opened most of them and unhooked their respective feeding tubes. *This is going to be Barf City in a few minutes.*

Matt ran toward Catherine. The lush forest and trees caught his attention for a moment, but he turned his focus back to Catherine. She struggled with the heavy lid but had it propped open a few inches. Matt shoved his hand into the void and lifted with all his might.

A small girl with porcelain skin lay in the fetal position; a dark bruise had formed on her temple, her dark-brown hair a sweaty, tangled mess. Matt tugged on her shoulder. The number 7 was embroidered on the left breast of her tank top. He jerked his hand back as if he'd touched something hot, then immediately closed the pod.

"We're too late, aren't we?" Catherine asked.

"No, it wasn't our fault," Matt said. "She's already cold. It was probably from the impact when the truck blew a tire. We couldn't have saved her." *I think.*

By now, most of the freed teenagers had gathered around them.

Catherine turned to the group. "We lost one. It's a damn shame. She lived through the cryofreeze only to die in a car accident. Let it be a lesson to us all. Safety is of the utmost importance."

"Who do you think you are?" Justin asked. "The spokesperson for us? You sure as shit don't represent me. For all we know, you killed her."

"What?" Catherine took an involuntary step backward. "I found the key. I *saved* most of you."

"Not me," Justin said. "That hick did. Hey, hick, where'd you get that accent?"

"Texas." Cody stared at the ground. A muscle ticked in his jaw. "This ain't helping nothin.'"

"Oh, it *ain't?*" Justin crossed his arms, a smirk plastered on his face.

"Look, everyone needs to calm down," Matt said. "Let's all get reacquainted—it's been a minute since we all met, and that was only for a short time before we were cryogenically frozen. Then we'll figure out what to do as a *group.* And yes, Catherine is the one who found the key. If not for her, we'd still be smashing in lids, trying to get you guys out. Who knows if your air would have lasted that long?"

Justin's shoulder's relaxed. Everyone else stared at Matt. *I guess I'm the leader, for now.*

"Um, hello?" a girl called out. "Hey, butt-face, you forget about me? Get me out of here, like now!"

CHAPTER 4

Matt leaned his head back and blinked hard. The blond who didn't want a scar in her scar. He had forgotten about her.

"Can someone please help her?" Matt asked.

"*Her* is Kim," the girl said.

Matt put a palm to his forehead.

"You just left her?" Catherine asked, walking toward Kim.

"She wanted someone else to help her with her feeding tube."

"I see," Catherine said. She reached into the pod. "I'll help you."

"No," Kim said, pointing to a huge guy. "I want him."

The boy lumbered over and gently caressed Kim's stomach. "Me? Little ol' me?" His initial smirk was now a full-on, smug smile.

I bet he used to be a jock.

"Puh-weese," Kim pouted. She actually stuck out her bottom lip.

He bent down and kissed her full lips, then pulled the tube from her stomach. "I never thought I'd see you again." He lifted her up and hugged her, and she wrapped her legs around his waist.

"Get a room," someone said.

"Gag me with a spoon," said another.

"Looks like they don't need reacquainting," Catherine said under her breath.

"Yes, we do. Like, all night long." Kim giggled.

"Okay, let's form a circle," Matt said, ignoring the PDA.

They all wore skintight, tan Save the Population Project uniforms. There was a light-blue number over the breast of each uniform.

"We'll go around and reintroduce ourselves one by one. I'm Matt Voorhees. I'm from—I was from Nevada, and like the rest of you from our cryocolumn, I'm seventeen. Last I knew it was the summer of 1985. I love movies, and I love quoting them even more."

"Voorhees?" a redheaded girl said. "Like from those horror movies?" She scrunched her nose.

"Yes! Exactly. Love that show," Matt said. *Maybe I shouldn't have mentioned my love of movies.*

He nodded for Cody to go next.

"Cody Anderson, Texas. That's where I got my *hick* accent from."

"Okay, okay, sorry." Justin held up his hands. "Maybe we got off on the wrong foot. I was just a little confused at first. Sorry, man."

"Apology accepted." Cody nodded.

"I'm Stacy King," the redhead said. "I obviously have strawberry-blond hair, and it's my favorite accessory." She twisted a frizzy curl. "And if anyone knows how to give perms, speak up, because I'm probably overdue."

"Looks red to me," Kim said.

"It's strawberry-blond." Stacy's eyes squinted, and her lips formed an angry, straight line.

"I'm Victoria Stewart," a petite girl said. She hugged herself with slender arms. Her long black hair was stick straight and cascaded down to the middle of her back. Black eyeliner had been smudged, and it looked like she had been crying. "I'm from Manhattan. My hobbies include getting the hell back to New York. Where are we?"

"I don't know." Matt shook his head. "What else?"

"I also like the arts," she meekly replied to Matt.

"I'm not sure *The Goonies* qualify as 'the arts,' but I think we can find some common ground." Matt offered her a smile.

"Kyle Owens. Hartford, Connecticut." The boy stood confidently, even though he was the shortest male of the group. His black hair was cut short, no-nonsense. "I'm a member of the Young Republican's National Federation. Alex P. Keaton is my hero, and I love to read. I was in the middle of the *Lord of the Rings* trilogy before I was called to go into cryosurvival with my family. So if you've finished the series, I'll ask kindly that you do not spoil it for me."

"Alex P. Keaton? Ha!" Kim laughed. "I'm Kim Baker. Okay, so like, I was and will always be a cheerleader. I grew up in Iowa, but I'm going to be a star in Hollywood. And this beefcake is Rhett." She pulled on his arm. He lowered his shoulder, and she kissed him on the cheek.

"Rhett Young. Washington. The state." He was the tallest of the bunch. Reminded Matt of a less muscular Hulk Hogan. "Would have been class of 1986 if we hadn't gotten frozen. Go Wild Cats! Woo-Woo!"

"Wait, how did you guys meet before this?" Victoria asked. "I mean, it's obvious you have a past."

"We met on the bus, the night before we were frozen. Had to go out with a bang, if you know what I mean." Kim smoothed her feathered hair.

Rhett smirked.

"Ew!" Victoria said.

"I think it's romantic." Stacy swooned.

"Enough of this," Kyle said. "We need to get down to business."

"What business, dork?" Kim asked. "The apocalypse is, like, obviously over. Chill."

"Chill? That's mental," Kyle said. "There's a dead female in a pod and a crushed elderly gentleman who was transporting us. For what? Huh? For what purpose? Where are we, and *when* are we? And where is the cryovault?"

CHAPTER 5

"Don't yell at her!" Rhett stood between Kim and Kyle. His deep voice echoed in the forest.

"Calm down, big guy." Justin placed a hand on Rhett's shoulder, guiding him back into the perimeter of the circle. "How tall are you anyway? Six-six?"

"Yup," he said, upper lip still twitching.

"Well, you got two inches on me, dude. Name's Justin's Lewis. Doesn't matter where I'm from, doesn't matter what I've done. I'm here, I have no fear, and I need a beer."

No one laughed.

Justin clapped once. "Not the response I was expecting. You guys need to calm down. Franky says relax!" He turned to a skinny boy the same height as him. It looked like he had hit puberty late and hadn't had a chance to fill out. "What's your name, kid?"

"Na-Nathan Mo-Mo-Moore. I'm from U-Utah." He turned his head to the side and whispered something into his hand. "So-sorry. I get a little nervous some-some-sometimes."

"It's okay," Catherine said. "I think we're all a little nervous. I'm Catherine Turner. I did gymnastics when I was a kid. I'd just started coaching elementary girls when we were recruited here."

"You're the one that found the key?" Stacy asked.

"Yes," she replied. "It was on the dead man's belt." Her curls had dried and were big and thick. She nervously tucked a section behind her ear.

"Gross." Stacy wrinkled her nose. "But thank you. You saved our lives."

"I couldn't have without Cody and Matt. They got me out to begin with."

"How did you get out first?" Justin crossed his arms and pointed to Cody and Matt with his chin.

"I was out first," Cody said. "The old man unsealed my pod and woke me. He was dang near frantic. Somethin' about the truck wrecked, and a meltdown . . . I don't know, I was just tryin' to get my bearings. It happened so fast. He ran back to the truck, and there was a loud crash. I unhooked my feeding tube, and that's when I saw him crushed. Matt's was the closest cryopod to me, so I cracked it open. But I didn't have the key. Heck, I didn't *know* there was a key or how to open it. So I grabbed a branch and beat the sh—pardon me—the crap out of one until it opened."

"Who is he?" Rhett asked.

"I think he's the scientist," Catherine said. "I remember him. We met him the same day we all met. Right before we were frozen. He's so much older now. How long have we been gone?"

"You're right. That is him," Matt said. "But he's gotta be at least twenty years older. Maybe more."

"What?" Kim yelled. "Are you telling me that I, like, missed my twenties? I'm in my thirties? Almost"—she gagged—"forty!"

"No, you're still seventeen," Matt said. "Kim, stop crying! We didn't age. Time was suspended for us. Everything aged around us, but we didn't. Okay? That's how cryosleep works."

"I don-don't remember much of anything," Nathan said.

"Me neither," Stacy said.

"Sure you do," Victoria said. "The weather was destroying the earth, like some sort of apocalypse. Then a bunch of scientists got together and decided to detonate an H-bomb in the Mariana Trench to tilt the world's axis one degree. But all it did was boil a bunch of fish and mammals and prolong the inevitable." She shrugged. "Sorry, animal lover here."

"That's awfully shortsighted of you to say," Kyle said. "It did fix the weather—for a while."

"Oh really, Mr. Republican?" Victoria raised an eyebrow. "All they did was kill a bunch of defenseless whales and fish!" She was yelling at this point. "And some hypotheses are that they actually *sped up* the weather patterns."

"Here we go." Kyle pinched the bridge of his nose. "A conspiracy theorist."

"How are hundreds of thousands of cooked fish a theory? I'd call that proof. The ocean died that day, and you know it. *Your* people caused it."

"My people?" Kyle took a step forward.

Matt grabbed Kyle's arm. "We all caused it. Now, everyone stop. What's happened is done. We were lucky, we were chosen in the lottery to live. Raise your hand if you are the only one from your family that was picked."

No one raised their hands.

"Okay, so we all have family. This is good," Matt said. "Now we just have to wait for them. Surely there'll be another truck coming with pods. We'll flag them down, and they'll send for help."

"I dunno, buddy," Cody said. "We've been here a good hour, and I haven't heard a peep from either direction."

"Someone has to know we're gone, right?" Catherine asked.

"Of course—I mean, I think," Matt said.

"What about over th-there?" Nathan asked.

"Where?" Victoria stared in the direction Nathan had pointed. She jumped twice, then said, "Please, pick me up, I'm only five-two. I don't have a good vantage point."

They gathered next to Nathan to see what he was talking about. Across the forest, they could barely make out a pitched rooftop.

"Is that a house?" Stacy asked.

"Um . . ." Victoria started. "Usually a house in the woods is called a cabin."

"That's true," Justin said. "It's a cabin."

"I think we should stay put," Matt said. "All my Scout training says to stay in one place so you can easily be found."

"No way," Kim said. "Listen, I didn't survive the apocalypse to just sit on a roadside hoping for a ride, like a hitchhiker."

"Maybe there's a phone we can use down there," Cody suggested.

"True," Matt said.

"Who died and made you leader?" Justin asked. "Screw this. All in favor of heading to the cabin, follow me. Those who want to stay and eat dirt, go for it."

"Wait," Matt said. "We need to stick together. I relent. Yes, let's go to the cabin, but if there's no phone, we need to all agree to stay put for a few days, so when people come they'll find us."

"Whatever, chief," Justin said. "Let's go."

"Wait," Matt said. "Let's leave a note. And we need to bring the scientist and girl. They deserve a proper burial."

"I'll try to find something to write on," Catherine said.

"I'll see if there's some rope in the truck," Cody said. "I'm pretty dang good with knots. We can put them in the lid of the pods and drag them behind us."

"I'm not doing that," Stacy said.

"You won't have to," Kyle said. "The girl is still in her pod."

"Ugh, this is going to suck," Kim said. "We, like, don't even have shoes. I can't walk that far barefoot."

"It'll b-be fine," Nathan said.

"Speak for yourself," Stacy shot back, then she smirked at Kim.

"Found some!" Cody stood in the bed of the truck with rope above his head.

"Great. Let's get the man loaded up," Matt said.

Rhett and Kyle helped Cody with the ropes while Nathan placed the deceased scientist into a pod.

"We ready yet?" Justin asked.

"Yes," Matt said. "Wait! The tapes!"

CHAPTER 6

Matt tripped over a broken branch in the rush to retrieve the nine generic black VHS tapes that had been haphazardly placed in his pod. Cody followed him and took the ones Matt couldn't carry.

"What are these for?" Cody asked.

"I'm not sure. Did you have any in yours?" Matt said.

"I don't think so."

"I doubt I'm the only one with them." He turned back toward the group. "Guys, check to see if you have videos in your pods."

"Oh, great call." Justin rolled his eyes. "Then we'll just play them right . . . ah, crap! I forgot my VCR."

"Maybe there's a VCR at the cabin," Victoria said.

"Hold on." Kyle rummaged around, tearing out gray padding. "This is weird. At the temperatures we were kept at, the tapes would have shattered. No, this was done after we were removed from the cryovault and started to thaw."

Everyone froze.

"You're right." Matt rubbed the back of his neck. The prickly hairs on his neck tickled his palms. "Did anyone else have tapes or anything else in their pod?"

"No."

"Why you?" Justin asked.

Yeah, why me?

"I don't know." Matt deposited the precious videos into the pod with the girl, then pulled on one of the ropes. "Let's just get to the camp and out of the open space."

"Camp?" Stacy asked. "How do you know it's a camp, *Voorhees?*"

"Fine, cabin. Whatever." Despite the hot, humid air, a chill sent shivers down Matt's spine. "It doesn't matter. We need to leave."

"Something is wrong." Victoria closed her eyes and titled her head toward the sky. "The energy feels off. Does it feel creepy to anyone else?"

"The only creepy thing is Matt *Voorhees* taking us to a camp in the middle of nowhere." Stacy laughed. "Did you bring your hockey mask?"

Kim joined her in laughter. "You know, Stacy, I think we're going to get along just fine."

"Matt!" Catherine yelled.

He jogged to the passenger side of the truck. Catherine held her head in her hands, her shoulders hunched.

"What's wrong?" Matt heard footfalls behind him. Over his shoulder he saw Kim, Cody, and the others following his lead. He took another step toward Catherine.

A boy—no, man—lay slumped on the green Naugahyde seat. He wore the same tan uniform tank top and shorts as them, with the addition of a thick Everlast leather weight-lifting belt. Matt had seen athletes wear similar ones in the weight room at high school. His light-brown hair was to his shoulders and feathered, like Kim's. Almond eyes and an underdeveloped jaw revealed crowded teeth that poked out of his relaxed mouth.

"Is he . . ." Catherine whispered.

"Why is he so filthy?" Kim asked, looking down at her clean tan uniform.

Matt gingerly placed two fingers on the man's neck, expecting nothing but coldness. "No. He's got a pulse. It's strong." Matt shook the man's shoulders; his head flopped without resistance. "Hey mister, wake up."

"Maybe he's hurt?" Cody offered. "Probably shouldn't shake him much."

Matt gave the man a quick once-over—no obvious signs of head trauma or open wounds.

"I don't think so." Matt propped him back in the seat. "Maybe he's just passed out."

"Now what?" Stacy asked. "Ew, he's gross. Leave him."

"Are you crazy?" Kyle stepped up. "*Obviously*, we're not leaving him. Can someone help us?"

Kyle stomped off; Catherine followed. They returned with a heavy cryopod.

"If he's been in the truck this whole time"—Catherine wiped her brow—"then he knows where we are, right? He looks older than us."

"Maybe," Matt said. "But he's wearing the same uniform as us. It looks like he might be from another age column."

"But why's he out of his pod?" Justin asked.

"I don't know, let me ask him." Matt rolled his eyes. "Look, he was probably supposed to help the scientist lift our pods. See his belt? I'm guessing he passed out during the wreck."

"When's he gonna wake up?" Rhett asked.

"I have no idea. I literally have the same info as you," Matt snapped. "Nathan, can you help me move him? Justin, Cody, you two want to pull the scientist and the girl? We'll all swap out and take turns, okay?"

"Aye-aye, captain." Justin saluted him.

"Yes"—Nathan paused and bit his lip, suppressing a stutter—"I can help. Is your stomach okay?"

"I think so." Matt lifted his tank top to check his belly button. A soft clot had formed in the void. "Not bad."

They followed the dirt road toward the camp. The soft ground was unlike any dirt Matt had ever seen. Dark brown with red undertones. Tall redwoods towered over them. Lush green ferns and flowery bushes filled in the gaps between trees.

"I hate to be an ingrate, but I hope there are real clothes at this place." Victoria crossed her arms over her flat chest.

"What's wrong with these?" Kim frowned. "They're just like the bloomers we wear under our cheerleading skirts."

"Exactly," Victoria said. "They're undergarments. I'd never leave my apartment in a sports bra or shorts this tight. Not even in Manhattan."

"I think I grew when I was frozen," Rhett said. He took the ropes from Matt and Nathan and pulled the pod holding the unconscious man by himself. "Mine are too tight."

"Physically impossible, you big dumb animal," Kyle muttered too quietly for anyone but Matt to hear.

"Shh," Matt said. "Do you hear that?"

Silence.

"I think you're losing it, chief," Justin said. "I don't hear jack."

"Exactly," Matt said. "It's silent. We're in a forest, and we don't hear birds, insects, or anything. Not even rustling leaves from the wind. Victoria is right. It kinda feels sterile, or like something is lacking."

"Maybe the apocalypse killed them off?" Catherine said. "And it's a calm day. We should be thankful for that, given everything that happened."

"No way." Matt picked up his speed. "I've never seen a forest like this without a single animal. And how are the trees so big?"

"You need to take a chill pill," Kim said. "It's a new world. Post-apco whatever. We beat it, that's all that matters. Learn to live in the moment."

"I'm just trying to figure this all out, that's all," Matt said.

"N-no problem," Nathan said. "K-Kyle, should we take a turn?"

"Absolutely. We all need to contribute and pull our weight. Thanks for pulling this far." He took a rope from Justin.

"Wait," Catherine said. "Nathan, you rest, you've had a go already. I'll pull the girl; you get the scientist, Kyle."

"Ma'am." Cody tipped his imaginary cowboy hat at Catherine before giving her his rein. "Thank you much."

"Don't mention it."

Matt listened for sounds of life, anything to give him comfort, but all he heard was chatter amongst the other survivors. No insects, no birds. Nothing buzzed near his ear. He stared at the road. No creeping or crawling things. Something else was missing, but he couldn't put his finger on it at first. Then it dawned on him.

"Guys—"

"I'm a woman, thank you very much," Victoria said.

"Don't you think it's weird there aren't any tire tracks on the road?" Matt asked.

"Of course there are," Kyle said. "How else did they build the cabins?"

"But no *recent* tire tracks. They've eroded away," Matt said. "Seems like no one has been here for a while."

"All you do is focus on the weird stuff," Stacy said. "Look! There's the entrance. Let's go!"

CHAPTER 7

Matt walked through an archway. Tall wooden spires jutted high into the air, then gradually shortened one by one until they leveled out and formed the perimeter. A huge, rusted metal sign connected the two poles at the top, with the words *New Beginnings* painted on it. Paint had chipped away on the sign, giving their visit to Camp New Beginnings a haunting welcome. The panoramic backdrop was a lone snowcapped mountain. The single snowcapped peak was jagged.

"Is that the Matterhorn?" Matt asked.

"I don't know what kind of janky Disneyland you've been to, but this definitely isn't it," Kim said.

"News flash, Kim," Kyle said. "The Matterhorn is based off a real mountain in the Swiss Alps."

"Whatever," Kim said. "Wait, does that mean we're like, in Switzerland? My parents promised to take me on a European vacation when I graduated."

"I don't think so." Kyle pointed. "The Matterhorn has more of a spike at the top. That one is pretty rounded."

"Great, so you don't know where we are," Justin said. "Thanks for the history lesson."

"You mean geography," Catherine said.

"Yeah, yeah," Justin shrugged, "whatever."

Matt took a couple of steps forward. "Let's check it out."

Inside the grounds, the same reddish-brown dirt lined the pathways. But someone had taken care and lined them with glittery quartz rock. Pale pinks, whites, and a few purples glinted in the sunlight. In the middle of the camp, a huge main cabin loomed. Matt guessed it housed the mess hall and stage for plays, presentations, and performances. At least, that was how it had been at summer camps he'd attended. Beyond the main house were a dozen modest cabins. Untouched and overgrown with moss.

"Here's to our new beginning." Justin laughed. "How lame."

"Totally," Stacy said. "This new beginning is bogus."

Tall grass had overgrown in the areas between paths. The trees inside the camp weren't as large as the redwoods outside. Colorful bark like nothing he'd ever seen grabbed his attention. It reminded him of the story of his parents' honeymoon in Maui. His mom had fallen in love with the rainbow eucalyptus trees, and his dad was bound and determined to grow one for her at home. This led to many failed attempts and dead trees in their Nevada yard. His heart sank. *They'll find us. They have to.*

"I think I'll stay out here." Victoria splayed her arms out, head toward the sky, and turned in a circle. "I need to be one with the Earth. Get reacquainted with this new post-apocalyptic world."

"You can, soon." Matt scanned the area. The hair on his neck stood at attention. "We need to stick together. It seems like this place was abandoned, and I honestly don't know what that means for us."

"Even better—no adult supervision required." Rhett smirked.

"Hey, there's a lake," Kim said. On the far side of the cabin, beyond some overgrown ferns and grass, was a lake. "Let's swim."

"Pardon me, everyone." Cody stepped up onto the stairs in front of the building and faced everyone. "But Matt ain't wrong. We need to scope this place out first. Look for some help, find a phone or radio—"

"Who would we call?" Kyle asked.

"The Youn-Young Republican group?" Nathan folded his lips in, suppressing a laugh.

"Federation," Kyle corrected him.

They stared at each other for a moment before erupting into laughter.

Matt joined Cody on the creaky steps. "Let's get in there, find a VCR so we can see what the hell's going on, then bury these two. After that, whatever. Split up, do what you want. I'm done being the babysitter."

"Sorry," Victoria said. "I wasn't trying to be difficult. I'm just scared."

"M-m-me too," Nathan said. "I was just trying to tell a joke."

"It's fine, I get it. But let's do this as a team," Matt pleaded. "Okay?"

"Great, chief. Team New Beginnings." Justin walked past Matt and slapped him on the shoulder on his way up the stairs. "Go team, go!"

Matt gritted his teeth but stayed silent. *I will not stoop to his level.*

"What do we do with this one?" Kim pointed to the man resting in a pod. His chest rose and fell steadily. "I think we should name him. He looks like a Lance."

"Rude," Catherine said.

"That guy is better?" Stacy asked. "Lance it is."

Matt massaged the back of his neck as he climbed the stairs. "Let's make sure it's safe inside first, then we'll bring him in."

Red stain had chipped and worn away the wide staircase. Both railings, heavily warped and bowed, showed signs of water damage. The covered wraparound porch seemed better for the wear, though most of the planks had scratch marks, and the exposed wood had grayed over time. Tumbleweeds blocked the grand front doors.

"I'll take care of those." Catherine grabbed two of the straw-colored weeds and tossed them off the side. Nathan joined in and cleared the rest. "Thanks."

"Should we knock?" Cody asked. "Wouldn't be right to go bargin' into someone's home."

"I don't what kind of house you grew up in, Tex, but this isn't a home," Justin said.

Matt knocked despite Justin's comments, then turned the brass handle. The connection was loose, but it still clicked open. The termite-eaten door creaked loudly, announcing their arrival.

"Hello?" Matt stepped through the threshold.

The enormous A-frame room was lit only by the light flooding in through the tall windows. On the left side of the entrance was a stage that encompassed the length of the gym. Heavy, dust-covered, black curtains were tied back and exposed the depth of the stage. On the opposite wall was a huge floor-to-ceiling fireplace. Bricks had crumbled away in spots, revealing mottled cement. Peeled-up varnish on the hardwood floor exposed a basketball court, but the rims and backboards were retractable and currently faced the ceiling. Along the walls were roughly a hundred wooden folding chairs, stacked five to a spot.

"Guess they were into the arts too, Victoria," Matt said, his voice shaky.

"Let me see." She caught up to Matt and stood flush with him. "Huh, looks like the one we had at my school. Pretty standard. I'd like to get a closer look, see what type of lighting system they have. Any chance there's electricity?"

"Let's have a look." Cody flipped a switch.

"Dang," Matt said. "Nothing."

"That means no phone." Stacy's voice rose to a high pitch. "And that means no TV or VCR. Those tapes are probably just stupid home videos anyway." She paced. Her breath was so heavy, her entire chest cavity puffed up and deflated at an alarming rate. "We are stuck here. Where's here? The middle of nowhere, and no one knows we're here. We have nothing! Nothing at all. No malls, no fast food—food! What will we eat?"

"Stop it!" Kim slapped Stacy across her cheek. "Snap out of it!"

Stunned, Stacy held her cheek.

"I didn't think you'd be the first to crack," Kim said. "Get it together, like, now, Stacy, or I can't be associated with you."

"Guys"—Catherine pointed out the window—"what's that?"

CHAPTER 8

Matt paused, giving someone else the chance to confront whatever Catherine saw. Everyone was a tough guy until it came down to brass tacks. Matt rolled his eyes and approached the smudged window.

"What?" he asked.

"That." Catherine pointed.

A ripped blue tarp covered a construction-yellow rectangle. The word *CAT* was visible from the tear in the plastic.

"I think that might just be our salvation for the night. Cody, come with me. Everyone else, search the place for a TV and VCR. It's probably going to be in one of the nearby rooms. If you find one, bring in the tapes. Oh, and grab some of the chairs and set them up, okay?"

"Whatever, chief," Justin said. He ran a hand through his messy hair.

"Can a few of you bring Lance up here?" Matt ignored Justin, again, and exited the building, Cody in tow.

"What did you see?" Cody asked.

"I don't want to jinx it. Let's look before I say anything more."

Matt ran down the stairs, gripping the railing, then toward the side of the building. Rhett and Nathan followed after them but stopped at Lance's pod.

Old, rotten leaves crunched under Matt's feet. With each step he unleashed their musty, mildewy scent. He kicked branches, garbage, and pine needles out of his way to fully expose the tarp. Crusty and frayed bungee cords weakly held the plastic in place over the machine. He pulled it free and exposed it.

"Yes!" Matt fist-pumped toward the sky. "It's a generator. It's huge, I've seen cars smaller than this bad boy." He slapped the side of it; something inside the machine rattled. "I think it's commercial-sized, like what they have at hospitals. And look! It's been retrofitted for the apocalypse. Rad."

On the back of the generator was a bicycle seat, pedals, and handlebars. Below it, an old oil puddle had stained the ground with chips of yellow paint on top, like confetti.

"What's the bike for?" Cody asked. "I'm a decent mechanic, but I ain't never seen nothin' like this."

"I've seen this in my techie magazines. But they were just ideas; I didn't know it was real. You pedal the bike, and it charges the batteries. Once it has enough stored-up charge, the generator runs, no gas required. This is new stuff. Like high tech. Who were these people?" Matt asked. He rubbed his hand over his short hair, then stared at his hand. Dried blood had flecked off onto his palm.

"I didn't want to be rude, but maybe you should wash that blood off your face and head," Cody said.

"Sure, yes. After this. Let's give it a try," Matt said.

Matt walked around to the covered control panel. A rusted silver lever fought with him, but he cranked it up and revealed the inner workings. "See this key?" A small, white rubber keychain dangled from it. "It turns over just like a car ignition. Once I've pedaled for a few minutes, fire it up and we'll give it a try."

"Should we get others out here to take turns?" Cody asked.

"Not yet. I don't want to get their hopes up until we know it still works."

As he climbed onto the machine and settled onto the uncomfortable seat, Matt was flooded with flashbacks. Riding down the street with his friends had been his favorite pastime when he was young kid. They'd attach discarded playing cards from local casinos in between the spokes with clothespins and whir around, pretending they were on motorcycles. Once they got older, they'd ride out to the desert. Wrecking on sand was preferred over asphalt. Building jumps and roller tracks. Summers seemed endless when Matt was on a bike.

His feet settled onto the pedals like an experienced rider. The chains cranked to life, slow and angry at first. After a few revolutions, the dirt and rust had given way to a smoother ride. The handlebars were old, like from a Mongoose pit bike. It felt right. Normal. It was a weird juxtaposition: the world had mostly died, and here he was, riding a "bike" like nothing had happened.

"Matt," Cody called. "Where'd you go, buddy?"

"Huh?" he shook the cobwebs from his head. His legs felt like jelly. The smell of hot oil wafted into his nose.

"I've been calling your name for five minutes. You were somewhere else. Thought I was gonna have to shake you."

"Just remembering how it was before. I loved biking. My parents got after me for watching too many movies, so they bought me a bike to get me out of the house. It became my second favorite thing to do."

"Never been much of a cyclist myself," Cody said. "Do you think it's okay to try the gennie?"

"Go for it." Matt pulled his feet back and let the pedals slow on their own to a stop. He panted and wiped his brow with his forearm, smudging the newly moistened blood.

Cody grasped the key, took a deep breath, and turned it to the right. The machine sputtered, then moaned. The moaning started strong, then slowly dissipated and grew weaker by the second. Eventually it lost all hope and gave way to a steady *click, click, click.*

"Not enough," Cody said. "You want me to give it a ride? Take a break?"

"No." Matt pulled off his tank top. The number *20* on the breast side flashed by his face as he yanked it over his head. "Give me a few minutes. I can get it. I know it."

Matt used his shirt to wipe his face and head before discarding it amongst the leaves and trash. Then he jammed down on the pedals and got the crank gear spinning.

While falling into sand dunes wasn't hard, biking on the gritty earth was, and he was prepared for this. He shifted forward on the handlebars, white knuckled the rubber grips, lifted his backside off the seat, and hovered as his quads burned and did the work. With each revolution he gained more momentum. Sweat poured down his brow and past his cheek and dripped onto the machine below him. The humid air didn't quench his lungs, but it didn't matter. He was running on pure adrenaline. Ridges from the metal pedals ground into his bare feet. He stared forward, finding his zone, his happy place.

"You said you're good at fixing things?" Matt said in between breaths.

"Yes sir. Had to learn when I was a young'un. Growing up on the farm and all."

"How much longer do you think I—" he swallowed hard "—need to go?"

"I'd guess just a few minutes," Cody said. "Actually, rest now. I can feel the power radiatin' from this baby."

Matt slumped back onto the seat, fell forward, and rested his head on his sweaty forearms.

Cody turned the ignition, and the engine groaned at first, then turned over with a loud boom. Old belts whined in protest. Then the machine roared to life.

Lightbulbs lining the porch popped and exploded.

"Yes!" Cody said. "You did it, Matt!"

"I just hope it lasts longer than a few minutes," he replied.

"Oh, I'd guess you powered it up for at least an hour, maybe two. Depends how many hours this gennie has on it."

"Hey!" Catherine called from an open window. "We've got power in here. What did you do?"

CHAPTER 9

Matt and Cody rushed back into the main hall.

"Wait." Matt abruptly stopped. "What is that?"

Gears grinding and popping encompassed the air around them, but nothing in sight made the noise.

"Maybe it's the generator." Cody walked back and pressed his head on the machine. "It's running. But I don't think it's coming from this." He pounded on it with a fist. The ruckus ceased. "Huh. That's my move. Works every time."

"Good work," Matt said. "Let's get back to the group."

Matt sidestepped a broken plank and walked into the cabin. Now with the room fully illuminated, they could fully appreciate how rundown the main cabin was. Matt walked over to a poster that had fallen to the ground. He lifted the frame away from his body and dumped the broken glass onto the floor. It was of Hulk Hogan tearing his yellow T-shirt off his overly tan body. He straightened a Magic Johnson poster that hung askew on the wall and hung up Hulk Hogan next to him. The basketball court curled at the edges.

"This looks like a lot of water damage," Matt said.

The stage area sagged in the middle. Wooden folding chairs were rickety, likely termite food until the world went to pot.

"What did you do out there, chief?" Justin asked. "On the first day, Matt created light."

Rhett and Nathan laughed.

"We found a generator." Matt shimmied his skintight tank on over his sweaty body. "Its power comes from an independent bicycle. We'll have to take turns charging it. But I think it'll work for now."

"Yay." Kim twirled her hair. "Can I go swimming now?"

"Fine," Matt said. "Do whatever. How's Lance?"

"Still asleep." Catherine pointed to the stage. "We found some blankets and put him up there. He doesn't seem to be in distress, just out."

"Maybe you should kiss him, like Snow White." Stacy laughed. "Are you his Princess Charming?"

"I'll leave the making out with strangers to you, Stacy," Catherine said.

"We found an entertainment cart," Victoria interrupted. She plugged an orange extension cord into an outlet in the nearest wall. A black, metal-framed cart on wheels housed a thirty-inch tube television and both a VCR and Betamax player on the middle shelf. "Should we see what's on those tapes?"

Matt grabbed a black plastic tape marked *1* from the pile. "Kim, if you guys want to go swimming, go ahead. Or maybe dig graves for the scientist and the girl? If not, then try to find the mess hall and find us something to eat or drink while you're at it."

"Excuse me," she said. "I'm not your maid. I won't be doing any digging. And if I stumble upon some Hi-C, then I do, but it's not because you asked me to do your bidding. Rhett, Stacy, Justin . . . and you, artsy girl, Victoria, you coming?"

"Yes." Victoria stood. "I need to get centered, if that's okay."

"You don't need my permission," Matt said.

"Whoa, whoa." Justin stood so quickly his wooden chair toppled over. "Are we just supposed to trust you to watch these videos and what, report to us?"

"Stay if you want," Matt said. "I'll be just as surprised as you to see what's on them."

"I'm gonna stay for a bit. See for myself what these mysterious tapes have to offer. Doesn't anyone else find it strange he just happened to have these tapes in *his* pod?" Justin righted his chair, then sat. "I'm not sure I trust you, chief."

Matt ignored Justin and powered the TV to life. Fuzzy black-and-white snow covered the screen. He pressed the power button on the VCR, then put Tape 1 in and pressed play. The video started for just a moment before the screen returned to snow static. The machine whined as it rewound the tape.

"Of all the times someone wasn't kind and didn't rewind," Catherine sighed.

"Speaking of kind, can you kindly wash that blood and gore off your arms and legs?" Stacy asked. "Gross me out the door."

"Totally." Catherine crossed her arms. "You find me a shower, and I'll get right on that."

An audible click ended the tension in the room, and Matt hit the play button once more.

The scientist, albeit a couple decades younger and sans beard, sat on a simple black stool. He wore the same round Coke-bottle glasses that were now crushed into his face. His white lab coat was new and pressed to starchy perfection. Behind him, stacks of twelve-inch, gray computer monitors with green screens flickered. Many of them had graphs and charts; the others had DOS coding on them. Matt even recognized *King's Quest* on one in the corner.

"Hello," the man said. "If you're seeing this, one of three things has happened."

CHAPTER 10

The man adjusted his glasses, then said, "First scenario: the apocalypse is over, and you all survived. Congratulations. It was my pleasure to maintain the cryovault and your cryopods throughout this time. Although it is lonelier than I anticipated, you all kept me busy. Normally a mixture of cooling liquids flowed through you, keeping your cells in a near-halted growth state. But you still may have had small growth changes, like sloughing skin cells and slightly longer fingernails. To stop this process completely, I added a little cryo cocktail," he grinned, "of my own invention to each of your cryotubes. This stopped hair and fingernails from growing. Overall result: your growth process stopped entirely."

Matt rubbed his fingers over his buzz cut. *He was a brilliant scientist.*

"Dear listener," he continued, "I hope the apocalyptic weather is quick and I can be here when you awaken. I look forward to meeting you all if scenario one comes to fruition."

He cleared his throat. "The second scenario: I have grown too old or sick to continue to take care of the necessities, and I've woken up my successor, Darin. Darin, you have all the information already, and I recorded these tapes mainly for posterity. Thank you for carrying on.

"Third situation: something terrible has happened with the vault. This is highly unlikely, but I must be prepared, for all humanity rests on my shoulders.

"I will be documenting some of my day-to-days as well as giving updates every few years. I supposed I'll record a few times when I'm in need of conversation as well. Please do not judge me too harshly, and know my intentions and actions have been valiant from the beginning."

"Geez," Stacy said. "How long ago was this video taken? Looks like the guy's aged a hundred years. Cave air must be bad for your skin."

"Tha-that's rude," Nathan said. "He's been looking after u-us and keeping us alive." He stood and walked toward the door. "I'm going to dig a grave. It's the right thing to do. If anyone wants to help, meet me at the west side of the bu-building. I think I saw a shed."

"I'll help." Kyle followed him out. "Fill me in on what's on the tapes, okay?"

"Sure." Matt nodded. "Thanks for doing the heavy lifting."

They walked out, and Matt could have sworn that the seemingly mild-mannered Nathan slammed the door. Stacy was out of line, and he hoped she got the message.

"Until next time," the scientist nodded, "I bid you adieu." He stood from his stool and walked toward the camera, and it blinked off.

Matt pressed the fast-forward button while he craned his neck toward the screen. A few moments later the black screen was filled with a close-up of the scientist.

"There's been a breach!" the frantic man yelled. An alarm droned in the background. "I'm not sure how, but something is wrong with the pods in age group seventeen." The man turned the camera around. Against a wall were pods stacked on shelves from the floor to ceiling. He panned in closer, and Matt saw his pod, number twenty. He absently rubbed the embroidered *20* on his tank top.

"See?" The man continued. "Everything looks fine, but the alarms sounded as I replenished the food. I was rummaging around, and I felt a small tremor. Maybe it was a large tremor. It's hard to tell; they've become so frequent these days that I believe I've become desensitized to them." He turned the camcorder back toward himself, inches from his face. Sweat ran down his temple onto his cheek. "I'll fix it. I know I can."

The tape stopped, and gears turned loudly inside the VCR. It clicked and automatically rewound.

"That's it?" Catherine said. "What happens next?"

"Like, that's easy. He let us out. Duh! Story over." Kim made her way to the door. "Have fun with your boring tapes. Spoiler alert, we live. Time to celebrate our 'new beginning.'"

"She's right. What else will we learn that we aren't already living?" Justin asked.

"I'd like to know where the rest of the people are. Like my dad and mom," Matt said. "Doesn't anyone else wonder where their parents are?"

"I do," Victoria offered, meekly. "Are we all an only child?"

"No," Kim said. "I have two older brothers. All five of us were on the plane together; they must have split us up on the bus."

"Only child," Justin said. "They stopped with perfection."

"I have a sister," Rhett chimed in.

"I'm the baby," Stacy said. "I have five siblings."

"I had a brother." Cody's voice caught in a hitch. "He died when I was twelve."

"That's terrible," Catherine said. "How?"

"Texas rodeo. Got stomped on bull ridin'. Name was Wildman—the bull, that is. My brother's was Brock."

"I'm sorry, Cody," Matt said.

"You said the rest were coming, right?" Cody said. "That's why we needed to stay put?"

"I mean, I hope they are." Matt rested his arms on his knees and leaned forward. "I don't have the answers. I'm just going to keep watching the tapes and hopefully *get* some answers. If anyone else wants a break, feel free. I'll let you know what I watch."

"You do the nerd work," Rhett said. "If you come across some reruns of ALF, then I'll tap in."

Justin led Stacy, Victoria, and Kim and Rhett, who had already looped their arms around each other's waists, out the door.

Only Cody and Catherine remained.

Matt hoped he'd be able to give them some answers.

CHAPTER 11

Buzzers blared and strobe lights blinked. Chaos. The camera jiggled, then someone controlling it zoomed out and panned around the room. A dark, ridged wall came into focus. Pods stacked twenty high on shelves remained still, but a bright-red sensor blinked on each one.

"Where is that?" Matt squinted.

The camera zeroed in on the pods, then the scientist came into view. He ran from pod to pod, unplugging wires and checking tubes of fluids. Shockwaves sent the man falling to the ground. Neon-green fluid spilled onto his stained lab coat.

"It was a meteor!" the man said breathlessly. "It hit the side of the mountain and interfered with the seventeen-year-olds' pods. It took me all my courage and secret passages, but I went outside and saw for myself. I'm trying to save these kids, but I don't know if I can. I'm sorry." He pulled on the sides of his thinning hair. "I couldn't have predicted this. No one hypothesized objects from space barreling into the earth in addition to this disastrous weather!"

The man disappeared behind the camera, and the screen blinked to black. Before Matt could react, it started back up.

"I think it's fixed." The scientist sat on a stool, his hair disheveled and flaking with dandruff, his cheeks flushed, eyes bloodshot. His face and hair had seemingly gone on a diet.

"What happened to this guy?" Matt whispered, leaning to the TV screen.

"The alarms go off every hour, on the hour, but I checked the vitals, and they seem correct. I'm not getting much sleep, as this has been occurring for the last week. I'm worried about the breach. The children's health is good for now, but I'm concerned that the pod system is failing. The impact to the mountain was too great. Oh, dear listener, you don't know that you're in a cave inside a mountain, do you?

"I was forced to wake my protégé, Darin. I think I may have mentioned him." A foamy crust had formed in the corners of his lips. "He tried to repair the mountain on the outside. But the weather is too harsh. He hurt his leg, and I've been helping him mend. None of this is going to plan.

"I hope I don't fail you. I'll do my best to find a way to fix the system." The room rattled. "Fantastic, another tremor. Or maybe meteor strike. Off to see what fresh hell awaits me." He exhaled loudly and walked toward the camera. "Please know, I am trying my best, and my intentions are good."

The tape clicked.

"Holy crap," Catherine said. "Are we . . . did everyone else die?"

"I doubt it," Matt said. "Only our section was failing. Wait, did you realize we were in a cave within a mountain?"

"Nope." Cody shook his head, his gray eyes wide.

"I don't even remember the plane ride." Catherine flipped her long, black curls over her shoulder.

"Do you guys remember anything from before?" Matt pressed his palms into his eyes. "I can remember things from way before getting frozen, the escort to the plane . . . then it's just blank. Completely gone. After that I remember waking up when the bus ride was over, meeting you guys briefly, then getting into my pod."

"I remember getting on the plane and being given a glass of juice," Catherine said. "They said it was for nausea and nerves. I didn't want it since I don't get sick on planes, but the stewardess wouldn't leave until I downed it. Does that ring a bell?"

"Kinda," Matt said. "Why would they drug us?"

"Yeah, wouldn't that make it harder to get us from the plane to the bus?" Cody asked. "It don't make a darn bit of sense."

"Before we start Tape 3, let's see what the others remember." Matt walked out to the covered wraparound porch, peered over the railing, and saw no one in the lake.

"Hey," Nathan yelled. "We're over he-here."

To his surprise, everyone—including Kim and Stacy—were digging two holes. Only a few had shovels; the rest used hammers, hoes, and other random items to claw at the ground.

"We'll be right there," Matt called back. He turned to Catherine and Cody. "I know you guys are skeptical. I am too. But I don't want to freak them out. Stacy has been all over the place—happy, excited, snarky, and downright mean. I think she's on the verge of cracking."

"I don't disagree." Catherine carefully made her way down the rickety porch stairs. "But I'm not going to lie."

"That's not what I'm saying. I just think we should tread lightly."

"Agreed," Cody said. "I can get behind that."

"Okay, I'm on board." Catherine fell back and let Matt lead them around the building.

Two large rectangular holes, not quite deep enough to house bodies, were formed at the edge of the camp perimeter. Someone had draped the tarp from the generator over the bodies.

"What did the second tape show?" Kyle wiped sweat from his brow with his forearm.

CHAPTER 12

"What do you guys remember about the transport here? I'm talking from the beginning to the end." Matt changed the subject.

"Why are you asking that?" Kyle asked. "The bus ride"—his face twisted in confusion—"I don't remember it. They told me I had been on one; I never questioned it."

"I remember the bus ride." Kim winked at Rhett. "It was, like, totally excellent."

Rhett wrapped his arms around her small waist and kissed the top of her head.

"Great." Matt looked to the group. "Does anyone else remember getting off the plane, or onto the bus or off the bus?"

No one spoke up.

"Okay, Rhett, Kim, spill it. Because we think we were drugged on the plane. Does everyone remember being given a glass of juice?"

"Yes," Victoria said. "It was orange juice with lots of pulp. I love pulp."

"I don't know." Kim smirked. "I guess I just saw this guy, and that's all I remember."

This is going to be like putting socks on a rooster.

Matt turned to Rhett.

"I was seated across from Kim. She kicked me, and it woke me up. She said I was stirring, and it was annoying her."

"No," Kim corrected him. "I kicked you because you were, like, talking in your sleep. It was weird. I was the only one awake. I hate pulp, so I dumped half of my juice into my mom's cup, which, I guess, explains why I woke up sooner."

"Rhett, how much do you weigh?" Cody asked.

"Two eighty-eight."

"Must have metabolized it quicker than they anticipated, or they calculated it wrong," Kyle said.

"*Anyway*, I kicked him hoping he'd tip over into the empty seat next to him and shut up. But then he looked at me with those baby blues. I was putty in his hands."

"Okay, okay." Catherine rolled her eyes. "We don't need the intimate details. What did you see outside the windows?"

"Nothing. I wasn't looking. It was dark," Kim said.

"Same," Rhett echoed.

"All I remember is when the bus was slowing down and the interior lights turned on. I think everyone else was waking up then. And we were already in the building." Matt huffed. "No one else remembers anything. Anything?"

"What are you getting at, chief?" Justin asked. "What was on that tape?"

"Yeah," Stacy echoed. "What are you hiding?"

"Nothing. I'm not hiding anything. I'm just trying to piece it together. Our cryovault and pods were in a cave inside a mountain."

"What?" Stacy yelled. "What are you talking about? No they weren't. The bus was in a warehouse, and we all exited in a *warehouse* with horrible, abusive fluorescent lighting."

"We think that building was actually the inside of a mountain," Catherine said.

"How would that even work? This is ridiculous." Stacy's voice was an entire octave higher than normal, and she waved her hands.

"That's what the tape said. And a meteor hit the side of the mountain, causing damage to the system in our pod unit." Matt held up his hands, stifling any more interruptions. "Things were bad enough that he woke his protégé, Darin."

"Do you think Lance is Darin?" Kyle asked.

"I don't know. Probably not. The scientist looks at least ten years younger than when we last saw him. Lance doesn't look that old. I'd say early twenties. We haven't seen him on tape yet because he's recovering from an injury he sustained trying to repair the damage. That's as far as we've gotten. The scientist looks haggard and tired, and he's losing hope on saving our cryopods."

"This isn't happening." Stacy burst into tears and paced in a tight circle. "Where is my mom? If I don't have my mom, who will pay my credit card bill? That means no salon." She was ranting so quickly that Matt had a hard time understanding her. "And my hair. My hair! What man will want me without a fresh perm? How will I find a husband? I'm too pretty to be in this situation!"

"A. Husband." Victoria crossed her arms. "That's her concern."

"Hey, hey now." Justin gently grabbed Stacy by the shoulders and crouched so that he was at eye level with her. "It's all going to be okay, all right? Calm—"

"Do not tell me to calm down!" Stacy screamed.

Kim stalked over to her and pulled her into a hug and whispered something into Stacy's ear, then held her hands. "Okay?"

Stacy nodded, eyes empty and wide.

"We're going to swim, lay out, and like, relax." Kim nodded her head toward the holes. "All this manual labor and talk of—whatever it is you're implying—has gone too far. Also, the dead bodies three feet away are, like, freaking us out to the max. We're going to enjoy the next few hours. Nathan, Kyle, you got this?" She waved Justin and Rhett toward her.

"Su-sure," Nathan said.

"Yeah, you go swim, that'll solve the major problems we're facing." Kyle picked up a shovel and aggressively slammed it into the ground.

"Great." Kim smugly smiled at him, turned, and skipped toward the lake with Stacy, the two of them still hand in hand. Justin and Rhett followed.

"It's not that bad, really. Darin knows that the scientist moved us and will come looking for him—us." Matt turned to Kyle. "We'll help with the graves."

"No, it's fine," Kyle said. "Go see what's on the next tape. And we're going to need to figure out our food situation. I didn't dare say anything in front of Miss Basket Case over there."

"I'll search for some chow. Mess hall can't be far," Cody said. "I'll meet ya back in the main cabin."

"Okay," Matt said. "You ready, Cher?"

"Very funny." Catherine brushed past him and flipped her hair. "Let's go, Sunny."

"Aren't they divorced?"

"Exactly." She tossed her head back and laughed.

CHAPTER 13

"Thanks for that." Catherine flipped on the light switch in the main hall.

"For what?" Matt said.

"The Cher thing. Made me laugh."

"I can be funny sometimes," Matt said.

"It really threw me off at first, though."

"Honestly, when I first saw you out of the pod, my brain was still so jumbled. Your hair, even matted down, looked just like Cher's to me. I guess I just blurted it out." Matt rummaged through the tapes and pull out one marked 3.

"I took it as a compliment."

"It was."

Matt ejected the second tape, the TV hissed with white noise until the VCR swallowed the third tape. The wooden chair groaned under his weight when he sat. His hands were slick with sweat, breath pensive.

The scientist came into focus. "Good morrow! I don't believe I've formally introduced myself. My name is Dr. Westbrook. Jim Westbrook." He rubbed his stubbly chin. His brown hair was streaked with gray, but overall, he looked healthier. Rested. "Things are much better these days. My dear seventeen-year-olds have persevered. Strong ones. Kids are resilient. I believe the breach in the mountainside has been fixed. You see up there?"

The camera panned up to the ceiling, then zoomed in on the dark rock.

"That must be Darin running the camera," Matt suggested.

The recording focused in on thick, black foam as it snaked its away across the roof and onto the side of the cave.

"That, my dear listeners, is carbon foam. I invented it long before I was one of the only humans on earth. It was a backup, a last resort if you will. I tried all other approved options to repair the cave. Darin's youth and agility has proven invaluable. My old back doesn't bend like it used to. Darin, return the lens to me."

The camera settled into its tripod, and it focused back onto the scientist.

"The foam not only filled the cracks and holes, but because it's carbon, it actually binds to the stone and becomes rocklike. Once I began the patch work, I realized some of the steel beams had been compromised as well. No matter, carbon foam to the rescue. See?"

This time Darin zoomed out as far as the lens would allow and went from one side of the room to the opposite. The true expanse of the cave finally came into view—thousands of columns stacked with pods lay dormant in the cave, each section marked by a white circle and the age group painted in light blue.

"There must be five thousand pods in there," Matt said.

Catherine's mouth was agape, but she said nothing.

"How was one man monitoring that many pods? Feeding this many people? Even with two people . . . it's too much."

"I don't know," Catherine said. "If he's smart, I'm sure most of it's automated."

"Where's the power coming from?" Matt cringed. "Never mind. Solar. I forgot the government scientists found ways to save and store solar power."

"Matt," Catherine put a hand on his knee, "it's okay to question things. No one expects you to have all the answers. Okay?"

Dr. Westbrook gave the full tour of the cave. Darin remained the silent cameraman. Walls slick with humidity glistened in the artificial light. Nondescript pods filled enormous floor-to-ceiling shelves. The shelves themselves were on a wheeled track, so he could easily manipulate them if he needed more space in a particular area.

"Weary traveler, thank you for watching my videos. And remember, my intentions are good, even if I fail." Dr. Westbrook saluted the camera, and the screen blinked to static storm.

"Okay, so things seemed to have been fixed, for now," Matt said. "But why are we out?"

"How many tapes do we have left?" Catherine asked. "I need a break."

"Me too." Matt followed her out onto the balcony.

Happy screams and laughter echoed in the distance near the lake.

"They really don't have a care in the world, do they?" Matt asked. "Look at them. I don't get it."

Nathan swung from a rope swing and splashed into the water. *Guess they finished the graves.* Stacy was on Justin's shoulders, and Kim was on Rhett's. The two girls chicken wrestled, trying to knock each other into the water.

"We're all wired differently, Matt. Accept it. Yikes," she pointed to the graves, "look at those mounds. I don't think they buried them deep enough."

Two dark-red dirt mounds covered the resting places of the girl and Dr. Jim Westbrook.

"Honestly, I figured we'd need to rebury them. That's probably too close to the cabins anyway. But we'll give them a better burial later. For now, let's watch one more video, then get everyone up to speed."

Catherine rubbed her face and nodded. "Okay, *one* more."

The next tape garnered them no additional information. Westbrook continually talked about carbon foam and how he was sure it was working. That should have made Matt feel better, but the more the scientist talked, the more apparent it became that he was trying to talk himself into believing his own words.

He took them on the same tour, showing off the size of the cave, the pods, but nothing that they hadn't seen before. Finally, it ended with him talking into the camera while eating canned chili. Tomato juice dripped onto his white beard, staining it.

"As always, I bid you adieu—and know that my intentions are good."

"Why do you think he keeps saying that?" Catherine asked.

"My guess is in case he fails. He wants to be remembered as someone who did his best. Not the man responsible for killing the entire human race." Matt awkwardly laughed.

CHAPTER 14

Cody entered the room with a large army-green duffle slung over his shoulder. "Found some grub. Mostly canned stuff and MREs."

"How old is it?" Catherine asked.

"Who knows? We don't even know what year it is. But the labels are pretty faded." Cody stuffed the bag in the corner of the room. "As long as they ain't dented, or hiss when you open them, you'll probably be fine. Found these iodine tablets too. Course, we're probably better off boilin' that lake water and using the tablets together. Rhett seems like the type to pee in the water."

"Good call," Matt said. "Did you have Scout training too?"

"Nope," Cody said. "Real-life training. My daddy took us camping a lot. Made us rough it. One time he dropped me off in the middle of nowhere and told me to find home. Left me with only with a flint, backpack, and compass. He got real freaked out when the weather stuff happened. Wanted me to survive. Learn how to live off the land. He'd already lost one son; he wasn't going to lose another."

"That's pretty intense." Catherine crossed her arms.

"He was nearby, makin' sure I was fine. Taught me good stuff."

"I guess." She turned her attention toward the doors.

Justin and Rhett had entered the room, dripping water everywhere.

"What did you find out, chief?" Justin asked.

"Not a ton," Matt said. "The scientist is named Dr. Jim Westbrook. He believes he fixed the breach caused by the meteor strike with carbon foam. Still doesn't explain where we are and where everyone else is."

"A meteor strike? Chyeah right!" Rhett said. "Did little green men show up too?"

"Whatever," Matt said. "You can watch later if you want."

"Is Lance still out?" Justin asked.

"Yeah," Catherine said. "I just checked on him a little bit ago. His pulse is strong, breath is even."

"Why isn't he waking from his cryosleep?" Rhett asked.

"He's just out of it, I guess." Catherine shrugged.

"Why don't you guys take a break?" Justin asked. "Come swim. It'll seriously clear your head."

"I could use a time-out," Catherine said. "Come on, Matt, please."

Matt looked back at the TV, then Catherine. "Okay," he relented. "Just for a little."

"You coming, Cody?" Rhett asked.

"Sure," Cody said. "Never cared too much for swimmin', but I could use a little sun."

* * *

Catherine made a pit stop at the shed and met them at the lake. She carefully dipped a galvanized bucket into the water and walked downhill from the lake and rinsed the scientist's blood off her arms and legs. Once clean, she ran past Matt and dove into the water.

Matt followed her in but jumped feet first instead. Cool water rushed over his body until he was completely submerged. He gently touched his belly and hurried to the surface. *I can't be in the water with an open wound.* He crawled onto a wobbly wooden dock just big enough for two people.

"Not in the mood to swim?" Catherine bobbed up and down near his legs.

"I figured it was a bad idea to bleed in our drinking water." He pointed to his stained tank top. "It hasn't reopened, but I don't want to take any chances."

"Or get some weird infection," Catherine said.

"Good point. Looks like they're over it too." He pointed to Stacy, Kim, and Victoria, who were lying on the soft grass next to the water. Cody, Rhett, and Justin skipped rocks. Kyle and Nathan remained in the lake. "I really do think our parents are coming."

"I do too," Catherine said. "Dr. Westbrook fixed the breach and restored our column's functionality. He wouldn't remove us for no reason. The apocalypse must be over and—wait, no." She turned pale as a ghost and pulled herself out of the water and onto the dock. "What if Darin can't leave the pods unattended?"

"He will," Matt said. "If they planned on the apocalypse outliving Dr. Westbrook, and Darin was to take over, surely there is another person next in line. Logic would state that he'd wake them, have them take over, and come looking for us."

"Sure." Catherine stood, walked along the shore toward the girls; Matt followed. "Let's see how everyone else is doing."

"How's the tan?" Justin plopped down next to Kim.

"Need baby oil." Kim rested her forearm across her eyes, shielding them from the light.

"I don't feel like I'm getting any sun," Stacy said. "It feels different than it used to. It's hot out, but it doesn't feel like the sun is what's making it warm."

"Must be the post-apocalyptic sun," Victoria said. "I never get a tan anyway."

"You're pretty pasty." Stacy laughed.

"Yeah." Kim sat up. "You're right. It does feel, like, different. This new sun totally sucks. Let's go. We're wasting our time."

"How about we split up, search the cabins. See if they're suitable to sleep in, report back to the main hall, and we'll reconvene in say, twenty minutes?"

"Whatever," Kim said. "Check for clothes too. I'd like something dry to change into. Maybe some silk pajamas if they have them."

"Wh-what if there are people in the cabins?" Nathan shuffled his feet. "Bodies. Dead people."

I should have thought of that.

"Make note of it and move on. Don't disturb the dead." Matt turned to leave before anyone else could ask questions he didn't have answers to. "And if it smells like something's rotting, don't bother going in."

CHAPTER 15

Matt watched everyone pair off and decided to crash Kim and Stacy's party of two. For one, they were the most likely to freak out (which was why he guessed that Justin and Rhett had separated themselves from them), and he wanted to calm them down before they spread fear through the entire group. And two, they were also the most likely to claim they smelled something funny and not bother checking any of the cabins.

The long path was dry. Dust kicked up with each step. Overgrown grass spilled onto parts of the path, but the quartz lining the walkways did a decent job of keeping most of it at bay. The first cabin they came upon was deeply overgrown with moss. It wicked up the sides, spreading like cancer.

"Not exactly a luxury suite," Stacy said. "We used to vacation in Aspen for every New Year's Eve. Our cabin was bitchin'. Not like this hunk of J-U-N-K."

"Aspen?" Matt kicked branches out of the alcove leading into the entrance. "Wow. I didn't think people actually went there. Who's your mom? Goldie Hawn?"

"Ha ha." Stacy rolled her eyes.

"Holy crap." Kim placed her palms on Stacy's shoulders. "Is she?"

"No." Stacy shrugged Kim off. "My dad's a lawyer. 'Ambulance chaser' is what the guys at the country club call him. I think it's royally rude to call him that."

"So you're just, like, rich?" Kim asked.

Matt turned the handle on the front door. Their chatter was a good distraction. They seemed at ease.

"Yeah," Stacy said. "I got a Beamer for my sixteenth birthday."

"Shut up!" Kim said. "Me too! A red one! My parents are orthodontists. Or were orthodontists? Who knows now? Matt? Matt! Get out here!"

Matt waited, forcing them to come after him. The modest room held four sets of bunk beds stacked along the east and west walls. In the middle was a table with a lamp hanging from the center beam. Puzzles and board games were stacked neatly on the edge. Their colorful cardboard lids, with pictures of kids playing the games, had faded under a layer of dust. Posters of teen heartthrobs from *Tiger Beat* were tacked to the wooden walls with plastic pushpins.

"This has to be the girl's cabin," Matt said.

Along the back wall was a small kitchenette: a porcelain sink, a tiny fridge, and a hot plate on top of a chipped Formica countertop. To the right of the kitchen, a toilet, sink, and shower made up the smallest bathroom Matt had ever seen.

"Geez," Stacy said. "Talk about roughin' it."

"Let's open some windows," Matt said. "Air it out. It's a little musty."

"This is like *Little House on the Prairie* BS." Kim picked up a blanket off a bed and shook it. "Huh, I expected thirty years of dust to fall out. Not too bad, I guess."

"Can we see if there's a better cabin?" Stacy remained at the door's threshold, only poking her head inside.

"Sure," Matt said. "But don't get your hopes up. They're probably all identical."

The next three cabins were, in fact, the same. The only difference was the posters still clinging to the walls.

Matt's head started to throb.

Kim and Stacy went back to comparing stories of luxury vacations and constantly one-upping each other. He doubted any of what he'd heard was true.

"A yacht?" Matt rubbed his temples. "Who charters a yacht? Come on, even I don't believe that."

"It's true!" Stacy insisted. "It was just like that one on *Overboard*!"

"You're only saying that because I asked if you were related to Goldie Hawn." Matt cleared tumbleweeds from the entrance of the next cabin. "Give it a rest."

"Yeah, Stacy." Kim's snotty factor was off the charts. "Stop lying."

"I'm not!" Her face reddened. She rushed to the door and opened it, stepping inside first.

I guess humiliation makes her actually contribute. I'll have to remember that.

"What is this?" Stacy called out. A small thud followed.

"Is it Goldie Hawn's yacht?" Kim smirked.

Matt ignored Kim and stepped inside. A massive trunk had been tipped on its side. Musty clothes spilled out onto the brittle wooden floor.

"Nice work! Kim, get in here, Stacy found you some clothes."

"Yeah, Kim." Stacy held out a royal-blue top with yellow piping. "You owe me."

"Is that . . ." Kim froze, mouth agape.

Stacy nodded.

"Suit up, cheerleader," Matt said.

"Get out of here, perv! I need to change." Kim pushed Matt out the door before he could had a chance to leave on his own volition.

He waited outside, listening to high-pitched squeals and laughter. "Girls, can you hurry up? We need to meet up with everyone."

"Just a second," Stacy yelled. "We found it first. We get first pick."

The door clicked open, and Kim twirled. Yellow and white adorned every other pleat on her skirt.

"A cheerleading uniform! Like, can you even believe it?" Kim smoothed down the front of the loose-fitting sweater. A yellow stripe dipped across the front and continued on the sleeves. "It fits me perfectly. I feel so—so me again."

"Just don't check the zipper in the back. It's a little snug," Stacy mumbled. Stacy wore pleated, acid-washed jeans, rolled at the ankles. A short, puff-sleeved, light-pink sweater topped with a pearl necklace completed her preppy outfit. "Necklace is fake. But what do you expect? These must have been costumes for their plays. Or lost and found? I dunno, I found a few scripts at the bottom."

"Great. You guys look great and seem happy. Let's pack up and bring it to the main hall; we're late."

"You didn't see the best part," Kim said. "We have shoes! Look, they even had Kaepas."

On the sides of Kim's white cheer shoes were two small plastic triangles that matched her blue-and-gold uniform.

"They look a little big," Matt said.

"I'm not going to, like, wear ones that don't match." Kim twirled her hair. "They'll do just fine."

"Don't you want to change?" Stacy asked.

He did but thought better of it. They'd probably just take off back to the group, leaving him to carry the heavy trunk by himself. Plus, it was getting dark. An orange hue cast the entire camp in a strange glow. It wasn't like the colorful sunsets from *before*.

"Nah, let's pack it back up, and one of you can help me carry. Take turns, okay?"

"But I don't want to get anything on my sweater." Stacy pouted. "And it's the only light-pink top in the trunk. It suits my hair and skin tone."

Matt took a deep breath and shot her a stern look.

"Don't have a cow," Kim said. "Calm down. I'll take the first shift."

CHAPTER 16

"Drop it here," Matt said. "Kim, can you ask your boyfriend to bring it up?"

"No problem." She smiled. "And he's not my *boyfriend*. Not yet, anyway."

Matt climbed the rickety stairs to the main cabin, his body slick with sweat. He wasn't used to the humidity. *But it's a dry heat,* his mom would say when he complained about the desert heat.

He found the rest of the group sitting on folding chairs, oddly quiet. Victoria's porcelain face seemed paler somehow, weary.

"Great news." Matt lightly clapped his hands together to draw their attention to him. "We found a trunk of clothes. Some are pretty theater-ish, others are leftover normal clothes. And Cody found some food."

"No, he didn't," Justin said. "We got back here before him; I don't see any food. You're losing it, chief."

"He found it earlier."

"Why didn't you tell us?" Justin balled his fists by his side. "We're starving, and you're hoarding food? I knew I shouldn't trust you."

"What gives you the right to make that decision for us?" Kyle asked.

"Whoa." Matt took a defensive step backward. "We don't have a ton at the moment, and we don't even know if it's still edible. I didn't want to pig out on what's left or get sick if it was contaminated. Plus, there are several things we need to go over before anyone starts eating. This stuff is like twenty or thirty years old."

"What's there to go over?" Rhett dropped the trunk on the floor. It bounced and dented the old wood. "I remember how to eat."

"Hang on." Catherine stood next to Matt. "You guys have been looking to him for all the answers. Then when you don't like it you give him a hard time. Either let him lead and stop giving him so much crap or—"

"Or what?" Justin took a step toward them. "Huh?"

"Or take the reins and actually do something, Justin!" Catherine squared up to him. Her long curls cascaded over her shoulders, her jaw set.

"G-guys," Nathan said, "stop fighting."

"No one is fighting," Justin said. "Trust me, if we were, you'd know."

"Is that so?" Matt puffed out his chest.

"Don't test me, *chief*. It would be over in two hits. Me hitting you, you hitting the floor."

Everyone froze.

Matt bit his lip. Nervous laughter bubbled up until he couldn't contain it for another second. He erupted into full hysterics.

"Oh, you think that's funny?" Justin gritted his teeth.

Matt held his stomach, hoping his scab on his belly button wouldn't burst open. He coughed, trying to regain his composure.

"You forgot I'm a movie buff. You stole that line from *The Breakfast Club*. Nice try." Matt laughed, then said in a mocking tone, "Me hitting you, you hitting the floor. Okay, sport-o!"

Justin's face reddened. "Where's the food."

It wasn't a question.

"Whatever, man." Matt pointed to the duffle bag in the corner. "Be my guest."

Justin stomped over to it and pulled out a can of Dinty Moore stew. "I need a can opener."

"It's at the bottom of the bag," Cody said. "But can't you wait? Matt and I have some survival training. We just need to inspect the cans and tell you what to look for, so you don't puke your guts out . . . or die."

Die.

They'd witnessed death within moments of awakening in their pods. But this was the first time anyone had talked about *them* dying. They'd survived the apocalypse and cheated death. Yet the threat of their demise lingered.

Justin twisted the silver handle on the opener; the can hissed.

"If it hisses—" Cody started.

Justin locked eyes with Cody and dumped the contents into his mouth. His eyes bulged. Cody ran over and knocked the can out of his hand. Justin doubled over, spitting out thick black goop.

"What the—are you trying to kill me?" Justin wiped his mouth with his tank top. "Don't ever slap something out of my hand again, got it?"

"This is what I was trying to warn you about," Cody said. "If the can hisses, odds are it's contaminated with botulism."

Rhett blinked blankly.

Justin had pulled off his shirt. Rock-hard, six-pack abs flexed while he tried scraping his tongue with his shirt.

"It means it can make you sick. Sick enough to die." Matt rolled his eyes.

"I think I weeded through most of the bad ones," Cody said. "If you see one that has dents or is bulging, don't open it. Once open, if it's foamy or discolored, don't eat it. I think we should go through the canned stuff first and save the MREs."

"What's an MRE?" Victoria asked.

"Meal Ready-to-Eat," Matt said. "The military uses them. If we end up leaving, they're lighter and easier to carry." He turned to Cody. "Do you know how to make a fire?"

"Way ahead of you." Cody nodded. "I grabbed a few flints from the supply closet. Here." He handed Matt a heavy black-and-silver flint. "Justin, get in that bag and hand me a pot."

Justin reluctantly complied.

"Can someone help Cody gather some wood for a fire?"

"It's hotter than crap out there," Kim said.

"We need to boil water from the lake," Matt said. "We're all dehydrated."

"I'll help," Kyle said. "Sorry I snapped at you, Matt. This is all so confusing and stressful."

"It's fine. Anyone else who doesn't know how to start a fire and wants to learn, go with Cody."

Nathan said nothing but followed them out.

"Justin, do you want to help me divvy up the food?"

"Nope." Justin crossed his arms over his thick chest. "You said it, you're our fearless leader. You do it, chief."

CHAPTER 17

Matt sorted through cans while the others found clothes in the trunk. Faded labels of SpaghettiOs, Campbell's soups, Manwich, Dinty Moore stews, Starkist Tuna Fish, Green Giant vegetables, and Libby's fruit in sugary, sweet syrup reminded Matt of his life *before*. Cody had undersold what he'd found. He flipped over a can. Embossed on the bottom was the date *09/84. It would be helpful to know what year it is now.*

Matt sectioned out nine cans of chicken noodle soup and nine cans of peaches next to nine metal cups. That seemed like a decent dinner. Plus, they hadn't eaten real food in years; best not to start with something too heavy. Not only that, but Matt guessed that Justin wasn't going to try the stew again tonight.

Matt smiled and studied the rest of his group. Their clothes all seemed to match their personalities well enough. Rhett wore jorts and a red T-shirt with the number *14* heat-pressed onto it. Justin's sweatpants were high-waters, so he'd bunched them up at the knees. His hoodie looked like something a wrestler would wear before a match. Victoria smoothed her black, ankle-length, muslin dress, her pale skin a sharp contrast. *Like a modest Elvira.* The bell sleeves swished when she moved her arms. Catherine surprised Matt. He'd expected her to wear something modest and unassuming. While her white polo was nondescript, it exposed her midriff. Bright green-yellow-and-red-striped shorts grazed the tops of her thighs.

"Guess it's my turn." Matt sorted through the clothes. "Rhett, will you ride the bike on the generator for a bit, just until the others are back with the water? Catherine, can you and the others set up the chairs in front of the TV? We can eat and watch the next tape together when Cody, Nathan, and Kyle return."

"Yup." Rhett exited the room without another word.

"Sure," Stacy said.

"Great." Matt decided to press his luck since Stacy was in the helping mood. "And put a metal cup, can of soup, and fruit on each chair?"

"Kim can do that," Stacy said.

"Ugh, whatever, fine," Kim said.

Matt settled on a pair of tapered jeans, a Commodore 64 T-shirt, and a jean jacket, then changed in a nearby room. When he returned, a big pot rested on a piece of fabric on top of the wooden floor.

"The guys are back," Catherine told him. "Cody said the water is still hot, so we need to wait a few minutes. I told them to change into real clothes."

Cody was the first out.

"Nice shirt," Matt said to Cody. He wore a western plaid shirt with pearl-snap buttons, tucked into tight jeans with a belt. "Too bad you couldn't find a belt buckle."

"Those are earned. Gotta win one. Only poseurs buy 'em."

"I wish there were an iron." Kyle tried straightening his collared shirt.

"Dude," Justin said, "you look like you're going golfing with my grandpa."

Kyle wore khaki shorts, a white Lacoste polo, and loafers. Justin wasn't wrong.

"I suppose you'd prefer I wear pajamas?" Kyle looked Justin up and down.

"NASA, gu-guys." Nathan pointed to his shirt. "I was su-supposed to go to space camp the year everything went to hell in a handbasket." He cringed. "S-sorry for cussing."

"Cute," Kim said. "Aren't you worried you're going to get those white shorts dirty?"

"They were the only ones that fit," Nathan said. "But yeah, they'll prob-probably be wrecked in an hour."

Now that everyone was dressed, Matt was slightly bummed that none of them wore a costume and they had all opted for regular clothes. Although he did agree with Kim and was happy there were boots and shoes that seemingly fit everyone.

"Let's all fill our cups, grab a chair, eat, and start the next video," Matt suggested.

"Are you sure there aren't any videos of ALF?" Rhett asked.

"Sorry, bud." Matt laughed.

Lance moaned.

Matt was first on the stage; Justin and Catherine were in tow.

"Hey, are you okay?" Matt crouched on the floor next to Lance. He groaned, then rolled to his side.

"What's wrong with him?" Justin asked.

"I don't know. It seems like he was trying to wake up," Matt said. "Let's get something under his head for support."

Cody tossed Justin a balled-up sweatshirt from the trunk. Catherine pulled the blanket off Lance and fluffed it.

"Wait," Catherine said. "Let's take off that belt. I'm sure it's uncomfortable."

"Good idea," Matt said. He reached for the buckle. "I can't. Look. There's a small padlock on it."

"What?" Justin pushed Matt out of the way. "Why?"

No one spoke. Matt felt a shiver down his back. He covered Lance and returned to the circle of chairs by the TV and sat silently.

"Well, this is awkward," Stacy said.

"Why don't you tell us what's on the menu, chief?" Justin asked.

"This is condensed soup, but we're fresh out of bowls at the moment. If you want, you can mix it in your cup with some water." Matt held the can opener. "Or just eat it straight from the can. I think it tastes better that way anyway. Remember what Cody said: if the can hisses when you open it, or if it's foamy, discolored, or smells rancid, then toss it."

"Like I said, I think I weeded out most of the cans with rusted-out bottoms and the ones that were bulging or had dents. But double-check them anyway, okay?" Cody said. "Actually, maybe I should go around and open everyone's can and show them what to look for this first time?"

"I'd appreciate that," Kyle said. "I don't plan on eating canned food forever, but the information is good to have."

Matt handed Cody the can opener and prepped the fifth tape for viewing. Before he pushed play, he paused. "Let me catch everyone up."

CHAPTER 18

Matt paced. "We all saw the first tape together, so I won't bore you with that. At some point there was a breach. Dr. Westbrook, the scientist, didn't know what had happened. He thought it was a malfunction of the system but quickly realized that something bad had happened. Alarms went off in our section every hour on the hour. He unfroze his successor, Darin, and had him help. Remember how terrible and crazy the weather was before we were saved?"

"Yeah," Cody said. "There was an F-5 tornado in the middle of a blizzard in Texas. It didn't make no sense."

"New York had completely flooded," Victoria said. "Even if I could get back to Manhattan, it wouldn't matter. Last I saw, the ocean had swallowed the entire city. Only the tops of a few skyscrapers poked through the water."

"And remember how the temperatures would shift throughout the day? You'd wake up and it'd be one-hundred degrees, then by noon it'd be negative twenty, and by late afternoon it was seventy. All the plants died." Catherine rubbed her left shoulder. "The air got thick; it was terrifying."

"I just remember when the roof on the mall blew off," Stacy said. "We had to take cover in a tornado shelter for two days. My Beamer had blown away . . . It was horrible. A police officer escorted me home. My parents were pissed."

"Exactly," Matt said. "So when the whole mountain shook, Dr. Westbrook thought it was an earthquake. But when he couldn't find any cracks in the ground, he started looking up. It wasn't an earthquake; it was a meteor. It struck the side of the mountain, and the cave had a crack in it."

"What?" Nathan said. "Sp-space?"

"No way," Kyle said. "That's too much. The solar system is waging war against us too?"

"I think it was just a coincidence with incredibly terrible timing," Catherine said. "Go on, Matt."

"Right, okay, then Jim—Dr. Westbrook, tried repairing it, but nothing worked. He had developed something called carbon foam and used it to fill in the holes and repair everything, even steel beams. Darin did most of the actual repairs since he was younger and more agile. The thing is this—and maybe some of you knew this already—but when they showed the repairs, we saw how large the cave was."

"What are you getting at, chief?" Justin asked.

"There were thousands of pods. *Thousands!*"

"You didn't tell me that." Justin spat his words.

"I am now." Matt said. "It all makes sense. You'd need that many people to start a new population. But it was unnerving to see. One man—well, two now—taking care of that many people."

"I wonder if we're the only cave people are stored in?" Victoria asked.

"Shut up!" Kim said. "That's, like, more than my brain can handle right now."

"She's probably right. We might not be the only seventeen-year-olds in our column. I vaguely remember there being more of us. We might have been the first ones out, then the truck—well, you know. But who knows? Hopefully we'll get that, and more questions, answered either from the tapes or Lance when he wakes up." Matt turned to Cody. "Everyone's soup okay?"

"I think so," Cody said. "Only had to replace one."

"Tastes weird," Rhett said. "But not disgusting."

"Great." Matt pressed play, sat in his chair, and smelled his soup. *Mom used to make me this when I was sick.*

He stirred it with a metal spoon. It felt thick, gelatinous at first, but once it was mixed it wasn't too bad. He gingerly took a sip; a slimy noodle fell back into the can. The salty broth tasted familiar but was overshadowed by a metal tang. It wasn't great, but it would do. He downed his water, not realizing how thirsty he was until his cup was drained. *I'll save the peaches for after the video.*

Dr. Westbrook sat on a stool in his usual spot, in front of the bank of computer monitors. He'd aged at least a decade, Matt guessed. His hair had completely grayed. His face was hollow and thin, though he seemed in good spirits.

"Everything has been stable, but the apocalypse is still ongoing." He sighed. "Darin, show them the feed."

The camera zoomed in on a computer monitor behind the scientist. Grainy black-and-white footage showed feet of snow along with a lightning strike. Moments later, a comet zoomed across the sky, blinding them for a moment. Then the camera shook.

"Holy suck!" Rhett yelled.

"Ah." Dr. Westbrook smiled. "Another meteor strike. They're becoming more frequent these days. I can't deduce what it means without additional information. Maybe things are getting worse, irreparable. Or not. I can't say, unfortunately."

A row of monitors blinked out behind him. A voice off camera alerted him.

"I bid you adieu, but remember, my intentions are good." Dr. Westbrook stood and walked slowly and carefully toward the monitors, slightly hunched and shuffling his feet. It reminded Matt of how his grandpa walked. The scientist pulled cables and cords out of the monitors just before the footage ended.

"Wow," Stacy said. "These tapes are boring. I think I'd just like your CliffsNotes version in the future."

"He's really gotten old," Nathan said. "H-h-how long were we frozen?"

Matt's head spun. "Hang on, this doesn't make any sense. The apocalypse was still happening when this was filmed. And Dr. Westbrook didn't look much older after the crash than he did in the video."

"So what?" Justin said.

"So, how are the trees so big? How has this entire place regrown? Those redwoods are at least a few hundred years old. No way that much time has passed."

"Maybe the entire world wasn't hit with the erratic weather." Justin shoved a syrupy peach into his mouth.

"I doubt that," Matt said.

"But you don't know, do you?" Justin asked. "How could you know? You got eyes and ears everywhere? No. Obviously this area wasn't hit too hard, and nothing was destroyed. How else do you explain the cabins and stuff, chief? Huh?"

Matt chewed on his bottom lip. "New York City is now part of the ocean, and you think this place was untouched?"

"Look around." Justin stood and splayed his arms out. "Unless we're all tripping on mushrooms, then yes."

"What do you think?" Kyle turned to Catherine. "You saw all the other tapes."

"Justin's right, this place does seem untouched. But logic, and what Dr. Westbrook has said . . . it doesn't make any sense."

The room fell silent.

CHAPTER 19

"It's getting late. I think we should sleep on it and have clearer heads tomorrow." Matt rested his elbows on his knees and hung his head. His chair squeaked.

"Gotta find a way to prove you're right, don't you?" Justin asked. "Fine, take all night. But you can't deny what's around you."

"Justin, I'm not the enemy. Yes, this is all here, you're right. I'm just having a hard time connecting the dots, okay? This all seems strange to me. The only logical thing is that the apocalypse is over, and he was moving us here to live. We were moved first because our column was the most in danger. I'm sure Darin will be bringing others soon. From the cryovault . . . from the cave."

"I'm scared," Stacy said.

For once, Matt thought she was being genuine. "I don't want to split up."

"Me either," Kim said.

"M-maybe we should all sl-sleep in here tonight?" Nathan asked. "Together?"

"Safety in numbers—good idea." Cody stood and clapped his hands together. "I think I saw some sleepin' bags in one of the backrooms."

"I saw them too," Kyle said. "I'll help."

"Great," Matt said.

They set up their sleeping bags in a circle, heads toward the middle. Once the sun had set, it was pitch-black outside. Matt stared out the window. No stars, no moon. Justin insisted that it was just cloudy; Matt silently disagreed. A green lantern in the center of the group illuminated the room. Awkward conversation only lasted a few minutes before it was lights-out.

Matt felt the tension. He knew he wasn't the only one questioning things. But he understood why people sided with Justin. Instead of sorting it out now, Matt closed his eyes and drifted into his first natural sleep in a few decades.

The hard floor beneath Matt vibrated. His eyes flashed open. "Does anyone else feel that?"

Before anyone could answer, gears popped loudly.

"I think it's the gennie," Cody said. "Like what we heard before."

"This loud? In here?" Matt asked.

The grinding grew louder, and the entire room shook. Metal screeched and groaned.

Victoria screamed.

"What the—" Matt stood. Then everything stopped. "That was weird."

"Wh-what w-w-was th-th-that?" Nathan's voice trembled.

The grinding and popping started again, but this time the room remained still.

"I'm going to turn off the generator." Matt lit the lantern. "See if that helps."

"I'm coming too," Justin said.

"You guys aren't leaving us." Kim stood, put a blanket over her shoulders like a shawl. "No way. That's like, literally the start of every horror movie, Voorhees."

"Yeah, I'm coming too." Stacy mirrored Kim and wrapped herself in a flannel sheet.

"Okay," Matt said. "Let's all go."

"Not me." Rhett turned on his side, eyes sealed shut. "Too tired."

"Rhett, get up!" Kim kicked his legs.

He groaned but didn't move.

"Fine," Kim said. "Then I'll find someone else to keep me safe."

"Okay, okay." Rhett stood, wiped the sleep from his eyes.

Matt led the group down the stairs, the lantern his only source of light. No crickets, grasshoppers, or cicadas buzzed, just the sounds of their footsteps on the dirt ground. Fog curled around their ankles. The heavy air felt thick in his lungs. Around the corner, the yellow beast hummed.

"I'll turn 'er off." Cody switched the key to off, and the whole unit shuttered to a stop.

"That's it?" Victoria asked. "Just like a car?"

"Yup," Cody said. "But always leave the key in the ignition. These suckers are easy to lose."

Matt held his hands out like he was surfing. "Whoa!"

The grinding shook the ground below their feet.

"I thought you turned it off," Rhett said. "What the hell?"

"He did," Matt said.

"I guess it had a bit of stored energy still in it?" Cody's voice cracked on his last word.

"An earthquake?" Kyle suggested. "Maybe the apocalypse isn't over."

"Dude, we already talked about this." Justin ran his hair through his messy blond hair. "Look around, it's over. We've had normal weather all day. What else could it be? I'm going back to bed."

Justin took the lantern from Matt and started back toward the cabin. Matt wrestled with what to do, but ultimately followed the group. It was too early in the morning to have a real conversation. The hairs on the back of Matt's neck stood erect. The generator had been turned off, but the noise and tremors still happened. It didn't make any sense. He said nothing on his way back to the cabin and kept his head down. *If I panic, they panic.*

Kim clicked on the light switch. "Ugh, can we turn the generator back on? It totally freaks me out not having power. Like, what if something happens?"

"We just shut it off." Justin crawled into his sleeping bag. "We'll deal with it in the morning."

"No," Kim protested. "Seriously, like, I can't deal with this. I'm going to have a panic attack."

"Does anyone else mind if we have it on?" Matt settled into his sleeping bag.

"No," Kyle said. "Let's have it on in case of an emergency. If the ground rattles again, we know it's just the generator. Nothing to worry about."

"All right," Cody said. "Nathan, you wanna grab the lantern and I'll show you how to turn it on?"

"Su-sure." The tall, thin boy held the lantern and walked side-by-side with Cody as they exited the room.

The silence was deafening. Now with the room completely devoid of light, Matt shivered. No matter how much he told himself things were fine, he couldn't shake the ominous feeling. He wrapped his arms around his legs and waited for his friends to return.

CHAPTER 20

"I'm wired," Catherine said. "I don't think I'll sleep anymore tonight. What time is it?"

"I dunno," Matt said. "The sky is barely purple, maybe four?"

The door creaked open. Nathan nodded in Matt's direction.

"Gennie's on," Cody said.

Stacy quietly cried in her sleeping bag.

"It's okay." Catherine rubbed Stacy's back. "We're going to be fine."

"I'm so scared," Stacy said. "That sounded purposeful. Like someone is after us."

"You watch too many movies," Justin said.

"Speaking of movies. How about you put on another episode of Jim Westbrook: boring-est and only man alive? That'll put us to sleep," Kim said.

Matt felt her sarcasm but took the opportunity to watch the sixth tape. He crossed the room and pushed the black plastic cassette into the VCR, hoping for an answer.

With the lantern off, the TV cast a flickering white light on the room until the video started.

"Greetings, gentle listener." Dr. Westbrook sat on a stool in front of a stack of pods. "I'd like to show you a bit of what I do up close. See this?" He moved to the side and held a thin, clear tube connected to a pod. Green lights lit up at the base, one by one, toward the top. "See how quickly they move? This is a good feeding tube. Connections are strong, delivery is consistent and effective. Not like this one." He pointed to the one above it, then disappeared from the frame. The camera shifted up toward it, then zoomed in. "See how sluggish the lights are, indicating the flow? And the last two don't light up. The tube is getting clogged with crud and must be replaced."

Dr. Westbrook came back into view and climbed a small ladder with a clear, plastic replacement in his teeth. He pushed a button on the side of the pod, and it hissed and steamed. The tube fell free from the top, and he worked quickly, securing the new. Blue lights lit up.

"I've got six different colors of lights to use. Currently green are the oldest and blue are the newest. I haven't had to dip into the other four reserves yet. You see, I must check 5,253 apparatuses every single day. This helps me move quicker, although I still must check the newer ones in case they are defective."

He disappeared behind the camera, and the lens moved toward the base of the shelf. Once back in view, Dr. Westbrook pulled a thick foam piece from a trap door on the galvanized frame. When he held it up to the camera, Matt recognized it as an air filter. Black dust covered it.

"We recycle the air, but it gets old and stale. This acid kills the dust, and the oils stimulate serotonin when inhaled."

He used an ordinary spray bottle, like the one Matt's mom used to keep the cat off the countertop, and sprayed the filter. Neon-yellow specks dotted it; one more spray and it was coated. The concoction looked alive. It rolled and zoomed around the surface. A yellow ball formed and twisted with black gunk. Finally, it rolled around the entire surface and fell off like an old piece of Silly Putty detaching itself from the ceiling. The filter was clean as new.

"Whoa," Matt said.

"This task isn't as hard, since one filter services eight to ten people. Admittedly, it's my favorite. There's something deeply gratifying about cleanliness." He picked up the ball of gunk and tossed it into a wastebasket.

The scientist was now behind the camera. "Now, this chore is my saddest one." The camera was set on the ground, and the tripod came into view. The camcorder moved unsteadily, then was seemingly placed securely in the cradle. He stood in view again with a flashlight. "I'm checking the door for cracks. The air quality is beyond hazardous at times, and I don't want it, or the erratic temperatures, leaking in. You see, this job saddens me because this was Darin's favorite task. I'm sorry to inform you, dear listener, that Darin has perished."

Matt's heart sank.

"Went mad, really. As the young people used to say, he had a freak-out. Couldn't take the isolation or pressure of the job. He exited the cave and is presumed dead. You see, he left during a lava flow wrought with acidic rain activity. It was one hundred fifty-eight degrees outside. Not only did he leave in horrible, impossible conditions, but he did it in his underwear. Marched to his death, really."

Matt felt the words form on his lips but didn't recognize his own voice. "Darin is dead."

"Dear Darin, how I miss you. I often wonder, if I had known your internal struggles, would I have unfrozen you? Could I have done this without you? And that is the reason why I won't awake anyone else unless I am near death. I wasted a life. Please forgive me. My intentions were good, and yet Darin has died."

Click.

The light from the TV now cast gray tones across the room. Loud snow on the screen. Matt swallowed hard, unmoving.

CHAPTER 21

Matt stood and slowly paced the room. He'd never even seen Darin, yet he couldn't get the image of a deranged man, clad only in his underwear, clawing at the door, desperate for an escape. *Is that what I'm doing?* He knew he had to choose his words carefully.

"I think we should go." Matt took a deep breath. "Darin is dead. There's no one left to get us. We need to find the cave and figure out how to maintain or unfreeze everyone."

"Okay, chief, let me get this straight. You were the one who insisted we stay, now you want us to go?" Justin snickered. "Sounds like you're losing your marbles. I never believed in you to begin with. Now I trust you less."

"Justin, stop," Catherine said. "Matt was right to have us stay. How could he have known Darin was dead?"

"He couldn't." An orange glow from the sunrise cast a menacing glow across Justin's face. "Just like he can't know if the scientist woke someone else up later."

"True," Matt said. "I don't. But he said he'd only do it in an extreme case."

"Like death?" Stacy said. "Because that happened."

"But he didn't know," Matt said. "He died in an accident. He wasn't sick."

"How do you know!" Justin's voice boomed. "That's right, you don't. How about this: you leave, I'll stay."

"I'm not trying to split us up. I just want to make sure our parents and brothers and sisters aren't unattended in a cave somewhere, dying. Don't you care?"

"I don't have a savior complex, chief. What I do have is a roof over my head, food, water, a few hot babes to flirt with, and best of all, a righteous lake. So while you're busy trying to fix a world that isn't broken, I'm going to take care of me."

"What a prince," Catherine said under her breath.

"Maybe we should have some breakfast?" Victoria said. "I think we might be a little hungry."

"Go ahead." Matt took the can opener and unsealed his peaches from last night. "I'm going to pack up some stuff and walk to the truck, see if it's salvageable. If it is, I'm following its tracks and driving back to wherever it came from."

"Good riddance," Justin spat.

"I'm coming," Kyle said. "The hostility in here is uncalled for. And I'd like to make a decision based on evidence I see with my own eyes."

Cody rummaged through the duffle bag and picked out a few supplies and deposited them into two green canvas backpacks. "You guys go ahead. I'm going to turn off the generator. I don't want anyone messing with it if the noises return."

"Anyone else?" Catherine asked. "Once, twice, no? Then it's settled, Matt, Cody, Kyle, and me."

"Nathan, will you check on Lance throughout the day? Make sure he's breathing," Matt said.

Nathan parted his lips but said nothing. Instead he simply nodded.

"Wait," Victoria said. "I'm not a good hiker, and I can't fix anything. I won't be any help . . . but you guys are coming back, right?"

"Yes," Matt said. "We'll be gone all day—overnight at the latest. If it's farther than that, we'll come back for you guys with the truck. But we'll be back, we won't abandon anyone. Not even you, Justin."

"Whatever, chief. You're burning daylight."

Matt stormed out of the cabin. His emotions had gotten the better of him, and he slammed the door shut behind him.

"I don't claim to have the answers. I have the same information you all have. I'm just looking at things logically. *Logically!*" Matt kicked a rock; it bounced into the tall grass. "Dr. Westbrook is dead. Darin is dead. The other girl from our cryopod column is dead. There could be others stuck dying in their pods. We still don't even know why he was moving our cryopods. We can't sit idly by and hope another successor was awakened before Dr. Westbrook was crushed."

"My daddy used to say, 'Hold out two hands, shit in one and hope in the other, tell me which one fills up first.' I know it's crass, but he ain't wrong, and neither are you." Cody said. "Gennie's off."

"Matt, you're not doing anything wrong." Catherine jogged beside him.

"We need to find our parents," Kyle said. "Maybe I should have stayed behind and watched the next tapes, maybe get some more answers."

"If you want to go back, then I understand." Matt stopped and faced Kyle. "But ever since I realized the vault could be unattended, all I can think about is my parents suffocating. And if not that, then severe dehydration is likely starting to set in."

"I think it was all automated," Kyle said. "Isn't it?"

"We think, but as Justin pointed out, we don't *actually* know. We only know what he showed us." Matt walked under the *New Beginnings* arch into the forest. "You saw all the checks Dr. Westbrook did every single day. I have to err on the side of caution. My conscience won't let me assume everything is okay. The entire human population could be on the line."

"Don't worry about that," Cody said. "I'm pretty sure Kim and Rhett are already workin' on repopulating the earth."

Matt laughed. He stopped and grabbed his stomach. Frustrated tears streamed down his face while he laughed.

"First of all, that's disgusting," Catherine said. "Secondly, we needed that. Thank you, Cody."

Matt wiped his eyes.

"You don't have the entire world on your shoulders." Catherine faced Matt. "I know it feels that way, but you're doing your best. We all are."

"Even Justin," Kyle said. "He's a dick, but he's just as clueless as the rest of us. You know? Some people just handle it better than others."

"You're right," Matt said. "Looks like the sun is fully up. I guess we better hurry. *We're burning daylight.*"

CHAPTER 22

"Did you guys notice the lake?" Kyle asked. "It was higher this morning."

"Now that you mention it, yeah. I thought it looked fuller," Catherine said. "Like it might crest the banks."

"How?" Cody asked.

"Maybe it rained last night?" Kyle said. "It would explain the fog."

"But the ground wasn't muddy. Not even damp," Matt said. "Are you sure it was higher?"

"Either that or the rope swing got longer," Kyle said. "It's almost touching the water."

Matt looked at the snowcapped mountain in the distance, through the massive trees.

Curious.

Another mystery he had no way of solving. Not yet anyway. His shirt clung to his body. He removed his jacket and hung it on a branch close to the path. *I'll pick it up on the way back.*

"Kyle, you said you were from Connecticut?" Catherine asked.

"Born and raised."

"You don't have an accent," she said. "Not even a hint."

"You'll hear it in my *o*'s on occasion, but not anywhere else. My mom was a WASP; I wasn't allowed to have one."

"Honestly, I thought you were snobby at first," Catherine said.

"I get that a lot," he said.

"What did you do up in New England for fun?" Matt asked.

"Normal stuff. I was class president every year of high school. Raised enough money for both a prom and a class trip. First class to ever do that. Took the entire class to the Hamptons for a day of ice skating."

"Oddly specific, but sounds fun," Matt said.

"You'd have to count me out," Cody said. "I'd never seen ice or snow until the apocalypse. Wouldn't know how to skate if I tried."

"Not true." Kyle proudly puffed out his chest. "We had coaches on site for the unfortunate ones who didn't know how. Everyone had a wonderful time."

"I bet you play tennis in the summer too," Catherine said.

"Of course I did. I wasn't meant to be the next Andre Agassi, but it was fun, nonetheless. Great for networking."

"You're a funny guy, Kyle." Cody patted his back. "We grew up very differently."

"And it's a good thing we did," Kyle said. "Our diversity is what keeps the group moving forward. So many different skills in a small group. It's a true melting pot. Just like our founding fathers intended."

Matt stifled a laugh; the kid was more intense than he'd realized. It was nice getting to know him outside the influence of Justin.

"Does anyone remember how much farther the truck is?" Kyle asked.

"I don't think it's far." Matt wiped sweat from his brow. "Has anyone else ever changed a tire before?"

"I have," Cody said. "Lots. Trucks, cars, farm equipment. Even a golf cart once. That sucker was harder than I expected."

"I have too," Catherine said. "My dad made me learn when I got my license. Then I'm pretty sure he sabotaged my tire to hammer in the point; I got a flat soon after. But I changed it and ruined a perfectly good sweater in the process."

"Great. That's awesome." Matt shifted his canvas bag on his shoulder. "Not about your shirt, though. Sorry."

Catherine shrugged.

"This will be an excellent opportunity for me to learn and stay out of the way. But I'll pay close attention." Kyle frowned. "I wish I had brought something to take notes."

"I don't think we'll be changing many cars' tires in the future," Matt said. "Unless there is a fleet of solar-powered vehicles."

They laughed, then walked in silence. For a minute, it felt like they were roaming the halls on the first day of school and they were all the new kid. Backpacks on their shoulders, awkward, forced conversation that quickly led to commonalities and friendships. It felt normal. Like *before.*

Matt's calves burned as he hiked up the last hill. He recognized the area. Red dirt stained his white shoes. As he crested the top, he saw the truck; it sat cockeyed. And behind it, a puddle of dried blood. Dr. Westbrook's final offering lay baking in the sun. He stared at it while he caught his breath.

"I wonder how different this would all have been if he'd lived. If he hadn't blown a tire. If he hadn't been crushed." Matt said.

"I know, buddy." Cody rested his hand on Matt's shoulder. "But all we can do is be thankful he got me out before it happened, or else . . ."

Matt fell silent. Cody was right.

"Let's get to work, then eat after?" Matt asked.

"Sure," Kyle said. "But I'm starving."

"With this many people, it ain't gonna take long," Cody said. "It'll be done lickety-split."

"Guys, I don't see a spare," Catherine said.

CHAPTER 23

"Crap." Matt's hands shook with nervous energy. "I didn't even consider that."

Matt checked the back of the truck. Nothing. He closed his eyes and took a deep breath. Searched his brain. His eyes flipped open. "It's underneath. I've seen this before, in a movie."

The truck sat cockeyed on its front passenger side where the tire had blown. Looking under the cargo area revealed a large, full-sized tire and jack wedged against the fuel tank. All of the parts under the truck had a white *B-35* painted on them.

"I'll help." Cody slid underneath on his belly, then flipped onto his back. "I wonder what that means?" Cody asked, pointing to a number.

"I dunno." Matt loosened the jack, and it landed on the pine-needle-covered ground next to him.

"Cody"—Matt lay next to him, wedging his fingers under the tire—"when we first met, you mentioned a meltdown. Dr. Westbrook said something about the truck and the meltdown. What did he mean?"

Cody froze. "Gosh, I guess I forgot he said that. Let me think."

Matt chewed on the side of his lip. *How could I have forgotten about that?*

"I—I guess he didn't really say much. Just that the truck had wrecked, and he needed me to help him get the pods open. There was an emergency. He said something, like maybe he was having a meltdown, I think."

"Are you sure?"

"Geez, I just don't remember. It was so hectic." Cody jostled the prongs, and the tire came loose.

Matt grabbed the side of it when it broke free; Cody had the other side.

"Kyle, Catherine, take this." Matt shoved it toward them, then grabbed the heavy rusted jack. "It's okay, Cody. I get it. It was crazy. I forgot about the conversation until we were back here. If you remember anything, let me know."

Matt shimmied out from under the vehicle and paused. The air felt different, still heavy and hot, but almost electric. Gooseflesh broke out over his skin. He still hadn't seen the sun. It was a disorienting feeling. Catherine had rolled the spare and propped it against the bumper. Matt concentrated on his conversation with Cody, hoping to trigger something. Maybe he'd heard him wrong, but it felt like there was something there. He handed Cody the jack.

The steel frame moaned as the jack lifted it to the proper height. While the rubber had ripped free, the lug nuts remained on the wheel. Cody worked quickly, unscrewing them.

"Did you feel that?" Kyle asked. "The ground, did it just move?"

"No," Catherine said. "Stop being paranoid, you're gonna freak me out."

The last lug nut fell and hit the ground.

Pop!

Gears ground and metal groaned, echoing through the forest. Matt whipped around.

"What *is* that?" Catherine asked.

Matt's blood turned to ice. He shook his head. "This is impossible. We're nowhere near camp."

A crack of thunder boomed, and a streak of silver lightning ripped across the darkening sky. Thick, puffy clouds formed out of nowhere, colliding. Rain poured from the pluming clouds.

"Hurry," Catherine said. She rolled the tire to Matt.

Matt pushed it on, his hand slipping in the wetness.

Cody walked to the edge of the hill.

The lug nuts became slick, but Matt shoved them on one by one.

"Water!" Cody ran toward them. "It's a flash flood."

"What?" Kyle yelled over the rain. "Impossible."

"It's coming!" Cody reached for the passenger door. "Get in!"

Matt stripped the final lug nut and wiped his brow. A fruitless effort in the downpour.

Matt jumped onto the driver's seat. Catherine, Kyle, and Cody piled onto the front bench seat. With shaky hands, he twisted the ignition; the engine hummed and clicked. He turned it again, this time pumping the gas. "Come on." It sputtered and turned over. "Yes!"

Water had already flooded the road. His dad had always told him to never drive into water. Flash floods were common in Nevada. But nothing like this. *Sorry, Dad.*

Matt backed the truck up a few feet. Water lapped at his ankles. The vehicle lurched forward. Creeping forward, he felt the tires sink. He floored it, but the truck was no match. The force of the flowing water slammed the truck into the trees.

"There's too much," Cody said. "We're stuck."

"Get on the roof," Matt said.

"We'll get swept away," Kyle said.

"What do you suggest?" Matt forced the door open and climbed from the sidestep to the hood, then onto the roof. "Come on." Matt reached for Catherine's hand and pulled her onto the hood.

Cody met Matt on the roof from the opposite side and pulled up Kyle, who immediately lay flat on the roof.

"Stand up!" Catherine yelled.

"No!" Kyle lay flat on his stomach. "This is safer."

The ground below them became a raging river in a matter of seconds. Logs and forest debris roared past. It was like white-water rafting on the Colorado River. A tree trunk smashed through the windshield, rocking the heavy vehicle.

"We need to get in a tree!" Matt jumped up and slipped, landing on his left wrist. Pain shot up to his elbow.

Cody planted his feet and slowly stood. He held onto a nearby limb and held his hand out. Matt reached up on unsteady feet.

"Go!" Matt yelled.

Cody climbed onto a thick branch, then up one more, and sat.

Matt grabbed Catherine's hand and boosted her into the tree. Heat radiated through his wrist.

"Can you climb up to Cody?"

She nodded.

The truck lurched again. Matt held on for dear life.

"Kyle!"

Kyle still lay flat on his stomach, holding the edge of the interior roof.

"Come on, you have to get up!"

"Just—just give me a second." Kyle's voice trembled.

Water rose rapidly.

Matt climbed fully onto the branch. He extended his arm down toward Kyle.

Kyle released his grip on the headliner and reached up.

Matt grasped Kyle's hand. "I got you."

Rain beat down even harder. Kyle's slippery hand squeezed Matt's so hard it was hard for Matt to hold it back. He pulled, his shoulder felt like it was coming out of his socket. Catherine or Cody had yelled something at him, but he couldn't make it out over the roar of the flood.

"Don't let go!" Kyle screamed.

"You have to get up!" Matt shouted. "I can't pull you into the tree."

Kyle tried to stand and lost his footing, pulling Matt with him. Matt squeezed his thighs around the branch. Bark cut into his legs. Matt felt a hand on his shoulder.

"Matt, stop!" Cody yelled into his ear. "He's gonna pull you into the water."

"Get up!" Matt yelled at Kyle, ignoring Cody. "Hurry! The water's rising!"

Kyle grasped Matt's hand.

A clap of thunder cracked so loudly Matt's teeth vibrated.

Matt turned his head, looking up the tree at Cody. "Pull!" Both of his shoulders were pulled in opposite directions. He screamed.

The newly-formed river raged harder than ever. A huge downed tree smashed into the side of the truck.

Pure horror was etched on Kyle's face. He thrust back as if someone had jerked him from behind. His grip on Matt was severed. Eyes wide with shock, he bounced off the roof of the truck and splashed into the water.

"No!" Matt screamed. "Kyle!"

CHAPTER 24

A wave rushed over Matt's entire body. He wrapped his arms around the branch and felt it fracture.

"Kyle!" He desperately scanned the area.

The limb sagged dangerously low, but Matt didn't care. He dangled his arm in the water, feeling for his friend. Sharp, jagged debris crashed into his soft skin.

"Come on, Matt!" Cody tugged on him a final time. "Get up here."

The branch cracked, and he relented. Matt followed Cody up onto the closest branch, then onto another one near Catherine. His wrist protested, but adrenaline pushed him through.

"Can you see Kyle?" Matt yelled over the raging river.

The truck tumbled under the water. A tire surfaced as the truck rolled, then slammed into two trees, wedging itself between them.

"No," Catherine cried. "The log, I saw it hit the truck. Kyle—he just—he just fell into the water. I haven't seen him surface."

"Maybe he grabbed onto a tree," Cody said. "He can swim."

Matt leaned forward, resting his head against the trunk of the tree. The rough bark dug into his forehead. His chest heaved as he caught his breath.

The rain quit as suddenly as it had started. Clouds parted, and the sky was bright again. The river swirled and receded. Like someone had pulled the plug on a bathtub.

"This is so weird," Catherine said. "I know it's the new normal, but it isn't normal to me at all."

"I don't get it either," Cody said.

"As soon the river is at tire height, let's climb down. We have to find Kyle," Matt said.

He scaled the tree when Catherine stopped him.

"Is it safe? Should we wait in case it rains again?"

"Kyle could be hurt. This is my fault." Matt jumped into waist-deep water. "Kyle!" he yelled.

Cody and Catherine soon followed and spread out. The water had completely receded, and Matt's feet stuck in the mud like a suction cup with each step.

"Anything?" Catherine called out.

"Nope," Cody said.

"No," Matt whispered to himself as he pulled a piece of material off a fern. He held the alligator logo from Kyle's polo. "Guys, over here."

Matt stared at the ripped hunk of shirt, willing Kyle to be okay. He held it out for them to see.

Catherine opened her mouth to speak but said nothing. Instead, she searched the area and called out his name.

Matt parted thick bushes, hoping his worst fear wouldn't be confirmed. Then he saw a shoe sticking out of scrub brush.

"Kyle?" He gingerly touched the shoe, hoping it was empty.

It felt hard.

Then he saw the other foot. He grabbed hold of both legs and immediately dropped them. Cold. Kyle was cold to the touch. *Maybe it's just from the water.*

A voice he didn't recognize yelled for Catherine and Cody. His vocal cords strained as he called out again.

Everything felt like it was in slow motion. He watched Cody pull Kyle from the foliage. Kyle's shirt had ripped free of his body. Blood seeped out of dozens of cuts on his chest and bruised ribs. His arm bent in an unnatural way; his skin was purple. Worst of all was his face: frozen, horrified, and wide-eyed. Catherine ran to his side and crouched next to him.

"Hey, hey, are you okay?" Catherine shouted. She tilted his head back and parted his lips, then gasped. "No, no, no."

Matt stared in disbelief. She shoved her fingers into his mouth and produced a fistful of wet leaves. Then she placed her left hand over her right, interlaced her fingers, and straightened her elbows.

Chest compressions.

She counted to fifteen, then pinched his nose and breathed into his mouth.

"Come on." Catherine pressed on his chest again. Sweat dripped down her temple. Again, she filled his lungs with air. "Kyle, wake up! Wake up!"

"He's gone." Matt put his hands over hers. "There's nothing we can do."

Catherine leaned into Matt's chest and sobbed. He wrapped his arms around her and stroked her long, black curls, streaking them with his muddy hands.

"Catherine, I'm sorry. You have to get up. We need to get back to camp."

"Camp." She jumped to her feet. "Crap! I forgot about them. I was so—so. I'm sorry."

"Don't be." Matt turned to Cody. "Are you okay?"

Cody's pallor wasn't much better than Kyle's. He turned and retched. Acidic bile and last night's dinner wafted in the humid air.

"Sorry 'bout that." Cody nodded, as if he were tipping his cowboy hat at them. "Seen a lot of dead livestock in my day, but nothing like this. What do we do, Matt? Bury him or leave?"

"Let's carry him to the truck and come back for him after we check on the others. We'll bury him after we check on everyone else." He cringed. "I know that sounds bad, but we don't have a choice right now."

"Okay," Cody said.

Matt held Kyle's wrists, and Cody held his ankles. They shimmied over to the truck, which was now wedged between two trees. The windshield had been obliterated. A tree poked out of the grill. Radiator fluid leaked, staining the wet ground.

Kyle's lifeless body lay next to the truck. Matt closed Kyle's eyes, like he'd seen in so many films. But his eyelids popped open. This wasn't the movies.

They walked in silence for a few minutes. Puddles from the left-over flash flood dotted the landscape along with trees and ripped branches. Parts of the path were nearly impassable with the debris.

"Dang it," Cody said. "That flood washed away the truck's track marks."

Matt rubbed his face. "I didn't even think of that. This sucks."

The ground rumbled under his feet. His heartbeat quickened. Then he heard the dreaded pop and grind.

CHAPTER 25

"Get in a tree!" Matt screamed. He laced his fingers together to create a step. Catherine's shoes dug into his palms, and he boosted her up. Pain again shot through his wrist. "Cody, you're next."

Cody waved him off and took a running start toward a thick redwood. He jumped and caught the branch, swinging until he had enough momentum to pull himself up.

Matt tried the same but missed. He found purchase on the side of the tree as the ground rumbled again. Popping and grinding. As if the earth was awakening.

"Climb higher!" Matt shook his left wrist and grimaced.

Camp!

He climbed up until branches were too far away or unstable, then leaned out as far as he could. No clouds in sight; Matt shielded his eyes from the bright light.

Then he saw it.

It wasn't the camp they'd left.

A newly formed lake encompassed the entire valley. Chimneys from a few cabins poked through the water. The only building exposed was the top half of the main hall.

"Are you guys seeing this?" Matt asked.

"Yes," Catherine said. "The flood, it happened so fast. I hope . . ."

Matt sat on his branch for a few minutes, still searching for signs of life and monitoring the sky for weather.

"How long should we wait up here?" Catherine asked.

"I guess we can get down now?" Matt guessed. "It just seems like every time we hear the noise something terrible happens."

"It didn't last night," Cody said. "But I'd rather be safe than sorry."

"Me too," Matt said. "But I guess something should have happened by now. Careful when you climb down."

Pain radiated through his left arm. Matt ignored it. Kyle was dead; no one wanted to hear about a sprained wrist. He waited for his friends to dismount the tree before he brought up the next topic.

They walked for a few minutes toward camp. Catherine silently cried. Cody's eyes were wide, blank, and expressionless. This wasn't a good time to bring it up, but he had no choice.

"I feel the closest to you two." Matt took a deep breath. "And I hope you guys feel like you can trust me."

"Sure, buddy," Cody said, putting his arm around Matt's shoulders.

"I don't want to freak anyone out, but—"

"The apocalypse." Catherine interrupted him. "It's not over, is it?"

Matt bit his lip. "Maybe not. But maybe so."

"Why would he unfreeze us?" Catherine asked. "It doesn't make any sense."

"It had to have something to do with the initial breach, right?" Matt asked.

"We gotta get back and watch the tapes," Cody said. "Hopefully he has the answers there."

"I doubt it. If he was as panicked as you said he was, I'd be shocked if he took time to record a message." Matt misjudged the depth of a puddle and post-holed up to his knee in mud. "That's the other thing. Camp is flooded. We don't know if anyone else is hurt, or . . . or like Kyle. And the tapes! I hope they didn't get ruined."

"Crap on a cracker," Cody said. "Maybe we can dry them out."

"It won't matter if the TV got fried." Catherine kicked a rock. "Ugh, how is this happening? Why did Dr. Westbrook do this to us? We came so far, and now he just leaves us here to—what? Die one by one?"

"He didn't mean to leave us," Matt said. "Catherine, he was crushed. I'm not saying the apocalypse isn't over, but I'm also not saying it is. That might have just been a random flash flood."

Matt hoped she believed him. He wanted to believe himself. But deep down, he knew something was very, very wrong.

"Have you noticed that?" Cody took a deep breath. "It's not fresh. I used to love the smell of rain. The plants ain't blooming; the birds ain't chirpin'."

Matt inhaled the heavy air and smelled nothing. He rubbed a hand over his prickly hair and stared at the ground. His head swirled.

The ground quickly became a slippery, muddy mess on their final descent down the hill. At the bottom, a couple feet of water still remained. Matt slogged through it, wishing he'd opted for shorts. Water wicked up his pants. He paused at the *New Beginnings* sign.

"No matter what, we stay together, and we stay calm. Okay?" Matt managed to keep his face expressionless, but a muscle ticked in his jaw.

"Roger that," Cody said.

Catherine nodded. "So much for our new beginning."

CHAPTER 26

The flood in the camp hadn't fully receded like it had elsewhere. But it made sense, since it was in the valley. Debris from the cabins floated in the knee-high water. When they'd first jumped into the raging river to find Kyle, they'd only encountered organic material. But here, old clothes, waterlogged folders and papers, along with mattresses, sheets, and pillows, floated in the newly formed lake that was Camp New Beginnings.

They waded through it, tripping every few feet on unseen trees and rocks below. Matt's foot caught something hard, and he fell, arms out to catch himself. His left wrist buckled immediately upon impact, leaving his right arm to take the brunt of the fall. Murkiness clouded his vision. He felt someone pull the back of his shirt and lift him out of the water.

"Thanks," Matt coughed.

"You're weak," Catherine said. "We need to eat."

"We will." Matt trudged carefully through the muck.

"Is that . . ." Cody squinted.

"Rhett!" Matt called.

The large boy paddled a small yellow canoe through the water. The front end sagged. It would be a matter of minutes before it would be rendered useless. Water swirled and rapidly retreated, draining into a low spot between the main cabin and the lake.

Matt high-stepped it toward him.

"Hey! You guys made it back," Rhett yelled. He stood and exited the watercraft.

"We're so happy to see you," Catherine said. "The others, are they . . ."

"They're in the cabin." Rhett yanked off his shirt, wrung it out, then slipped it back on with a shiver.

"What happened?" Matt asked.

"We were swimming, and all of a sudden it started to rain big time bad. Kim," he rolled his eyes, "got all freaked out because she thought she saw some lightning. Then Stacy joined in. Total hysterics. They demanded we take cover inside. I mean, have you ever met anyone that's been electrocuted?"

Matt furrowed his brow. *Big dumb animal, isn't that what Kyle whispered? He had him pegged.*

"So we walked toward the hall just to shut them up, and the lake leaked into the camp."

"Leaked?" Catherine folded her arms. "You mean, it crested its banks? Major flash flood?"

Rhett smiled—big straight, white teeth. As if he was posing for a team photo.

"Rhett, it was serious." Catherine continued, "We were stuck in trees and saw that the entire camp was underwater. All the cabins, sheds—everything except part of the main structure."

"That was the thing. The girls were already up the stairs. We got caught in it the last few steps and swam up to join them in the cabin. Where's Kyle?"

"The cabin didn't flood?" Matt ignored his question. He only wanted to recount that story once.

"Oh yeah, follow me." Rhett waved them toward him. "It flooded a bunch. Past the deck and into the gym. Probably two or three feet high."

"But everyone is okay?" Catherine asked. "You all made it to safety."

"Yep." Rhett walked up the first few steps and out of the water. "Even the sleeping guy is okay."

Catherine turned to Matt. "How is he so casual about all of this? He has no idea how bad this could have been and *was* for us."

Matt's spine stiffened. "Do you think the lake flooded before? Maybe that's why the floors inside are so warped? Same with the railings and porch?"

"Maybe." Cody turned white as a ghost. "That means it'll happen again."

Matt shrugged and trudged up the stairs, his mind reeling. The swollen door caught on the deck when he forced it open. Inside, Kim, Stacy, and Victoria huddled in a corner, faces tearstained. Justin lay on the stage; Nathan sat on the ground below him. A waterline on the exposed logs was two feet high.

The door scraped loudly when he released it. All eyes were on them.

"You made it back, chief." Justin sat, dangled his legs off the stage. "Where's my ride?"

"We got caught in the flood," Matt said. "The truck is wrecked."

"Way to go." Justin slowly clapped. "Not another car on the street, and you still managed to total our only vehicle."

"Shut up, Justin," Catherine said. "You have no idea what we've been through."

"Yeah, you look pretty rough," he said. "You been rolling in the mud or what?"

"We got there and changed the tire; it was sunny skies. Then . . ." Matt rubbed his face. "I don't know. Suddenly it was raining, bad—like how it would rain right before we were frozen in the cryovault. Without warning, there was a flash flood. We got in the truck, drove a few feet, and within seconds there was water in the cab. The river smashed the truck against a tree. We got out onto the roof—"

"No way," Nathan said. "Th-th-the lake was up to the tr-truck."

"Doubt it," Cody said. "I reckon it was just a flash flood. Coincidence."

Matt stared at the floor. It was still damp, the wood curled worse than before. "It all happened so fast. We climbed onto the trees, and Kyle . . ." Matt's shoulders slumped. "He was still on the truck. He was swept away by a wave."

"What?" Victoria jumped to her feet and ran to the door. "We have to go find him."

Matt stopped her and held both of her shoulders. "We found him. Kyle is dead."

CHAPTER 27

"Get out," Stacy said.

"I'm sorry," Matt said.

Everyone approached him; he held his ground.

"What do you me-mean dead?" Nathan asked, his eyes filled with tears.

"He drowned." Matt took a small step backward.

"This is your fault." Justin balled his fists. "It was your idea to go to the stupid truck in the first place. Now look, you have no truck and Kyle's blood is on your hands."

"That's not fair," Catherine said. "Kyle panicked. He wouldn't let go of the truck and climb onto the tree."

"He wouldn't have been there if it weren't for you three," Rhett said.

"And what if we had stayed here?" Cody stood next to Matt. "There's no sayin' where he would have been or if he would have made it back to the cabin in time. Least we were out looking for a solution."

"Where is he?" Victoria's voice was barely above a whisper. "His body."

Catherine took Victoria's hands into her own. "He's still there. We saw camp was underwater and ran here first to see if you guys needed help. We'll go back and get him. Bury him like we did with Dr. Westbrook and the girl. Okay?"

"I hope you jerks do a better job burying Kyle than you did the scientist and the girl," Justin said. "We saw a body float by about twenty minutes ago."

"So-sorry." Nathan hung his head. "You gu-guys left us to swim. Kyle and I did our best."

"Now Kyle gets to join them, thanks to Matt," Justin said.

Victoria sobbed quietly.

"Now what, *chief*?"

"That's enough!" Catherine shouted.

"The tapes, where are they? Are the TV and VCR okay, or did they get wet?" Matt asked.

"Can you, like, shut up about the stupid tapes already?" Kim screamed. "You act like they're going to give you a secret code to this crap. Like, enough already!"

"Yeah," Stacy said. "All you've done is boss us around, coddle the tapes, and get Kyle killed."

That stung.

"Hey, that ain't fair," Cody said. "If it were up to you, all you would have done is swim and frolic in the sun. He directed us to find food, clothes, and shelter. Isn't that somethin'?"

"Not worth a life," Stacy muttered.

"Here's the 411: none of us are safe." Matt's face flushed. "Justin could have died when he ate the rancid stew. Heck, you could step on a nail and die of tetanus. There are things we can avoid, like drinking tainted water or injuring ourselves. What we can't avoid are natural disasters. I'm done fighting. Where are the tapes?"

"Whatever." Kim turned on her heel and walked away.

"Bottom of the TV cart." Justin smirked. "But I don't think you're going to be happy."

The cart had been shoved in the corner near the stage. Matt stalked over to it. He patted the TV and VCR. Both felt dry to the touch. At the bottom were all nine tapes. Water pooled at the bottom of the tray.

Matt cursed.

"We gotta get these dried out, see if they still work." He picked them up. Water leaked out of the holes.

"Dude, take a chill pill," Stacy said. "It's not like we have anything else to do."

"Nathan, did you see any screwdrivers in the shed?" Matt ignored her.

"Ye-yes," he replied. "What kind?"

"Phillips. Bring a few. The screws are pretty small." He turned to Cody and Catherine "Help me bring these outside?"

"Sure." Cody grabbed four tapes.

"I'm going to stay here, try and explain this again to them, okay?" Catherine whispered to Matt. "You're not the enemy."

Matt nodded, rummaged around the backroom for a towel, took the remaining tapes, and left.

The waterlogged wood stairs felt soft under his feet. Like they were made of foam. It was only a matter of time before the supports rotted out and the wraparound porch collapsed. That was a problem for another day.

"That rain really cooled it down." Cody shivered. "Wind picked up too."

"Yeah, it did." Matt yelled toward the shed, "Nathan, we're on the east side of the cabin."

"Won't they dry faster in the sun?" Cody asked.

"I don't think the tape can be in direct sunlight. I mean, that's how camera film works. Well, they can't see light at all. But these are like cassettes. I think they'll fare better in the shade. Hopefully they're not completely soaked and the breeze helps dry them out."

Nathan met them with six screwdrivers. One had a grease-stained handle that was still neon orange on the very top and bottom. It said *Trav's Auto Care 555-2744* on the side grip. The other five were clear plastic, standard green.

Matt reached for the colorful-handled one first. "Hope this works."

On top of the faded *Gremlins* beach towel, all nine tapes lay ten inches apart. Matt carefully unscrewed one side of the tape, and the other. He wedged his fingers in the small space and evenly applied pressure, careful not to break the plastic.

Pop!

He placed the casing directly below the tape, laid the screws in it, then examined the innards as if he were doing an autopsy.

"Okay, see?" Matt pointed to the reels. "This was completely rewound. That was in our favor. The roll is tight; it looks like only the first few layers got wet. And they might still be playable. Cody, you start on that end, Nathan the middle. If it is partially unwound, let me know and we'll decide what to do. If you're feeling nervous, open one of the tapes we've already seen first. We cannot break Tapes 7 through 9."

Matt removed four more black plastic covers and discovered the same thing: all had been completely unwound or rewound.

"You guys doing okay?" Matt asked.

"I cracked the back piece on Tape 3," Cody said. "But if we need to rewatch it, we can swap it out with one that's intact."

"That's okay," Matt said. "Nathan?"

"A-all good."

"I think this is the best spot for them to dry. If we hear any popping or grinding, our first priority is to meet here, grab the towel, and bring it inside and up high. Hopefully that's a nonissue today. For sure, we'll bring them in at night."

"Works for me," Cody said. "What about the generator?"

CHAPTER 28

"Crap," Matt said. "I guess let's see if it starts. Nathan, do you want to help or see if you can find some smaller pieces of wood that have dried out already? We need to get a fire going."

"Sure," he said. "I'll see if any-anyone else wants to help."

Matt rounded the side of the building with Cody in tow. Broken trees, mattresses, and bedding from cabins had crashed into the side of the generator.

Stale, wet mildew wafted from the soaked mattresses. *This isn't the first time it's flooded. Who cleaned up last time?* He pulled one off the machine and dropped it onto the ground. Cody dragged a heavy branch from the back end of it.

"I dunno," Cody said. "I ain't ever tried to start one after a flood."

"Should we wait? Will it damage it?"

"Might. But I have an inkling this one is different, considering the modifications from the bicycle."

Matt pressed his hand against the side with his good hand. No humming. His heart sank.

"I hope it's not ruined." Matt kicked the side. Water trickled out of one of the seams. "I guess we can wait until tomorrow. Let's help with the fire in the meantime. At least get our bedding dry before night."

Matt stared at the clear blue sky. Afternoon had faded into a deep blue, as if the sky was preparing itself for the sunset. He and Cody grabbed branches and broken limbs on their way back to the front of the cabin. Nathan waved at them and pointed to his small pile of wood.

Two logs of similar size had been speared into the ground, six feet apart from each other. Stacy stood on one side of the makeshift clothesline with a rope near the top of the log. Kim mirrored her on the opposite side.

"Ready," Stacy said.

Catherine pressed a nail through the coarse rope and pounded it in, then did the same on Kim's side.

"Great idea, ladies." Matt turned to Nathan. "Any of the wood dry enough to burn?"

"Ki-kinda," Nathan said. "Justin is looking for dry paper to use as kindling." He continued to break small twigs and stack them in a cone.

"Can't believe he's actually helpin'," Cody said.

"He said he wa-wants a dry blanket." Nathan rolled his eyes.

Victoria traipsed down the long staircase, arms overflowing with matted sleeping bags.

"Here," Matt met her halfway up the stairs, "let me help."

The sleeping bags were considerably heavier than they had been before. He draped one over the clothesline. The line sagged in the middle at first but righted itself once more bags had been evenly spaced over it.

"This is great. Can you make a few more like this?" Matt asked Kim and Stacy.

"I guess," Kim said.

"I'll help." Victoria touched a post. "These shouldn't be too hard to find. How many more should we build?"

"Three or four, I reckon." Cody yelled toward the cabin. "Rhett, Justin, get down here."

"What?" Justin yelled from the balcony.

"You find some paper?"

"Yeah," he said. "We'll be right down. Keep your shorts on."

Matt and Cody placed the bigger logs near the fire pit while they waited for Justin.

"All we could find were old playbills from the cabinets in the dressing rooms by the stage," Justin said.

"That'll work." Matt tore the black-and-yellow magazines into long strips and placed them between sticks. "We'll have to rotate these logs and branches near the fire. Get them dry."

"The bags are too far away," Rhett protested.

"An-any closer and they'll melt," Nathan said.

Rhett shrugged.

Matt pressed his hands near his pocket and felt the outline of his flint. He pulled it from his pocket, thankful it hadn't been lost in the chaos. He struck the metal across it; a small spark jumped from the end. One more strike and a tiny fire erupted.

"Hand me a few sticks," Matt said. He gently blew on the fire then placed a few thicker sticks near it. "That's right. Burn baby, burn."

The girls returned and built four more clotheslines. Rhett used an old, rusted ax to break them into smaller logs.

"It's getting dark," Catherine said. "I'm going to grab us some dinner. I haven't eaten yet today."

"Me neither." Nathan followed her up the stairs. "Sh-should we check on Lance too?"

"Good idea," Matt said. "If he doesn't wake up soon . . ."

Catherine nodded.

The remaining teenagers sat in a circle around the fire. Shadows danced across their faces as the sky faded from orange to black. Rhett held Kim as she sobbed quietly. Justin tried to comfort Stacy, but she rebuffed his advances. The breeze from the afternoon had turned into a gusty wind. Matt wrapped his arms around himself, wishing he still had his jacket.

And Kyle.

CHAPTER 29

They all ate metallic-tasting stew except for Justin. He opted for Spa-ghettiOs and complained there wasn't any Tang to chase it down. Cody had boiled water for everyone, then boiled a second batch to be stored in the cabin.

Cutting the wood had helped it dry out considerably faster. The fire roared; Matt held his hands out, catching the warmth.

"Guess we should bring the tapes in before we turn in," Matt said. "Just in case."

"Ugh!" Kim yelled. "Can you, like, shove it with those tapes? I wasn't kidding before. I've had it with your heinous ideas. Come on, Rhett. Let's take a walk."

She stood, holding Rhett's hand, and pulled him up from a log. He waved goodbye but said nothing. Within a few seconds, they disap-peared into the darkness. A few minutes later, Matt heard the distant opening and closing of a cabin door.

"N-n-no stars or moon again tonight," Nathan said, craning his neck toward the night sky.

"Hmm, the sleeping bags aren't quite dry yet, but mostly." Cath-erine flipped them one by one until each one's damp side faced the fire.

"It's okay. We can hang out a little longer." Justin winked at Cath-erine.

I guess he's moved on from Stacy to Catherine.

"I'll be back," Matt said, in his best Terminator voice. "Cody? Nathan? Will you bring a lantern with you?"

"You're breaking my heart, chief." Justin put an arm around both Catherine and Stacy's shoulders. "You leaving me out?"

"Nope." Matt balled his fists at his sides. "Just leaving you to tend to the fire."

"I'll keep 'em warm." Justin smirked.

Matt's nostrils flared, but he thought better of saying anything and walked away. He led Nathan and Cody to the east side of the main hall. Nathan held the light while Matt held one end of the towel and Cody held the other. They carried their precious cargo and walked slowly, careful not to lose any screws or disturb the open reels. As the stairs had dried out, the wood had curled more fiercely and made it even more precarious to climb.

"Careful," Matt said.

"I ain't one to complain," Cody said, "but this porch has seen better days."

Nathan opened the door and illuminated the dark hall. "Now where?" he asked.

"Um, how about one of the tables up on the stage by Lance?" Matt replied.

Nathan again led the way, and they placed the towel on the stage. Matt jumped up first, and Cody followed. He froze.

"Wh-what?" Nathan asked.

"Hang on." Matt jumped down and placed his hand on the ground as if it were train tracks and he was feeling for an oncoming train. "Nothing. I thought I heard something."

"You did," Cody said. "I heard it too, but it wasn't as loud this time."

"Maybe it's nothing," Matt said.

"Wh-what do you mean?" Nathan asked.

Matt made eye contact with Cody.

Cody nodded.

"We heard those popping and grinding noises out by the truck, right before the rain and flash flood. It might be related." He quickly returned to the stage and helped Cody place the towel and all the VHS tapes onto a rickety card table. "But we heard it again later and nothing happened. Okay, these tapes should be good."

"How'd they look?" Nathan asked.

"They're still pretty wet," Matt said.

The front door slammed open.

"Hey," Catherine said. "Get out here!"

"What?" Matt jumped down and jogged toward Catherine.

"It's snowing."

Matt shook his head. "No. No way."

Loud footfalls echoed up the stairs.

"Believe it, chief," Justin said. He held several sleeping bags. "Guess I'm not getting my own room tonight."

Victoria and Stacy followed behind him with the rest of the bags. Matt slammed the door shut.

"We've got to find Kim and Rhett." Stacy shivered.

"Forget them," Justin said. "They know where we are."

"I agree with Justin," Matt said. "We need to move the dry wood into the shed. The fire should burn out on its own. We should only go in and out if it's absolutely necessary; we've got to save the heat in here. Lighting the fireplace should be a last resort. We have no idea the last time it was serviced or if the flue is blocked. Anyone who wants to help with the wood, follow me."

Everyone followed. Victoria held the lantern. Ice-cold wind whipped the snow around their feet. Luckily it was only flurries. They had to keep the firewood dry.

"Ow," Stacy said. "This bark is sharp."

"Suck it up, buttercup," Justin said.

"Kim," Stacy yelled. Her voice cut through the wind. "Kim!"

Catherine and Victoria joined in.

Matt trudged back and forth with Victoria leading the way. Wind bit at his exposed skin and seeped through his shirt. He tucked his head down. Finally, most of the wood had been safely tucked into the shed. He looked in the direction of where Rhett and Kim had run off to. Smoke snaked its way from a chimney in a nearby cabin.

"Look," he yelled over the wind.

"I can't believe that Rhett figured out how to make a fire," Catherine said. "And what are they burning?"

"Who cares," Matt said, and he ran toward the main hall.

He raced up the stairs and waited until everyone was behind him before he opened the door, then quickly slammed it once they were all tucked inside.

"Holy crap," Cody said. "It's like Alaska out there."

"I don't think the apocalypse is over," Catherine said.

Matt bit his lip. "I don't know. It—nothing makes any sense."

"I found a few candles in the stage area yesterday," Victoria said. "Can you use your flint to light them?"

"I think I can handle that," Cody said. "Good find."

Three red candles jutted up in a tarnished silver candelabra. Once lit, Victoria extinguished the kerosene lantern. An eerie crimson glow filled the room.

Stacy walked to the window. "Why is it so damn dark? I hope Rhett and Kim are okay."

"It's just a little snow," Justin said, putting a hand on her shoulder.

"It's barely even accumulated. It's just the wind that sucks. I'm sure they're keeping warm in a cabin, if you know what I mean."

"Gag me with a spoon," Stacy said. "I'm going to bed."

"Good idea," Matt said.

They placed their sleeping bags in a small circle again, this time short three people. One by one they fell asleep. Catherine rested her head on Matt's shoulder.

"I'm scared," she whispered.

"Me too." Matt wrapped his arm around her and fell asleep.

CHAPTER 30

Matt slowly blinked sleep out of his eyes. The candles had burned down, leaving a waxy puddle under the candelabra. Bright light shone in from the windows, the kind that only sun reflecting off fresh snow produced. He gently shook Catherine, waking her.

"Hm?" She held the back of her neck and sat.

Matt shimmied out of his sleeping bag and approached a window. Three feet of fresh powder covered the ground. Trees white with frost. His breath fogged up the glass. Lazy wisps of smoke from Kim and Rhett's cabin rose in the cold air.

"I wonder how long they're planning on staying there?" Matt tapped on the glass in their direction.

Bang! Bang! Bang!

"What the—"

"Is that Kim?" Stacy bolted toward the door.

Matt stepped in front of her. His hands trembled as he palmed the knob.

"Or Rhett?" Stacy's voice cracked.

It wasn't.

"It's not coming from the door." Catherine slowly approached the stage. "It's Lance."

The tall man rolled on his side, scratching his throat and pounding the stage with a closed fist.

"Water," Matt said. "Get him some water!"

Cody dipped a metal cup into the saved water and presented it to Lance, who greedily drank it down.

"Are you okay?" Matt stood in front of his group, an arm's length away from Lance.

"I think—" His voice caught in a coughing fit.

"Move," Justin said to Matt. He reached for the cup and left to refill it. He returned and handed it to Lance. "There you go, drink it down."

The man's hands shook, and he only sipped the water this time.

"I feel so weak," he said. "Where am I? How long was I out?"

"We'll get you some food," Matt said. "You've been unconscious for as long as we've known you, so almost three days now. We're at a camp called New Beginnings."

"What's your name?" Cody handed him a can of Manwich and a spoon.

"Thank you." He focused on his meal and ate. Orange stained the sides of his lips. "Where did you get this?"

"Found it in the mess hall," Cody said.

"Thanks—" He froze. "Where's Westbrook?" He threw his blanket off and pawed at the Everlast weight-lifting belt.

"He's—he's dead." Matt held his hands up defensively.

"Dead?" Lance's eyes grew wide.

"Calm down. It's going to be okay. He was crushed by a pod—"

"The key, where's the key!" he shouted.

"What key?" Justin asked. "Are you looney or what?"

"The one that opened the pods. I need it."

Catherine pulled a silver chain tucked into her blouse from her neck. "This?"

"Please." He held out his palm. "I'll die without it, and so will you."

"Who *are* you?" Matt spat.

"I'm Darin."

CHAPTER 31

"No way," Matt felt the color drain from his face. "The protégé? No, he died."

"Died? I didn't die. What are you talking about?"

"Yes, that's what Dr. Westbrook said in his video. You went crazy and died." Catherine palmed the key.

"So you are cuckoo for Cocoa Puffs," Justin said. "Great."

"What?" Darin shook his head. His feathered hair swished. "No, I'll explain everything—just give me the damn key."

"After you explain," Matt said.

"This belt is an explosive device, and I have no idea what detonates it. Let me take it off so we're safe. Okay?" Darin's tone had softened, and his words were even.

Catherine didn't hand him the key but instead unlocked the padlock on his belt, then placed it back around her neck. "Good thing I saved it."

"Yes." Darin exhaled loudly and removed the belt. "Is it safe to go outside? We need to get it out of here. As far away as possible."

"Yeah, it's fine right now. And you're not leaving," Matt said.

"I'll take it." Victoria gingerly picked it up. "Is the forest okay?"

"No," Darin said. "Too much potential shrapnel. Are there any barren spots in camp?"

"May-maybe the back of camp, opposite of the entrance?" Nathan suggested.

"Yes," Matt said. "Good idea."

Nathan jumped off the stage and reached up to Victoria to take the belt. "Let's go."

"I can do it," Victoria said.

"What if it starts to snow again?" Nathan asked. "P-p-pairs are better."

Matt nodded, and they left. A cold gust of wind bit through the air when they opened the door.

"Snow?" Darin asked.

"Don't change the subject," Justin said.

"How are you not dead? And you're not old enough to be Darin from the video. If he had lived, he'd be like thirty or forty." Matt sat on the stage floor and stared at Darin.

"Let me explain. I was in the twelve-year-old column when I was frozen. One day Westbrook woke me up. I had no idea what was going on. He said I was to take over for him if the apocalypse outlived him. He seemed perfectly healthy, but I worked with him day in and out for years. Maybe ten or so? I'm not sure. He was—odd, to say the very least. As young as I was, I still felt like something was off about him. He called me defiant and ordered me back into my pod, said I wasn't ready, that I had disappointed him. The last thing he said before he put me in the cryopod again was, 'Darin, you are dead to me.'"

"That doesn't explain why you're here now," Matt said.

"Why *am* I here? Where is here?" Darin stood on wobbly legs. "You said there was snow. How bad?" He stepped down and approached a window.

"Pretty bad. We got like three feet," Catherine said. "It came out of nowhere. We're worried the apocalypse isn't over. Look, we need to find our families."

Matt put a hand on her shoulder. "And we want to know why Dr. Westbrook woke us up if it wasn't safe."

"This isn't bad," Darin said. "Snowstorms aren't unusual. Look, you can see the sky. The air isn't hurting my lungs. It's worse in some spots. On our way here, it was just as bad as before. This must be some sanctuary. I wonder how he found this place?"

"I've had it!" Stacy yelled. "Tell us right now what's going on or—or I'm going to kill you. You got it?"

"Calm down, Stacy." Matt turned to Darin. "We aren't going to kill you. That's insane."

"Westbrook was insane." Darin stared at the ground.

The room fell silent.

"He woke me up—I guess three days ago. He was manic, frenzied," Darin continued. "Fifteen years must have gone by; he looked so much older. He didn't give me a second to acclimate. The moment I stood, he put the belt around my waist and told me to help or else. The alarm was buzzing so loud, warning strobe lights blinking reds and greens. It was chaos. I refused to help until I knew what was going on. Then he told me that the column that I—he told me that the column that had broken when I was first awake was failing. That the seventeen-year-olds were dying. We needed to move them and wake them up. I asked why the weight belt. I'd use a forklift to move the pods. He said it was a bomb—insurance, really, so I'd be forced to help. If I didn't, he'd detonate the device and kill me and anyone within a hundred feet."

"Why didn't he trust you to help?" Matt asked. "We were dying."

"I didn't fully trust him when he put me back to sleep. I was the only one awake, and where could I go? Out into the apocalypse? Let's just leave it at that. Anyway, he'd backed the emergency truck into the cave, and I moved as many pods as I could fit into the cargo area. Once it was full I jumped into the cab. No idea how we were going to unload the pods or where we were going. I honestly assumed we were just going to a different area of the cave." He stared blankly out the window at the snow. "But he drove to a big set of doors, made me open the right side. I was afraid he was going to lock me out. As soon as I opened the door I was hit with intense heat. The air was so thick and polluted. In the few seconds it took for him to pull the truck out and me to shut the door and get back in the truck, I was coughing up black mucus. The sky was an orangish-red. Wind swirled. Tornados everywhere. Lightning strikes shook the truck; I was worried about the pods. It was terrifying. We were on a death drive. Once I caught my breath, I tried to ask Westbrook where he was taking us. Out of nowhere, I felt a sharp pain in my thigh. A huge needle was plunged into my leg, and the next thing I knew, I was here. See?"

Darin pointed to a round bruise on his upper thigh.

"This doesn't make any sense. Dr. Westbrook was trying to save us. Maybe he tranq'd you to calm you down. Are you sure you weren't the hyped-up one?" Matt paced. "He was good. He sacrificed his life for us."

"I knew a very different Westbrook," Darin said.

"What about the tapes?" Catherine asked.

"Oh, right! I forgot he used to document us. Wait, how do you know about them?" Darin's face twisted in confusion.

"I assume he put them in my pod," Matt said. "I guess to explain what happened, just in case. We've only watched six of the nine."

"You have power? And a TV?"

"Yep," Justin said. "We have it all."

"I need to see them. What did he tell you?"

"Does it matter?" Matt asked. "You were there."

"You don't get it." Darin raised his voice. "Whatever Westbrook told you was a work of fiction. His reality and actual reality weren't linear."

"No," Matt said. "No way. He was genuine and sincere. He looked over us for years all alone."

"You're right," Darin said. "But I was there. I saw him; he changed. The isolation unlocked something deep in him. Something—wrong. I want to see those tapes."

"Can't." Justin said. "They got wet during the flood yesterday."

"It flooded before the snow?" Darin scratched the bruised injection site on his leg.

"Yes," Cody said.

A rush of cold air filled the room, and Victoria and Nathan slammed the door behind them.

"Okay, it's done." Nathan wrapped a blanket around Victoria and himself.

"Kim and Rhett aren't out of their cabin yet," Victoria said. "I guess they'll join us when they're good and ready."

"Fine with me," Stacy said. "Kim was getting on my nerves."

"There are more of you?" Darin asked. "How many?"

"We gotta get back to the vault," Matt said.

"How?" Justin asked. "You got any snowshoes or a map?"

"No, I've got something better." Matt turned to Darin. "Do you remember the way?"

"I don't," he said. "I lost consciousness maybe fifty feet from the front doors of the cave. Besides, you guys, the air is *breathable* here. We must be really far—like hundreds if not thousands of miles from the cave. None of this looks toxic or volatile. How did Westbrook know about this place?"

"But the other seventeen-year-olds, they're dying. Our parents, everyone!" Matt said.

"Do you want to die trying to save them?" Justin asked.

"You don't care?" Matt asked.

"My parents were assholes," Justin said. "Good riddance."

"Look, let's just stay a few days." Darin said. "Let the snow melt, and we can reassess. You said Westbrook was crushed. How?"

CHAPTER 32

"The truck must have blown a tire," Matt said. "When he tried to pull the pods off the truck they fell off and crushed him. Luckily, he'd gotten Cody out first, before he was crushed."

"Where's the truck?" Darin asked.

"A little way up the road," Catherine said. "But it's totaled. The flood ruined it."

"So . . . we have no way to get there?" Darin asked. "I'm telling you, it's better here. Wherever here is."

"You seem a little too eager to stay and too happy about Dr. Westbrook's death," Matt said.

"Death is always sad. But trust me when I tell you, he wasn't well intended," Darin explained.

"How did you know he said that?" Matt asked.

"Because I filmed him for the better part of a decade. Sometimes he would send me on a task and would film while I was gone. He never let me see those recordings. I'm not saying he was evil, just troubled. Maybe it was the isolation. I don't know."

"What do we do?" Catherine asked. "Matt's right, we need to get back and pick up where Dr. Westbrook left off."

"Fine," Darin said. "But let's wait a few days. I need to regain some energy, and the snow needs to melt."

"No," Matt said. "I want to go now."

"Go where?" Darin asked. "I told you, I don't know how we got here. And I meant what I said. I'm not going back out there without a gas mask."

Darin padded toward the chairs and gingerly lowered himself. He hunched forward, resting his elbows on his knees. Victoria placed a can with a torn label in front of him with a mug of water. She paused but said nothing and sat next to him.

"Thank you," he said. "How many cabins are there?"

"I dunno," Cody said. "Probably a dozen or so. Plus, there are outbuildings."

"Maybe there are gas masks in one of them?" Darin asked. "Have you searched the place?"

"Briefly," Catherine said. "We were just looking for shoes and food. The cabins were pretty barren, but I suppose there could have been masks in one of them. I wasn't looking for that kind of thing."

"Me n-neither," Nathan said.

"I didn't see any," Stacy said. "Matt did most of the searching. Although I *did* find the trunk."

"Okay, then will you meet me halfway?" Darin asked. "Please, once the snow stops, let's search every building for masks. If we don't find any, then we'll come up with a plan B. I mean, look at me, I'm in no condition to even walk down the stairs. I just need a day or two to regain my strength. Being passed out for three days—it really messed me up."

Matt opened his mouth and found himself at a loss.

"I'm not trying to not help," Darin said. "I just want to do it right. What's the point if we just end up dying in the apocalypse?"

"It's snowing really hard again," Stacy said. "I vote we wait like Lance—um, Darin—said. It really looks gross out there."

"Fine." Justin smirked. "It's not like we have snowshoes anyway."

"Anyone opposed to this?" Matt crossed the room and held out a hand toward Darin. He shook it. "Then it's a deal."

CHAPTER 33

Matt spent the majority of the day staring out the window, willing the snow to stop. He overheard Stacy officially name Darin, Lance-Darin, which seemed to make Justin jealous. As much as Matt hated to admit it, Darin was right, and Matt's years of Scout training gnawed at him. *Scouts are always prepared.*

A hand on Matt's back startled him.

"You okay?" Catherine asked.

"Yeah," Matt said. "I'm just kicking myself. I should have searched the cabins better. Told everyone else to. No one should have been swimming when we could have been scouring the place for supplies."

"Matt, that's nuts. None of us could have known what was next. Honestly? It's been a lot the last few days. I think we could all use a day to just process everything."

"And just stand by when the entire human race could be dying?"

"Chill out, Matt." Catherine frowned. "Don't get mad at me. I want to find my parents as much as you—we all do. Well, maybe not Justin. But what can we do? We are snowed in, and that's that. Try and give yourself a break. I found some Stephen King books in the game closet, you should grab one."

"You're right," he said. "I'm sorry."

"Ma-matt," Nathan interrupted. "It's getting pretty cold in here."

"I don't have any experience with fireplaces or what to look for," Matt said.

Justin sat in a chair, legs splayed out. "I do, chief." He sprang to his feet toward the hearth.

"Awesome," Stacy said. "Why didn't you say something before?"

"No one asked." He lay on his back and stared up into the chimney. "I didn't grow up rich like the rest of you. Burning wood was the only source of heat in our house. I know how to make a fire too. But you didn't ask me about that either, did you?"

"Sorry," Matt said.

"That I'm poor?" Justin's voice echoed. He stood and was fully inside the large fire box now, with his head up the chimney, only his lower legs exposed. "Don't be, we're all on the same level now. Hand me a broom or something."

"No, I'm sorry I didn't ask." Matt rubbed his hand over his buzz-cut. "We're all still getting to know each other, so please speak up. I shouldn't have assumed no one had knowledge in this area."

"Here." Victoria crouched and angled a straw broom up the chimney.

"Thanks," Justin said.

Justin banged the broom so hard and loud inside the chimney that Matt wondered if Justin was smacking the bricks as if it was Matt's face.

"You doing okay in there?" Matt asked. "I really am sorry."

Justin emerged from the fireplace, face and hands smeared with soot. "No problem, chief. You know what they say about *assuming*. Everything looks clear. No nests or debris; we shouldn't smoke up the place. I'm going to get some firewood."

"Sounds like a plan," Cody said. "Count me in. I'm freezin'."

"I'll help," Catherine said. "I need some fresh air."

"M-me too," Nathan echoed.

"Have fun," Stacy said.

Just as they filed out, Stacy turned to Matt. "You shouldn't be so hard on him."

"Justin?" Matt furrowed his brow.

"Yeah. He seems like he's damaged. Had a hard life or something."

"I'm not! Are you *serious* right now? He's been the combative—you know . . . fine."

Matt stalked over to the theater stage, hoisted himself up and sat with his legs dangling. *This is ridiculous. How am I the bad guy all of a sudden?* He stared at the peeling varnish on the basketball court, lost in thought until he was smacked with a cold burst of air.

"How was it out there?" Victoria ran to the door and closed it behind Nathan, Cody, Catherine, and Justin. "Is it letting up?"

"Hell no!" Justin shook snow from his hair.

"Gettin' worse, actually," Cody said.

"Really?" Darin stood and walked to the window. On the third step, he collapsed.

"Lance-Darin, are you okay?" Stacy ran over and crouched next to him. "Justin, help me get Lance-Darin up."

"Easy, big fellah," Justin said, then lifted Darin.

"I want to see," Darin said.

"Okay, okay." Justin placed Darin's arm around his neck and acted as a crutch as they made their way to the window.

"No way we can travel in that," Darin said, shaking his head. "It's snowing sideways."

"Y-y-you're telling me," Nathan said. "I don't th-think anyone should go out alone. It's near whiteout conditions. Blizzard t-type weather."

Cody sat crouched next to the fireplace and struck the flint. Sparks landed on an old playbill he had wadded up for the starter. Soon the wood cackled and snapped, and flames danced in the fireplace.

Matt jumped down from the stage and walked over to the folding chairs. He grabbed them two at a time and set them up near the fire.

"Thanks for getting the wood," Matt said. "And Justin, it's awesome you knew how to check the chimney and stuff."

"Yep," Justin said. He deposited Darin in the chair closest to the fire. "You gonna be all right, man?"

"Yes," Darin said. "I think I just stood up too fast. I should be good as new tomorrow."

"Let's hope," Matt said.

Darin nodded and watched the flames.

It didn't take long to warm everyone, before the front door burst open and they were hit with another wave of bitter cold.

CHAPTER 34

"Um, like, hello?" Kim yelled.

Several feet of snow spilled in around her feet. Rhett pushed in behind her, then turned and tried to force the door shut.

"Kim!" Stacy ran to Kim and embraced her in a full hug. "It's so rude you just ditched me like that. I'm so glad you're okay."

"Sorry." Kim faked a frown.

"Glad you're back." Justin lifted his chin in Rhett's direction.

"Ran out of crap to burn," Rhett said. "Wait, is that . . ."

"Oh yeah, he woke up. *Finally*," Stacy said. "He says his name is Darin. But I call him Lance-Darin. You can too, if you want."

"I'll leave that to you," Kim said. "So what's your story, Darin? You getting us out of here or what?" She rocked back on her heels.

"You said you burned stuff," Darin started. "Did you come across any gas masks?"

"Uh, no. We only burned the furniture," Kim said. "And by we, I mean Rhett."

"Sorry." Rhett shrugged. "I didn't see any masks, and I searched the whole cabin pretty good. Why do we need gas masks?"

"Dang," Matt said.

"Come have a seat, and we'll fill you in," Victoria said. "How deep was the snow?"

"At least three feet," Rhett said. "I had to carry Kim."

"Just like the gentleman he is." Kim grinned ear to ear and sat next to Victoria.

Victoria proved to be an incredible storyteller and historian, as she recounted what had happened in perfect detail over a candlelit dinner of canned food and water.

"Guys, it's getting dark, I think we should sleep," Matt said.

"Looks like Darin beat you to it, chief," Justin said.

Darin slouched in the chair with his chin resting on his chest. An empty can of SpaghettiOs in a limp hand threatened to fall off his knee.

"He can use my sleeping bag," Kim said. "I'll share with Rhett."

"How nice of you." Catherine rolled her eyes.

"Hey, Lance-Darin!" Stacy shouted. "Get your lazy butt up and sleep in a bag, will ya?"

Matt laughed, still unable to get a pulse on the situation. Stacy either had a terrible way of flirting or outright hated this guy.

Darin seemed to be equally confused. He stood and rubbed his eyes. Everyone else shuffled to their respective bags. Most moved theirs near the warm fire. Rhett and Kim didn't, though that didn't surprise Matt, since Rhett had declared himself a "hot sleeper."

Matt stared out the window at the massive mountain then had an idea. He turned and saw that everyone was asleep. It would have to wait until morning.

CHAPTER 35

Matt woke before the others and waited anxiously for everyone to wake. With his patience thin, he faked an overly loud sneeze. Cody was the first up and met Matt near the picture window.

"Dang, look at those drifts," Cody said. "I ain't never seen one that big before. Hey everyone, come look! There must be twelve-foot snowdrifts out there."

Snow had piled up in huge mounds across camp. Despite the continued snowfall, the brightness of the morning was amplified by the glittering white powder. The wind pattern must have shifted throughout the night, as the drifts were in varying directions.

"Wow," Catherine said. "The wind *was* fierce last night, kept waking me up."

"Me too," Justin said. "And you're welcome. I kept the fire going all night."

"Well, aren't you just turning out to be the best little helper?" Stacy teased, and tried to squeeze his cheek before getting her hand swatted away.

"Look, it's not that. I—I just realized that maybe this isn't the haven I thought it was," Justin said. "I mean, look outside. I'm with Matt now. I think we should look for the vault once it's safe to leave."

"How are you feeling, Darin?" Matt asked.

Darin stood and did a full-body stretch, complete with an audible yawn. "Not too bad."

"Like, that could take, like, months," Kim said.

"Or just a day," Victoria said. "Who knows?"

"M-maybe," Nathan said.

"Where you taking us, anyway?" Rhett asked.

"Like I've said, I don't know where to begin looking," Darin said. "And we must have gas masks. I don't want to put my lungs through that again."

"But you and Dr. Westbrook said the cryovault was inside a cave within a mountain, right?" Matt said.

"Yes." Darin tilted his head to the side, confused.

"What about that mountain?" Matt tapped on the window. The peak of the mountain jutted high into the sky. Yesterday the jagged rock was gray with a small cap of snow. Now the entire peak was solid white. The green trees below were blanketed with heavy snow. A winter wonderland worthy of Christmas morning. "I wonder how long it'll take to get there."

"I—I don't know, but when we left, the air was terrible." Darin walked to the window and shook his head. "I don't know how the air would clear so fast."

"Well, it was like 90 degrees yesterday—now look outside," Kim said.

"Y-y-yeah," Nathan said. "It flooded, and the water disappeared within an hour."

"So," Matt eagerly concluded, "since the weather changes so quick—you know, apocalypse and all—why couldn't the air change and become nontoxic just like that?" He snapped his fingers.

Darin tipped his head to one side, then rubbed his chin.

"So then you agree?" Matt said. "The air here is fine, so if we don't find gas masks we can go as far as that mountain and see if the vault is in there."

"I mean, I guess." Darin's lips were in a flat line, his jaw set. "But if it starts getting bad, I'm turning back."

"It is the only mountain in the vicinity," Cody added.

"You're the only one who knows how to run the cryopod systems. We need you. Please," Matt said.

"Yeah, Lance-Darin, stop being selfish," Stacy said. "I'd like to see my family again."

A chorus of "me toos" followed.

A small smile formed on Darin's lips. "Okay, once the snow lets up, we'll go. I relent. I was just worried about our safety, not trying to be selfish. Trust me, my intentions are good."

TO BE CONTINUED

APOCALYPSE FALL

Tyler H. Jolley
Mary H. Geis

For my parents who let me grow up in the 80's.

CHAPTER 1

Matt Voorhees stared out the largest picture window in the main cabin of Camp New Beginnings. Outside was a picturesque winter wonderland worthy of a tacky gilded frame placed above an afghan-covered couch. If only he had a couch, and a home, and parents.

Well, technically, he *did* have parents. They were just cryogenically frozen inside a cave—somewhere. And hopefully still alive.

"Is the snow ever going to let up?" Matt crossed his arms over the *Commodore 64* logo on his shirt. The roaring fireplace was nice, but it only really kept them warm if they were close. "This is getting ridiculous. It's probably snowed another foot."

"Better, like, watch out, Victoria," Kim said. "Much more snow, and it'll be deeper than you are tall."

"Very funny." Victoria stood with pin-straight posture and smoothed her long, black Gothic dress. "I'm not that short." She looked down at her shoes, away from Kim's judging glare.

"Chill out," Stacy said. "Besides, we have a bunch of buff guys here who can carry you—if the snow ever stops."

"I can manage myself," Victoria said. "Catherine, will you French braid my hair?"

"You should tease it up like Elvira and plop it on top of your head like this." Stacy gathered her frizzy, strawberry-blond curls on top of her head. "It'll give you a few inches."

"Come on." Catherine motioned with her chin toward the hearth. "Let's do it over here. You know, I've never had my hair braided. It's too thick and curly."

"I can try after you do mine," Victoria said.

Catherine waddled toward the fireplace, holding up an oversized pair of gray sweatpants over her striped shorts. Most had just opted to use blankets, but a few layered on what they could find in the tattered trunk of old clothes. Once they were closer to the crackling flames, Matt couldn't hear their conversation, but Victoria's shoulders relaxed, and a small smile crept onto her pale face.

Cody sidled up to Matt and pressed his forehead against the window, leaving a greasy smudge.

"First time I saw snow in Texas, I thought it was neato burrito," Cody said. "Now it's the ugliest thing I ever done seen."

"No joke," Matt said. "It's so frustrating. We're stuck. Mother Nature wins again."

"How you feelin'?" Cody turned to Darin.

"I just needed a day to get myself right." Darin shifted in his folding chair. "I'm still not a hundred percent, but I'm getting there."

"Good. I'm glad." Matt stared back out at the flat gray sky, willing the non-existent sun to shine.

The only shirt large enough to fit Darin was a navy-blue polo with the word "Counselor" embroidered onto the left breast and a pair of too-short, pleated khaki shorts. Matt found a small bit of comfort in the counselor shirt. It seemed to tell everyone that Darin was in charge, and it took the pressure off him.

"Wh-what's the plan?" Nathan asked. He had a blanket slung over his shoulders. Only the *AS* was visible on his NASA shirt.

"I guess as soon as it stops snowing, we go," Matt said.

"No, not th-th-that." Nathan shifted his gaze to the floor. "The bodies."

"Right." Matt pinched the bridge of his nose. "Justin, you said you saw the bodies in the flood water?"

"What's that, chief?" Justin cupped his ear but made no attempt to come closer to Matt.

Matt walked toward Justin, Rhett, Stacy, and Kim. Cody, Nathan, and Darin followed behind him.

"You said you saw Dr. Westbrook and the girl, um, float by?" Matt asked.

"Yep." Justin shuffled a deck of cards. "They were pretty bloated too. Good job on burying them, Nathan."

"I'm so-sorry," Nathan said.

"Nah, I'm just giving you a hard time," Justin said. "I wasn't exaggerating, though. They're pretty messed up."

"Sick!" Kim said. "That's, like, totally disgusting, and I won't listen to this. Come on, Rhett. Bring me a sleeping bag or something."

Kim turned on a heel. The pleats on her cheerleading skirt flashed yellow and white. Rhett shrugged and followed her toward the theater stage.

"We'll need to bury Kyle too. Pay our respects, you know." Cody gripped the spot where a rodeo belt buckle should have been and nodded at Matt.

"Yes, we'll do that first. Before we go to the mountain," Matt said.

"I thought you were in a big hurry," Darin said. "I'm not complaining, just saying."

"I'd like to get them buried before they . . . I can't even believe I'm saying this, but we probably should do it before they thaw out," Matt said.

"Th-three graves is a l-lot of work," Nathan said. "And we have to go deeper this time."

"Yes," Matt said. "All hands on deck this time."

"Or we could just do one big hole," Justin said.

"What?" Stacy gasped. "That's uncivilized."

"For once, I agree with you, Justin," Matt said.

"It does seem a little, I dunno, disrespectful," Cody said.

"Well, cowboy, we're fresh out of coffins and backhoes," Justin said.

"I agree," Darin said. "You guys can put it to a vote if you'd like."

"No," Matt said. "It's not ideal, but it has to get done, and done quickly. They're rotting—we have no time to waste."

"Then it's settled," Justin said. "Pop a squat, let's play poker."

A loud gust of wind rattled the door. Matt secretly hoped it was someone coming to rescue them, but he knew better. This was up to them.

* * *

Neither Matt nor Darin was in the mood to play cards. Plus, Justin was on Matt's side at the moment. He didn't want to sully the relationship by whipping him at poker. The large gym had finally started to warm up. The fireplace was big, but the room was bigger. He passed by Kim and Rhett on the stage. They lay facing each other, with their legs intertwined. Kim brushed a lock of Rhett's blond hair off his forehead. They looked like dirt-covered Ken and Barbie dolls. Only this Ken doll was 6'6", with big blue eyes and a big, dumb brain. Kim whispered into Rhett's ear, and he laughed, then responded by tickling her.

"You think they ever get tired of playing tonsil hockey?" Matt asked, pointing his thumb toward them.

"Have they been like this the whole time?" Darin asked, hoisting himself onto the stage next to Matt.

"Before, actually. They woke up on the bus ride to the cryovault. They say they didn't see anything because they were too busy doing that." He pointed at them.

"Wait, are we sure they didn't see anything?" Darin asked. "Maybe they know where the vault is."

"We asked them a few times," Matt said. "Trust me, we got more relationship details than I cared to hear, but nothing useful. Ah, here we are."

Matt did his best Vanna White impression and presented the tapes to Darin. Eighteen black rectangular halves and the spools lay splayed out on a *Gremlins* beach towel. Small screws and three screwdrivers lay amongst the organized chaos.

"I hope these still work," Matt said.

"Me too," Darin said. "Good idea on taking them apart to dry out."

"Thanks. I accidentally spilled water on my mom's new Neil Diamond cassette once and used this same method to dry it out. The case cracked a little, but it still worked." Matt tightened the tape on the reels, then carefully placed the back piece over it. "Hand me a Phillips, will ya? I like the orange-handled one best."

"Trav's Auto Care." Darin examined the screwdriver and his face darkened. "I'm here. Alive and breathing. Whoever this Trav was, he isn't. Gone. Dead. Like everyone else in the world. It's kind of surreal when you think about it."

"Yeah." Matt took the tool from Darin and slowly replaced the screws. "It makes me wonder how and why we were picked."

"Me too," Darin said, bowing his head. "Me too."

"You know, with all the snow, it's too bad we can't go sledding," Matt said, changing the subject.

"I haven't been sledding since I was a kid." Darin laughed. "We could use the canoe."

"My parents drove me to Tahoe a few times with our dog. He was a Chesapeake Bay Retriever. You know what they look like?"

"No. I'm not a big fan of dogs," Darin said.

"What? How is that even possible? Dogs truly are a man's best friend."

"Not when they're chasing you," Darin said. "I used to deliver papers."

"A paperboy?" Matt laughed.

"Hey, I was only twelve when I was frozen, remember? Anyway, a few would chase me relentlessly. I got bitten once. It scared me."

Statements like that were odd to Matt. Darin had been put in cryosleep just like them, but he'd been awakened for nearly a decade before he was forced back to sleep. Actual time had passed for him. He'd aged. Somehow getting older than Matt, despite being born five years after him.

"Saber wouldn't have done that," Matt said.

"You named your dog Saber?"

"Yep." Matt beamed. "I love movies. *Star Wars* is one of my favorites. Anyway, Saber loved the snow. I grew up in Nevada, so we had to drive to the mountains to see snow. Saber would ride on the sled with me, all eighty pounds of him. We'd fly down those hills. It's one of my favorite memories."

Matt's voice cracked, and his eyes filled with tears. He turned away from Darin and wiped his eyes.

"You really liked that dog, huh?" Darin asked.

"It's not that." Matt cleared his throat. "It's everything. I need to make sure my family is okay. And after that, I want to rebuild. Have a dog again. Live normal. Not eat expired canned food. And none of that can happen while the sky vomits snow all over us."

"I know," Darin said. "We all do. Well, maybe not those two." He pointed to Rhett and Kim. "They're about three seconds away from actually *showing* us how babies are made. Hey! You two cover up or get a room!"

Matt laughed and dried his eyes one more time. "I think this tape will work." He used his index finger to spin the reels. "Cody, can you fire up the gennie?"

CHAPTER 2

Matt rolled the TV cart closer to the fireplace. Catherine and Victoria placed the folding chairs in a semicircle around it. Once everything was in place, all they could do was wait.

"Matt, do you have a sec?" Catherine nodded her head toward the opposite side of the room.

Matt made eye contact with her and followed her to a corner away from everyone.

"I don't want to freak you out—and take this with a grain of salt. I mean, we're all under a lot of pressure right now and we've been through a lot." Catherine twisted a long, black curl. "But it's Darin."

"What about him?"

"I honestly wrestled with whether I should say this or not, but I've had a weird feeling all day. I just can't shake it." Catherine pressed her eyes together and released a sharp breath. "He was talking in his sleep last night."

"What do you mean?" Matt pinched his eyebrows together. "What was he saying?"

"He was, I dunno, apologizing. He kept saying he was so sorry and that he didn't mean to—didn't know it would happen."

"Is that all?" Matt asked.

"No." Catherine shook her head. "He kept saying something about Jim. And how Jim had tricked him. Or maybe Darin tricked Jim—Dr. Westbrook. It was . . . so weird."

"I knew it. I *knew* it!" Matt whispered. "Something felt off from the second he woke up with that bogus story about a bomb being strapped to him. I knew he was lying. What else is he hiding?"

"Matt"—Catherine placed her hands on his shoulders—"it may have just been a nightmare. Don't confront him on this, please."

"Why not? He might hold the answer to where we are. Where our families are. He's holding something back. I felt it in the beginning and you just confirmed it."

"Maybe." Catherine bit her lower lip. "Or maybe it was just a nightmare. I dunno, it *did* feel really intense. But if it's nothing, then you're going to divide the whole group with an accusation like that."

"Fine," Matt agreed. "I'll stay quiet, for now. But caution signs are up in my mind."

"Come on, let's go watch the tape."

"Hey, did the power kick on yet?" Matt called, walking toward the group. Catherine followed.

"Nope. Like, this is not going to work. No way," Kim said. "I can't believe you made my boyfriend go out into that heinous storm."

"Did you expect Cody to trudge through the snow by himself?" Catherine asked. "Besides, he volunteered. So did Darin, Justin, and Nathan."

"Who said anything about Na-Na-Na-Nathan?" Kim laughed, then fluffed her feathered blond hair.

"So rude," Victoria muttered. "I think it's great. The more people who know how to run the generator, the better."

"Then why aren't you out there?" Stacy asked.

"I will, once the snow melts," Victoria said. "I've never ridden a bicycle before. Now isn't the time for me to learn."

"It's not a real bike anyway." Kim rolled her eyes.

"A stationary bike is still a bike," Matt said. "Victoria, I'll teach you. It's pretty easy, and you don't even have to balance."

The front door slammed open. Darin stood there, covered in snow. "Anything?" he asked.

Matt clicked on the TV. Nothing. "Nope."

"You got the gennie dug out?" Catherine asked.

"Mostly," Darin said. "The engine turned over, but they only pedaled for a few minutes. We'll take turns. I'll be back." He flipped the light switch to "on." "Let me know if the lights turn on, okay?"

"Sure thing, Lance-Darin," Stacy said.

Darin opened his mouth to say something but instead shook his head and turned to leave.

"Bye-bye." Stacy waved just the tips of her fingers.

"Ugh, this is, like, so dumb," Kim said. "How much longer is it going to be? And why aren't you out there helping, Matt? You're the only guy who didn't volunteer."

"He told you already!" Catherine yelled. "His wrist is still sore from when he slipped during the flood. He doesn't want to risk reinjuring it."

"When you killed Kyle?" Kim raised an eyebrow. "I mean, let him die?"

"Shut up, Kim! You don't know what you're talking about." Matt gritted his teeth. "If you're so bored, why don't you go shovel? Or better yet, go back to your cabin."

"You wait until I tell Rhett. He's going to kick your—"

The lights in the room flickered like a dying flame then went dark.

"I better tell Lance-Darin," Stacy said, breaking the silence and skipping to the door. She pulled it open and stepped out onto the wraparound porch. "Hey! Lance-Darin! The lights came on for a second."

"Way to let all the cold air in," Matt said. "The place just finally warmed up."

"Sorry." Stacy shrugged, shivered, and closed the door once she was back inside.

The lights flickered again, but this time stayed fully illuminated. Matt walked past Stacy and outside, careful to shut the door behind him. He made his way around the porch above the generator.

"Good job, guys," Matt said, peering over the edge at Justin, Cody, Rhett, and Darin. Darin sat atop the modified generator on the bike. He pedaled fast; his hot breath hung in the frigid air. "Lights are on."

"You guys go in." Darin huffed. "I'll be right behind you."

Matt watched Justin, Cody, and Rhett trudge through a narrow path they'd created in the deep snow. They used their shovels as walking sticks. The same shovels they would use to create a mass grave when the ground thawed.

Once inside, the boys removed their shoes and outerwear and replaced them with blankets and fresh socks.

"I ain't never been this cold," Cody said.

"Except when you were cryogenically frozen," Victoria said, smiling.

"That's true, little lady. Very true." Cody huddled in front of the fire.

Darin filed in a few minutes later. He dusted snow off his feathered brown hair.

"There should be enough stored power to keep it going for a few hours," Darin said. "You guys are going to need to find some oil or something for the gears—everything seems really tight."

"We'll see what we can find," Matt said. "I'm gonna start the next tape if anyone's interested."

"Not me," Kim said. "Rhett come here. I need to talk to you."

"I want to see the tape," Rhett said.

"Rhett!" Kim placed a hand on her hips and stomped a foot.

Rhett let out an exhausted sigh and lumbered over to Kim on the stage area.

"Good riddance," Matt said. He picked up a tape marked "7" and pushed it into the VCR. "What do you have to tell us today, Dr. Westbrook?"

The snow on the screen was replaced by jarring alarms and the scientist's red face. Gauze had been taped over his ears with white athletic tape. He held his head and muttered, "Dear listener, I regret to tell you, I've made the difficult decision of killing myself."

CHAPTER 3

"The alarms, they've been blaring for—well, it seems I've lost count. I've done everything to fix the underlying issue. It's the seventeen-year-olds. They're failing again. My attempts to fix the column have been unsuccessful." The man looked to the ceiling and released a desperate breath. "Sometimes, during the busiest parts of the day, I get used to the constant ringing of the alarm. Then all the feeding machines stop, the filtration systems rest, and the computers go to sleep, but I don't! I haven't slept since this started. Not one wink."

Dr. Westbrook began muttering incomprehensible sentences and paced. Soon, he was behind the camera and showed the seventeen-year-old column. Stacks of pods on shelves all blinked yellow. Warning. The sound was deafening. Matt pressed the fast-forward button while straining his neck to stare at the screen. In a flash, he saw the man's living quarters. An unmade bed and stacks of half-empty canned food littered the room. It looked like a hoarder's paradise. Finally, the camera settled onto the tripod, and Dr. Westbrook came back into frame.

"He looks terrible," Matt said.

"In the military, they use sleep deprivation as a form of torture. Did you know that? Of course you don't, why would you? I'm in a room with over five thousand people, and I've never felt more alone. Dear listener, do not feel guilty. I took this position on willingly. I thought I could be your savior." He removed his coke-bottle glasses and hung his head, revealing a small bald spot on the crown. "But the alarms are making me go mad. Please know, my intentions—from the very start—were good. Now, I must bid you adieu." He held his finger and thumb in the shape of a gun and pointed it at his temple before the tape went black.

"No!" Matt jumped up and smashed the fast-forward button in with his thumb.

Nothing but black.

"There's the crazy Westbrook I knew," Darin said.

"Stop it!" Matt said. "Look at all he went through to save us."

"Like he said, he volunteered." Darin stood, and his chair tipped over. "And he obviously didn't kill himself."

Matt squinted at him. Darin was right.

"Remember, he woke me up to help transport you guys? You saw him dead. Crushed, I think was your exact word."

"Then what happened?" Justin asked. "I hear you, man, but he looked pretty crazy."

"How would I know what happened?" Darin righted his chair and sat. "He woke me up the same day he moved all of you."

"According to you," Matt said. His conversation with Catherine about Darin echoed in the back of his mind.

"Whatever," Darin said. "I'm not going over this with you again. I don't know anything."

"It's late," Catherine said. "Maybe clearer heads will prevail tomorrow."

She walked toward the rolled-up sleeping bags on the opposite side of the room. The varnish on the basketball court had peeled away years ago. Much of the wood had curled up and made it uneven. *A tripping hazard and lawsuit waiting to happen,* Kyle would have said. Catherine picked up a nylon bag and unrolled it in the center court, where kids from years past tipped off the start of a basketball game.

"I'm with Catherine," Stacy said. "Lance-Darin, wanna keep me warm?"

Justin furrowed his brow and crossed his arms in front of his chest.

"I think I'll sleep by the fire." Darin stared at Matt for a moment, then said to Stacy, "Alone."

"Your loss," Stacy said.

Matt wanted to interrogate Darin, but no one else seemed interested. They didn't know what Catherine had heard. Deep down, he was certain Darin was holding something back—maybe he knew the location of the cave. Instead, Matt lay next to Cody and Justin on the warped court.

"How about we get some mattresses from the cabins next time we go out, chief?" Justin asked.

"Do whatever you want." Matt rolled over and pressed his eyes shut.

"Chill out, man," Justin said.

"Sorry." Matt cringed. "Yeah, a mattress would be good right about now. Maybe after the snow melts."

"No worries, chief," Justin responded.

Matt found sleep quickly, but it was fitful. He was in his back-yard standing on his AstroTurf lawn with a soggy tennis ball in his grip. Dutifully sitting, with his tail sweeping from side to side, was his beloved Saber. His eyes were fixed on the toy, pink tongue hanging from his mouth. Matt threw the ball but his dog didn't chase after it. Saber stared at him with familiar and comforting green eyes and led him into the house. "Wait!" Matt ran after him. "Come here, buddy." Before Matt opened the back door to let them both in, he knelt down and pet Saber. "I missed you."

He slid the sliding glass door sideways and walked in first. When he turned, Saber was gone and the kitchen phone was ringing. Matt ran across the faded linoleum and picked up the yellow receiver. "Hello?"

"Matt!"

"Mom?"

"Matty, where are you?"

"I'm—I'm home. You called me at home." Matt stretched the cord as far as it would go around the corner, searching the house.

"Matt, your father and I have specific instructions for you."

"Mom, I miss you and Dad so much! Please, you have to come home."

"We want that more than anything. But we can't come home until you finish your dinner."

"My what? What are you talking about? Mom, this is serious."

"Just make sure you eat all your food."

Click!

Matt held the phone up to his ear until he heard an operator come on and say, "If you'd like to make a call, please hang up," followed by aggressive beeping.

Matt replaced the receiver on the wall unit and turned around. "What the?" The empty kitchen table had been filled with cans. Bulging and swollen cans. He picked one up. The ripped label for green beans slipped from his fingers. Black sludge oozed from the top. He dropped it and stared at the massive pile of leaking tins. "No!" He opened a cabinet, and dozens of cans tumbled from the overly full space. He tugged on the dishwasher and gagged. Black muck sprayed out of the water line; he struggled to close it.

"This isn't happening. Mom! Dad!"

Matt ran into the living room and tripped. He landed in a wretched sea of foaming black residue amongst thousands of cans. He looked toward the ceiling and saw it had been replaced with a stories-high skyscraper of canned food. It swayed back and forth unsteadily. Matt tried to get to his feet but kept sliding and falling. Landing on his back, he heard the tower crumble, and all he could do was place his arms around his head.

"Matt." He felt a hand on his shoulder, but the voice sounded miles away. "Matt, wake up."

He blinked hard. "Catherine. Oh man."

"Nightmare?"

"Yeah," he said miserably.

"Me too," Catherine said. "Darin's not the only one, right?"

"Yeah," Matt said. "I guess."

"Forget about that right now." Catherine stood. "Come look outside."

Matt used the back of his hand to wipe the sleep from his eyes then jumped to his feet. His muscles were stiff. On one of the earlier tapes, he'd heard Dr. Westbrook wondering what fresh hell he was in store for that day. That statement resonated with Matt more than ever. He stared out the window into a sea of white. Nothing but snow. Deep snow. So much so that he wasn't sure where the snow stopped, and the buildings began.

"Come on, help us decide," Catherine said.

"Where is everyone?" Matt scanned the empty room.

"Outside," Catherine said. "You were sleeping really hard; I didn't want to wake you."

Matt wrapped a blanket around himself, slipped on his shoes, and stepped out onto the frigid porch. Snow was up to his mid-thigh.

"Whoa," Matt said.

"Whoa is right, partner," Cody said.

"Ma-Matt, can you see the sun?" Nathan asked.

"What?" Matt shook his head, still not fully awake. "That's why I'm out here?"

"Yes," Catherine laughed. "I know it's silly; call it cabin fever. But there's no sun."

"Yes, there is," Kim whined. "See that brighter spot, like, behind the clouds? This is so lame. I'm going in."

Matt squinted at the sky. "I mean, I'm sure there's a sun. But like Kim said, it's behind the clouds."

"Then why haven't we seen a sunset?" Cody asked.

"I know," Rhett said.

Everyone turned to the jock.

"You-you do?" Nathan asked.

"I grew up in a small mountain town in Washington. We were actually in a valley. Mountains surrounded us, so we never saw the, um"—he snapped his fingers—"what do you call it? The horizontal? So it just got slowly light then slowly dark out. Never saw the sun rise or set."

"There you have it, folks," Justin said, walking toward the door. "Mystery solved by my buddy Rhett. Waddya say we get some breakfast."

Matt turned to Cody. "That was weird."

"We was just stallin'." Cody led Matt back into the main cabin. "Everyone was waking up and bein' loud. You've seemed really tired lately, so Catherine and I devised this distraction. Only lasted a few minutes, but I swear, those extra five minutes on the snooze button are the best sleep I ever got."

"Oh geez, an alarm clock." Matt walked in and shook the snow from his tapered jeans. "Talk about a blast from the past."

"Chief, you want to watch another one of those tapes of yours?" Justin yelled.

"Sure," Matt said, but he had a sinking feeling in his stomach. The hollowness in your abdomen that formed when you knew you were about to get grounded or run into an ex.

"Br-breakfast?" Nathan handed Matt an MRE of powdered eggs. "Is this o-okay?"

"Thanks, Nathan," Matt said, "but I think we should probably keep these for when we leave camp, you know? They're lighter."

"Sorry," Nathan said.

"Don't apologize." Matt turned to the group. "Hey, everyone, grab yourself a can of whatever you want. Please don't eat the MREs. We'll save those for when we travel to find our parents, okay?"

"Ravioli for breakfast?" Kim stuck out her tongue.

"Gag me with a spoon," Stacy echoed.

"Keep it up, and I just might," Catherine whispered, then handed Matt an open can of sliced pears. "Here."

"Thanks," he said. "Well, tape eight or bust. Wait, where's Darin?"

"Lance-Darin? He's clearing the snow and riding the generator bike," Stacy said. "He said he didn't want it to become fully buried again. Someone else might need to take a turn when he gets back, so it's fully charged."

"Sh-should we wait?" Nathan asked.

"Nah," Justin said. "He can watch—"

"I don't want to watch," Nathan said. "I'm going to switch with him."

"You okay?" Justin asked.

Nathan's shoulders slumped, and he walked out of the room. His tall frame seemed thinner today, more slight somehow.

The shuddering sound of gears popping and grinding interrupted Justin.

CHAPTER 4

Matt looked to Catherine and Cody. They stared back, wide-eyed. Then they ran to the window and waited.

After a few minutes of nothing, Matt turned to the group. "Let's get the tapes watched while we can." Matt powered the TV and VCR on and slid tape eight in.

The scientist appeared, smiling—almost jovial. Alarms sounded, but he seemed unbothered. His wiry hair had long since lost its color and was fully gray. His face was plump, and he looked healthy.

"Look at that deranged man," Darin said.

"How's the gennie?" Matt asked, ignoring Darin's insult. *This man saved our lives, there's nothing deranged about this.*

"Not too bad." He had a blanket wrapped around him. Snow dripped from his feathered light brown hair. He pointed at the TV with his narrow chin. "His eyes—look, they're crazy."

"He seems happy." Matt deflected Darin's comment.

"Good morrow, gentle listener! Today is my birthday—I've lost a few days here and there, but I'm confident today is the day. I am seventy years old. I've celebrated the last forty birthdays here. Isn't that remarkable?" Dr. Westbrook smiled like the Cheshire cat. "The first decade or so were quite fine. The loneliness didn't get to me until sometime in my forties; that's when I started documenting my days. Youth is something to be desired. You're resilient and can handle any-thing. If only my dear Darin had been as spirited as promised."

Everyone turned to Darin. He rolled his eyes and shrugged in response. The front door opened, taking the attention off him. A blast of freshly chilled air swept into the room. Nathan's clothes and head were caked in snow.

"The generator is as charged as it's going to be," Nathan said, then walked to the fireplace. "It's really coming down hard out there. I couldn't pedal anymore; the gears are frozen."

"But I digress," Dr. Westbrook continued on the screen. "Weary traveler, you have been with me for three decades in a matter of minutes through my recordings. And you have been my motivation to remain. The alarms have been constant for some time now, but I've grown used to them. Come, see what travesty has transpired."

He turned the camera toward an empty column. Then panned to an area with pods piled carelessly on the ground. Next to them were black body bags stacked neatly on top of each other.

"You see, the fifteen-year-olds didn't make it. Not a single one. We lost all one-hundred and six of them."

"Stop the tape," Rhett said.

Nathan jumped up and paused it.

Rhett sat hunched over in his chair. His shoulders heaved, but he made no sound.

"Rhett, it's okay. Like, tell me what's wrong so I can help you," Kim said.

Tears streamed down Rhett's face. "My sister, she was fifteen. She was in one of those body bags, like trash!" He cradled his face in his hands. "She was so smart, not like me. When I was failing math, no one could get through to me like her. She is—was—so patient and nice. Never made me feel stupid. Secretly, she was my best friend. I can't believe the last time I hugged her before cryosleep was—was the last time ever!"

"Oh, Rhett, babe, I'm so sorry." Kim rubbed his muscular back.

"Rhett . . ." Matt tried to find the words, but nothing came.

Kim led him off toward the opposite side of the room, where they'd slept the previous night. He lay on a sleeping bag over Kim's lap, and she stroked his hair while he cried. For once, she didn't make a situation about her.

"We need to know what happened to everybody else. I need to see what happened to my family. Can we just watch the stupid tape?" Stacy said.

Nathan clicked it back on. The scientist continued.

"My dear seventeen-year-olds were the problematic ones. The reason for the initial breach. Troublesome as they were, I ultimately got them stabilized. But it must have triggered something, because as soon as they were fixed, the fifteen-year-old column quit. Died immediately. There was no saving them. But I won't let that happen again."

Matt's chest tightened. He looked around the room and saw eyes wide, mouths frozen open in horror, and others shifting in their seat toward the person next to them. It was as if they were watching a slasher film, and not real life.

The camera shook, and a loud bang followed. Overhead lights flickered behind Dr. Westbrook.

"Ah yes, the apocalypse is still in its full fury. There is no stopping it! I will be moving my unstable columns to a site called HZRD. The first ones to move will be my hardy seventeen-year-olds. I'll take ten at a time, or at least that's the goal. Once they're all successfully relocated, I will move the rest of the pods. Over five thousand in total. 'Tis a massive undertaking, but I am up for the challenge."

"Wait." Catherine stood and paused the tape. "Why move the stable ones? That doesn't make any sense."

"Because he's crazy. Like Jack Torrance in *The Shining* crazy," Darin said.

"Or maybe he needs to have everyone in one spot to take care of them," Matt said. "Play it up."

"But where's HZRD? Is this HZRD?" Catherine pressed.

"Hell if I know," Darin replied.

"Hang on. Before, when he was talking about Rhett's sister, he said 'we,' Darin," Matt said. "Were you there?"

"What? No." Darin's face contorted as if he'd eaten something rancid. "He also called you weary traveler. No one has traveled in over forty years according to him. He's nuts. He probably uses we, I, and us interchangeably, depending on what personality he's using that day."

"It just seemed like maybe someone was there. He said 'we,' not 'I,'" Matt said.

"Like I said, he was crazy," Darin replied. He sat with his legs splayed out, slouched so far down in his seat, it looked like he might slip off his chair. "I wasn't awake. Period. End of story."

"Let's get this over with." Stacy started the tape. "And no more interruptions. We need to know what happens to everyone else. And for the record, *I* believe you, Lance-Darin."

"Unfortunately, the test site, HZRD, doesn't have the freezing capabilities, and I will be forced to wake you all. But I will take care of you. Become your leader. It is time to get to work. Goodbye for now. And as you'll soon see, my intentions are good."

"There were ten of us, including the girl who died," Matt said. "That means there are others in our column waiting to be moved."

"Or he already mo-mo-moved them, and we were the last," Nathan said. "The other seventeen-year-olds cou-could be at HZRD."

"Maybe this place is HZRD," Catherine said.

"Then he would have known about the power and VCR, right?" Victoria asked. "I don't know, this seems . . . calculated to me."

Darin stared intently at the floor, avoiding all eye contact.

"Did you guys notice the way he looked?" Cody asked. "I know Darin and I were the only ones to see him alive after our initial freezing, but don't you think he looked the same age?"

"Yeah, he did," Darin said. "This was filmed shortly before he woke me and moved you guys."

"Wait, you were there," Matt said. "Were we the first or the last?"

"First." Darin looked down. "He was shutting things down when he unhooked you. I don't think the others in your column are still alive."

CHAPTER 5

"So that's it?" Catherine gasped. "We're the only seventeen-year-olds left?"

Darin stared forward and nodded.

"No way!" Stacy yelled. "No way they're all dead!"

"What about the other age columns?" Matt stood.

"As far as I know, and from what I could see," Darin swallowed, "they were all still alive."

"Yeah, but that was days ago," Justin said.

"And what about HZRD?" Cody asked, pressing his palms into his eyes.

"I-I can't believe so many people have perished." Nathan wrapped his arms around himself. "Wh-why did we get to live?"

"Let's see what the last tape says." Matt nodded in Victoria's direction.

"I need to know what happened to my parents!" Victoria pressed in the final tape. "Shh."

"Hello, gentle listener, greetings to you all. I've been very busy these last six months. First, I must start with the grim news. I spent much of the time prepping and burning the corpses from the fifteen-year-old column. It was a task that had to be done. My dear seventeen-year-olds have held strong. I will move them first. Come see." He panned over to a pod with "#20" on it. Matt recognized it immediately and rubbed the area above his heart where his old uniform had the same number embroidered on it. "Here are eight recordings of our time together. I'll place this final one in once I'm done. Number twenty, whoever you are, you will have our history for when we start this new life together."

Dr. Westbrook used a key around his utility belt to unlock the cryopod. Matt lay inside in suspended animation. Staring at himself, so still and helpless, sent shivers down Matt's spine. The doctor carefully placed the tapes around his body, like lining a coffin with flowers.

Everyone turned to Matt. "Now we know how I got the tapes," he said.

"Guess you weren't lying, chief," Justin said. "It really was random."

The scientist continued. "You'll be transported in this fine piece of equipment. I had to add a few modifications, like the solar panels, but it seems to be up and running just fine."

The lens zoomed in on the same Army-issued truck they'd first seen when they escaped their pods just days ago. The same truck they'd found Darin passed out in. The same truck Matt had stood on and lost his grip on Kyle. Matt rubbed his wrist; it was nothing more than a dull ache now. But Kyle was still gone, and Matt carried that weight.

The camera rested on what Matt guessed was the tripod, and Dr. Westbrook stood—something he rarely did in his videos. He wore a white jacket over his shirt with a yellow bandana hanging from his neck. Long, tan cargo pants housed a utility belt of treasures. Matt recognized the Swatch around the doctor's wrist from when he was crushed. A boxy yellow rectangle, the size of a loaf of bread, hung awkwardly off the belt. A Geiger counter. Matt had only seen them on the news after the Chernobyl meltdown. On the face of the Geiger counter was a round circle with a needle-style gauge.

"My calculations were correct," Dr. Westbrook said, beaming. "I can fit exactly ten pods onto the bed of the truck. I will take you all to the HZRD site and will give you further instructions or record another tape for you to review while we move the remaining pods. Oh, this is an exciting day indeed. It's your first day of your new life. Cryosurvival is no longer sustainable. I will move each and every one of you myself—all five thousand of you—minus the fifteen-year-old column, of course. Now we must survive together. Gentle listener, you will soon see how well-intended I am. I can't wait for you to meet me."

He removed the camera from the tripod and captured a quick shot of the truck before ending the recording.

"What the?" Matt sprang from his seat and to the VCR. "Was that?"

Matt rewound and hit play, then pause. He pressed the pause

button repeatedly, moving it frame by frame, wrenching his neck to see the shot.

"See?!" Matt said.

Darin was paused on the screen near the back of the truck, mid-jump, holding a length of rope. Around his waist was the brown Everlast weightlifting belt that Darin had claimed was a bomb.

"And?" Darin said. "Yeah, that's me. I told you I was there. I was securing a pod."

"Right, sorry," Matt said. "I think I'm just grasping at straws. I just really want you to have the answers, or at least more information."

"Yeah, well . . ." Darin paused. "I don't know anything that would be helpful."

Matt stared at him but said nothing.

"Okay," Stacy said. "If anything, this video proves he was there just like he already said."

"I honestly don't care if you guys believe me or not. I know what happened, and I've told you everything. Believe it or not. That's not on me," Darin said.

"So that's it?" Victoria asked. "That was the last video?"

"Looks like it," Cody said. "Never had a chance to film the instructions for us."

"Now what?" Victoria asked. "We're snowed in. What can we do?"

"We need to find the cave," Matt said.

"I agree." Darin sat forward. "But where do we even start searching? The air was terrible when I left there, the weather was deadly, and worst of all, we're not going anywhere for days, maybe weeks. The snow is so deep."

"Well," Stacy said, standing, "while you guys figure that out, I think the rest of us should go sledding."

"I've never been sledding," Victoria said.

"Really?" Justin asked. "There's a lot you haven't done."

"And plenty I have!" Victoria nervously twisted her long braid. "I've been to five continents, eaten at countless Michelin star restaurants, learned Spanish and Portuguese, flown in private jets, met Reagan and . . ." She broke down in tears. "None of that matters. I can't do basic things. I can't do survival things. I only know my Manhattan life. Look at all of you. You all have skills. What am I good for?"

"Oh, Victoria," Stacy said. "I'm just as useless as you. And it turns out we have a lot more in common than I thought."

"Do-don't feel b-bad." Nathan hugged Victoria. His tall, lanky frame encompassed her petite body. "Stop crying. These gu-guys will help. Cody taught me how to use the ge-generator. And Matt sho-showed me the flint."

"Victoria, we'll teach you anything you want," Matt said. "Come on. Let's go out to the deck for a few minutes. Get some fresh air, and I'll explain the basics of the flint and steel wool. We can practice on the existing fire inside after, okay?"

She dried her eyes on Nathan's shirt and nodded at Matt with red-rimmed eyes. "I'd like that."

"Hey, listen up." Matt clapped his hands. "Anyone who doesn't know how to make fire, grab a coat or blanket and meet me on the deck."

"No *thanks*," Kim yelled. "I've got my beefcake, and he'll take care of me."

"Kim!" Stacy yelled. "Come on, if I have to do this, so do you."

"No way." Kim's eyes grew wide, and she tilted her head toward Rhett, whose head was still in her lap. "Like, I'm not leaving him in his time of need."

"It's fine," Matt said. "I'll show you later. Or Rhett can if he knows how."

Matt tossed a blanket over his shoulders and waited at the door for Stacy and Victoria.

"I'm coming too," Catherine asked. "I think I could figure it out in a pinch, but I'd like a lesson."

"Of course," Matt said. "Maybe we should have everyone get a refresher so Rhett and Kim can be alone. He seems really heartbroken about his sister."

"I'll tell everyone," Catherine said.

Somewhere in the distance, gears popped and grinded. The floor under Matt's feet trembled. He pressed his ear to the door but only heard the wind. Soon, everyone but Rhett and Kim joined him at the entryway.

"Ready?" Matt asked.

"Yep," Justin said. "Even though this is a waste of my time, chief."

Matt stepped outside, and his breath was immediately stolen by the glacial air. Snow fell so quickly, it seemed unreal. Like a movie set.

"Whoa!" Justin pushed his way to the railing on the deck. "Check out this drift. It's hardcore."

"No way," Matt said. "It's as high as the deck railing. This isn't good."

"Why?" Stacy asked. "We can totally sled off the side of the deck once it's nicer out. Victoria can finally have her first experience."

"Seriously?" Matt held the bridge between his eyes. "It means we're going to be stuck here for a very long time."

"Sorry," Darin said. "I know you guys wanted to get out of here ASAP."

"What's with this 'you guys,' mantra, man?" Justin asked. "You never refer to yourself as part of the group."

"I—I dunno," Darin said. "It's just—wait. Nathan, are you okay? What are you doing?"

Nathan stood frozen, his trembling arm pointed straight out. Matt peered in the direction he indicated. Snow cascaded down the mountain face in what looked like a large, pluming cloud and enveloped the trees. A small cabin on the outskirts was swallowed within an instant, nothing more than an appetizer for the incoming avalanche.

"Get inside!" Matt yelled. "Hurry!"

CHAPTER 6

"Nathan, get inside!" Matt desperately pulled on Nathan's shoulder, trying to wake him from his trance.

Nathan stared back at him with blank eyes.

"Please!" Matt pleaded. "Help!"

"We got you," Justin said. Darin followed behind him.

"Come on," Darin said. "Snap out of it."

Darin bear-hugged Nathan, locked his arms behind him, and pushed forward. Nathan's hips swung back toward Darin. Next, Darin stepped his right leg out and behind Nathan's long legs. Nathan fell onto Darin's thigh and instinctively reached out for him.

"What are you doing?" Matt asked. "Don't hurt him."

"He's okay. Westbrook taught me that move," Darin said. "Drag him in!"

Justin, being the strongest, slipped his arms under Nathan's armpits and pulled. Matt held a foot and Darin the other. It was only a few feet away, but Nathan was dead weight and Matt's forearms burned.

Catherine stood at the door, ready to slam it shut behind them.

"Get something to block the door," Matt yelled, looking frantically around the gym. The open space didn't have much to block the entrance.

"On it." Rhett and Kim had rejoined the group by the entrance. He rolled the TV cart toward the door. "Get some chairs."

"Here." Victoria handed him a folding chair.

Rhett wedged it under the door handle, then tipped the TV cart on its side and shoved it next to the door. The TV smashed against the hardwood floor, shattering the screen.

"Now what? What do we do?" Stacy asked, her face stricken with panic.

"I don't know. Find a tub? Like you do for a tornado?" Catherine suggested.

"No," Matt said. "The stage—no windows, it's our best bet. Run!"

The low rumble became a freight train in his short sprint to the stage. The entire ground below him shook. His ears rang, the room spun, and Matt fell onto his hands mere feet from the stage. He crab-walked backward, looking at the window. A wave of snow smashed against it and swallowed the cabin. Snow caked the windows. He felt hands pulling him onto the stage and faintly heard someone yelling for Nathan.

Nathan had come to his senses at some point and was running across the gym. His thin arms thrust forward like windmills, his gait was overly large, and his eyes were so unnaturally wide, Matt thought he looked like a caricature of himself. The roof creaked under the weight of the snow.

The tall, lanky boy from Utah stopped dead in his tracks and look up at the support beam that ran along the center of the A-frame cabin. It splintered in the middle of the roof, and one half came careening down like a cricket bat—Nathan was the ball. He ducked, then sprinted toward the stage.

Nathan hadn't planned on the centripetal force.

"Duck!" Matt screamed.

Smack!

The log connected with the back of Nathan's legs and butt, throwing him forward. He landed with a sick thud.

Matt jumped down to help him, then he heard the other half of the log break free from the center. It came swinging down toward the stage. Matt dove to the left of the theater area. The log bounced against the stage, denting it.

"Nathan!" Victoria called.

"I'm okay." Nathan slowly stood. "I'm just a little worse for the wear."

Matt heard another sick creaking noise and watched in horror as the left side of the aluminum roof collapsed, bringing mounds of snow down onto his friend.

But it didn't just cave in. It folded inward as if it was connected to a hinge on the long side of the cabin. The metal bang was deafening as it connected with the wall. Snow plumed, creating a hazy white cloud. Before it completely settled, the opposing wall fell in a similar fashion.

"Nathan!" Victoria called out.

Matt jumped down next to her and grabbed her. "No! It's not safe."

"We can't leave him!" Victoria said.

"Avalanche!" Catherine screamed.

Matt gripped a handful of Victoria's long dress and heaved her up onto the stage, then scrambled up after.

"Get back!" Matt yelled.

Before he could react, the front wall of the cabin toppled onto the rubble. He found himself as far back on the stage as he could go.

"We're going to die!" Stacy cried.

A wave of snow pinned Matt to the cinderblock wall so hard, he thought he might actually break through it. Frigid snow filled his ears and nose holes like quicksand. As soon as he felt the momentum shift, he pressed his hands against the wall and pushed himself backward. He fell and found himself staring at a drift against the wall.

He frantically reached into the drift for his friends. Justin and Rhett had gotten themselves out on their own.

"Help!" Matt yelled at them.

He'd been in this same situation before. Only last time it was pods, and Catherine and Cody were out. He punched his hand into the drift and felt for anything. A hand gripped his forearm. Matt pulled back as hard as he could without falling. Frizzy, red hair popped out of the snow. Stacy gasped for air, then immediately melted into a puddle of tears.

Matt turned to his left and saw that Cody and Darin had been pulled to safety. As soon as they caught their breath, they became part of the search team.

"Catherine! Victoria!" Matt yelled.

He reached into the snow again, but this time came up empty-handed. With each punch, the skin on his knuckles tore little by little, leaving pink streaks behind.

A hand and wrist reached up from the snow.

"I'm coming!" He ran to the hand and pulled.

Justin reached over the side of Matt and joined in. Finally, the face appeared.

Catherine.

She rolled onto her side and coughed.

"We've got Kim and Victoria," Rhett announced.

"Is that everyone?" Matt asked.

"No." Victoria sat up, and brought her knees up to her chest. "We're missing Nathan."

Matt sucked in a cold, dry breath. The silence was deafening. He slowly walked to the edge of the stage, trying to process the scene. He felt his chest tighten and tried to focus and calm his breath. The temperature had dropped at least fifty degrees, and every breath felt like tiny, sharp icicles were gathering in Matt's lungs.

The last he'd seen, the green metal roof had split down the middle. Each side came to rest against the long wall on its respective side. Now, after the second avalanche, he saw the true destruction. It had completely downed the front wall. For a brief moment, Matt was thankful it hadn't been pushed into the theater area where it would have crushed them. It, like the roof, hadn't broken or splintered. The avalanche simply tipped it forward into the room.

All support for the cabin was gone. It appeared the east wall had caved in first. It lay at an angle on top of the front wall. The west wall had fallen last. The mounds of snow were the icing on top. Only the cinderblock wall, backstage, remained. And it was likely to cave at any moment.

"Nathan." Matt jumped down onto the snow pile of rubble.

There was no excitement behind his voice. He knew. This wasn't a rescue mission.

It was a recovery.

Cody was the next one down, followed by Justin, then the rest.

Matt tried to push on the wall, but it was useless. Not even with all their might combined could they move the snow-covered walls and roof.

Matt crawled under a beam and reached around blindly. He held onto it and pulled as he shimmied out. Freezing snow slid up his shirt. He felt a thick cord. He pulled on the cable, but it wouldn't budge.

"What is this?" Matt said to no one. "What is this connected to?"

He clambered to the top of the pile toward another black cable poking out of the snow. The source was an eyelet screw that connected it to a log on one of the walls. Matt's face twisted in confusion.

"I found him!" Victoria yelled. "He's right here. Hurry! Help me!"

Matt dropped the cable and carefully walked to the spot from where he heard her voice. Rhett's legs poked out from the rubble next to Victoria's.

"Victoria, let go," Rhett said. "You're making this harder."

Victoria emerged first, her black dress caked with snow.

Rhett shimmied and stopped inch by inch until he was out. Two feet peeked from the rubble. The same way Matt had identified Kyle. He sucked in a sharp breath.

"Is he going to be okay?" Victoria asked. "He is, right?"

"Victoria . . ." Catherine pulled her into a hug.

With one hard yank, Rhett pulled Nathan free from the rubble.

A dusty white haze filled the cabin. They all huddled together around their dead friend's body.

CHAPTER 7

Before Matt could even gather his thoughts, the clouds parted and the sun shone brightly through the rubble. As if someone had flipped a switch. Intense heat coupled with swiftly melting snow created an unnatural and intense humidity.

Snow melted at an incredible speed. The scene reminded Matt of watching a National Geographic movie about Yellowstone in biology class. It had been a time-lapse video of winter melting away and spring beginning and turning into summer. The snow had evaporated, and a small green bud popped through the earth. In a matter of seconds, it had grown into a tulip, then died and wilted in the summer heat.

"What in the French toast is happening here?" Cody asked.

"This is insane!" Stacy said.

"Whoa," Matt said. "What the French is right."

What lay before Matt made him question his own sanity. Dozens of thin black cables hung loose from a pulley apparatus above them. All that remained of the cabin was the cinderblock and rebar-reinforced stage area. The rest of the cabin lay folded in on itself.

"What the hell?" Justin cupped his right hand over his forehead, shielding it from the bright light. "This is straight out of a sci-fi movie. Is some alien playing cat's cradle, and these pullies are the yarn?"

The cabin destruction left from the avalanches was showcased under powerful light and the blue skies above. Water flowed into cracks, melting snow as quickly as it came. All the water pooled toward the spot where the fireplace had been.

"We need to get out of here now," Matt said. "This place is unstable."

"Follow me," Cody said.

"What about Nathan?" Victoria cried.

"I'll get him," Rhett said. He nodded at Justin.

Justin held Nathan's limp wrists, and Rhett lifted Nathan's ankles.

Matt leapt over a cable, then ducked under another. He tripped and bashed his knees on what used to be the roof. He ducked and rolled, avoiding cables.

"You guys, watch out for the cables." Matt looked over his shoulder at Justin and Rhett. "They're everywhere."

Then he saw it.

Nathan's face. He'd been avoiding it since they pulled him from the wreckage.

Blood oozed from his nose, mouth, and eyes. His crushed, sagging body looked like a wooden marionette doll that bounced and jiggled with each step Justin and Rhett took.

Matt turned away and swallowed bile that had gathered in this throat. *I shouldn't have left him behind. But what could I do?*

Matt followed Catherine on the partially intact wraparound porch to the backside of the cabin—technically the theater area. From the outside, the cinderblocks had been covered in logwood siding, concealing the industrial look. A support beam had fallen on the porch, and the deck angled sharply toward the ground.

"Victoria, you're the lightest. You go first." Darin pointed to the steep ramp. "We need to see if it'll hold."

"Excuse me?" Kim said. "I'm the thinnest. I'm a flyer for my squad, thank you very much."

"Fine!" Darin yelled. "Then you go!"

"Screw you. I'm not your guinea pig."

"Kim, if you don't shut your mouth—" Catherine started.

"No!" Victoria yelled. "Stop it! I can't take it!"

Victoria ran down the wobbly deck, screaming the entire time. It shifted from side to side with her erratic gait but held. She got to the edge and lowered herself down three feet until she was firmly on the ground.

"This is all our fault!" Victoria yelled. "All this fighting and finger pointing. Nathan is dead because we couldn't come together. This is *all* our fault!"

Matt swallowed hard and locked eyes with Catherine. She was next down the ramp, and once at the bottom, she embraced Victoria and stroked her hair.

One by one, they made their way down onto the ground, where muddy water squelched up over their shoes and surrounded their ankles. The heat intensified, and Matt guessed it was over ninety degrees. His skin was slick with sweat and the air felt thick. Finally, Rhett and Justin gingerly carried Nathan's body over. Matt's palms sweat as he watched what was left of the porch bow and creak with each step.

"Where should we put him?" Justin asked, bowing his head.

"I don't know," Matt said. "Somewhere safe until we can bury him."

They all looked around, their faces mirroring what Matt was thinking. Was any place safe?

CHAPTER 8

"None of this makes any sense." Stacy collapsed onto the wet ground. "This has to be a bad dream."

"Poor Nathan." Matt ignored her, and instead walked around to the front of where the cabin had been. It wasn't like he had the answers.

Everyone but Stacy followed.

"He didn't have a chance," Darin said. "There was no way he could have survived the collapse like that. And I fear it's going to keep happening."

"What do you mean by that?" Matt asked.

"I mean, the apocalypse is obviously still ongoing. We're encountering more crappy weather." Darin held the bridge of his nose. "Look, fifteen minutes ago, it was a full-on blizzard. Now, it's ninety degrees, and most of the snow has melted. And why isn't it flooding? Where is all this water going?"

"This is just like the flood." Matt shook his head. "It's like it drained or something. I don't know!"

"Look at that!" Cody pointed to the side of the mountain filled with downed trees.

A few drifts that still remained looked like someone spilled chocolate-infused piña coladas, but most of the snow had melted, creating a sloppy mess. The avalanche chutes were clear. The largest scar carved through the forest, remnants of the avalanche that killed Nathan. Matt hung his head.

First Kyle. Now Nathan.

They hadn't even had a chance to give Kyle a proper burial before this mess unfolded. Now they had another body to add to that count.

"Matt," Catherine whispered into his ear. "I'm scared. What is this?"

He stared back toward the mountain. The scent of moist dirt and pine filled the air. Loud creaking echoed in the otherwise silent valley. One by one, trees sprung back up like someone had turned the page in a pop-up book. Needles cascaded to the ground from the swaying trees as the forest around righted itself to normal. Matt shook his head, trying to make sense of it all.

"I—I don't get it! I wish you could just get us out of here and back to the cave, Darin!" he screamed.

"Back off, kid." Darin stood almost a full head taller than Matt and was nearly as muscular as Justin. "I've been patient with you guys and your unrelenting questions—*accusations*, really. I know you think I have some sort of information that's going to explain this all away, but I don't. I'm just as puzzled as you."

"Then what is this place?" Kim's voice trembled. "Like, what is happening? Holy crap, half of the cabins are, like, wiped out!"

"We know we're at HZRD, according to Westbrook. But who knows what HZRD is?" Darin said. "Westbrook royally screwed us when he brought us and left us in a forest."

"I thought you loved this place. Said the air was good and whatnot." Matt crossed his arms.

"The air *is* good. But this place is a natural disaster zone. He just should have kept us frozen," Darin said.

"And let us die?" Cody asked.

"Looks like that's gonna happen one way or the other here." Darin walked back toward the backside of the cabin, where Stacy had remained.

Matt looked to his friends. Kim had buried her face in Rhett's firm chest, and he hugged her, but his face was blank, expressionless. Justin stood tall, overlooking the camp. Cody rubbed the back of his neck.

Catherine turned to Matt, hugged him, and whispered, "I'm sorry. I'm going around back. I need to say goodbye to Nathan."

Rhett and Kim followed her.

Justin ran a hand through his sandy-blond hair and said, "Darin's right. We're screwed."

The adrenaline had worn off, and Matt was overcome with emotion. He felt his chest tighten, and tears spilled from his eyes. He crouched against the wall, brought his knees up to his chest, and wept like he hadn't done since he was a little kid.

"Hey, I didn't mean it, chief," Justin said. "It's probably not that bad."

"It's not you," Matt said in between sobs, "it's everything. None of this makes any sense. You saw it with your own eyes. The cabin, the trees, the avalanches, and the quick shifts in the weather. Now Nathan. Nathan, who wouldn't hurt a fly, was crushed to death. Pinned. He was so scared. I'll never get his desperate cries out of my head. I should've saved him."

"You saved the rest of us," Cody said. "You were right to have us wait. We're lucky we all weren't crushed. What happened to Nathan is a tragedy, but it's not your fault."

"Look how many have died. Dr. Westbrook, girl number seven whose name we don't even know, Kyle, and now Nathan. Darin's right. We're all doomed."

"Look, chief, you gotta pull it together," Justin said. "Everyone looks to you for answers—"

"Darin too," Cody interrupted.

"Yeah," Justin shifted, "*Lance-Darin* too. If you crack, everyone is going to lose it."

Matt pressed his palms into his eyes and stood. A wet spot from the melting snow stained the seat of his pants. Justin was right. Matt had to figure out something—even if it just meant getting them somewhere safer and leaving Camp New Beginnings.

"Should we go around back? Pay our respects to Nathan?" Cody asked.

"You go," Matt said. "I need to take a walk. I'm not ready to see him like that again."

Matt trudged through the mud. Behind him, the once large main cabin was now smashed flat. With the force of the avalanche, many of the cabins in Camp New Beginnings didn't have a chance. Something odd pulled at the back of his brain. Most of the collapsed cabins weren't piles of splintered sticks, but instead, they seemed to have just folded in on each other.

But that wasn't what drove him forward. The trees had sprung up like nothing had happened, and no one said a word. Maybe he was the only one who'd seen it happen. Or maybe they were too traumatized. Matt walked to the first trees near the edge of the camp. An old conifer that was once laid out by an intense avalanche now stood tall and erect. He couldn't make sense of it. What apocalyptic phenomenon had the force to flatten a tree, then revive it back to life?

CHAPTER 9

Once at the tree, Matt dropped to his knees. Pawing at the earth, he was positive he'd find something, *anything* to explain what he'd witnessed. Either that or he was going insane and imagining all of this. He paused for a moment and considered that. *Is this real? Are my friends real? Am I even here? Is this a dream in the cryosleep?*

A dull ache thumped in his left wrist. He rubbed the spot. *No, not a dream. I don't think you feel pain in dreams or hallucinations.* He dug like a frantic dog looking for a bone. The soft earth caked his hands with rich soil. Pine needles poked at his palms and fingertips, but he put it out of his mind and continued to dig.

"Where is it? What lifted you back up? Huh? Tell me!" he yelled. "Who did this? Is there someone underneath? Who are you? How'd you do it? Is this real? Of course it is. Nathan is dead. Kyle is dead. That's real!" Matt screamed until his throat was raw. He pounded the dirt.

A gentle hand touched his shoulder. Matt snapped back to himself.

"Matt, you gotta calm down," Cody said evenly. "You saw what happened to Nathan when he lost it."

"I did!" Matt stood. "And now we have to bury him. And Kyle. And Dr. Westbrook and some random, nameless girl—if we can even find them."

"Whoa, chief," Justin said. "Come back to reality with me for a minute, 'kay?"

Matt blinked hard, trying to calm his breath, wishing they hadn't seen him like this.

"I can't explain what's happening either," Justin said. "But let's just take a step back."

"A step back?" Matt scoffed. "I'd like to take a leap back. Back to when things were normal."

"None of this has made sense from the beginnin'," Cody said. "We were dropped off outside a camp that just so happened to have some food, water, a generator, and a dang VCR."

"Exactly!" Matt desperately splayed his muddy hands out in Cody's direction. "That's what I've been saying!"

"But maybe it's not meant for us to know," Cody said. "Like God. I don't understand why He decided it was time for an apocalypse, but it's not for me to understand. I just kept on livin' and trustin' He'd take care of me."

"All right, let's not drag religion into this," Justin said. "We all know that's garbage."

"Is not," Cody said.

"Yeah, I bet the other bazillion people who died didn't feel taken care of by your God," Justin replied.

"I hope you find Jesus Christ in your heart before it's your time," Cody said. "I'm more than happy to help get you there."

"Whatever." Justin rolled his eyes. "But the cowboy makes a good point. We're here, and things don't make sense, but neither did the apocalypse. Maybe this *is* the new normal. I'm not sure. But not everything has an answer, you know? Like women. Geesh, good luck ever trying to figure any of them out."

"Yeah," Matt said.

Justin smiled. Matt bet his smile got him out of a lot of trouble *before.* "And I know my parents sucked, but I don't want them to die. I want to save them. And everyone else. This place isn't all we thought it was cracked up to be."

"I know," Matt said. "We have to find everyone else. Wherever *that* is."

"Let's try and keep you out of the looney bin," Justin said. "While this pains me to admit, you've had the best plans so far." He cleared his throat. "You figure anything out with that tree?"

"No, the ground is still frozen under the surface. I need a shovel. Couldn't get past the topsoil." Matt wiped his hands on the logo of his *Commodore 64* shirt. "I need a shovel to see what's really down there."

"Speaking of that—" Cody said.

"I know," Matt said. "Come on, let's get this over with."

They walked in silence, which Matt was thankful for. He was still trying to make sense of everything and get his mind right. During the walk back, he closed his eyes and thought about his parents. When he entered high school, he started having "little episodes," as his mom called them. He'd get so overwhelmed that his chest felt tight, and he couldn't catch his breath. His mom taught him to fix his attention on something still, like the tile floor, and focus on breathing. She said it was sort of like meditation, and deemed it "Matt-itation." It became his saving grace, and he couldn't believe he'd forgotten about it until now. The moment he felt the tightening in his chest, he'd do his Matt-itation. He smiled at the memory.

The humidity from the melted snow combined with the intense heat made the air thick. Matt stared at the rubble and thought back to the first time he saw the cabin. He was so full of hope. Now he was filled with dread.

"Where'd you go?" Catherine met him where they'd had the fire-pit the night before.

"I needed a minute," Matt said. "How is everyone?"

"Kim seems a little shaken, but no worse for the wear. Rhett is really upset, almost withdrawn. I can't imagine seeing your sister tossed away in a heap of garbage bags." She nodded her head toward the two, who were holding each other on the ground. "Stacy is sad, Darin is withdrawn, and Victoria is traumatized. She hasn't left Nathan's body and keeps talking to him. I don't get it. They weren't close."

"She's sensitive. Plus, this is the first time she's probably ever witnessed death. Honestly, probably the first time anyone has, except you and Cody."

"And you," Catherine said.

"Right," Matt replied.

He followed Catherine to the back of the building until he reached Nathan. All color had drained from him. Victoria stroked his brown hair and quietly sang a song Matt didn't recognize. He knelt by her and Nathan's body.

"What are you thinking, Victoria?" Matt asked.

"Life's precious." Her gaze remained fixed on Nathan's face.

"It is," Matt said. "Do you think it would be okay if we moved him away from the cabin?"

"Why?" Victoria finally looked at Matt. "He seems peaceful here."

"He's gone, you know that, right?"

"Yes." She covered her face and cried quietly into her hands. "I suppose he needs a proper burial like the others."

"Absolutely. As soon as the ground is fully thawed—and that'll be really soon—we'll have a funeral. Until then, maybe take a break. Didn't you promise to braid Catherine's hair since she did yours?"

Victoria touched the long plait that ran down her back.

"Come on." Catherine pulled Victoria to her feet. "Good luck braiding this curly mess."

The girls walked hand-in-hand, and it brought brief comfort to Matt.

Then he remembered the grisly task that awaited him.

"Rhett, Justin, can I get your help?" Matt called.

Darin followed the two over. Matt gritted his teeth.

"We need to get him out of here. Let's put him under a tarp until we can dig the graves. Anyone object to that?" Matt turned to Darin.

"I'll get the tarp," Darin said.

CHAPTER 10

Matt returned to the group, wishing they had a working faucet. He desperately wanted to wash his hands and get the smell of death off him. One of his neighbors from *before* hunted deer. Every year, the neighbor would hang his deer's corpse in the garage. On hot days, the smell would waft out, filling the block with a scent Matt couldn't describe other than death.

If Matt didn't get everyone buried soon, the same would be true for Camp New Beginnings. He guessed the ground would be thawed in the next hour and made a mental note to make that a priority. In the interim, it was time to make a plan.

"Can everyone gather around?" Matt asked. "We need to talk about what's next."

They all formed a circle around the remnants of the firepit. The rubble from the main cabin sat behind them.

"What now?" Kim groaned.

"Geez, Kim," Catherine said. "It's not all about you all the time."

"No, no arguing, please." Matt rubbed a hand over his buzz cut. "If you want to stay at camp forever or do nothing, fine. If you want to help, come join me over here. I can't take the fighting. I've had enough."

"What*ever*," Kim said.

Rhett put an arm around Kim and guided her toward Matt and the rest of the group.

"Let's break up into teams, okay?" Matt said. "Things have gotten real serious, real fast."

"You can say that again," Stacy said.

"Teams for what, chief?" Justin asked.

"We need to search camp for supplies," Matt said. "Go to all the cabins that didn't get demolished from the avalanche. And just like Darin suggested, we've got to be thorough. Anything and everything that might be helpful. Even if it seems weird, grab it. Let's check every cabinet and under beds. All the outbuildings and sheds need to be checked too. Whatever you find, bring it back here, so we have it all in one spot, okay? Pack it up, bring it here."

"What are we packing for?" Rhett asked. "Are we finally going to go to the mountain?"

"Yes," Matt said.

"Then gas masks are key," Darin said. "We absolutely need them."

"Great, fine," Matt said. "Everyone, please meet back here in the next hour or so, even if you're not done. Just to report, you know?"

"You mean make sure we didn't die?" Victoria asked. "That's the real reason, isn't it?"

Matt hesitated. "Split up. I'll see you all back here in an hour."

"I'll check the shed and any other outbuildings," Darin said.

"Lance-Darin, I'll help you," Stacy said, sidling up to him.

Kim rolled her eyes.

"Great." Darin blinked hard. "You guys got the cabins?"

"Sure," Justin said. "Cody, Victoria, and Rhett, you guys in?"

"Yes," Rhett said.

Kim frowned and pushed his arm off her waist.

"Sounds good to me," Cody said.

Victoria nodded.

"I'll check the infirmary, or at least I think it's the infirmary," Matt said.

"Count me in," Catherine said.

"All right, then," Cody said. "Kim, what are you gonna do?"

"Me?" Kim did a backbend and kicked her feet over. Her colorful pleated skirt fluttered and reminded Matt of every pep rally he'd ever been to. "I'm going to sit my pretty little butt right here and relax. Have fun."

"Kim, come on," Catherine said.

Kim sat on a log that had served as a bench the night before. "Come on what? Keep pushing me, and I'll make Rhett stay here and fan me. How about that?"

"No." Rhett shook his head. "I want to help. I have to find what's left of my family."

"Whatever." Kim rolled her eyes. "I guess you can go."

Catherine opened her mouth and hesitated.

"It's not worth it," Matt whispered in Catherine's ear.

Matt called back to his friends. "Hey, guys, try to find a place we can sleep tonight. One of the other cabins that didn't get destroyed."

"Sound good," Darin said.

"See you in an hour, chief," Justin said.

* * *

Matt led Catherine to a cabin on the edge of the avalanche chute. It wasn't much bigger than the other bunkhouses in this area of camp. To their right, Justin pushed his shoulder on a door, and entered a cabin. The door slammed behind him. Victoria followed Cody into another. They entered more cautiously than Justin, easing the door open and peering in first.

The door in front of Matt and Catherine had a white square with a chipped red cross painted on it. He turned the handle but was met with resistance.

"Is it locked?" Catherine asked.

"No," Matt said. "I think there's something blocking the door. Probably from the flood."

He turned to his side and thrust his shoulder into the door. It budged, but only an inch.

"Help me," Matt grunted. "On three. One, two, three!"

They took a small step back and slammed themselves into the door. It crashed open, and a chair flew across the small space, smashing into a doctor's exam table. Matt fell on his back; Catherine landed next to him on her side. He stared at her for a moment and tucked a tight black curl behind her ear. *Just like in the movies,* he thought. She smiled at him and held his hand.

"I'll be honest, that kinda hurt," Matt said, breaking the tension.

Catherine rolled onto her back and laughed. "This whole thing is so messed up, I'd expect nothing less. And hey, if you're injured, we found the infirmary."

Matt stood and stretched. Dusting himself off, he smoothed his filthy shirt. In the middle of the small room was an old exam table with a tarnished metal top. The table paper had long since been destroyed, but a thick, rotting cardboard spool from a roll still remained at the top. Across from it was a sink, soap, and two jars—one with matted cotton balls, the other with cottons swabs with long wooden handles. Below the countertop were four small drawers. Matt ran to the sink and lifted the faucet's handle.

Nothing.

He waited with his hands under the faucet, willing water to come out.

Catherine stepped up to his side and said, "We can go to the lake if you'd like after."

"Yeah, that'd be good."

Matt looked at her. Even in the physical state they were all in, dirty and bruised, he still thought she looked beautiful.

They held each other's gaze.

Catherine cleared her throat. "I'll check the cabinets under the counter." She opened a white metal cabinet on the opposite side of the table.

Matt shook his head and calmed his breathing. The first drawer, just left of the sink, squeaked like a bike wheel void of oil.

"Are you finding anything?" she asked.

"Kind of." He scooped the contents out of the old drawer. "I've got Band-Aids, ACE bandages, and instant ice packs. You?"

"Some pills . . . um, this one says liquid iodine." She handed it to Matt. "And some Lortab and some antibiotics, I think."

The heavy, brown glass jar of iodine was still intact and didn't appear to have been damaged in the flood. She set the cloudy orange pill bottles on the counter next to him. He tilted them from side to side, ensuring they weren't one big, wet pile of pill mush. They'd work in a pinch.

"And scissors." Catherine dropped them on the exam table. "Arts and crafts in the infirmary?"

"No, those are hemo-something. I can't remember. Here, let me check something." Matt stepped onto the exam table and reached into the very top of the cabinet while Catherine moved out of the way. "If they're here, I bet there are needles and sutures too. Jackpot!" He held a plastic pack of curved needles and thread. "You may have just saved someone's life, Catherine."

"I had to have stitches in my hand once. It was not fun. The way the doctor pierced my skin—I don't even like thinking about it." She shuddered. "Did they teach you how to use those in Scouts?"

"Heck, no," Matt said.

"I don't want to be the guinea pig." Catherine smiled, and placed them in a green canvas bag she'd brought.

"Cody grew up on a farm and ranch. I'd bet a thousand bucks—if money mattered—on him knowing how to use them."

"I'll take that bet, Voorhees." Catherine held out her hand.

Matt shook it, then held on for a moment. "Uh, we should probably get back to the main cabin."

"Yeah." Catherine blushed and looked away. "Good idea."

Matt gathered up the rest of what they found from the drawers.

"Can we take a detour by the lake so I can wash off a bit?" Matt asked as they left.

"Sure thing," Catherine replied.

She looped her arm in Matt's and started to skip toward their water source.

Hopefully, everyone else had been this fruitful. Regardless, for the first time in a long time, Matt felt something strange.

Hope.

CHAPTER 11

As Catherine and Matt made their way back to the meeting spot, Justin came out from in between cabins.

"Hey!" Justin shouted. "Matt, you got a free hand?"

Matt stopped short and handed his canvas bag to Catherine.

"I'll meet you over there," he said, then jogged to Justin. "What's up?"

"Here, take these." Justin plopped a bunch of harnesses in Matt's outstretched arms. "I think it's for rock climbing. This camp must have been a pretty rad place back in its heyday."

"Schweet," Matt said. "Which cabin were you guys in? I'll drop these off and bring Catherine to help."

"Nah, this is the last load. We'll meet you by the firepit as instructed!" He saluted Matt then turned away.

The coarse harnesses dug into his arms while the carabiners clanked as he walked on the reddish-brown dirt. Surprisingly, glittery quartz rocks remained untouched and still lined the path perfectly, like some kid had glued them on a life-sized diorama.

Matt frowned at the damage once again. The main cabin was wrecked, along with a half dozen smaller cabins. All of the cabin roofs had become void of the moss that was so prominent when they arrived just a few days ago.

Matt adjusted the rope and climbing equipment on his shoulder. He figured they probably wouldn't be climbing the face of the mountain, but it was still a good find, nonetheless.

Piled next to Kim was a different kind of mountain. Stacks of hiking boots, carefully folded clothing—all army green—and tons of tools. Axes, shovels, and sledgehammers were the most common among the pile of tackle.

"Hey there," Darin said. "Nice find on the med supplies."

"Thanks," Matt absently replied. He picked up a crowbar. "Whoa, where did you guys find these? How the heck did we miss all of this?"

"Good question," Kim said. "Like, did you even try before?"

"Shut up, Kim," Catherine said.

"*You* shut up." Kim had her back against the supplies and was flipping through an instruction manual like it was the latest issue of *Seventeen Magazine.* "Seriously, Matt, some leader you are. All this junk was, like, at our fingertips, and you were only worried about dumb crap. Let's bury bodies, watch boring home videos, don't go swimming, I'm going to the truck," she mocked.

"I never said I was the leader," Matt said through clenched jaws. "You're welcome to offer up suggestions whenever you'd like. That is, if you can pull yourself away from your afternoon nap, Madame."

"Princess," Kim corrected him, never looking up from her yellowed instruction manual.

"Anyway," Stacy said, "check out what Lance-Darin and I found. We made a really solid team." She winked.

She's a chameleon, Matt thought. She took on whatever personality granted her approval. He highly doubted her stories of being rich and popular. Whatever the case, he liked this version of her a lot more than when she hung out with Kim.

"We got these Special-K knives—"

"K-bars, not the cereal," Darin interrupted.

"And axes," she said, ignoring him. "Plus more shovels, flashlights, backpacks, these hideous clothes—and oh! We found an office! Check out the Trapper Keepers."

Stacy held out a Lisa Frank organizer with a rainbow background and a unicorn on the front. She lifted the top, and the Velcro ripped away from the bottom sticking to it. Plastic ripped a little and she shrugged.

The death of a Trapper Keeper, Matt thought. He knew it well. His last year of school, his had a red Lamborghini on the front, and it tore after the second week. Every time he pulled it out of his backpack, the top would fly open and papers would spill out. He finally resorted to using a large, blue rubber band to keep it closed.

"I searched the desk pretty good," Darin said. "Couldn't find anything that identified the owner of it. But we grabbed a bunch of these pencils, lead, and notebooks."

Matt examined the yellow Pentel mechanical pencils and gently shook one. The lead inside the walls of it bounced around. Aside from the yellowing pages, the purple notebook he held look brand new. He uncapped the eraser from the pencil and started erasing a line on the cover.

"This works better." Darin handed him a flat pink one with the words "Blackwing 602" scrolled across the front, printed in block letters.

"Thanks." Matt continued his work with the flat pink eraser until he had etched his name onto the cover. He grinned. "Sorry, I couldn't help myself."

"I used to do the same thing," Cody said, returning with Victoria.

"Did you cover your books with paper grocery bags too?" Victoria asked. "I always heard kids in the suburbs did that."

"Never did. Never cared," Justin said. "What kinda fancy school did you attend?"

"It wasn't fancy," she said. "It was just forbidden. Teachers would tear off any book covers and give you detention. We were required to keep our books pristine or else. No paper bag coverings. Looked too trashy, I guess."

They laid out more rock-climbing gear next to the pile of supplies.

"This is great," Matt said.

"Any gas masks?" Darin asked.

"No," Rhett said. "You said you found flashlights?"

"Yes. They're pretty old." Darin held up a bulky green rectangle with "Dyno Torch" embossed on the side. "Squeeze the handle over and over and you create light. No batteries needed."

"Cool," Rhett replied. "We found compasses. I don't know how to use them."

"Not a problem," Matt said. "I can teach you. You don't have to be a rocket scientist to learn how." He palmed the round metal and watched for the needle to find a steady point. It bounced around, never stilling. "Hmm, that's weird." He tapped the compass's clear face. "It won't find a fixed point. Doesn't matter. I'll try the others later. Now that we've got our supplies, and more shovels, I think it's time."

"What about Kyle?" Victoria asked.

"As bad as this sounds, we're going to have to go search for his body. After that avalanche, who knows where it ended up and what condition he's in. And moving it might not be an option anymore," Matt said.

"Come on," Darin said. "Let's stick to this task first."

"Do we even, like, know where any of the corpses are?" Kim asked.

"Sadly, yes," Justin said. "We found them when we were searching the cabins. We used a couple bedspreads to drag them over to Nathan's body. Honestly, they were pretty bad. Skin falling off, completely bloated, the girl's arm looked like it had been ripped almost completely off her body and the smell—"

"No need to get to graphic," Cody said. "The point is, they're with Nathan and they've been wrapped in those blankets so no one else needs to see them."

"Everyone, grab a shovel or hoe. Let's do this together," Matt said.

"Even me?" Kim said.

"Especially you, Kim," Rhett said. "Nathan was my friend."

"Ugh, fine." She finally stood and toward the bodies. "Let's get these stiffs in the ground."

CHAPTER 12

Arguing ensued before they agreed to bury them by a crop of trees on the edge of camp. All in one grave. The girls stayed behind and dug while the guys dragged the bodies to the burial site. When Matt returned, Catherine, Stacy, Victoria, and Kim had made a decent sized dent in the grave site and were sweaty—all except Kim, who looked fresh as a spring daisy. Matt guessed she'd leaned on the hoe the whole time.

"Wow." Catherine gagged. "They're . . . fragrant."

"Yeah," Matt said. "Let's get this done quick."

He joined in the shoveling. After twenty minutes, his back ached, and his forearms burned. Sweat dripped down his back, making his shirt cling to him. It always looked so much easier in the movies. Even with nine people digging, it was slow going.

"Whoa!" Cody said. A loud clang followed. "Whoa. Musta hit a rock."

"We're almost done," Darin said. "Don't worry about digging it out. Just go around it."

"That's a hell of a stone." Catherine leaned over Cody. "Matt, check this out."

Matt wiped his brow with his forearm and stared down at an object with sharp angles. "Wait. That's no rock." His face twisted in confusion. "Is it metal?"

They chased the object down a few more inches. Matt jumped in the hole and scooped dirt out with his hands, excavating the artifact like a fossil from an archeological dig.

"Kinda looks like a jacked-up hubcap," Rhett said.

Matt dropped the piece of metal on the edge and climbed out of the hole.

"Weird." His face twisted with confusion. "It's a gear."

They all stood at the edge of the hole, staring down at a large, rust-colored gear.

"What do you think it is?" Catherine asked.

Matt knelt down to get a better look. He squinted. "I have no idea."

"Looks like someone just threw a bunch of giant junk out here to rust away," Darin suggested. "I mean, I saw a picture one time of a tree that grew through a bicycle, and several years later, the bike was about seven feet up and totally incorporated into the trunk."

"Yeah," Cody said, "that could be it."

They let an awkward silence settle in until Kim blurted out, "I'm gonna gag to death over here."

Matt turned and said, "Okay, I think this is deep enough. Let's bury them."

They grabbed the tops and bottoms of the tarp and blankets. Matt did his best to respectfully lower them into the grave, but his back strained, and it was too deep. He braced himself for the sickening thud the bodies made as they were dropped into the hole.

When Nathan, Dr. Westbrook, and girl number seven were all in the open grave, Matt said, "Anyone want to say a few things?" He suppressed a gag and pressed his index finger to his nose.

No one spoke.

"Okay—" he stammered.

"I'll go," Kim said, perking up. "The worms crawl in, the worms crawl out—"

"Kim, stop," Catherine whispered.

"The ants play pinochle on your snout," Kim sang. "Your stomach turns a moldy green, and pus comes out like whipping cream!"

"Kim!" Stacy shouted.

"What the hell's wrong with you?" Victoria asked. "Show some respect."

"What do you expect from me," Kim laughed. "I barely knew Na-Nathan and didn't know the other two at all. Sorry you froze up and got squished by beams? Sorry, scientist, for abandoning me in this hellhole? Sorry, girl who probably could have sold me some jeans at the Gap? I'm outta here. See you back at camp." She walked away.

"I don't know what you see in her." Matt turned to Rhett and shook his head.

"Maybe that's how she grieves," Cody said. "It's still extremely rude but . . ."

"I've got something to say!" Rhett blurted out. "Nathan, I'm sorry my girlfriend mocked your stutter. I really liked you and thought you were a big dork. But in a good way. I wish I could have saved you." He hung his head.

"Sorry, Nathan, and girl." Justin placed a hand on Rhett's shoulder.

"Nathan, I saw the look of fear in your eyes, the sound of terror in your voice. No one should lose their life like that," Victoria said. "Sweet girl, I didn't know you, and I hope you weren't panicked. We didn't get to you in time. And Dr. Westbrook, you gave up your life for us, thank you." She dropped a wildflower into the grave.

Catherine and Stacy followed suit and said a few nice words. Matt turned to Darin.

"I've said all I needed to say to Westbrook," Darin said.

"Dr. Westbrook," Matt said, "you did so much for us. Even up to the end when you gave your life so we could live—"

"He wasn't Jesus," Darin interrupted.

Matt continued, "I don't know if you had a wife and kids or what you left behind, but it's admirable. I'm so thankful I have a chance at a second life. Nathan, what can I say? You were great, and we all liked you. And girl number seven, I hope you didn't suffer."

Matt was the first to take a shovel full of dirt and toss it in the hole. It bounced off a floral comforter and rolled down the sides.

He looked to the group and nodded at them to do the same. After a few minutes, the hole was almost completely filled in. Soon, the only thing left was a large mound over the bodies.

"We'll need to make a proper marker for it when we can," Cody said. "Wouldn't be right to have an unmarked grave."

"Now what, chief?" Justin asked.

"Would it be okay if I gave a crash course in compasses?" He took the one Rhett had given him out of his pocket. "This is so weird; do you have more of these?"

Rhett handed him two more.

Matt shuffled through the three compasses. "Okay, so maybe they got ruined in the flood, but they're all kinda working the same." The needles were going wild. They spun back and forth, never fixing on a given direction.

"I don't know," Matt confessed. "Compass class is canceled. I guess let's call where the truck wrecked north. The trail sort of splits the camp, the lake is east, and the mountain is south." He pointed. "That makes the main cabin just west of the pathway. Any questions?"

"What's the urgency to go?" Stacy said. "I'm feeling pretty sad."

"I made a promise to Kyle," Matt replied. "And the sooner we get him buried, the sooner we can find the cave and our families."

CHAPTER 13

Matt and the gang headed back to the collapsed main cabin.

"Me, Catherine, and Cody will go north, try to find Kyle's body, you know . . ." Matt said. "We can bury him at the truck once we find him."

"I'm good with that," Cody said.

"I just feel like we need to give him a proper burial before we go to the mountain," Matt said. "It's the right thing to do."

"Do you need help?" Darin asked.

"I think with the three of us, we should be good," Matt said. "We'll head to the mountain right after we get back."

"Okay," Darin said. "I'll get everyone packed up for the trek."

"Taking on the role of camp counselor already," Matt said, a tinge of sarcasm laced in his words.

"More like babysitter," Kim said.

Matt, Cody, and Catherine packed backpacks for their day trip. Matt's bag consisted of a couple of cans of food, a knife, a canteen of water, and a wool blanket.

"Ready," Catherine said to Matt.

"Yeah, you got the supplies?" he asked.

"Yep."

Matt turned to the group. "Three hours max. We will be back."

"I'm, like, going swimming," Kim said.

"Figures," Matt said.

The three left their friends on the porch, walked down the red-brown dirt path, and passed the Camp New Beginnings sign that now lay on the ground next to the toppled archway. Matt looked back at the destruction the avalanche had done and held the bridge of his nose.

"You comin'?" Cody asked.

Matt jogged to catch up to Catherine and Cody, who held three shovels. Cody handed one to Matt.

"I'm so glad to have a break from Kim," Catherine said. "She's insufferable."

"I know it ain't right for a man to speak ill of a woman, so I'll just nod and say nothin'," Cody said.

"Sorry, not trying to gossip," Catherine said. "But I've had enough."

"Me too," Matt said. "Honestly, after her performance at the funeral, she can leave the camp. Too bad Rhett is so attached to her. We can't lose him, and he's actually pretty cool."

After twenty minutes, they had ascended the hill close to the truck. A deep scar of freshly churned-up dirt confirmed the avalanche had swept through the area. All smaller plants and scrub brush that had grown between the trees remained but had been trampled.

Then there was the truck. When they'd last seen it, it was wedged between two trees with Kyle's body propped against it. Now it was flipped upside down between the same set of trees. Painted white numbers and a letter stenciled on its undercarriage were now visible. The windshield was obliterated, the axles on both front and back were broken in half, and the driver's door was ripped off. Kyle was nowhere to be seen.

"Holy crap," Matt said. "How big was this avalanche?"

"That was no avalanche," Catherine said. "That was something else. It needs a different name."

"An apoca-lanche." Matt shrugged.

"I like it," Catherine said.

"Look at that." Cody walked swiftly toward the truck. "See this? We saw it a little bit when we was changin' the tire." He outlined the painted letters and numbers on the bottom of the truck. "B-35."

"Okay, we need to remember that," Matt said. "Don't know why, but I'm writing that down. We need to note the position of the truck, the painted number." He retrieved the Trapper Keeper from his backpack. First, he drew the location of the mountain and Camp New Beginnings. Then he sketched a rudimentary image of the truck: two circles under a rectangle. On the rectangle, he wrote "B-35," then scribbled the question: *What does this mean?*

"Man, I thought the truck was toast from the flood," Catherine said. A stump had wedged into the radiator. "Look at it now."

"It's gonna be hard findin' Kyle," Cody said.

"Probably," Matt said. "Let's get searching."

He and Cody fell silent.

"I mean . . ." Catherine's eyes darted side to side. "I just—I'm not blaming anyone. But Nathan and Kyle—I don't want anyone else to die."

"I know what you mean," Matt said. Still, he felt such guilt and overwhelming responsibility for both losses. The pit in his stomach grew as he worried about what the future held. They'd have to be extremely careful and watch each other's backs. "Let's stick together instead. I think the best bet is to follow the avalanche chute. It probably carried his body off. Maybe just fan out like ten feet apart from each other. We should be able to cover more ground that way."

With Catherine to his right and Cody to his left, he walked and used the shovel to push away the damaged foliage. He'd done something similar when he earned his search and rescue badge, never expecting to actually use the learned skill. They explored in awkward silence for half an hour before Matt paused to wipe his brow. The only thing they found was a couple halves of the cryopods. The lining had been torn out, and the padding spilled out, soaked with melted snow. The other half was cracked, and a portion was missing, leaving the pod a jagged heap of broken plastic.

"This feels weird," Cody said. "Like we should be callin' out his name or somethin'."

"Makes me sad," Catherine said. "What if I'd climbed up just a second or two quicker? Then Matt could have helped Kyle. That's all it would have taken."

"You can't blame yourself," Matt said. "If it's anyone's fault, it's mine. He was scared, and I was yelling at him. We did the best we could. Who would have predicted a flood and avalanche like this? We need to be on guard. And guys, you know we're not finding his body, right? It's long gone."

"Matt," Catherine said.

"Now just wait a goll durn minute," Cody said. "You didn't create the rain. This is no one's fault. It was an accident. Trust me. I've been down this path with my brother."

"I forgot," Matt said. "I'm sorry."

"No sorry needed." Cody swung his shovel, mimicking Matt. "I blamed my brother for bull riding—a stupid sport, I might add. I blamed the bull, who was just being a bull. Heck, I even blamed God. Let me just tell you, none of that made me feel better. In fact, I felt worse. Kyle's gone, and that's that."

Matt shook his head. "You're right, and thank you. I need to stop making it about me and blaming myself. Look over there, see it? What is that?" Matt pointed to his left. "Something is shimmering over there."

CHAPTER 14

Cody chopped through thick scrub with his shovel and ran ahead toward the glinting object. Matt sprinted closely behind. Ferns whipped Matt in the face, but he put it to the back of his mind and forged ahead. He looked over his shoulder and saw Catherine following right behind him.

The small group came to a skidding halt. Matt stumbled into the back of Cody, and Catherine ran into both of them. Before them was an enormous gray metal door hanging on hinges that were mounted into granite stone. Embedded in the door was a square window reinforced with diamond-pattern silver wire.

Matt took a deep breath of the thick, sweet-smelling, humid air. "What the . . ."

A generous hill loomed in front of them with a seemingly random door in the forest beckoning them to enter. Overgrown brush and tree branches hung over the door, concealing most of it. But the sunlight hit the window just at the right angle, exposing its location.

Matt cupped his hands on either side of his eyes and peered into the glass. "I can't really see anything. Looks abandoned."

"Is it a cave?" Catherine asked. She knocked on the door. Matt jumped back.

"Geez, you could've warned me." Matt rubbed his forehead.

"Sorry," she said. "Just thought it was worth a try before we do a little B&E."

Matt pulled down on the metal handle.

"Locked." He jiggled the handle harder this time. "What do you guys want to do? We can keep searching for Kyle, but I think he's long gone. Or we can see what's in here. I'm guessing we've only got about an hour, maybe an hour and a half before we need to head back to camp."

"I dunno," Cody said. "I feel terrible givin' up. But I think you're right."

"Well, if you two are on board, let's commit the 10-62 and get past this door," Catherine said.

Cody removed his backpack and rummaged around, producing the Dyno Torch flashlight. "Guessing there ain't a generator in there."

"This could have the answers for us. Heck, this could be the entrance to the cryovault!" Matt said.

"Don't get your hopes up," Catherine said. "Dr. Westbrook drove us out of the cryovault. Remember the video? And there's no way a truck is fitting through that door."

"There may be a truck entrance somewhere." Matt grabbed a rock and hit the door handle. "I don't know. It's something. It's gotta be. If someone took the time to build into a hill, completely conceal it, and lock it, then there's something big behind these walls."

Matt dropped his canvas bag and produced a hatchet. "Watch out."

He lifted the hatchet over his head and swung, connecting with the window. Vibrations stung his forearms, but he kept swinging. The futile attempts of trying to break the window didn't even leave a crack.

"I guess we'll have to do this the hard way." Matt raised the small ax again, but this time came down on the handle.

Catherine took the map from the Trapper Keeper in Matt's bag and started scribbling on it. "What should we call this place?"

"How about Hillside Bunker?" Cody asked.

Matt's hands ached with each blow to the handle. He was doing no favors to his recently injured wrist. But the handle was no match for the hatchet, and it finally gave. It fell to the forest floor amongst a bed of leaves. The only things left were holes where mounting bolts were inserted and a spring that protruded from the larger hole where the inner hardware for the handle was. Matt cleaned the chipped metal debris and spring from the hole and felt around with his finger. Pressing the small metal latch past the strike plate, he thrust the heavy door inward with his shoulder.

"Ready?" Matt said.

Cody and Catherine nodded.

Matt sucked in a sharp breath and shivered. He stepped through the threshold and was hit with the unmistakable odor of chemicals. Coconut sweetness of gamma-nonalactone and the strong fruitiness of isoamyl acetate encompassed with hints of the pungent rotten-egg aroma of sulfur.

Memories of high school chemistry lab flooded his mind.

Simpler times for sure.

"Ugh," Catherine said. "That stings my eyes."

"What is this place?" Cody grabbed a chair from a stack propped against the wall and wedged the door open.

Outside light flooded in from the open door. In what looked like a small reception area were six black steel drums with a skull and crossbones stenciled across the front in white paint. Across from that were two plastic blue barrels labeled "Potable H2O" with curled-edge stickers.

Matt ran to the blue barrels. He rubbed his hand over the sticker, then knocked on the side.

"Could it still be good?" Catherine asked.

"If it was properly sealed, it would be," Matt said, shaking a barrel. The liquid sloshed around inside. "This looks legit. I had these old neighbors, nicest couple I ever met—they were Mormon—and they stored water like this."

"Why?" Catherine asked.

"I dunno." Matt used his canteen to wash off a two-sided, cloudy-white corrugated hose. "Something with their religion and storing food and water . . . for the apocalypse." Matt laughed. "I didn't really ask much after they told me that. Besides, I was there for the lemon meringue pie, and let me tell you, it was the best I ever had. When we find my mom, please don't tell her I said that."

Matt unscrewed the white lid and sniffed the liquid inside. "Smells like water. Whatever water smells like."

He snaked one side of the hose into the hole and screwed an orange siphon onto where the cap had been. Cody pushed and pulled the pump's lever up and down several times until water sputtered out, then streamed with each time Cody depressed the handle.

Matt rinsed his hands in the liquid, then cupped his hands underneath, letting it pool. He sniffed it again and dipped the tip of his tongue into it.

"How is it?" Catherine asked.

"Tastes a little bit like plastic, but better than the lake water," Matt said, lapping up the rest. "Give me a little more. I'll drink it, and if I don't get sick, we'll know it's good."

"Good idea," Catherine said. "This is a game changer, guys. How big is that barrel?"

"Fifty-five gallons of glorious H2O," Matt said. "Okay, I'm going to put this on the map. Let's see what else is here."

There was a spot for a desk, but if it had been there, it was long gone now. In the middle of the room was another metal door with the same stenciled writing as the truck: "NO ADMITTANCE A-67."

Matt checked the handle. To his shock, it turned. Cody pumped the old flashlight, giving them a steady beam of yellow light. Catherine held the door and propped it open with a chair just as Cody had done.

"Last thing I want is to get locked in here," Catherine said. "We can't take any chances."

Cody walked to the center of the room and spun in a slow circle, casting light on the darkened areas. The windowless room was fully inside the hill. It was at least twenty degrees cooler than outside. Six butcher-block black lab tables were evenly spaced apart. Atop them were forgotten Bunsen burners and beakers with crusted chemicals in the bottom, flasks turned on their sides, and graduated cylinders of varying sizes.

"Looks like someone had been conductin' experiments and abandoned it midway through." Cody picked up a flask and held his flashlight up to it.

"Dang." Matt held his nose. "Guess we found the source of the smell."

Mounted to the wall on the right side of the room were an eyewash station and an emergency shower. Matt recognized both from his high school days. He had been tempted to pull on the long triangle handle whenever an unsuspecting classmate stood under the large showerhead, but never did.

"Why is there a lab in the middle of the forest, buried under a hill?" Catherine asked. "Was this like a nerd summer camp?"

"Maybe," Matt said. "Could have been a multipurpose summer camp. Sports for half the summer, then academics in the other half."

"What's with all the No Admittance and locked doors if it was just for a summer camp?" Cody asked. "I ain't never heard of a camp that specialized in both school and sports. Course, I only ever went to church camps."

"Good point," Matt said. "I don't know why all the secrecy and the numbers A-67 and B-35. I got it all written down. Cody, what's piled up over there?"

"Looks like them cryopods." Cody crossed the room.

On the opposite wall of the eye wash were three older-looking pods. Matt rushed over to them.

"Looks like gen one," he said. "Definitely older than ours."

Matt searched the outside of the pod, looking for a release handle. The surface was rough, and the overall shape was less egg shaped and more pine-box-coffin shaped. His palm located a lever. With a swift turn to the right, the cryopod clicked. The corroded plastic lid snapped and creaked under the strain. Hinges that probably hadn't been used in years resisted Matt lifting the lid. With some effort, he swung the lid open.

"Shine it here," Matt said. "Whoa, look at this. Are these feeding tubes?"

Inside the rectangle was a raised bed like Matt had in his cryopod, but it wasn't nearly as plush. Crusty yellow tubes and exposed wiring lay in a tangled bundle.

"Glad we weren't stuck in those," Catherine said. "They look like a prototype or something."

"Rhett never would have fit in there," Cody laughed.

"For sure," Catherine said.

"This is weird," Matt said. "Why would the pods be here?"

"I'm freaked out," Catherine said. "This is creepier than the Fratellis' basement."

Matt and Cody both laughed at her *Goonies* reference.

"Let's hope Sloth isn't hiding down here," Matt said.

"Honestly, though," Catherine said, "I could go for a Baby Ruth right now."

Matt walked back across the lab. "Baby Ruuf."

"Head down that a way," Cody said, shining the flashlight.

Another hallway jutted off the other side of the lab. Four doors lined the hallway. Two on one side and two on the other, all metal, all painted drab green. Matt turned the handle to one, revealing an office.

"This is like breaking into the principal's office," Matt said. "Almost feels like we need a lookout."

Cody handed the flashlight to Catherine. "Wanna give it a try? My hand needs a break."

"Sure." Catherine took it from him and began pumping the handle. She shined it on a large bank of shelves behind the desk. "I wish we'd brought the lantern."

The modestly plain office had a desk in the middle with all the usual suspects. Decades of dust covered the metal "mail in, mail out" tray, stapler, boxy computer in the middle, and tape dispenser.

Propped up against the desk was what looked like a movie poster secured with a rubber band. Matt slid off the rubber band, which disintegrated in his hand, then he unrolled the poster-like paper and laid it out over the desk, covering the computer keyboard. What stared back at him was faded blue-gray paper with dark blue lines. At the top, it had a red rubber stamp on it. *TOP SECRET* and A-67.

"Blueprints," Matt said.

CHAPTER 15

They gathered around the desk and stared at the blueprints.

Matt traced the outside of a mountain with a small entrance noted at the base. He turned the extra-large paper over and saw the plans for a warehouse inside the cryovault. The warehouse had a large opening—large enough for a bus—and gradually, the building led down.

"Holy shi—" Matt dropped the blueprint and took a step back. "Guys, this is it. These are the blueprints to the mountain, the warehouse, and the cryovault!"

"Does it say where?" Cody asked. "It's gotta be nearby."

Matt flipped a page. "No, not that I can see."

"A-67 . . . is that what it's called?" Catherine reached in front of Matt. "See, it's on the top of every page. That must be what the site is called. A-67. And what's this? Why are the words at the bottom blacked out?"

"We can't see. You're hogging all the light," Cody said.

Matt and Cody huddled around her like she was holding the flashlight and telling a scary story.

"Look, the cryopod columns—this is what we saw in Dr. Westbrook's videos." Matt pointed. "So assuming this is cryovault A-67 . . . then we're not alone."

"Not alone?" Cody asked.

"I'm following ya. The truck said B-35." Catherine twisted her thick curls into a knot behind her shoulders. "This blueprint is for cryovault A-67."

"And the truck has B-35," Matt interrupted.

"Exactly," Catherine continued. "So we must've come from cryovault B-35."

"For sure!" Matt punched the air.

"No way." Cody shook his head.

"Yes way," Matt said.

Catherine rummaged through a metal tray. "See this?" She held up a piece of letterhead. The top right corner had black marker with lines over it. "It's redacted. Just like on the blueprints. They only do this for serious stuff, you guys."

"Let's not get ahead of ourselves." Matt approached the bank of cabinets. "We are for sure onto something. We need to do a good search of this office and the others."

On the back wall of the office were three robust steel closets. Matt yanked on the handle, and it barely budged.

Gears screeched off in the distance.

The ground tremored slightly.

Everyone paused.

Catherine gripped the edge of the door frame as if she were in an earthquake. Matt locked eyes with her before ducking under the desk.

"Ya'll heard that, right?" Cody asked.

"Yeah." Catherine nodded. "I hope it's nothing. But maybe you should find a doorway or something."

Matt felt his heartbeat in his ears.

Pound! Pound! Pound!

If it was another flash flood, they'd be trapped inside the hill. One way in, one way out. Drowned.

Like Kyle.

Matt knew he needed to Matt-itate, but finding anything to focus on seemed impossible. He swallowed hard. "Co-Cody, can you run out and see if anything is happening?"

"Ten-four," Cody said.

Matt heard Cody's footfalls become more distant. "Catherine, are you okay?"

"I should be asking you the same. This—whatever it is—is traumatizing. I can't live in constant fear."

"It's just so, I don't know, unpredictable." Matt emerged from under the desk. "Sometimes it's something, and other times it's nothing. Or at least nothing here. Maybe the weather is bad far away."

"Nothin'," Cody said, running into the room. "Everything seems to be right as rain."

"Well, that's a relief," Catherine said.

"For now," Matt mumbled. "Thanks for checking, Cody."

"Glad to help."

"Time's a wasting," Catherine said. "Let's see what's in the cabinets and bounce."

Matt shrugged. He planted his feet and pulled with both hands. The closet hissed as he broke the sealed connection, revealing its contents. Catherine shined the yellow flashlight beam on floor-to-ceiling boxes.

"Jackpot!" Matt exclaimed.

Organized neatly were hundreds of white boxes with black print that simply said "Potato Chips" across the front. On the bottom, it stated if they were plain or flavored and that there were two packages per container.

"Open one. See if they're still edible," Cody said.

The top of the box was sealed like a cereal box, and just like every other time Matt had tried to open one, he accidentally tore it, ensuring it'd never close right again. Inside were two small silver pouches. He pulled the seams apart, and the aroma of greasy potato chips caused his saliva glands to fill his mouth with spit. The chips looked perfectly preserved, albeit generic.

Matt turned one over in his fingers, inspecting every inch. "They're not black, so that's good."

Cody rolled up the blueprints. Matt dumped the chips onto the desk.

"No bugs," Catherine said. "Seems good. Who's going to try it first?"

No one budged, but Matt licked his lips.

"Oh geez," Catherine said, then popped one into her mouth. "Holy crap, these are fresh."

"The cabinet, it was sealed," Matt said. "They must've preserved all of this. Open the next one."

Matt and Cody opened separate cabinets at the same time. Matt's had "Vanilla-Filled Sponge Cakes" and "Chocolate Cream-Filled Cakes" in them.

"Twinkies and Ho Hos?" Matt shrugged. "Don't mind if I do."

He tore into the knock-off Twinkies and handed one to Catherine before greedily shoving a whole one into his mouth.

"Oh, Twinkies, you really did withstand the apocalypse," Catherine giggled.

Cody presented them with movie theater-sized boxes of various candies simply labeled "Chocolate" or "Non-Chocolate." They opened one, and inside were individually wrapped red spheres. Cody indulged first, and his face turned deep red.

"Atomic Fireball?" Catherine asked.

"Yep." Cody spit it into a trashcan. "Too hot for me."

"Try and reseal the cabinets," Matt said.

He pushed on one. When it clicked, a stream of air released from all four sides, like when his mom would "burp" Tupperware.

"Okay, last one. Any guesses as to what's inside?" Matt pulled on the door.

"Gum?" Catherine said.

The cabinet was split into two columns. One side had white cylinders with black print that read "Cheese-Flavored Balls." On the other side were hundreds of white aluminum cans labeled "BEER."

"Wow," Cody said. "Didn't expect that."

"Me neither." Matt resealed the door. "Let's see what's in the other three offices. Hey Catherine, you still creeped out?"

"Buzz off," Catherine said. "The junk was good, but it just raises more questions. Why is it here? Why are there sealed cabinets?"

"Maybe they were planning on waiting it out here," Matt said. "We all knew the apocalypse was inevitable. Heck, they froze *people*. Why not ensure there are food and supplies for when they defrost them?"

"Defrost?" Catherine laughed. "Now you're starting to sound like Darin."

Catherine led them into the second office, where the desk was barren, but the cabinets revealed similar nondescript, black-and-white boxes of dried meats. Most were normal, like chicken and beef, but there were more exotic ones like alligator and ostrich. Cody said he'd had alligator jerky before and claimed it was pretty good.

Matt took over with the flashlight duties for the last two offices—if you could call them that. The office in the back corner had no desk but a cabinet full of freeze-dried vegetables. A shiver ran up Matt's spine.

"Let's hurry with the last one and get out of here," he said.

"Bets on what type of food we'll find?"

"Dairy?" Cody guessed.

"Got that covered in the cheese balls," Matt said.

"Grains is my guess," Catherine said.

"Oh, I hope so," Matt said. "I'd love some toast—it's probably my favorite food. Lots of butter and honey, or with cinnamon and sugar, maybe some peanut butter."

"Toast is your favorite food?" Cody yanked a cabinet open in the final office. "I woulda guessed pizza."

"It *is* bread!" Matt said when he saw inside the cabinet. "Pita bread, but hey, that works."

From top to bottom were white boxes that read "Flatbread." The one next to it housed "Nut Butter" and "Fruit Spread." Catherine tore open a box. Inside were small pouches. In the last two, they discovered "Thin Pasta" and "Tomato Sauce." The sauce was in the same packets as the peanut butter. Matt guessed it was a better way to store it over canning.

"Okay, let's grab some PB&J, maybe some chips, and head back to camp for dinner," Matt said. "This is a great find! Once we have everyone, we can move some supplies back to the cabin. But I think it's best if we keep them sealed up here. It's not a bad walk, maybe thirty minutes?"

"Do you think we can trust the others?" Catherine asked. "Like, Kim won't come up here and steal all the Ho Hos?"

"What can we do if she does?" Cody asked.

"True," Catherine said. "I just worry this might . . . I dunno. People can get weird with resources."

"I'm not gonna lie about it," Matt said. "Remember how pissed Justin was because we didn't tell him about the canned goods in camp? I just got him on my side, sort of. I hope we can just all be a team and not screw anyone over."

"All right." Cody walked out of the beam of light. "Lead us out of here. I'm with Catherine. This place is a little creep-tastic."

CHAPTER 16

"Wait," Matt said. "What's that?"

He shined the light on a brown legal file pocket. Next to it were a few papers, as if someone had left in haste. He picked it up and headed for the exit. Once outside, he removed the black rubber string that secured the large flap.

"I think we should name it the Research and Development Lab instead of Hillside Bunker," Matt said. "Or R&D for short."

"I was thinking 7-Eleven, or the Sev, like me and my friends used to call it. But R&D is good." Catherine removed several packets of peanut butter from the top of her bag before extracting her Trapper Keeper. Then she smoothed the paper and clicked her mechanical pencil a few times.

"I'm cool with the Sev," Matt said.

Cody raised his hand. "I vote for that as well."

Matt thumbed through the file, expecting more papers. What he found were pictures.

"Guys." He dropped to the ground and splayed out the fading Polaroids. "Construction pictures."

"No way!" Catherine dropped her pencil on top of the map and abandoned it for the time being.

"Look. The truck." Cody shook the picture toward them. "ARMY CORPS OF ENGINEERS" was stenciled on the side of the green construction vehicle. "This is military. Our government built the vault."

"Well, I mean, I figured that," Matt said. "It wasn't like we had any time to prepare for this. Some guy in a black suit showed up at our house, talked to my parents, and told us to be ready for transport in three days. I always assumed it was the government."

"Right," Cody said. "But now there's no mistaking it."

"Not just military." Catherine stood, her hands trembling. "Demo Trench. See? These workers, their orange vests say 'Demo Trench.' They hired a private company. We now know there are at least two cryovaults—A-67 and ours, B-35—both inside caves, inside mountains. They must have taken years to build. How did they keep this a secret?"

The ground lurched, and gears scraped against metal. Matt paused and looked around frantically, but nothing happened.

"Same way they kept Roswell secret. And JFK's killer," Cody said. "Everyone in Texas knows Lee Harvey Oswald didn't do it on his own. Tarnished the whole state's reputation."

Matt thumbed through the pictures. He saw huge excavators moving dirt and rock. Then equipment was hauled in on flatbeds of semis. Steel beams and rods that made up the columns were shiny and free of rust.

"Come on," Matt said. "Let's get back to camp. It's starting to get dark, and I want to see if Darin knows anything about this. Maybe Dr. Westbrook mentioned it to him."

They hurried back to camp while keeping their eye out for Kyle's body. Guilt tugged at Matt. He'd promised they'd come back and bury Kyle right after he'd died. Matt hoped they'd get the chance to search again, but knew he needed to resign himself to the fact that they might never recover him before they left to go to the mountain. He had to stop letting the guilt get to him.

"It feels like we're so close, but I have more questions than ever," Matt said. "I miss my parents. I just need to see if they're okay."

"I know," Catherine said, stepping over the New Beginnings sign. "We all do."

The rest of the group sat on the wraparound porch of the main cabin.

"What the . . .?" Matt said. "Guys, am I hallucinating?"

"No," Cody said. "It's—"

Catherine shook her head. "Unbelievable!"

"I've got no words," Matt said.

"You guys rebuild the cabins or what?" Cody yelled toward the group.

"No!" Darin answered. "It was like this when we got back."

He stood as Matt, Catherine, and Cody approached.

"Wait! What?" Matt asked. "The main cabin just reconstructed itself?'

Darin stretched his arms out wide. "That's what I'm saying. You didn't see anyone else that could have done it? And I'm telling you we didn't do it. It was fully erect when we got back from our walk."

Matt shook his head. He couldn't believe what had happened. It made zero sense.

"Where did you go?" Matt asked. "I thought you guys were going to pack?"

"We went on a walk," Justin said.

"I needed a break from the cemetery," Stacy said.

Justin rested against the railing of the porch. "You're not going to believe what we found!"

"Huge, big metal things," Rhett said.

"What are you talking about? Like equipment?" Cody asked.

"No, like gears. Like the guts of a machine. But a gigantic machine," Justin said.

"It was totally lame," Kim said. "I could have been attacked by a bear. And it was really sweaty."

"Not now, Kim," Matt said. "There's a what? A huge machine?"

"No, just parts," Justin replied.

"You can let these two brainiacs try and tell you, or you can apologize for being rude, and I'll explain it," Kim said.

"Sorry?" Catherine said. It came out as a question.

"I meant them." Kim pointed at Rhett and Justin. "Anyway, there are, like, these gears and junk like that. Did you ever see the cover of Queen's *News of the World*? Not the cassette, the vinyl."

"Yes." Matt shook his head. "Why does that matter?"

"Like, my parents always played that crap to torture me." Kim twirled her hair. "It has this huge, ugly, metal-looking giant on it. In his hands are dead people he's crushed. It looks like that bald weirdo destroyed a giant car or something and hurled the gears into the ground."

"Can someone tell us what's really going on?" Catherine rubbed her temples.

"No, she's right," Justin said. "There are enormous pistons and fans and hydraulic arms just—I don't know—plunged into the ground. I've never seen anything like it."

"Okay, wait," Matt said. "Start over. Darin, what is going on?"

"Listen." Darin stepped in front of Matt. "You gotta quit asking me that!"

Matt relented. "I understand. Okay, so why did you leave camp?"

"I needed to get away from the grave," Stacy said, raising her hand. "Like, mourn, you know? I asked them all if we could just go on a little hike or something to, like, get the thought of Nathan and stuff out of my mind."

"So you went on a hike . . . and what?" Catherine asked.

"Like I said," Justin replied, "enormous gears and junk. A junkyard made from giants."

Rhett cleared his throat. "I've never seen anything like it. Kim is kinda right. It's just like that record cover."

"We didn't even tell you the best part," Justin said. "We found some cargo trucks! We tried to start them, but they were dead. Cody, you're good at fixing crap. Do you think you could get them running?"

"What!" Matt exclaimed. "This could change everything!"

"No guarantees, but I'll give her a try," Cody said.

"That's an amazing find," Matt said. "Let's go. We might even be able to find the cave tonight."

"It's almost dark," Justin pointed out.

"He's right," Cody said. "I need full light to see what I'm dealing with. Plus, they might be solar. *Hopefully*, they're solar."

"Right. We'll go at first light then," Matt said. "But tell me about the elephant in the forest."

Justin raised an eyebrow. "Huh?"

Matt pointed to the main cabin. "What's the story with this?"

"Like I said, they were like this when we got back," Darin repeated.

The main cabin and all the other bunkhouse cabins that were destroyed by the avalanche were put back together. Fully erect.

"Are they safe to sleep in?" Catherine asked.

"I don't, like, see any avalanches in the distance, do you?" Kim asked. "Stay outside if you want."

"I'm exhausted," Matt said. "We have a big day tomorrow. But for now, let's eat."

"Great, more weird-tasting, metallic food," Victoria said. Then she sighed. "I'm sorry. I shouldn't be so negative."

"Girlfriend"—Catherine wrapped her arm around Victoria's shoulder—"what if I told you we had some peanut butter and jelly sandwiches with a side of chips with your name on it?"

CHAPTER 17

The group settled into the cabin for the night. After the sun went down, it cooled off dramatically. Catherine filled the rest in on what they'd seen and found north of camp at the R&D lab.

"We're calling it 7-Eleven, or the Sev," Catherine informed them.

"Sounds wonderful," Victoria said. "There's really all that food?"

"Yeah," Catherine said. "And it's not too far from here."

Justin lit a fire while Matt unloaded and portioned out sandwiches and chips for everyone. Victoria and Stacy filled a large pot with water from the lake.

"Let me." Darin took the water from both girls. "Justin, you ready for this?"

"Give me one sec." Justin propped up a metal grate above the fire for the pot to rest.

"While we wait, let's gather around, if that's okay," Matt said.

Folding chairs were set up as they readied to eat. Rhett's chair creaked as he took a seat next to Kim.

"I can't believe you found food," Darin said. "Oh, this jelly is so sweet. Peanut butter's a little weird. Tastes like the almond butter they had at the cafeteria in school."

"Whoa." Matt held out his free hand. "No one said *peanut* butter. Just nut butter."

"So weird," Kim said. "My parents would have never bought this garbage."

"No one is forcing you to eat it," Catherine said.

Kim placed her half-eaten pita bread on the ground next to her feet and crossed her arms.

"Don't mind if I do." Justin plucked it from the dirt.

"Sick," Kim said under her breath.

"I grew up on this stuff. Government commodities," Justin said. "And look where being a snob got you: a seat right next to me. Only difference is my belly is full. Mom used to make Tuna Helper when things were tight—which was most of the time. It was so gross, yet so good at the same time. I'd give anything for her cooking."

"Sick!" Stacy laughed. "That makes me want to gag just thinking about it. Canned tuna, blech! Although, speaking of tuna, I could go for some sushi. My dad, he used to take me once a month. It was our thing, you know?" Stacy's voice cracked and she cupped her hands over her face.

"We'll find them." Victoria rubbed Stacy's back. "And you're right. Sushi is the best. We had so much good food in Manhattan. When my parents bought the apartment above us, they renovated both apartments into a two-story home. They cooked so rarely, they got rid of both kitchens." She laughed. "We only had a mini fridge and wet bar."

"No way," Kim said.

"Believe what you want. It's actually pretty common. No one in the city cooks—too much goodness around every corner."

"Do you think we'll ever have something like that again?" Catherine asked.

Matt didn't think so, but he wasn't going to say it.

An awkward silence filled the room.

"I wish we still had the TV." Rhett changed the subject. "We found a few older movies in one of the cabins."

"Me too." Victoria smiled.

"Whatever!" Kim shot to her feet. "I'm going to sleep."

"Hang on, babe," Rhett said. "I want to hear what Matt's plan is."

"Oh yeah, right. Guess we got sidetracked," Matt said. "Here goes. And I'm open to suggestions."

The fire flickered in the background, and all eyes were on him. For the first time, he admitted to himself that he was the leader.

"As you know, we all really need to head to the mountain and save our parents and siblings. Let's call that south. But I want to check out the junkyard as well. That can be east. So I say the plan for tomorrow is to pack up some supplies here, go east to the junkyard, and on the way to the mountain, we can swing by the Sev, which is a little north, and get lunch supplies and more gear for our trip to the mountain. Sound good?"

"I'm good with that," Catherine agreed.

Matt looked around the room.

"Isn't the Sev far from here?" Rhett asked.

"Yeah," Kim said. "The less sweating, the better."

"It's not too far," Cody said.

Rhett shrugged. "Okay, then."

"Did I tell you there are Twinkies?" Catherine asked.

"Yeah, a whole closet full of junk food," Matt said. "It's food heaven."

"That's it?" Victoria asked. "Junk food?"

"No, no," Catherine said. "There's all sorts of food, dried veggies, and bread." She held up her sandwich. "It seemed like we could get a well-balanced diet and no metal taste."

"Awesome," Justin said. "I can't wait. Then off to the mountain."

Everyone seemed to be on board. After dinner, Justin, Rhett, and Cody went to the cabins unaffected by the avalanche to retrieve more blankets and sleeping bags. The ones they had set up for the other nights were soaking wet. After everyone settled in to go to sleep, Matt approached Darin with the folder of Polaroids.

"Hey, Darin, can you explain these?" Matt handed Darin the brown file folder. "What do you know about construction of the cry-ovaults? Did you know there were multiple vaults?"

Darin opened the file folder and stared at the pictures, dropping each into his lap.

"I was a tweenager when they froze me." Darin stood. "Sorry to disappoint you, but they didn't trust top secret info with a kid."

"Fine. Fair. I'm not accusing, but you were awake for years," Matt said. "Dr. Westbrook never told you about other vaults?"

"No."

"Did you guys go to the other vaults to take care of those people?" Matt asked.

"I told you I didn't even know about them."

"I assume there are other scientists, like Dr. Westbrook? And other pods?" Matt asked.

"I have no idea," Darin said. "I have the same information as you. Hey, why do you think there's other cryovaults?"

Matt pulled the blueprints from the backpack by his chair. He unrolled them and said, "See here in the corner, stamped, it says 'A-67.' These are blueprints for, I assume, a vault A-67. The truck we came in on has 'B-35' all over the undercarriage. Painted on. So I assumed that these pictures and these blueprints are for a vault A-67 and that we must've come from vault B-35."

"Wow." Darin clapped Matt on the back. "Watch movies much? That seems like quite a stretch."

"Well, that's what it means." Matt vigorously rolled the blueprints, annoyed.

"Listen, Westbrook probably didn't even know how the caves were built or if there were others. He only cared about making sure his people lived so he looked good."

Or that the entire human race didn't die out.

Darin gave the folder back to Matt. "And what do your pictures prove? That it was constructed? Big whoop." Darin threw his hands in the air. "We all knew that. Do you think the cryocolumns just spontaneously appeared inside a cave? And are you really shocked there are other caves? Five thousand people isn't very many. I always assumed there were multiple. That way, if one failed—like ours did— the human race would still have a chance. Ever hear of not putting all your eggs in one basket?"

"What about the breach?" Matt tilted his head to the side, remembering what started the whole thing.

Darin stiffened.

"The one you were awake for," Matt continued. "The one that affected our column."

"I—I don't know. Meteor, I guess," Darin said.

How does he not know? He was there. They fixed it with carbon foam.

Dodgy answers like this frustrated Matt. Normal questions were met with vagueness or non-answers. Matt bit his tongue, while his suspicions about Darin spiraled.

"Lance-Darin," Stacy called, patting the floor next to her.

"Look, I'm on board with your plan," Darin said. "I absolutely want to find my parents too. I do. But it's not going to help them if I die in the process. So we need to be smart about this. I like the idea of getting more food for us. We have all the gear we need. We will need to carry water."

Matt took a deep breath and slowly released it. "Yeah, you're right. I'll see you in the morning."

"Yeah." Darin yawned. "See you tomorrow."

Matt crawled into his sleeping bag on the hard floor. The fire died down as he was faced with his own thoughts and guilt. Sleep was fleeting that night. He stared at the rafters of the massive A-frame. His eyes followed one cable to an eyelet as big as his fist, where the end was secure. In the other direction, the cable coursed through two pulleys and down to a bolt where the end was fastened.

Could those be why the cabin sprung back up? he thought, scratching his head.

"No, I didn't know! I didn't mean to. I didn't know what I was doing!"

Matt knew that voice.

Darin.

Matt tiptoed toward him and stared at the sleeping man.

"You're crazy." Darin thrashed from side to side in his sleeping bag. "You did this. It was a trick. I'm sorry. Please, no. No! Don't put me back in the pod!"

Darin's entire body tensed then relaxed. Matt watched him for a few minutes to see if he'd say anything else. Once satisfied the sleep-talking was over, he returned to his own sleeping bag.

Now for sure he couldn't sleep. His mind was reeling about what Darin had said and how the cabins in New Beginnings were recon-structed.

Repositioning over and over, he couldn't find a comfortable spot. Once he finally fell asleep, he had dreams about his parents—that he'd found them trapped in their cryopods. Frozen in death, their eyes wide with shock, like Kyle's had been.

His body jerked, pulling him from the nightmare, before his eyes fluttered closed once again. The Kyle nightmares began with his second wave of sleeping. Kyle army-crawled across the rugged ter-rain. Something was wrong with his legs, and they dragged behind him at unnatural angles. He kept calling out Matt's name. Begging him for help. Matt's own legs were encased in jagged lava rock, and he couldn't do anything. Kyle inched closer and closer. Then a flash of lightning ripped across the sky. Kyle's face was contorted, cheeks hol-lowed out, eyes deep set, and his lips dripped with blood. Kyle smiled wide—far too wide—and said, "You're next." Then he jumped to his feet with his hand outstretched toward Matt.

"Ah!" Matt sat up in his sweat-soaked sleeping bag.

He looked around the room, thankful he was the first one up so no one heard him cry out. The sky filled with dim light and brightened up the gym. Matt stared at a piece of peeling varnish on the floor and did his Matt-itation. His breathing and heartbeat slowed, returning to normal. Darin stirred in his sleeping bag, then rolled onto his back.

"Darin," Matt whispered. "You up?"

He nodded but didn't open his eyes.

"Meet me on the stage. Help me with the packs."

"Nightmares?" Darin hopped up onto the stage.

"Yeah," Matt said. "You?"

"Every night," Darin said. "I don't think I'll ever shake the ghost of Westbrook."

"I heard you talking in your sleep," Matt said.

Darin sorted through items, never looking up or responding.

"You kept apologizing, saying you didn't mean to. What's that about?"

"Living with, or rather under, Westbrook's rule was torture. I don't want to get into it, okay?"

"But what happened? What didn't you mean to do?"

"Nothing." Darin stared at the floor.

"You keep getting mad because I don't trust you, but you keep giving me reason not to," Matt said, trying to keep his voice even.

"It was—look, I can't. It was the worst trauma of my life. Shit went down and I had to—no, please. No. I'm not ready."

"How can I believe you when you keep hiding things?" Matt felt heat rise up in his chest.

"Do you want to relive the worst thing that's ever happened to you? Did I make you go into detail about how Kyle died? Blame you? No!" Darin's face was red and he was panting. "It happened. *All* of this has happened. We were all pawns in some weird game where Westbrook was playing both offense and defense. I know you don't believe me, but I will tell you—just not now."

Matt paused. He saw how upset Darin was. Whatever happened to him must have been really bad. Or he was hiding something really big. But Darin was right, this wasn't the time. "Let's just get everyone a backpack, okay?"

"Fine by me," Darin said.

"I think we just need to pack light—compasses, first aid, things like that," Matt said, shifting the conversation. "We can get food at the Sev."

"Fine," Darin said. "You distribute those. I'll pack some ropes, MREs, and whatnot."

"Cool, cool—"

Gears popped, and a small tremor shook the floor.

The rest of the group shot to their feet.

"Ugh," Kim said. "Nice wake-up call, Matt. Like, are you trying to put me in a bad mood?"

Matt said nothing and rushed to the nearest window. The sky was clear. He ran to the window near the front and watched the mountain.

But nothing came.

"Come on," Matt said. "Everyone grab a backpack on the stage. If you're up to it, take a hatchet, hammer, ax, or even shovel. Justin, you lead the way."

"All right, chief. Hold your horses," Justin said. "Let me drain the snake first."

"Disgusting!" Stacy said.

"No breakfast?" Kim asked.

"Do what you have to do, I guess, and let's meet at the lake in ten minutes. *Everyone.*" Matt glared at Kim. "Also, I'd suggest getting some new clothes on. More for protection. Cheerleading uniforms and dresses might not work."

"Screw you, Matt!" Kim said, stripping off her sweater and dropping her skirt. She strolled over to the trunk in her underwear. "You're such a jerk. I will always be a cheerleader!"

"Kim!" Stacy said. "Like, inappropriate."

She shrugged, throwing clothes in the air, searching for something that fit. "I don't care anymore," she pouted.

Matt turned away.

"I'll help you." Rhett stood between her tiny frame and the rest of the group, blocking them from her tantrum.

"Yeah," Kim said to Rhett, "I know."

Victoria cautiously approached the trunk, not knowing how Kim would react.

"You think I'm good, guys?" Stacy asked.

"I think so," Darin replied.

Rhett dropped his trousers and slipped into a pair of gray sweatpants. He took his T-shirt off and put on a mesh football jersey.

Catherine grabbed a pair of Guess jeans and a pale yellow *Return of the Jedi* shirt with three-quarter sleeves. She exited the gym to a room off to the side. Victoria quickly snatched up youth army-colored cargo pants and a black Billy Idol concert tee.

"Can I come with you?" she asked Catherine.

"Absolutely," Catherine answered. "I'm not as daring as Kim."

Catherine and Victoria returned within a few minutes. Kim, on the other hand, was taking her own sweet time. She held up a T-shirt, then tossed it onto the pile of clothes. She held a pair of jeans to her waist and shook her head.

"You good?" Rhett asked.

"Yeah," Kim replied, "just trying to find the perfect outfit."

"This isn't the first day of high school," Darin finally piped in. "We really need to hustle."

"Fine," Kim said. She slipped on white Jordache jeans and a purple top. Then she held her hair down with a lime-green headband. The white Kaepas with gold and blue triangles on the side completed the outfit.

"There you go!" Kim said. "Like, how do I look? Ugly? Horrible?"

Matt walked across the gym to the front door of the cabin. "Good enough, Kim." He was at his wit's end. He'd lost his patience for her a long time ago, and they had only been together a few days.

Matt set his backpack on the porch and took a deep breath. He rummaged through his pack once more, making sure he had everything he deemed necessary for their survival. Everyone was taking leaving the camp seriously. Matt could hear Kim asking Rhett if she had everything she needed. Hopefully, his annoyance and the gravity of the situation were sinking in.

Victoria left for the lake first. She sat on the dock, feet dangling above the water. Matt joined her on the old wooden dock. The water seemed lower than usual.

"How are you holding up?" Matt asked.

"I was just about to ask you the same thing." Victoria stared at the water.

"Me?" Matt raised his eyebrows.

"You've been the one taking the brunt of everything." Her long black hair, still in a frizzy plait from yesterday, hung lazily over her shoulder. "How are you coping?"

"I . . ." Matt paused. "I honestly haven't had a chance to think about *how* I'm doing. Okay, I guess." A hitch caught in his throat.

"You're strong, not like me." Victoria stood and smoothed her T-shirt.

"Stop—" Matt started.

"But we all have different strengths, and that's what makes us stronger together. Isn't that what Kyle said?"

"Yeah," Matt said. "Something like that."

"I see people. *Really* see them." She closed her eyes and tilted her pale face and upturned nose toward the sky. "Read people well, you know. Kyle was more than a Young Republican. He was eager to learn, unafraid to make mistakes. That's what I liked most about him. Nathan also wanted to learn, be better, but he was paralyzed with fear over letting you down. That's what made it so much worse when he died. That frozen look on his face wasn't terror. It was knowing he'd let you down in the worst way, Matt."

"I-I didn't know," Matt said. "What else do you see?"

"I'm not judging, Matt. Just observing," Victoria said. "Stacy wants to be liked. Craves it, really, and she'll conform to whoever's personality to gain it."

"Yeah, I can see that," Matt laughed. "She acts so different now that she's trying to get approval from Darin."

"Justin and Kim are the most similar. It's striking, really. They're both damaged, just in different ways. Kim was ignored, showered with gifts to make up for the neglect. Parents who bought her love.

The only thing handed to Justin was a slap to the face after being cussed out."

"He said that to you?" Matt's eyes grew wide.

"No. He didn't have to." Victoria pursed her lips. "Kim and Justin both claim to not care and push everyone away, Rhett withstanding. Isn't it funny that they're both drawn to him? Justin wants to be a good guy, but sometimes he just can't help himself. He wants to heal and create a new life. Rhett is exactly what we all see. Easy, unassuming, and wouldn't hurt a fly."

"What about me?"

"Matthew Voorhees, you aren't as strong as you look. You're stronger. You just don't know it. Not yet. But you will. Come on. The others are arriving. I'll fill you in on the rest later."

Matt hadn't realized how thoughtful Victoria was. He had looked at her as sensitive, if not weak. This was his first time one-on-one with her, and he regretted not doing it sooner. He wondered what she saw in him that he neither saw nor felt in himself.

CHAPTER 18

They spent twenty minutes trudging through the underbrush, following Justin and Rhett, and Matt only counted seventeen times where Kim complained about something.

"It's just over here," Justin said. He jumped over a large tree trunk and landed unsteadily on his feet. "Careful, the ground is slick."

Matt opted to climb over it and take his time. His wrist finally felt better, and he didn't want to risk re-injuring it. Or worse.

"Holy . . ." Cody said.

"Wow!" Catherine exclaimed. "What is this place? It's like we shrunk."

Kim's description had been spot on—even though Matt was reluctant to admit it. Among the bright green, overgrown grass and dark green shrubs were enormous pieces of a machine unlike Matt had ever seen. Untarnished hydraulic arms plunged out of the ground and soared twenty feet into the air. Matt counted six enormous gears. It was like being on another planet. He climbed up in the middle of a gear and held his arms outstretched.

"Dang," Matt yelled, his voice sounding like he was in a tin can. "I can't even reach either side of this baby." He jumped to try to reach the top.

"What are these things?" Stacy asked. "It's like that movie *The Incredible Shrinking Woman* that came out a few years ago."

Matt hopped up onto a smaller gear that was lying on its side. "Whoa, Stacy," he said. "I didn't see you as the movie type."

"Well, I'm just going off the title," she giggled.

"I think this is a piston," Darin said. "A giant piston. Westbrook showed me a couple mechanical things like this. Out of one of the broken-down trucks. This is crazy."

In the center of the mess was a twelve-foot-wide, six-foot-high metal casing with a long, shiny pole slid into the center. At the top was an eyelet. It reminded Matt of his dad's beer opener.

In between the pistons were flasks and beakers on 'roids.

"These things are huge." Cody pressed his face against the side of the oversized chemistry glassware. Residual gray and brown water filled them three feet high.

"I bet all six of us could fit inside that beaker," Stacy said. "Lance-Darin, did you bring a ladder?"

"Nope," he said. "Just an ax."

Matt pulled himself up onto another gear to get a better vantage point. Off to his right was a metal fan bigger than his childhood home. It made no sense. Just like everything else at Camp New Beginnings. Next to it was a cart of some sort.

"Guys, come over here. I think I found something," Matt said.

"Is it, like, more trash in this junkyard?" Kim asked.

"Come on. I'll give you a piggyback ride," Rhett said.

Kim tiptoed toward Rhett, and a small smile formed on her lips.

A tram of some sort was on its side, and a pile of tracks were in front of it. Pine needles and dirt were piled in the bottom of the carts. The tram had three cars that sat cockeyed. Its vinyl-covered benches had torn, and the mustard-yellow stuffing was rotted out of them.

"These look like really unsafe rollercoaster cars," Matt said.

"Why would they be out here?" Rhett said.

"Why is any of this here?" Justin clapped Rhett on the shoulder. "Why do people pin and cuff the bottom of their jeans? Why did the Bears make a Super Bowl Shuffle? Where *is* the beef? Life is just full of mystery."

Pop!

Grind!

Screech!

Matt swallowed hard and turned his attention to the sky. Dark clouds formed south of them in the direction of the mountain. To the north were big, white puffy clouds.

"I don't get it," Catherine said. "This place looks like a giant took apart a car and left it to rust in the forest."

"It doesn't explain the oversized chemistry set or that fan," Victoria said. "Someone, or *something*, put it here, and I'll bet it wasn't a giant."

"Let me know when it's time to go," Kim said. "Come on, Stacy, let's see if we can find some flowers for our hair."

"I don't know." Stacy turned to Darin.

"Why are you looking at me?" Darin's eyes moved nervously from side to side. "I don't care what you do."

"Oh, okay." Stacy's face fell.

"Hey," Justin's voice echoed. "Guys, the trucks are over here!"

"Finally, isn't that what we came here for in the first place? Like, get me outta here," Kim said. "Justin, yell again so we can find you."

"Marco!" Justin's voice called out from behind Matt.

"Polo!" Catherine sang back.

They climbed over smaller machine parts and around the enormous ones until they found him.

"Look, they say 'Demo Trench' on the side," Justin said. "They must've dumped all this stuff here. Has anyone ever heard of these guys before?"

"Demo Trench was on some papers we found at the Sev." Matt shifted. "Don't know why. We'll show you when we get there."

"Well, the truck's had better days," Victoria said.

"What the heck, Justin?" Kim kicked a flat tire. "This hunk of junk hasn't run in, like, decades. This isn't going to get us to the mountain any faster than if we walked."

"But maybe we can fix it?" Justin asked.

"I doubt you guys can fix this one, Cody." Darin poked his head under the bed of the truck. "Rims are bent, axle is destroyed, and I doubt we'll find any gas or oil for it. But maybe the others?"

"Way ahead of you." Cody poked his head up from under the green, rusted hood of a cargo truck. "We had to piece things together on the ranch some days. Town was far—an hour round trip. I'm pretty good at robbin' from Peter to pay Paul. If anyone knows what a radiator line looks like, see if you can find an intact one on another truck."

"You're on your own, buddy," Justin said. "Not my forte."

"Mine either," Matt said. "These trucks remind me of that movie *Commando*."

"That movie was sick!" Rhett said. "A bunch of guys from my football team snuck in to watch it."

"Ah, yes," Matt laughed. "The forbidden R-rated movie. My dad took me, made me swear I wouldn't tell Mom."

"Your dad sounds like he was cool," Rhett said.

Was. Past tense. Matt's heart ached.

"Anyone find me a radiator line?" Cody asked.

"Sorry," Matt said. "I wouldn't know what I was looking for."

"Not a problem." Cody walked from truck to truck, peering under the hoods. Jostling wires, pulling and prodding. "This one seems to be the least rotted. Give me a few minutes and I'll know if I can salvage it."

Matt stared at his friends' faces. Each wore a different expression of anticipation or anxiety. If this didn't work, they'd wasted an hour and were no closer to finding the cave.

Cody hopped into the driver's seat and left the door ajar. "No one get your hopes up, but it's worth a shot."

Matt watched him turn the key, expecting to hear the truck struggle to life. But instead, he heard nothing. Not even the clicking of a dead battery.

"Damn it," Justin said.

"Let me check one more thing." Cody jumped down and lay under the vehicle. "That's odd . . ."

"What?" Darin asked.

Darin looked under the truck again along with Cody. "It says 'HZRD' on it. We've seen this before."

Matt swiftly grabbed the trapper. "HZRD, you say?"

"Yup," Cody said.

Matt scribbled on his map and took notes. B-35, A-67, HZRD. "Nothing makes sense."

The sound of gears revving up filled the air. The ground shook. Stacy grabbed onto Darin, who surprisingly didn't shake her off.

"Uh, excuse me," Cody said. "This ain't good."

"No duh. The truck is, like, useless. And what's with your stupid hick ain't bull crap?" Kim mocked. "Ain't ain't a word. And you ain't supposed to say it. If you say ain't five times, you ain't going to heaven."

"I wouldn't joke about that right now." Cody pointed to the sky. "Those clouds are about to collide, and we're looking at something bad."

A fierce gust of wind ruffled their clothes. A sudden cold bit at their skin. Black and white clouds swirled together, creating a deep gray overcast. Lightning streaked across the sky with a loud crackle. Another jagged bolt struck a tree nearby. Sparks jumped, and the tree smoldered. The clouds churned. Deep gray funnels riddled with electric bolts formed to the south until one stretched out like the devil's finger.

"Twisters!" Cody yelled.

"Run!" Justin shouted.

"No!" Cody held out his hands. "You can't outrun a tornado. They're unpredictable and faster than you can imagine."

"What do we do, then?" Matt said. He strained to hear Cody over the vicious squalls of air.

"We need to lie in a ditch or low area." Cody searched around desperately.

"There isn't a ditch!" All color drained from Victoria's already pale face.

"Then over here. Follow me!"

Cody ran toward a gear in the outer area, away from the glass flasks and beakers. The large gear was half stuck in the ground at an angle, creating a semi-shelter. Matt sprinted, but the wind had gotten stronger and pulled at him from every direction. He lost his footing, stumbling onto the hard ground.

"Matt!"

Someone's faint voice called his name.

Matt rolled over onto his butt and stared into the distance. A huge, mile-wide mass spun on the ground, picking up everything in its path and adding it to its deadly vortex. A tree was sucked up and spit out in sharp, thick splinters. Dirt and grass swirled in the black tornado. He froze at the sight. Someone yanked his shirt. He shook his head and half-sprinted and was half-dragged to the closest thing they had to safety.

"Are you trying to get killed?" Justin dropped him in a heap with the rest of the group.

"No, I . . ." Matt's chest tightened.

His breath came out in short spurts. He'd frozen just like Nathan. Matt's heart raced.

"Matt?" Catherine gently rubbed his back.

"I'm . . . okay," he stuttered. "Ju-just give me a sec."

Matt stared at the rusty brown surface of the gear and tried to Matt-itate. He counted to ten and back in his head.

"You better calm down, or you're gonna pass out, chief," Justin said.

Matt puckered his lips and slowly sucked in a deep breath, then closed his eyes. The air tasted moist, like petrichor after a rain. But there wasn't any rain. He thought about when his dad taught him to ride a bike. He'd been nervous then, but it was different. That was exciting. The air blowing through his brown hair. The instability once his dad removed his hand from the seat. The uneasy wobble that he managed to recover from. The purple and white streamers fluttering on the handlebars of his borrowed bike. "Once you prove to me you can ride, we'll get you your very own bike." His dad's words echoed in his head. All of it. Every moment calmed him and filled him with warmth. He blinked his eyes open to everyone staring at him.

Everyone but Victoria. She hadn't followed Cody.

CHAPTER 19

Matt stared at a small, pale, fragile girl, hunched under a downed tree. Her braid had come free, and long waves blew sideways across her face as she struggled to hold on. Her eyes were wide and filled with fear.

She yelled something to the group, but it was swallowed up by the ravenous, blowing wind.

"What happened to you?" Catherine asked, cupping her hands around Matt's ear.

He did the same to her. "I just had a freak-out for a second."

"Yeah, don't do that agai—" Catherine looked past Matt, her eyes wide.

Matt turned. The sky birthed hundreds of tornados. Some stayed up high; others lapped at the ground like a thirsty dog to water. At least half of the weather monsters connected with the earth, chewing up everything in its path. Cody had one thing right: They were unpredictable. The vortexes would shift and disappear, only to reappear closer to them. One sucked up a huge beaker, sending glass shrapnel everywhere. Matt ducked just in time to see the vortex being pulled back up into the sky as if it had satisfied its craving.

Victoria scrambled on all fours until she was out in the open. Exposed to the storm. She paused for a moment, looking back over her shoulder, then bolted toward the group. The fierce wind whipped her around, but still she trudged forward.

"Victoria!" Matt yelled, holding up his hands like a traffic cop. "Stop! Get out of the open!"

Broken branches clawed at her, knocking her around like a rag doll. She stood and tripped on a downed branch. Her green cargo pants tore from the thigh down. The fabric whipped around like a paralyzed appendage.

A piece of glass lifted off the ground and sliced into her leg, but she didn't falter. Bright red blood streamed down her thigh, a sharp contrast with her white skin.

Matt started and stopped over and over, weighing the risk to run out and help her, to pull her back in, to carry her. Anything to get her to safety. He was wrestling with what to do when, in a flash, the choice was taken out of his hands.

Rhett pushed past Matt, knocking him to his knees. He raced into the open area.

"Rhett! No!" Kim yelled, but her voice was swallowed up by the raging tempest.

Victoria's already shocked eyes somehow got wider. She trudged toward Rhett, her head down. The wind was too powerful for the thoughtful, delicate girl. A gust, swelled with dirt and leaves, hit her with the force of an oncoming bus. She was down, crawling. She outstretched a hand toward Rhett. The blood from her leg was stolen by the storm.

Intense pressure built in Matt's ears, so he pressed his palms into them. It felt like the world was going to explode. A deeper gray cast them into darkness. The sound of a freight train without the warning of a horn took Matt by surprise.

Rhett ducked.

Victoria didn't.

The broken-down truck they'd seen lying lifeless was now on a collision course. It spun violent and unpredictable in the tornado's funnel, tumbling over and over. Everyone screamed. Victoria stood and tried to run, fighting intense wind, unaware of what was chasing her. The truck flipped in the vortex just before its wheel well smashed into the back of Victoria's head. Matt ducked instinctively. Although the tornado was deafening, he swore he heard the sickening thud as it connected with her.

"Victoria!" Catherine screamed.

She took a step forward, but Justin grabbed her by the waist. She turned and buried her face in his muscular chest. Matt wanted to look away but was powerless. Dirt and leaves smacked him in the face, but his eyes remained fixed.

Victoria's head rolled toward them.

Eyes.

Hair.

Eyes.

Hair.

Eyes.

Her decapitated body remained upright for a moment then slumped. Blood poured down from her neck, leaving a crimson puddle around her body.

Matt's jaw slacked. Before he could fully process what had happened, the twister swept up what remained of their sweet, considerate, sensitive friend. He looked away.

"We gotta get Rhett!" Kim ran out toward him. "Rhett!"

Her baggy purple shirt wrapped around her slender body as she fought the wind. She fell and lay with one arm outstretched, her mouth agape.

"Come back!" Kim screamed, barely audible over the gale-force winds. "Please."

Then she was still. Completely unmoving. Rhett turned toward Kim, and he was hit with forest debris in the back. His large-statured body jolted and jerked like it was being shot, but he didn't fall.

Everything slowed. Motion and time didn't seem to matter.

"Get back here now!" Cody yelled, knocking Matt back to reality.

The force of the wind made it seem like Rhett was stuck in thick swamp mud. His face contorted. Another piece of debris connected with his shoulder, he lurched forward, and grimaced. Lightning tore through the sky, exposing hundreds of tornados that grew from the dark clouds.

"This is bad," Darin said. "Something's wrong."

"No shit, Sherlock." Tears streamed down Stacy's face.

"I—" Darin turned to Stacy, gently grasped the back of her neck, hesitated, and kissed her. Stacy's face reddened.

Then Darin ran to Kim.

"Lance-Darin!" Stacy yelled.

He was knocked back by a gust.

"No!" Stacy screamed. "Please, no."

Darin sat and pulled Kim toward him. Kim kicked at him. In one motion, he stood and placed his arms around Kim's waist, then heaved her over his shoulder. She pounded his back with closed fists in protest. He stood and ran back toward the gear.

"I gotta help Rhett," Justin said.

"No," Matt said. "It's too dangerous!"

Rhett dropped to his knees, then fell face-first onto the ground. A thick piece of jagged metal stuck out of his back. The storm had turned him into a wind-up toy. To never be wound again.

Even with all the commotion, wind, and tornadic activity, Matt still heard Kim's shrill cries over it all. She kicked her legs wildly but was no match for Darin. He ran hard against the wind and was only a few feet from the safety of their shelter.

Rhett pushed himself up and attempted crawling.

Darin ducked under the gear and dropped Kim onto the ground. He pointed at her and said, "Stay!"

"No!" Kim screamed.

Catherine and Stacy held her in their safe place.

"I can't take this." Justin ran toward Rhett but stopped suddenly.

A new funnel cloud snaked its way toward the ground, ready to strike Justin. He backed up and dove back under the gear, skinning his forearms. The skinny tornado quickly quadrupled in size and devoured everything in its path. It launched another piece of debris at Rhett, but he was prepared this time. He raised a massive forearm and blocked it, fileting his skin open in the process.

The twister then shifted its path and started to circle Rhett. Like a boxer sizing up its opponent. The rest were powerless. The choice to help was not theirs to make anymore. If Matt or anyone else left the sheltered spot, the risk was too high for both to survive. Matt had never felt such guilt in his life. His friend was only fifty yards away, and there was nothing he could do.

The tornado slowed and swirled in one spot, throwing up dirt in every direction. Rhett attempted to stand once again. He took one step, then two steps forward, but then, like a cobra, the tornado struck, sucking their 6'6" jock away, hurling him up into the sky.

Matt closed his eyes and focused on his breath. A collective gasp and scream echoed behind him. Kim's cries were unmistakable. He'd never heard such pain or agony come from anyone or anything. She lay on her back, Catherine and Stacy at her side. Clear snot dripped from her nose; tears streamed down her bright red face as she struggled to get free from the girls.

"Rhett!" Kim cried. "No, no, no, no, we have to help him!"

Catherine stroked Kim's blond hair. "He's gone, Kim. I'm so sorry."

"Rhett," Kim wailed. "This is all *your* fault. You did this!" She stared at Matt like a crazed animal.

Matt Voorhees snapped.

CHAPTER 20

Matt's temples throbbed, and his entire body felt hot. He ground his teeth and flared his nostrils. Kim wasn't the only one who had just lost someone. They'd *all* lost Rhett and Victoria. In the last few days, every single one of them had experienced the loss of four friends, a scientist who took care of them, and a girl they'd never known. And now Kim was assigning blame to Matt. It was more than he could take.

"Shut your damn mouth!" Matt yelled. "You're so selfish, Kim. This isn't about me or you—it's bigger than us. No one is to blame. I didn't create that storm! I didn't force Rhett to chase after Victoria!"

The storm slowed, and the winds died down. Everything felt eerily calm.

Kim turned to Cody. "You should have stopped him!" she screamed. She glared at Justin. "You should have helped him, Justin. He was your friend. And where were you?" She pointed to Darin. "Why didn't you save Rhett? You should have just left me out there!"

"Kim—" Stacy started.

"No." Kim swiped Stacy's hand off her shoulder. "You're just as guilty. What? You didn't want to mess up your stupid red hair? So you just stood by and watched him die?"

"We lost Victoria too," Catherine said. "I'm sorry, Kim. We all are."

"Shut up!" Kim stood.

"Stop this!" Stacy shook Kim. "Listen, like Matt said, it was Rhett's decision to run after Victoria. Rhett is a hero. That's why he tried to help her."

"You're so stupid, Stacy," Kim said in between sobs. "No one cares what your idiot mouth has to say."

Stacy's face fell flat. She raised an eyebrow and put a hand on her hip. "Is that so? First of all, my hair is strawberry blond. *Not* red. And maybe, just maybe, Rhett tried to save Victoria because he liked her more than you."

"You bitch!" Kim slapped Stacy.

Stacy held her cheek, stunned.

"Okay, that's enough! No one talk!" Matt said. "Kim, you especially should use this time to grieve. And be silent."

Kim's legs gave out, and she collapsed into a puddle of tears.

"He could still be out there," Cody whispered to Matt. "I've seen it on the news before. Someone gets swept up into a twister, and they find 'em alive and well two towns over."

Kim looked up at Cody with glassy eyes. "What did you say? You're stupid too. He had a piece of metal sticking out of his back. He's dead, you moron. Dead!"

"You know what? Ima listen to Matt and seal these lips." Cody put his hands in his pocket and looked toward the sky.

Matt sat with his knees up to his chest. He thought about how he'd barely had time to grieve the loss of Kyle and Nathan. Now he had to add Victoria and Rhett to the list. Four lives—four kids, really—who had survived the apocalypse, cryosleep, and a car accident only to die by the natural disasters that made it necessary for cryosleep to be invented in the first place. His friends had succumbed to the natural disasters. Rain, snow, and now wind.

Mother Nature was a murderer.

Catherine sat next to Matt. She leaned over and rested her head on his shoulder. "You know no one blames you, right?"

Matt shrugged.

"Matt, come on, be reasonable. Look at her." Catherine nodded in Kim's direction. "She's a mess. Hurt people hurt people. It's easier for her to hate us than deal with her feelings."

"I guess." Matt stared at Kim. She quietly wept in the fetal position, in utter grief. "I'm just tired of being her punching bag. I shouldn't have yelled at her. I feel terrible."

"Then apologize," Catherine said. "But you weren't out of line."

"Thanks for saying that." Matt hugged Catherine. "The sky is still dark, but it seems like the weather has lifted."

"Do you guys want to try to head back to camp?" Catherine asked. "We need proper shelter."

"The wind is starting to pick back up," Darin said. "It might be our only chance to run for a while."

"There still might be bad weather at camp," Matt said. "But at least we'd have more cover in a building. Not getting hit with debris every few seconds."

"I'm in," Justin said. "Should we leave it to a vote?"

"Nah," Cody said. "If you want to stay, stay. I'm leaving."

"I'm in," Matt said.

Catherine nodded.

"Me too," Justin said.

"Camp sounds good to me," Darin said. "It's only a thirty-minute walk, and if we run, we can make it there in no time."

"I trust you, Lance-Darin." Stacy weaved her arm through his.

Darin stiffened. Matt guessed he regretted kissing Stacy.

"Kim," Matt said, crouching next to her, "I'm sorry for snapping at you. Will you come with us? We can't leave you alone here."

"Rhett's gone," she cried. "Nothing matters anymore."

"It's getting pretty windy," Catherine said. "It might start up again. This is our only chance."

"We can't leave her," Matt mouthed.

"Scoot aside," Darin said. He picked Kim up and placed her over his right shoulder. "If you won't walk, we'll carry you."

Kim lay limply over Darin, still crying.

"Let's go." Matt jogged out from under the gear and was immediately hit with the earthy scent of moist air. He didn't see any tornadoes, so he waved everyone forward. "Stay in a group, but let's get there as fast as we can."

"I'll lead," Justin said.

"Thanks," Matt said.

Matt found his place firmly in the middle. Thirty minutes passed. Kim protested and said she'd run. But every time Darin placed her on the ground, she would just lay down and cry. With all the starts and stops, it was taking them longer to get back to camp than it did to get to the junkyard in the first place.

"Get up or be carried," Catherine said. "Kim, I know you're sad, and you can cry and grieve all you want once we're in the main cabin, okay? You can stay there for the rest of your life if you want."

"What's the point?" Kim rolled over into a puddle of mud, staining her purple shirt and white jeans.

"The point is you're hurting all of us right now," Matt said. "Get up, or I'll carry you."

Kim stood and shuffled her feet. She flat out refused to cooperate. *Is she trying to get us killed?* Matt wondered.

While Matt wasn't the strongest, he decided it was his turn. He scooped her up and held her like a baby, her muddy clothes staining his. She struggled at first, kicking her feet and flailing her arms. Matt briefly considered dropping her but thought better of it.

"Give me your hand," Stacy said to Kim.

Matt gently deposited Kim back on the ground, his back protesting the entire time.

"I'm sorry for what I said," Stacy said. "And I know *you're* sorry for slapping me. Run with me, Kim. Please."

Kim wiped away a tear, smearing mud on her cheek in the process. She gave a single nod and lazily ran, hand in hand with Stacy.

CHAPTER 21

Kim's improved attitude didn't last long—not that Matt expected much of her. She'd tripped over a log, and she lay on the ground crying, Stacy at her side. Branches creaked, and leaves rained down on them as the winds picked up once more.

"Come on, Kim," Cody said. "I ain't ever yelled at a lady in my life, and I'm not about to start now. But you have got to either run or let us carry you. This is getting so dang frustrating."

"I'm so sad," Kim said. "I've been, like, traumatized."

"We've *all* been traumatized," Justin said. "Enough is enough. Cry later. We're all hungry, tired, and cold."

Darin clenched his fists and stalked back toward Kim.

"Move," Darin said to Stacy.

Stacy jumped to her feet and out of the way. Darin crouched and scooped Kim up and over his shoulder once more.

"This is the last time I'm doing this," Darin grunted.

"No!" Kim protested.

Darin held her over his shoulder and clamped her thighs down with his left arm. Leaving his right arm free, he jogged. Matt matched his pace and ran next to him.

"Can you bring up the back, Justin?" Matt asked.

"You got it, chief," Justin said. "No soldier left behind."

"Let me down!" Kim pounded on Darin's back. Tears streamed down her red face. "You're kidnapping me!"

Kim's mud-stained feet flailed while she screamed. "I hate you!"

"You know what? I'm done." Darin said. "I can see the lake from here. I'm not screwing with this anymore."

He put Kim down. Kim kicked Darin in the crotch.

He doubled over. Matt could only imagine the flames of nausea coursing through Darin's gut after a kick like that.

"Kim!" Stacy yelled. "Did you kick Lance-Darin in the—the—you know?"

"He deserved it!" Kim wiped tears from her face. "He dropped me . . . again."

"Whatever!" Stacy chased after Darin. "We've tried everything. You're being completely ridiculous. Friendship over, Kim. Friendship over!"

Matt looked back. Kim was, once again, on the ground in the fetal position, sobbing. Catherine crouched next to her and held her hand.

Leaves whipped at their feet in the swirling wind. Matt waved Justin and Cody ahead.

"Come on, Kim. We're not leaving you," Matt said.

"Good luck, chief," Justin said. "Kim's being a real shit-eating brat right now."

"Tell me about it," Matt replied.

"We might just want to leave her, as hard as that is to say," Cody said. "Matt, she's slapped Stacy—twice, and punched Darin in the ole family jewels. Just because she's a girl doesn't mean she's allowed to hit us."

"You're right." Matt rubbed his face. "I just need to get her back to camp and have her chill out before I address it, you know?"

"Tick tock." Justin tapped his wrist on his non-existent watch.

Matt nodded and gritted his teeth. When it came down to brass tacks, Matt wanted to leave Kim in the woods. He figured she'd come running like a toddler whose parents threatened to leave them in a store during a tantrum. But he couldn't leave her to just die. She'd been hand-picked for the cryovault program just like himself. If nothing else, he'd do it for Rhett. His friend. His dead friend. He squeezed his eyes shut and pushed back tears. *Not now, Matt, deal with it later.*

Matt approached Catherine and Kim, who was now standing.

"Kim has agreed to come with us, as long as we don't look at her or speak to her," Catherine said.

Heat filled Matt's chest. He opened his mouth, and Catherine placed a palm over it.

"And I informed her that we will be respectful of her request because we *choose* to and not because she's demanding it. We acknowledge she's mourning. Kim has also agreed to keep her hands and feet to herself." Catherine glared at her.

"We need to have a serious conversation when we're back," Matt said.

"No talking!" Kim stomped forward.

Catherine rolled her eyes and hurried along, side-by-side with Matt.

Not much later, they were back at camp, just on the other side of the lake. The winds in camp were stronger than in the forest they'd just crossed. Above them, the sky swirled a menacing gray. Matt stopped at the bank of the lake.

"Welcome to Camp New Beginnings." Justin splayed out his arms. "Where the weather is just as dysfunctional as its residents."

"Very funny," Catherine said. "Come on, let's get to the main hall."

"Wait." Matt pointed toward the back. "Is that another . . . crap, it is. See the funnel?"

In the southeast part of camp, a small funnel cloud twisted and dipped toward the earth, then was sucked back up into the sky, growing larger each time it plunged to the ground.

"Now what?" Stacy asked. "Back into the forest? I can't run anymore. I'm exhausted."

"Cody?" Matt asked. "You're the most experienced with tornadoes."

"Well, I'd say let's give it a few minutes." Cody held his pants as if he were cupping a belt buckle in the front. "If it touches down and stays connected to the forest floor, we're better off laying on the low edges of the lake. The forest has too much potential for shrapnel. If it keeps going up and down like that, it'll probably dissipate—"

A loud rumble of thunder sent the tornado to the ground. It twisted, then slowly migrated to the east.

Boom!

A thick column of white smoke erupted from the ground and blossomed into a mushroom cloud. Fire erupted within the explosion, igniting a small cabin. Rain poured down without warning, and the twister was sucked back up into the sky.

"What the heck?" Stacy held Darin's arm. "Tornados are like bombs now?"

"No," Matt said, shaking his head, "that's impossible."

Everyone huddled together, staring at the smoke.

"I can't believe he did it." Darin slicked his wet hair back. "That crazy old bastard. He really did it."

"You think Dr. Westbrook did this? He's dead." Matt's face twisted with confusion. "That's laughable. You can't blame everything on him."

"Bro, that was my belt." All color had drained from Darin's face. "That psycho actually strapped a live bomb onto my body."

CHAPTER 22

"I'm not doing this here," Darin said. "Let's get out of the rain."

They ran, slipping on the red, muddy pathway on their way to the main cabin. Once inside, Justin started a fire. Catherine placed seven chairs around the hearth.

"My belt. It really was a bomb," Darin said. "I mean, that's what he told me. I was worried, but I never—not really—ever thought it was really a bomb. I mean, I knew there was a chance, but I figured he was just trying to scare me."

"We can't be sure that was what exploded," Matt said. "The people who buried it are . . ."

"Nathan told me," Cody said. "I asked him where. That was the general area. I just wanted to make sure it was in a good spot. Plus, I knew it needed to be reburied. They had only buried it under the snow, not into the ground. I liked him and Victoria plenty, but they didn't have a lot of survival instincts, you know?"

"No, they didn't, did they?" Kim said. "If that stupid goth girl had, like, any brains, my boyfriend would still be alive!"

"Kim!" Matt growled and pinched the bridge of his nose. "We'll deal with you later. For now, either zip it or go back to the stage like you were before."

Kim tried to cry but only managed to make her face red.

"It's the only thing that makes sense. The tornado picked up my belt and somehow detonated it," Darin said. "Westbrook could have killed us all."

Rain beat down hard against the roof and the south-facing windows.

"Why would he do that?" Justin asked. "He really didn't trust you. Why?"

"Because I wasn't a puppet," Darin said. "He did some things . . . I can't get into it, but there was distrust. And it wasn't on his end. He broke *my* trust. In the end, I was in a hostage situation. Forced, you know."

Matt held the exhaled loudly and started to walk off.

"Fine," Darin said. "Westbrook was eccentric when I first met him after he woke me the first time. I figured it was the isolation, plus I was only twelve. I didn't have enough life experience to realize he was completely deranged."

"Qualify that," Catherine said.

"It started off with little things that struck me as odd. Like he would count his steps as he walked. Then demand I did too. He'd make me give him my numbers throughout the day. That's what he'd call it: my numbers. If I lied, he'd actually know the correct number of steps I'd taken. Who does that? He was obsessive about everything."

"Maybe he was just bored," Matt said.

"No. It was more. Things started breaking, things that shouldn't. Like individual pods. Columns could go out, sure, but not one cryopod here and there. They were all connected. But he'd always manage to be the hero and save the day by fixing it. He was creating problems just to fix them."

"Are you positive?" Justin asked.

"It went on for years. I finally caught him one day when I was supposed to be on the other side of the cave. This was maybe a year before I was forced back into cryosleep. Which, honestly? I was thankful for. I didn't want to be a part of it and his sabotage any longer."

"No way," Matt said. "Why would he do that?"

"So he could be useful? Because he was crazy? Make himself our savior? Hell, I don't know," Darin said. "You're asking me to make sense of someone who made none."

"But you knew him. You knew him better than anyone else," Matt pleaded. "I just can't imagine this selfless man was . . . misguided."

"Did I really know him? Do we really know anyone? Westbrook was three different people. The valiant person he wanted to be—which is what you saw in the videos. The smart scientist who cleverly fashioned solutions out of his hat. But when the camera was off, he was the sick, scary man that I knew."

"The camera . . ." Matt started. "The videos."

"Wait," Catherine said, pacing. "What if Darin is right? If Dr. Westbrook truly was sick? I can't believe I'm saying this, but what if the cryopods weren't failing?"

"No, they were failing," Darin said. "I know that for sure. They'd almost failed in the past. I saw it with my own eyes."

"Then maybe he made them malfunction?" Stacy asked.

"Yeah." Darin's eyes darted to the left, and he stared at the floor. "Maybe."

"I believe you, Lance-Darin," Stacy said.

"Why didn't you tell us all this in the beginning?" Matt asked.

Darin kept his gaze on the wooden floor. "You had this image of him already in your head, and you'd never even met him, not really. It was clear from the word go you didn't trust me. I really didn't see the point in making the rift worse."

"Yeah, well, I think I almost trust you less now." Matt crossed his arms.

"Do you believe me? About Westbrook?" Darin asked.

"If that bomb hadn't exploded, I wouldn't have believed you. I guess I kinda do," Matt admitted. "But maybe you were the bad guy, and he had to threaten you."

"If I was the villain, why wake me?" Darin asked. "If I was that big of a threat, why give me a bomb? I could have detonated it myself and collapsed the entire cryovault and killed everyone."

"I . . ." Matt trailed off. "Wait a minute . . ."

"What?" Cody asked.

"This makes more sense. On the videos, he said that you had died." Matt scratched his head. "That means he lied. You didn't die. He just put you back in cryosleep."

"Well, there you have it. I didn't die. I'm here in the flesh. And he did lie about me dying."

"What were you, captain of the debate team in high school?" Justin walked by Darin and toward the window. "You got me convinced."

"Never made it to high school," Darin said.

"Oh right." Justin shrugged.

"This is a lot to process," Matt said.

"Darin, I'm with Matt," Cody agreed. "I believe you, but it's a lot to think about."

"I don't care who believes me," Darin said. "I was there. I know. And if he was telling you that I died, and I actually didn't, then you shouldn't believe him at all. I don't know what his motives are . . . or were. All I know is that we should do all we can to survive."

More gears pounded and shuddered through Camp New Beginnings.

This time, the grinding was pure metal on metal.

"Justin, is the cabin still burnin' out there?" Cody asked, his eyes darting from side to side.

"Nope," Justin said. "Smoldering a little, but the rain mostly took care of it. Also, it's not raining anymore. But the mountain is on fire."

"What?" Matt stood so fast, his chair screeched over the wood and tipped over.

He jogged over toward the window and stood next to Justin. Atop the highest peak of the mountain, smoke plumed. A small burst sent small red debris into the air.

"That's not a fire!" Matt's voice trembled. "That a volcano, and it's about to blow!"

CHAPTER 23

Several small bursts sputtered from the mountain, followed by more smoke. The gray sky had cleared to a pale blue. But now, smoke streaked through the blue and swelled until Matt worried that soon, the sky would be entirely darkened again.

"Okay, everyone, stay calm," Matt said. "The smoke could just be steam eruptions, meaning it's not going to erupt for a while."

"How can you, like, tell the difference?" Kim asked. "You're an expert on this too?"

"I can't," Matt said. "You're right. We need to leave. Pack up what you can carry, and we'll take off."

"Where are we going?" Justin asked. "Back to the gears?"

"R&D Lab—the Sev." Matt stalked back toward their supplies on the stage. "It's on higher ground and built into the hill. I think we should be safer there."

"You think." Kim sat in a folding chair. "But you don't know. All you do is guess and, like, get people killed."

"Kim!" Matt yelled. "If you're so unhappy with me, then don't follow me. No one is making you."

"Oh really? Then why did you drag me out of the forest? Force me to follow you?"

"Because I wasn't going to leave you to die," Matt said. "But if you want to keep fighting at every turn, then just leave me alone. I don't have the energy to fight with you anymore. Please."

Matt snagged a few lanterns, slipped on his backpack, and headed toward the door. As he palmed the door handle, the whole cabin vibrated violently.

Boom!

Matt flung the door open and ran to the edge of the deck. Giant plumes of black smoke were escaping the mountain. Small explosions within the smoke continued the momentum. It billowed higher and higher, blanketing the sky in darkness. Then covering the entirety of Camp New Beginnings.

Matt turned back to everyone in the gym. "We need to get out of the main cabin!"

Catherine screamed behind him.

Matt coughed and held his shirt over his nose. A fountain of red and orange lava erupted like a geyser. The top of the mountain burst open, allowing the column of fire to shoot straight up. Another explosion rattled the ground and sent shockwaves through the cabin.

"Get your packs!" Darin yelled.

"Let's get outta here!" Matt shouted, and grabbed Catherine's hand.

She locked eyes with him, panting, sweat dotting her brow, and nodded before running down the stairs.

The haze thickened by the minute. Matt counted six people. He inhaled acrid air that sent him into a coughing fit.

"Stay close!" Matt yelled. "We can't get separated!"

"Ah!" a female voice yelled. "I'm hit!"

"Keep going," Matt yelled. "Ahh!"

A thick piece of molten lava struck Matt on his arm. He instinctively grabbed the singed flesh, only to burn his hand and pull it back immediately.

Lava rained down at them like meteorites falling from the sky. It didn't make sense; Matt knew this wasn't how volcanos erupted.

"Help!" Stacy collapsed.

Without missing a beat, Darin picked her up.

"Stacy, are you okay?" Darin's voice was filled with genuine concern.

"No," she cried. "Please don't leave me here."

The sky was a burnt orange hue, casting them into what felt like hell to Matt. A piece of molten rock, the size of a basketball, crashed into the ground ahead of them, spitting steaming-hot dirt clods in every direction. The incoming chunk of lava left a crater three feet in diameter. The earth tremored again, and a blast sent them all tumbling to the ground.

Catherine winced and stood, holding her shoulder. She bit her lip, holding back tears. Justin pulled Cody to his feet.

"I'm burnt real bad," Cody yelled. He limped toward the lake and jumped in fully clothed.

Catherine followed suit. Everyone else joined in except Darin, who helped Stacy dip her foot in to cool it off. Even Kim swam out to the middle. Matt treaded water and stared at the mountain. It was like a scene out of a movie. Pieces of red-hot rock and lava shot down around them with intense force. A piece of liquid lava splashed into the water close to them, boiling the water as it sunk deeper. The cool water warmed rapidly.

"No," Matt said. "We're going to get trapped in here. We need to get out of the lake."

Matt swam to the edge and pulled himself out. His arm throbbed, and he smelled burnt flesh. He took note of everyone's injuries when they emerged from the lake.

Half of Catherine's hair had been singed off, and part of it was burned into her shoulder. Justin was pretty banged up, but Matt couldn't see any large burns. Stacy must have stepped on something hot enough to melt her shoe away and burn the sole of her foot. The back of Cody's thigh had a bright red mark where his pants should have been. Kim treaded water, her feathered hair swishing around her.

The sky around them reddened even deeper. Small fires broke out, blocking the path.

"Come on, Kim," Matt said. "We're not waiting. We have to go."

"No!" she screamed. "Look at you idiots. Every one of you is hurt. But not me! I'm still perfect. I'm not letting you drag me into danger. I'm safe here."

"Kim, please!" Stacy screamed. "We can't leave you."

"Scram!" Kim yelled.

A smaller piece of hot ash landed on Matt's shoulder, singeing his shirt. Sulfur steamed off the lake. Matt looked behind him.

"We're beggin' you," Cody said. "We gotta go."

"Then go!" Kim said. "How about you go—"

A high-pitched whistle zipped through the sky. Matt looked up and saw a bright orange ball careening toward the lake. Kim stared in shock. Before she could scream, the fireball smashed into the side of her face. Her skin melted, her hair burned off instantly, and her right eye became liquid and oozed down her face.

Stacy dove into the water and swam to Kim. She held Kim with one arm and swam backward with her free hand, legs kicking furiously. Lava bits cascaded down all around them, hissing the water's surface. Matt and Darin waded into the water and pulled them both to shore.

Kim's face was completely black. Her skin had melted off on point of impact, exposing her teeth like she was smiling. Her eye was gone, and her cheekbone was an open hole of charred bone. Gray brain matter leaked out of her exposed skull bone.

Stacy wailed.

Matt looked over his shoulder. The mountain released a river of lava that crept toward them.

"We don't have time for this," Matt said. "Grab your backpack! We need to move, now!"

"We can't leave her!" Stacy said.

"What choice do we have?" Catherine's voice trembled. "We can't carry her body and you."

Stacy nodded and sniffled.

Catherine quickly hugged Stacy and ran toward the north. Away from the volcano and toward the truck and lab.

In one day, Rhett, Victoria, and Kim had died. Matt felt such guilt with Rhett and Victoria, but not with Kim. He'd begged and pleaded with her all day. Maybe she willed herself to die. Maybe Mother Nature heard her call and obliterated her head with a chunk of lava rock. It was nonsense in its own way, and he couldn't play mind games with himself now.

Now, it was time to run.

CHAPTER 24

The lava crept toward camp as the fractured group climbed the hill toward the truck. Matt's thighs burned, and his mouth tasted like acid cotton. He hoped in the deepest parts of his heart that the lava wouldn't follow the same path as the avalanche.

"Hang on," Darin said. He gingerly placed Stacy down near the mangled truck where they'd all started their journey just days ago. "I need a second. That hill was brutal."

"I'm sorry." Stacy stood on one foot and balanced herself on Darin.

"Don't be." Darin was hunched over, and his hands rested on his knees. He looked up at Stacy and smiled. "I'm just glad you're alive."

"Really?" Stacy smiled, but it was a sad smile.

"Yeah." He stood and embraced her.

Matt looked down at camp. Lava still exploded from the top of the mountain in the distance. He wondered if there was even going to be a camp to return to. He squinted to see if any of the buildings were still standing, but it was too dark.

"I guess our plans of going to the mountain are canceled," Matt said. "We should probably get going."

Catherine winced when she stood.

"I gotcha." Justin took her pack from her. "I'm thirsty."

"There's water at the lab. It's not far," Cody said.

"You never mentioned water!" Justin said. "All right!" He greedily drained his green canteen.

"Justin," Matt said, facing him, "there's an even better surprise that I think you're gonna love."

"Right on." Justin wiped his lips.

They hiked past the truck and into the field toward the hill. The little bit of light that shone through the heavy smoke faded quickly as evening took hold. Constant coughing became their theme song. Matt stopped and lit one of his lanterns. They circled the base of the small hill until they reached the metal door to the R&D lab.

"We're here." Matt pushed in the door. "Welcome to the Sev."

The thick dust caused him to cough more.

Once everyone was in, Cody quickly closed the door and shoved a handkerchief in the broken handle, sealing the smoke out.

"Wow," Darin said. "What is this place?"

"Follow me," Matt said. "To your right are the blue drums filled with water. On the opposite wall are the black barrels. We think they're hazardous based on the skull and crossbones painted on them."

"Go, go, Inspector Gadget," Stacy said.

"I used to love that cartoon," Darin said, then blushed. "It's weird that I was younger than you when we were put in cryosleep, but now I'm older than you, right? Heck, I'm old enough to drink."

"Speaking of that . . ." Cody nodded at Matt.

"Water first," Matt said. "Grab your canteens."

Cody pumped on the bright orange top, and water sputtered out at first before he got a steady stream. One by one, they filled their canteens, drank them, and came back for more. After their thirst was quenched, Matt led them through the lab and into the back offices. He showed them the food closets and saved the larger office/junk-food room for last.

"Catherine, would you like to be my assistant?" he asked.

"Sure." She tried to force out a smile. Matt worried about how badly she was hurt.

"Behind door one, I present to you"—Catherine opened the door and presented it like she was one of Bob Barker's Beauties "—chips!"

"And behind door two, we have Twinkies and Ho-Hos!" Matt unsealed the cabinet. It hissed like a soda can.

"Door three," Catherine said, "chocolate and non-chocolate candy."

"Kim would have liked that," Stacy said quietly.

"And behind door four, the coup de gras!" Matt unsealed the final heavy cabinet.

"Is that? Sweet mother, is that *beer*?" Justin stood, mouth agape.

"And cheese balls. Wanna crack the first one?" Matt tossed him a plain white aluminum can labeled "BEER" in plain, black, blocked letters.

If it had been a few days ago, Matt would have made a crack

about Justin being able to read. But now, he was thankful he had a friend to lean on. He was glad they'd come this far.

Now that the adrenaline was wearing off, Matt's burned arm felt like it was boiling.

"How about we set up in here?" Matt asked. "I'll grab the packs."

"Wait, you think we're okay to have a couple of beers?" Catherine asked.

"Why not? I mean, technically, we're like forty-five or somethin'," Cody said.

"Don't feel like you have to drink one if you don't want," Matt said.

"No, I mean, you're right. We're technically of age," Catherine said.

"And who cares?" Stacy hobbled toward the cabinet and helped herself to a can. "It's not like there are any cops here to bust up this party."

"I meant, should we be celebrating? We lost so much today," Catherine said.

"It's not celebrating." Justin popped the tab on his can. "It's taking the edge off. I'm in a ton of pain. I'm sure you guys are too."

Catherine nodded.

Justin took a long drink from his can and burped. "Well, it's a little skunky, but not as bad as I figured. Glad it's not hot in here, or they'd be rank. Anyway, I think I'd like to have one before I clean out my wounds."

"That's not a bad idea," Matt said. "And I think we should eat, fix ourselves up, then we can all talk about . . . well . . . everything, I guess. It's been a hellish day. And now that we're sort of safe, I'm starting to really hurt."

Darin passed the plain white "BEER" cans around. He stood in the middle, held his up, and said, "To Kyle, Nathan, Rhett, Victoria, and Kim."

Everyone held their cans up and repeated the toast.

CHAPTER 25

Matt swallowed the last bit of beer from the can. He felt a pang of sadness. He'd never have a chance to finish his conversation with Victoria down by the dock. Or even really get to know the true her.

"That made me feel a little dizzy," Matt said to Cody.

"Me too. I ain't had one since the last branding at my daddy's ranch." Cody helped Matt sift through the contents of the backpacks, hoping for first-aid kits.

"Your parents let you drink?" Matt asked.

"Only at brandings," Cody said. "It's tradition. At the end of each branding, everyone has a Coors Original and Rocky Mountain oysters. I was only ever allowed one or two, but after bein' in the hot sun all day, and kicked by a steer here and there, it was pretty nice."

"Wow." Matt stacked a small first-aid kit onto another he'd found. "I'd never had alcohol until today."

"How's your arm feeling now?" Cody asked.

"Not as bad," Matt said.

"See? Just like Justin said, took the edge off. You findin' anything?"

Stacy's scream sent chills down Matt's spine.

"Just some basic kits. The good stuff is still at camp," Matt said. "You?"

Stacy shrieked again.

"Same. I guess let's see what we can use," Cody said. "I'll meet you in there. I'm going to double-check the cabinets in the lab."

"I hope Darin is able to get all of Stacy's shoe off. It looked like it had melted into the bottom of her foot. Pretty terrible luck, stepping on a molten lava rock like that."

"Yeah, it was pretty gruesome," Cody said. "But most of the shoe melted away. I think once he gets the edges loose, the rest will fall off."

Matt handed Cody his lantern in the lab, then followed the light emanating from the larger office.

"Hey," he said, entering the room. "We found a few things, but we'll need to head to camp tomorrow or once it's safe for the rest of our gear. Cody's checking out the lab right now for additional salves and bandages and whatnot."

Stacy lay with her head in Darin's lap. Her foot, propped up on Catherine's legs, was wrapped in a white lab coat. Blood seeped through, staining it red.

"How'd it go?" Matt asked.

"You heard," Darin said. "Did you find any pain pills?"

"No, the Lortab is still at camp," Matt said.

"Well, I'd suggest drinking a bunch of water and downing another beer, Stacy," Justin said. "You'll at least fall asleep."

"O-okay," Stacy whimpered. "You still have to clean it out, don't you?"

"I'm sorry," Catherine said. "We do."

Stacy sat, plugged her nose, and downed several large gulps, then leaned back on Darin. "I don't remember beer being so disgusting."

Catherine carefully unwrapped Stacy's foot. The top of her foot wasn't too bad, but the bottom was raw, red, and bleeding in several spots.

"Just do it," Stacy said. She squeezed her eyes shut and held Darin's hand. "Get it over with."

Catherine placed the lab coat under Stacy's foot and poured water from her canteen over it. Stacy squirmed and cried out. She begged for Catherine to stop. Within a few seconds, it was over. Matt handed Catherine a tube of antibiotic cream from the small hiking first-aid kit he had carried in his pack.

"Stacy, I'm going to put some salve on your foot, okay? It might sting at first, but it'll help heal it and keep infection away," Catherine said. "We don't have a ton, so I'm only putting it on the open wounds, okay?"

Stacy nodded. Her face was bright red, and tear streaks cut through the dirt on her cheeks.

Matt felt a little nauseated and decided to check in with Justin instead of witnessing this. He grabbed a white canister of cheese balls and headed toward Justin, who sat with his back facing Stacy.

"How bad are your wounds?" Matt asked.

"Not too bad. I was a running back. I did pretty good at dodging the debris. Only small burns. Lots of them, but nothing like the others got. My skinned forearms probably hurt the worst."

"You should still clean them," Matt said. "Our medicine is pretty limited back at camp."

"Do you think it'll still be there?" Justin asked.

"Camp? Or the main hall?" Matt asked.

"Either." Justin swigged his beer. "This whole thing is screwed up."

"I know." Matt removed the clear lid from his cylinder container and peeled back the silver seal. He tilted it in Justin's direction. "Cheese ball?"

"Thanks."

Justin took a handful and stuffed a few in his mouth. Matt did the same. He looked over his shoulder, and Stacy was lying on her side. Darin stroked her frizzy hair.

"How are you feeling?" Matt asked.

"I told you, I'm not too hurt," Justin answered in between bites.

"No, I know. Not that, the other thing," Matt said.

"I don't feel anything. It sucks we lost any of them, especially Rhett. He was my buddy. But I guess I figure we're all going to die soon, probably. We just have to try and delay it as long as possible."

"Yeah," Matt said.

The earsplitting sound of gears started up again. The sound encompassed them like the smoke.

The room fell silent.

"You guys hear that?" Cody burst into the room.

"Great, what's next?" Stacy cried.

"Maybe nothing," Matt said. "Maybe something. Either way, we're in the best spot. I think we'll be safe here."

"I hope," Catherine said. "I honestly don't think I can take any more natural disasters tonight."

"You know what? Let's actually live like tonight's our last night." Matt tossed a movie theater-sized box of chocolate candy in Catherine's direction. "Normally, I say we need to ration, be smart, don't overindulge—well, don't overdo it on the beer, but everything else? Eat it. Have fun. After you clean out your wounds, though. That's a non-negotiable."

"You're serious, aren't you, chief?" Justin asked.

"Why not?" Matt passed out more candy, Ho Hos and cheese balls. "We should celebrate. We can't sit here and keep focusing on what we lost. We need to celebrate what we overcame! We survived a flash flood, a treacherous snowstorm, monster avalanches, dozens of tornados, and a volcano eruption! We *did* that! Never mind we survived the cryosleep and car crash."

Plus, it could be our last night at this rate.

"Don't forget the bomb," Darin said.

"Oh yeah!" Matt said. "Darin lived through a live bomb being strapped to him. Who's in? Huh? Who wants to have fun? Eat, drink, and be merry, and tomorrow we live. No talk of death or what-ifs or Westbrook at all."

Darin locked eyes with Matt. It was the first time Matt had referred to the scientist by his last name only. Either Darin was a great liar, or Matt was starting to see the cracks in Dr. Westbrook's façade.

"Beer me," Justin said.

CHAPTER 26

Cody didn't find any additional medical supplies in the lab. But he did find an old boom box and batteries. The silver, boxy JVC stereo had two round speakers on either side of a tape deck. Above it was the radio station feature, complete with a twist knob for manual searching. Below the tape deck were all the usual buttons—pause, fast forward, rewind, record, eject—with play and stop being the largest buttons of all.

Matt put the batteries in and hoped for the best. The gray cassette inside had a white label and blocky print that ironically read: "mix tape."

"Here goes nothing." Matt pressed the play button. It clicked, but nothing happened. "Dang."

"Let me check," Catherine said. She opened the back of the boom box. "The batteries are in backwards, Matt!"

Catherine giggled, and she replaced them. She pushed play and squinted her eyes, waiting.

Loud trumpets ripped through the silence, then Gloria Estefan's upbeat voice, followed by snappy piano.

"The conga?" Matt laughed. He laughed so hard tears streamed down his face. "My mom *loved* this song!"

"Get up!" Catherine pulled Matt to his feet and placed his hands on her waist. "Darin, help Stacy, you guys lead!"

Matt stared at Catherine's shoulder. Her hair that had melted into her skin was gone now. But it left behind a deep, blistering burn. It glistened with antibiotic salve. Despite her injury, she looked like she was ready for the club with a trendy, off-the-shoulder *Flash Dance* shirt and an edgy haircut: long on one side, short on the other. She started out reminding him of Cher, and she'd now become his Jennifer Beals.

Darin gave Stacy a piggyback ride, and Catherine held Stacy's waist. They formed a conga line like they were at a wedding reception. Kicking feet out to the side. Moving forward and back. Matt's heart ached. Every time this song came on the radio, his mom would perk up and crank up the volume. At the time, it was so embarrassing. Now he'd give anything to relive that moment. He had to find her, but he was at a complete loss as to how.

"I cannot believe those batteries worked!" Darin yelled. "This is hilarious."

Cody was the first to drop off once the music ended. A piano chord progression started the next song.

"Well, this one's a downer," Justin said. "Journey? Lame. I wonder if they got any Metallica on there."

"Leave it for a sec," Matt said, taking Catherine's hand, placing it on his shoulder, and putting his hands around her waist. The slow-tempo lyrics of "Faithfully" took him back to his first high school dance. Steve Perry belted out the mesmerizing words. Catherine put her head on his chest, and they swayed back and forth. For the moment, all worry and pain melted away, and Matt was in the now.

The song ended with full electric guitar overlaying the grand piano chords. Catherine stopped him. "Matt, are you okay?"

"I'm just, I dunno, I feel really helpless. Our parents are stuck somewhere. We're no closer to them than we were the first day."

"Hey!" Justin shoved a silver bag of potato chips at him. "What about no being sad or whatever crap you said? Here, eat your feelings."

"I'm sorry." Matt sat and took a deep breath. "I can't help it."

Darin sidled up to Stacy. Catherine trimmed the wick on the lantern and joined the rest of the group in a circle around the light.

"I'm feeling pretty bad too," Stacy said. "Lance-Darin, you've been a dream, and I'm so thankful for you. But I can't get the image"—she burst into tears—"of Kim's face exploding like that out of my head."

"Or Victoria's," Matt said. "Her head was completely cut off. I know we said we'd try to find their bodies and bury them, but I hope we never find hers. I don't want to see her like that."

"I feel awful for saying this, but I hope all the bodies are just gone when we get back," Catherine said. "They were all so, so mangled. I honestly think I've been traumatized or something."

"If we can go back," Darin said. *"If."*

"You ain't wrong about that," Cody said. "But we gotta try. Most of our stuff is still back there."

"You want to go back?" Catherine said, her voice cracking.

"No, but we gotta go back, don't we?" Matt asked.

"I can't even walk!" Stacy said. "I'm a burden."

"No, you're not." Darin put an arm around her.

"Cody is right," Matt said. "A few of us need to try tomorrow and see what we can salvage. More clothes, supplies, and first-aid stuff. But I think this bunker is our new home."

"You Shook Me All Night Long" ended, and Tiffany's one-hit wonder, "I Think We're Alone Now" blared from the speakers.

"We really are alone now." Justin sat in the corner, his head cradled in his hands. "Screw this song."

"Not for long," Matt said.

Justin looked up; his long, sandy-blond hair was matted to his right cheek.

Matt lifted his chin and said, "We're going to find the cryovault. Mark my words." He hoped he'd make good on his word.

TO BE CONTINUED

APOCALYPSE WINTER

Tyler H. Jolley
David J. West

I dedicate this to Dinty Moore beef stew.
The heartiest canned stew on the market to this day.

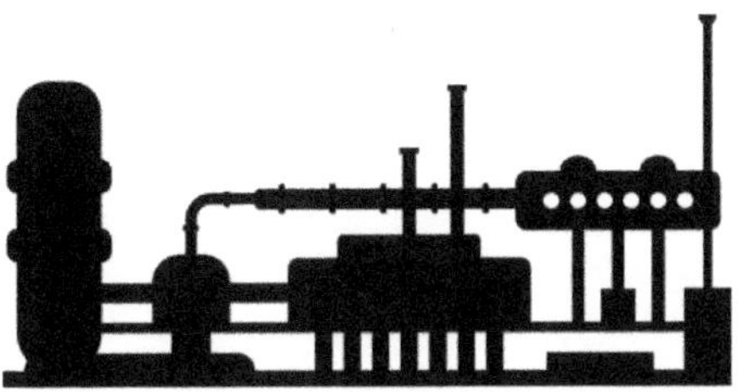

CHAPTER 1

Matt opened his eyes. The frosted glass of his cryopod obscured the people standing over him, watching him, shadowlike. Were they his parents? Scientists who worked at the cryovault? He panted, struggling to get enough air. Panic washed over him like a cold river. He banged on the glass, screaming, "Let me out! Let me out!"

The shadows remained, observing as if he were no more than a bug to be examined under a microscope. They did nothing to help his feeble attempts to escape his cryocoffin.

"Help! Help me!"

He gasped and sat up, his rumpled blankets tangled about him on the floor of a research and development building they had nicknamed the Sev.

We're still here.

The night before was numbing to say the least. They had lost three friends and drowned their sorrows and injuries with old beer and a dance party. The reality of today weighed down on Matt.

"Morning," came a voice.

Matt rubbed the sleep from his eyes.

Darin lay wide awake in a huddle of blankets, Stacy sprawled across him. "Rough night?" Darin asked.

"Bad dream. You?" Matt responded.

"Probably the best night I think I've ever had, actually," Darin said.

Stacy, still asleep, snuggled closer with a smile on her face, despite her injuries.

"Maybe we should go and get the supplies, first-aid kits, clothes, and things—and let them sleep it off?" Matt stood and weaved his way past a sleeping Catherine, Stacy, and Justin. The party from the night before had lingered into the early morning. He wandered over to get a drink of water from one of the barrels to try to shake the sleep out of him. "If we run, it shouldn't take the two of us too long."

Darin nodded as he pulled himself out from under Stacy. She murmured, her arm reaching for him like he was her pillow, but she remained asleep. "Wasn't sure I could move out from under her."

Matt nodded and offered a refilled canteen to Darin.

"Thanks." He took a good, long swallow. "I always wanted to party with the teenagers when I was a kid."

Matt looked at him with a raised eyebrow, trying to decide if he was joking or not. It *was* strange though, Darin was put into cryosleep at twelve—five years younger than Matt, but during his time out with Westbrook he'd aged to twenty years old. Making him Matt's senior.

"I really did," Darin reaffirmed.

Matt still wasn't sure if he was serious. "I figure if we hurry, we can get back with any salvageable gear and the first-aid kits before they're even all awake." He glanced around at the mess and the slumbering bodies strewn about the floor. "We did party pretty hard, didn't we?"

"Any harder and Spuds Mackenzie would have shown up."

Matt chuckled, remembering the party dog, and moved a bit of debris from the previous night's party from in front of the door.

Darin took the handkerchief from the doorknob hole, and when no smoke poured in through the broken handle, he opened the door. He squinted at the brightness of the morning, filtered through gray clouds. "You wouldn't even know a volcano went off last night. Where's the smoke?"

Matt stepped out and let the hazy light cascade across his face. "I don't know. I'm just glad it's gone. I wasn't sure I would ever see a day like this again."

Darin grinned. "When you see every kind of weather there is, there must be a good day once in a while."

"My dad used to say, 'A broken clock is right twice a day.'"

"He's right."

"Hey! Where are you guys going?" Catherine asked. "Don't go out there. It isn't safe."

Matt turned to the sleepy-eyed girl. "Take a look for yourself."

She met them outside, a blanket wrapped around her burned shoulder, and joined in their amazement at the calmness of the forest outside the Sev. "I can almost see the sun through the clouds." She pointed up, and Matt laughed. "What's so funny?"

"You pointed at the wrong spot. It's morning. The sun is over there."

"How do you know? That's not east," Darin countered.

Matt shook his head. "It's where I've noticed the most light every morning."

"Does your compass even work?" Darin argued.

"No."

"Then you don't know which way is east. Besides, I think the sun is over there." Darin pointed in an altogether new direction.

Catherine squinted as she looked up at the gray sky. "I think I can see *three* suns behind the clouds."

"Three suns is crazy. We aren't on Tatooine," Matt said with a laugh.

"Aren't we on a crazy alien landscape, though?" Catherine taunted. "I wouldn't be surprised if sand people tried to ambush us next."

Darin scowled. "Don't even joke about that. Last thing I want to do with this crazy weather is fight a zombie horde of freaks."

Catherine winced. "Sorry. I'd be happy to see almost any other people."

"Not if they were trying to kill you," Darin said.

Cody ambled up to the group. "What're you guys doin' up, anyway?"

"We're going to go get the first-aid kits and look for some food and clothes at the camp while the going is good. We'll be right back." Matt turned to Catherine. "You can stay here . . . if you want."

"You can keep an eye on things, especially Stacy, please," Darin added.

"All right, I will. You two be careful, though. This weather is bound to change any minute, you know."

"I'm going with them. And we'll be careful," Cody said.

They walked back along the path they had come on to get to the Sev, and Matt marveled silently at how yesterday, freak storms had destroyed everything and taken three of his friends' lives. How did Camp New Beginnings suddenly resurrect itself? It was like they were being played with by some terrible gamemaster. He turned to Darin. "Did you ever see a movie called *The Dungeon Master,* where the main guy was being transported into all kinds of worlds by this evil DM, and it kept changing? This reminds me of that in a way."

"No, I never saw it. Snuck into *Goonies* once."

"Well, this was a little different. Scarier, I guess, like *Nightmare on Elm Street.*"

Darin shook his head. "You all talk about all these pop culture references like it was yesterday, and for you guys, it was yesterday, but I was twelve. I didn't pay attention to a lot of that like you teenagers. I rode my bike and went swimming, but it was all over once I was with crazy old Westbrook. I didn't get to enjoy any of that stuff. It was all just work, work, work. Do this, do that. I didn't get a life like you guys."

Cody shook his head. "Sorry."

"It's all right now. I just feel out of place and alone." He glanced back toward the hill concealing the Sev from their view and said softly, "It's nice to be wanted."

"Stacy?" Matt asked.

Darin looked at him and muttered, "Yeah," before taking a few quicker steps, signaling an end to the conversation.

Camp New Beginnings had transformed into something out of *Mad Max*. Hardened black lava covered the back part of camp. A black brick road to destruction. The cabins had been burned, leaving piles of pullies and cables intertwined with scorched wood and hot coals. The trio rummaged through the buildings that had survived the apocalyptic crescendo and found a couple of first-aid kits, complete with salve for burns and extra bandages.

Darin found a couple of forgotten MREs. "You never know when these might come in handy."

Matt nodded. "Good call. Let's hurry back to the others."

They jogged along, keeping a good pace, then Matt paused. "Hey, wait up a sec."

Darin stopped. "What is it?"

"Something looks weird over there. Something is moving the grass, but there's no wind."

"An animal?" Cody asked.

"I haven't seen any animals this whole time," Matt said.

"Me neither, but if it's a rabbit or a chicken, it's going down." Cody crouched into a hunter's stance.

"Let's be careful," Matt urged.

"Right, we don't want to scare it away," Darin said.

"I don't think it's an animal. The grass is movin' too weird. Plus, it's where me and Nathan buried your belt," Cody said.

Darin stopped his crouching approach. "Then let's go back to the others. We've got people to take care of. Who cares about where the belt bomb went off?"

"I want to check it out." Matt crouched next to Cody and crept toward the swaying grass. "With all the natural disasters, we should make sure it's safe. I don't want to lose anyone else."

Cody nodded. "That's true."

"Plus," Matt said, "that's the way we have to go to get to the mountain, so we're going to pass it anyway. It won't hurt to make sure the ground's stable for us before we bring everyone over here."

Cody followed him.

At the edge of the billowing grass, Matt stopped dead in his tracks.

Darin caught up to them and looked down. "Whoa!"

Matt whistled. "That is one big sinkhole."

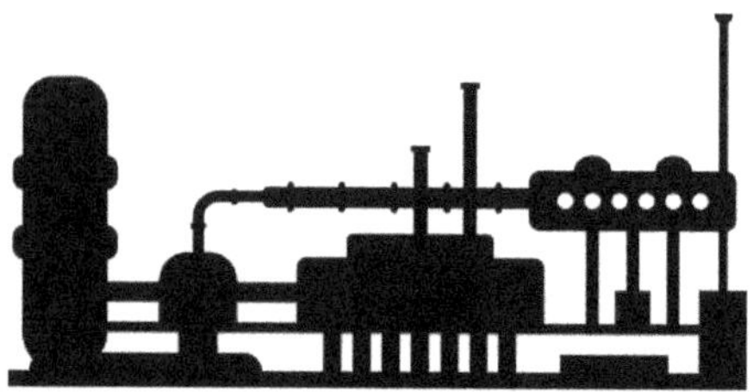

CHAPTER 2

Matt, Cody, and Darin stood around the forbidding black hole as if it were a gravesite. The ten-foot by ten-foot chasm—about the size of an elevator shaft—had no bottom in sight.

Cody whistled and looked at Darin. "Just think, you were wearing that thing."

"How did a weight-belt bomb make a hole that deep?" Matt asked.

Darin shook his head. "It didn't. Cody must have placed it right on top of a small volcanic fissure."

"But it's so big," Matt exclaimed. He kicked a small stone into the dark unknown.

It clanged far below, an oddly familiar sound of rock hitting metal.

"Maybe it's just a tunnel," Cody said. "A tunnel that goes to the Sev."

"Under the ground? So you think it's connected?" Matt asked. "We didn't see any tunnels running this far over when we explored the Sev, though."

"Maybe not to the Sev, then," Cody said. "But could it be connected to the cryovault?"

"I think that's gotta be too far away." Matt shook his head and pointed to the mountain. "I just know we need to get to the mountain and find my parents."

Cody put a hand on Matt's shoulder and smiled. "But . . . you want to investigate first."

Within the short few days they'd been together, Cody had unlocked Matt. His humor. His curiosity and ideas.

Matt nodded. "This all makes sense!" He continued to nod. "I didn't put two and two together until now. There must be a tunnel system or something. Cody, you're right. Back at the Sev, there was a blueprint with tunnels on it, but I didn't realize what it was. Maybe we can get to the mountain this way. Underground."

"I don't know about that," Darin said.

"Look," Matt said, "let me just take a look first. If it's not a tunnel, then we'll forget about it, but if it is, then wouldn't you think we would be safer underground?"

Darin shrugged.

"We've had so many people die up here that a tunnel might be safer. The natural disasters wouldn't touch us."

Darin examined the base of the hole. "Seems like a death trap to me. Even if you reached the bottom safely, you might end up just crawling around, not knowing where you are." He kicked at a cooled bit of lava rock that had reached the edge and dripped into the hole.

"It's worth a look," Matt persisted.

"Can you see the bottom? I sure can't." Cody peered down the hole.

They stood a moment longer. The breeze blowing up from the shaft stopped, and the grasses alongside the open abyss went still again. Matt looked at Darin and Cody and then up at the sky, wondering if some terrible new weather disaster was about to be sprung upon them. But the sound of gears grinding didn't come. For now, they were safe.

A moment passed, and Cody said, "Well, we better be getting back to the others and fixing up everyone's burns." He and Darin headed back the way they'd come.

We all agreed that we would go to the mountain. Everyone is injured. This could be a better and safer way, Matt thought.

He took a step after them but stopped. "Wait, we can't give up on this opportunity. I think it's still worth checking out."

"How?" Darin argued with gruffness. He held his fist up and whistled as he slammed it into the palm of his other hand, simulating Matt falling down the long shaft. "Splat."

"If I can find a safe way to get down there, can we check it out?" Matt propositioned. It felt like he was asking an older brother to take him to the movies or something.

Darin nodded with a chuckle. "Okay, I give. If you can find a safe way in there, I'll help you. But there isn't a safe way in. Done deal."

"Do you promise that *if* there is a way, though?" Matt asked. He didn't have an older brother, but he still felt like he had to negotiate with Darin and get his permission.

"I promise." Darin put his hands up in surrender.

"Good, 'cause I saw some rope back at one of those cabins before the snowstorm hit. I'll go find it, and we can go down and check out my theory."

Darin frowned as he peered into the abyss. "Better be a helluva long rope."

"I'll hurry. I know right where I saw it." Matt ignored his warning—even though his Scouts training told him Darin was right about the length of rope.

"I'll help," Cody said.

Matt and Cody raced across to where one of the cabins had been knocked down but now stood up again. He didn't want to think about how that had happened. It was too . . . crazy. Maybe the avalanche had only made it look like they had fallen over, and it had been an illusion because of the cold. But then, the lodge had fallen over and killed Nathan and was back up again. No, something didn't add up about old Camp New Beginnings. He shook the thought out of his mind. It was an apocalypse, after all. Nothing seemed right during an apocalypse.

Matt found the rope lying coiled in a heap beside a ramshackle shed. "Found it!"

Cody slapped his thigh. "Giddy-up."

Matt snapped the dirty old rope taut to check its strength. Dust and rope fibers floated up in front of his face. He shrugged. "Seems good to me."

"Let me help ya," Cody said as he picked up the dragging portion.

They rushed back to where they had left Darin beside the hole.

"We found a rope," Matt said.

"Good for us," Darin said. "One step closer to dying."

Matt and Cody piled the rope next to the hole.

"Let's go!" Darin chided. "Let's get the others."

"We're coming," Cody said.

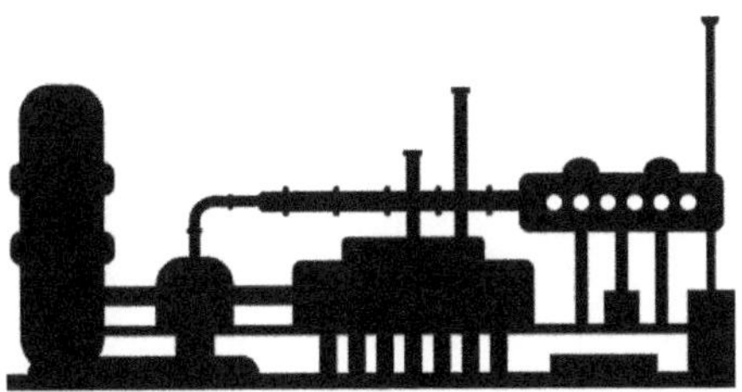

CHAPTER 3

"Where have you guys been?" Stacy asked as Matt and Darin came through the door.

"Didn't Catherine tell you?" Matt asked.

"She did, but I want to hear it from you guys. Is the weather getting crazy again out there?" she asked, brightening as Darin produced a first-aid kit and sat down next to her.

"No, it's actually pretty nice, you know, for the apocalypse," Matt said.

"Yo, chief, what'd you find for us?" Justin asked, wiping the sleep from his eyes.

Matt tossed him a first-aid kit. "Something to take care of everyone's burns a little better. Let's get everyone patched up, and then I've got something cool to show you guys."

"Somethin' cool." Cody nodded.

"It isn't cool. It's a hole." Darin rolled his eyes.

"A hole?" Justin asked.

"A hole?" Stacy repeated.

"A hole," Catherine said.

Darin, Justin, and Cody laughed.

"A-hole finds a hole," Justin said with a laugh.

Matt shook his head, trying to regain his composure. Why couldn't they see the importance of his discovery? "Look, guys, we should check this out. Darin has already promised he would help."

"Lance-Darin?" Stacy questioned, as if she were a disapproving mother.

"He wants to slide down a rope and look around. We'll all just help pull him back up." Darin smiled. "Now, let's take a look at your foot."

"Sounds dangerous," Catherine said.

Matt huffed and raised his voice a little. "It's worth it, and it'll just be me going in."

"We can't afford to lose anyone." She frowned.

"I think it's worth the risk," Cody said. "Could be a shortcut or something."

Darin broke in, "If the rope is long enough, he'll be fine. We can just pull him back up."

"Let me help you," Catherine said as Darin began undoing the old bandage on Stacy's foot.

Stacy gritted her teeth and squeezed Darin's hand until his knuckles turned white. Catherine gingerly applied salve and eased Stacy's foot into an extra-large sock and new shoe. Darin covered the shoe with a thick garbage bag and duct-taped it around her pants leg at her calf to keep it dry.

"We'll have to check your foot again tonight, put more salve on it, and change the sock." Catherine smiled at Stacy.

Matt applied ointment to Justin's burns that he couldn't reach himself. They looked worse than they had last night, but he held his cool better than Stacy had, only flinching a little at the salve application.

"It tickles," he said as Matt paused in applying the cream.

"Dude, I don't ever want to tickle another dude," Matt said. "Don't tell me that."

"Can I smear some of that on my shoulder?" Catherine reached for the jar.

Matt handed it to her. "Let me help you."

She slowly smiled, then nodded. She held his gaze a few seconds longer. Matt's heart quickened, and he smiled back.

He gingerly applied salve as he stared at her new hairdo. "It looks punk, but I like it."

Catherine flopped her head side to side, her hair swishing around her face. "Rock on! I never would have done anything this wild back in the old days. My parents would have freaked."

"Mine too," Matt said softly.

Everyone grew quiet, remembering their families and their loved ones.

"You look radical, like a member of The Clash or something!" Matt said, trying to turn things around before everyone broke down in tears. "We should all go."

The group followed Matt out of the Sev.

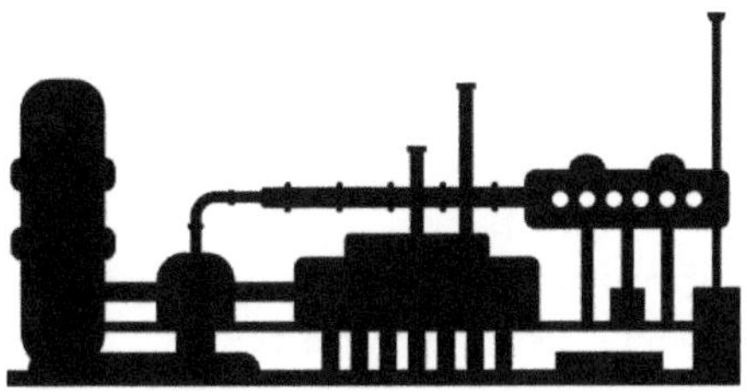

CHAPTER 4

At the edge of the big hole, they all glanced down into the dark.

"What did you find, chief?" Justin asked.

"Looks like we done found a basement in the woods," Cody said.

"This is, like, how horror movies start," Stacy added. "And I'm still stuck on your last name, Matt *Voorhees*."

Justin chortled. "We're already in a horror movie."

"What happened here?" Catherine gestured at the chasm.

"Darin's belt bomb," Matt said.

"Westbrook's, not mine," Darin broke in with a huff.

Matt nodded. "Right, Dr. Westbrook's bomb blasted a hole through . . . whatever."

"Maybe it's part of another base? Like maybe there's a C-85 or something," Catherine said as she leaned forward.

Matt grabbed onto her good shoulder to make sure she didn't lean too far in.

"This looks really dangerous, Matt," she said.

"It'll be all right," he said, guiding her back away from the edge and showing her his rope.

"I can't see the bottom, chief," Justin said. "Maybe this isn't such a good idea."

"That's what I said." Darin waved his hands.

Matt wrapped the end of the rope around the small steps of the cabin nearby.

"How are you even going to be able to tell if it reaches the bottom?" Catherine bit her lip, her eyebrows meeting to form a concerned V.

Matt gave her a friendly smile, doing his best Han Solo impression. "Trust me."

Catherine frowned.

"It'll be safe," he continued. "I want to get to the mountain and find our parents as much as anyone, but there's something down here that could get us out of all the weather. It could be safer."

"So how can you even test it?" Catherine asked.

"Simple." Matt took the end of the rope and hunted for a moment along the ground. When he found a good-sized quartz rock from the old Camp New Beginnings path, he wrapped it in a basket knot at the end of the rope. "I learned this in Scouts."

"A weighted end?" Catherine asked.

"If this touches bottom, we'll know the rope reaches the bottom safely," Cody said as Matt tossed the rope-knotted rock into the pit. The rope was pulled violently into the shaft, driven by the weight. The rough material slid through Matt's palms, threatening to chew them raw. He wished he had gloves. Just as he thought his hands would burst into flames, the clang of stone hitting metal sounded far below.

"How long is that rope?" Justin asked, looking at what was left of it coiled behind Matt.

"Almost two hundred feet," Cody replied. "I ain't never swung down anything that long before."

"I haven't either," Matt said, as he pulled the rope back up, "and without rappelling gear, this will be tricky. But I've got you guys to help me."

The end of the rope, minus the rock, plopped over the edge onto the ground next to the hole.

"Hey, where did your rock go?" Stacy asked.

"I think it broke when it hit bottom and came out of my knot," Matt said.

Justin shook his head. "What if it fell out of your knot, and you only thought it reached the bottom?"

"Don't worry about that. I'm positive it reached. I'll keep my feet cradled in the knot, and you guys lower me down and pull me back up."

"This will take everyone helping out except Stacy," Darin said with finality.

Catherine looked at Stacy, who only gave her a coy cock of the head.

Stacy brushed Darin's arm with her fingers and mouthed, "Thank you."

"Found these in the Sev." Cody shrugged, holding out a pair of walkie-talkies.

"Better hold onto this in case we can't hear you very good down there." Darin handed one of them to Matt.

Matt inspected the eight-inch, black, brick-style walkie-talkie with two dials on the face. He and his best friend, Jed, used to play with them when they would dress up in camo gear. He clipped it to his belt opposite the hand-crank flashlight and nodded his thanks.

"You mean we aren't just going to go with one tug on the rope means 'lower me down,' and twenty-two tugs means 'I have to make a pit stop,' and sixty-six tugs means 'pull me up now'?" Justin taunted.

Catherine scowled at him as he chuckled at his own joke.

Matt ignored him and prepared to be lowered into the hole, keeping one foot in his knot-basket and the other leg free to kick himself off from the torn-open sides of the pit.

"Hey, Stacy, you be in charge of talking to Matt." Darin handed her the other walkie-talkie.

For at least six feet, there was exposed dirt and rocks with a healthy section of roots splayed at the edges of the hole. "Okay," Matt said to himself. "A good old dirt hole so far." A bit of dirt and dust trickled down beside him as he gingerly descended. A jagged patch of dried lava reminded him of last night's devastation.

"Real easy on this first part," Matt said. "Just exposed ground from the bomb blast." He looked up. "Something changed. The dirt's gone."

His stomach rolled nervously. Had this been the right idea? Was it as safe as he'd assured the others? Was there really anything to be learned from this basement in the woods?

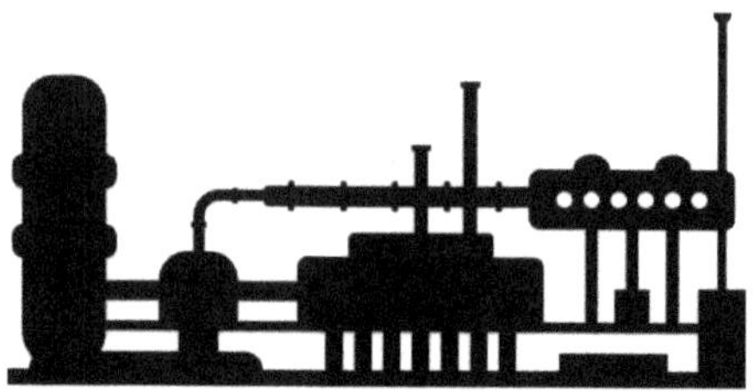

CHAPTER 5

Surrounded by the darkness of the pit, Matt looked up toward his friends and clicked on the walkie. "Hey, what's happening up there?"

"He's confused. He needs help. Pull him out!" Stacy said.

Matt yelled, "No! No, I'm fine. Everything's okay."

Darin leaned over the hole, looked Matt in the eye, and shook his head. "Keep lowering him down. He's fine."

Bits of dirt and vegetation debris rained down on Matt. Some of it fell past his collar into his shirt. He shivered.

Once he reached about twenty feet down, Matt pushed the button on the walkie-talkie. "Breaker one-nine, breaker one-nine, this here is the Rubber Duck. What's happening topside? Over."

"I love *Smoky and the Bandit*," Stacy answered. "Over."

"I'm talking about *Convoy*," Matt corrected.

"Oh yeah, I knew that," she said with a giggle. "'Eastbound and down, loaded up and trucking.' Over."

"That's still *Smoky and the Bandit*, but what I want to know is what is the weather like up there? I'm asking because I'm starting to hear something down here like gears moving and machines. Maybe fans starting up. I don't know."

"You've got to say 'over.' Over," Stacy reminded him.

"Over, Stacy, what is the weather like up there? Over."

"It's nice still. Did you find anything? Over."

"Not yet, have them keep sending me down."

Matt slid farther down, keeping one leg free to kick away from the edge. But after another slow twenty feet, his other leg grew restless, so he had his friends stop lowering him while he carefully switched his legs to keep the stationary one from going to sleep.

The clanking of machines grew louder, and a sudden blast of wind from below sent Matt crashing into the side wall. His cheek pressed against cool metal, and his heart raced with the thought of now being slammed into the other side by the buffeting wind.

"Are you okay, Matt? Over." Stacy's voice crackled through the walkie-talkie.

"I'm doing okay," Matt said. "Just a blast of wind or something. It kinda scared me for a second, and I hit the wall."

"Yeah, it startled us too. Over," Stacy said.

"Darin here. Did you say you hit the bottom?"

"No, I hit the side wall of the shaft."

"You guys need to be saying 'over,'" Stacy reminded them.

Matt shook his head at Stacy's observance of walkie-talkie protocol during an apocalypse. His heart leapt once more as his foot touched down on metal. He took the flashlight and cranked the knob a few times to get some light.

He hadn't reached the bottom, but rested on top of a thick chunk of grate, barring him from going down farther.

The rope went slack, as he was now fully standing on top of thick, crisscrossed metal bars.

"Hold on a minute. Over," he said.

"What happened?" Darin asked. "Did you find the bottom right after you said you didn't?"

"Not quite, hang on," Matt replied.

"Over," Stacy chirped.

The flashlight needed to be continually pumped, or the light faded quickly. He aimed the weak beam of light downward. A wide chunk of the grating had been eaten away by the lava from the night before. It was black and caked in the corner, but there was a big hole in the grating that he could continue down if he squeezed.

"I can keep going down, but I'll have to move where I'm at a bit. You guys probably ought to rearrange where you're lowering me from, too. It's a tight squeeze." He paused a moment before adding, "Over."

"Hold on." Darin's voice crackled through the walkie-talkie. "Are you saying the hole got smaller, and you want to keep going? I think that's a bad idea, dude. Too dangerous."

"No, the hole didn't get smaller. There's a grating over the shaft, but lava ate away at a section, and I can get through and keep going. It's all right."

"So you want to keep going down into a hole where you have to worm through a spot that lava opened up?"

"Yeah, it reminds me of the sarlacc pit that Boba Fett went into," Matt said.

"Boba Fett died in the sarlacc pit, chief," Justin said into the walkie-talkie.

"No, he didn't. In the comic, he climbed back out," Matt argued.

"Dude, I never saw *Jedi*, but climbing into a monster pit is not a good argument, no matter how you put it," Darin said.

"I read that issue," Cody said. "He went back into the sarlacc pit while fighting Han Solo, driving the Jawas' sand crawler. I think he died that second time."

"Okay. Bad analogy," Matt answered. "Over?" He angrily depressed the handle on the flashlight to keep looking around.

"We're gonna pull you up," Darin said. "This is way too dangerous."

"No, hang on." Matt stomped his foot in anger, and the grating beneath his feet fell away into the abyss. His stomach lurched, and he choked back a startled scream as he dropped about five feet before the rope went taut, holding him firm. The flashlight tumbled away in the dark, the light fading as the charge wore out as it followed the grating. The chunk of metal struck something below, the booming crash echoing through the darkness, followed by the crack of the flashlight breaking as it hit the ground. Disturbingly similar to what he imagined his bones breaking would sound like.

"What was that? Matt?!" Darin shouted into the walkie-talkie.

"I'm all right, just got seriously spooked. The grating fell to the bottom. I won't have to squeeze around it now."

"But you're okay?"

"Yeah, just about soiled my pants, but I'm all right."

"We'll bring you up."

"No. I really think I need to see what's at the bottom. There's something down there that the grate hit. Sounded like metal. It's only about another fifty feet. I'm just past halfway, I think. Let's finish this."

There was a long pause as the people at the top must have been discussing what to do.

"Cody says he's worried the rope is getting frayed, but if you really think this is something we should check out, I lost the vote," Darin said.

"Yes, I want to get to the bottom and investigate, so long as the weather above is holding out."

Darin sighed. "It's as nice as it's ever been, so yeah, but let's be quick about this, huh?"

"Agreed. Over," Matt said.

They gradually lowered him farther into the dark. He swung back and forth ever so slightly, like a pendulum.

The light from above was like a vague, square-shaped moon overhead. It gave light, but not enough to really see anything below. He found himself looking up toward it, then being blinded once he looked back down into the gloom.

His free foot traced along the slick edge of the metal shaft. Then it pressed against nothing but air.

Was he out of the abyss and into the antechamber below? He reminded himself to not look up at the opening so as not to become night-blind again.

"Hold up a minute. Let me see where I'm at. Over," Matt said into the walkie-talkie

"Thanks," Stacy said. "Over."

His eyes had to be playing tricks on him. Shadows coalesced out of the darkness. Forms moved and took the shape of wheels within wheels as the grinding of machinery creaked far away. Lights blinked in the distance—first white and then, farther away, red. They flashed everywhere to his right and his left.

After a moment, he realized he could see well down there, the same as if it were a starry night at home.

"Guys, I think you all better get down here. Over."

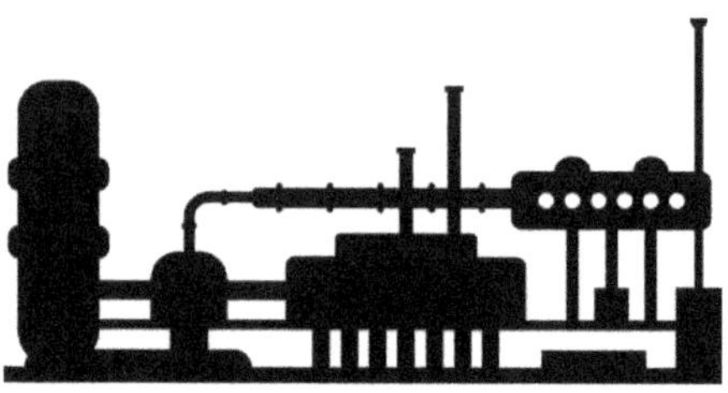

CHAPTER 6

In the eerie electric glow of the dim lights, Matt stared at enormous gears slowly turning like water wheels, flickering white lights off in the distance, blinking red lights on top of power boxes with coils of power cables stretching into infinity, pistons chugging up and down, and hydraulics pumping like heartbeats. "Everything is man-made," he said to himself.

He gazed in astonishment at the vastness of the place. "Guys, I think I'm in a building!" Matt yelled. He dangled and twirled slowly, eyes adjusting to the darker subfloor.

"Just like the Well of Souls where the Ark of the Covenant rested," Matt whispered to himself.

Not more than ten feet away was a catwalk and railing, the human highway for this place. If he swung hard enough, could he reach it and get a foothold?

"Catherine said she heard you shouting. Use the walkie-talkie," Darin reminded him. "Over."

Matt fumbled with the radio. "You guys need to see this. Get down here."

Darin's voice crackled over the walkie-talkie. "Why on earth should we do that?"

"Simple. This bunker is massive. I'm talking it has to be city blocks big. I can't see the end of it."

"Come again? Over?"

"You guys need to get down here and take a look at all of this. It's a whole big complex that stretches on and on. I'm seeing big gears and machines, cables and pumps, and electrical conduits. This is so big. It makes sense why nothing up on top is normal. There's something going on down here. Like maybe the underground vaults are way bigger than we thought."

"They are big," Darin answered, "but not as big as you're saying. Trust me."

"Trust *me* and come down here and see for yourself. I think there are machines down here running the weather and stuff up there. All of you need to come down and see it, now!" Matt snapped. "This is so crazy! Just like out of a sci-fi movie. Listen, I think these machines are running everything up there. I really think it'll be better down here. No natural disasters could touch us." It was unbelievable. The catwalk stretched on as far as he could see in either direction. Massive gears and pulleys groaned in the distance as cables and light fixtures sparked dully.

"Going down a rope is one thing. What about coming back up?" Darin asked.

"This place is so big, there have to be multiple exits farther down. Heck, maybe it even connects to the cryovault."

"No way," Darin broke in. "That's gotta be way too far."

"You guys have got to see this place. It's probably safer traveling down here than up there anyway. It's so big. This air vent is not the entrance. There must be lots of doors somewhere else."

"We'll put it to a vote," Darin said. "Give us a minute."

Matt waited in the dark. The flickering lights played with his senses. In another time and place, they might have been fireflies at night or the dim red light of someone's boom box playing music at a block party. But no, he was inside the vast dominion of a machine, something man-made and secret. A government bunker of sorts to protect mankind during the worst thing to hit the planet since the dinosaurs were annihilated.

Darin broke the silence with his walkie-talkie response. "It makes sense with an air vent that big that there must be a huge complex down there. I never saw anything like that when I was with Westbrook, but there are plenty of places he didn't let me go and see. It seems like it should tie into the Sev, but everyone here is excited to go and see it, so we'll come down."

"I think we're finally going to get some answers," Matt said.

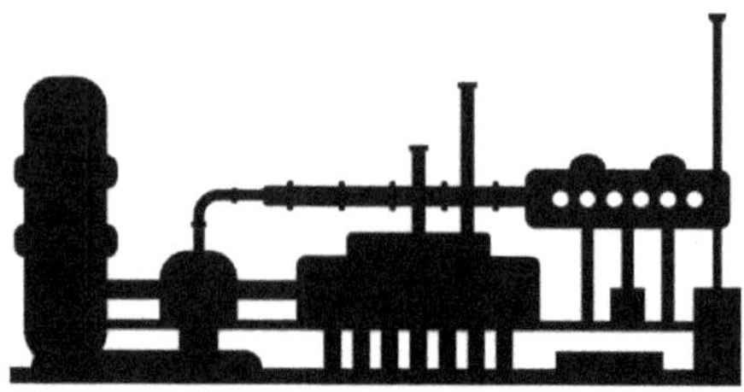

CHAPTER 7

They eased Matt down another foot. He reached for the catwalk but couldn't quite get a hold. He said into the walkie-talkie, "Let me get my footing on the causeway and then you guys will have an easier time coming down after me. I'm going to need to swing a bit, back and forth, to reach it. Over."

"Copy that," Darin said.

"Be careful. Over," Stacy said.

Matt swung in the cradle with his free leg. It reminded him of using a regular swing, except now he only used one leg to pump back and forth to get momentum to move him closer and closer to the catwalk.

As his swing widened, he noted that the rope would occasionally pinch above him as it hit the corner where the shaft met the ceiling. It wouldn't stop him from swinging and reaching his goal, but it did make things a little harder. He had to pump extra hard to keep the momentum going.

"We're holding on to you really good," Darin said through the walkie-talkie.

Matt appreciated that but couldn't respond as he worked his leg back and forth. He was so close, but the walkway remained just out of reach. Another foot and he could grasp it with his free hand.

Almost making it was more demoralizing than realizing he could never make it at all. He had to work at keeping the swing going because the rope rubbing on the corner above was stealing his pendulum power. Finally, he concluded he could not reach the elevated steel path from this position. He got back on the walkie-talkie. "New plan, guys."

"Pull you back up?" Darin asked.

"No, maybe lower me another five feet. I need just a little more slack to reach it, since the rope keeps hitting the ceiling corner where the antechamber and the shaft meet."

"So down just another five feet?"

"Yeah, I think that will do it. Over."

"Roger that," Darin said.

Matt heard Justin in the background while the button was still depressed. "Ask him if he ever saw the movie *C.H.U.D.* and if he sees any down there?"

"What is a Chud?" Darin asked.

Then there was silence again as they left Matt to attempt his stunt.

Matt had seen *C.H.U.D.* but didn't want to think about any cannibalistic humanoid underground dwellers right now. He had to concentrate on grabbing the edge of the suspended walkway. And as he reached for the cold metal rail, it didn't help to think that a green-faced monster-man might try to sink blood-stained teeth into the back of his hand.

He swung back and forth, now able to pump his leg easier. But with more length, he now had to reach up above his head to grasp the iron railing.

He strained and caught the lowest rung of the causeway's safety rail with his right hand and held on for all he was worth. He struggled to grasp the walkie-talkie with his left hand and depress the button to talk. "Hey, guys, I've got it, but need you to pull me up a little so I can climb up. Over."

"Understood. Over," Stacy said. "Guys, pull him up a few feet."

Matt expected them to pull the rope a couple of feet. Instead, they yanked him up six feet. He flew end over end, and his foot came loose of the knot.

He fell, gravity pulling him down, the rope out of reach.

"Ah!" Matt screamed.

He flailed his arms, but there was nothing to grab on to. The walkway he had struggled so hard to get to became his lifeline as his hand made contact with the metal handrail just as his body slammed into the side of the suspended path.

"Are you okay?" Darin shouted into the walkie-talkie. "We just pulled a little, and all your weight is gone! Are you all right? Matt. Matt. Matt!"

Catherine's garbled shouts came from far above. "Matt! Are you okay? Did you fall?"

Matt couldn't depress the button to respond. The walkie-talkie was the last thing on his mind as he threw all his energy into holding on to the causeway. The whole thing swayed as he pulled up and threw a leg over the handrail. Had the floods, avalanches, and volcanic eruptions destroyed its stability?

Scratchy voices continued spouting from the walkie-talkie in a chaotic cacophony as the others argued over what to do.

Matt got his foot over the side, then struggled to move his entire body to the cold metal floor. He took a deep breath, fully realizing how close he had come to death, then grasped the walkie-talkie. "I made it, guys."

"You're all right?" Catherine asked.

"Yes, just catching my breath. Give me a minute to find something to snag the rope with, and I'll secure it for you guys to come down."

"Are you sure that's a good idea, Matt?" Stacy questioned.

Glancing down the catwalk, he found a spare piece of a crossbeam from a pile of scaffolding. It was awkward, but he slung it over the edge of the causeway, reached the dangling rope, and let it slide down the piece of scaffolding into his waiting hands.

Back on the walkie-talkie, Matt said, "All right, guys, you're good to go. Come on down."

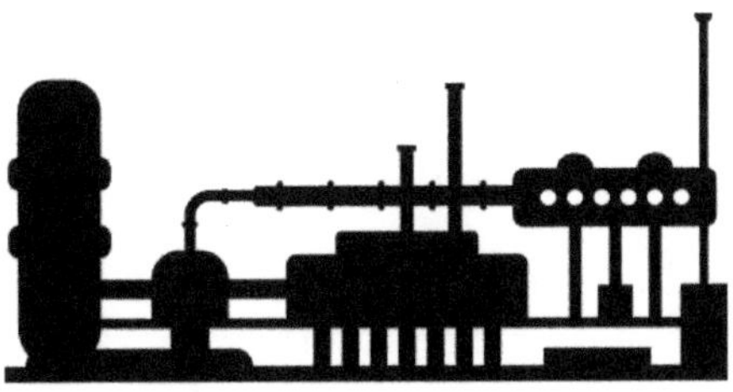

CHAPTER 8

"Can you see any better down there now?" Darin asked.

"Yeah, it's like a big subbasement, maybe ten stories down."

"Okay," Darin said over the walkie-talkie.

"I think I *am* in a building!" Matt exclaimed. "You gotta come see this. That means this is so big, we can go all the way to the mountain. There's a tram track next to the catwalk I'm on. I think we can take that. I've tied the rope onto the edge of the metal railing. So as long as you guys go slow and easy, you can get right to where I am, no sweat."

There was a pause, and then Darin answered back, "All right, we all agreed that it may be the best way to go. Less natural disasters. More protected, if you know what I mean. No more obstacles to survive. It might be a lot better to go to the mountain from down there."

Matt clapped his hands together. He truly believed they would have a much better chance walking down in a creepy industrial basement than out there in the crazy apocalyptic weather. "Great, who's coming down first?"

"Stacy is. Cody has rigged up a harness to help us get down. We'll all help ease each other down, and I'll go last since I can just climb down myself," Darin said.

"All right, let her rip," Matt responded as he got ready to help Stacy once she reached the railing.

It took longer than he expected, but it was a lot to ask of people who had never done anything like this before. How many other teens had slid down a rope, hundreds of feet, into a dark pit inside what must be a gigantic underground bunker?

The rope jerked a little as Stacy was eased down, her legs clasped about it and her arms held in a harness.

"This does not feel good. My arms are gonna get pulled from the sockets. Am I almost there, Matt?"

"Yes. Almost. Just a few more feet, then you need to let go of the rope with your shoes and touch down on the top of the railing. I've got you."

"Okay," she said reluctantly.

She started to move one leg from the rope, then hesitated, squeezing her eyes shut and clamping her legs tighter around the lifeline.

"Let me help you." Matt took a gentle hold of Stacy's uninjured foot and guided it to the railing. "Now you're touching the catwalk. I've got you; you can climb on down now."

She gingerly reached out and put her hands on his shoulders as he eased her down. As soon as she stood solidly on the catwalk, balancing most of her weight on her unburned foot, she pulled her arms out of the harness and exhaled a big breath of air. "That wasn't so bad—for a horror movie."

Matt got back on the walkie-talkie. "Stacy is down, and we're good. Go ahead and have Catherine come down."

The rope harness disappeared back up the hole. They took turns, and soon enough, both Catherine and Justin had made it. Matt continued to help each person down as the others moved along the catwalk a short distance to take in the bizarre imagery of the underground facility.

"Which way should we go?" Justin asked.

"To the left." Stacy stood facing him and Catherine.

"Which left?" Justin asked. "Ours or yours?"

"It's always the left of the person who said it," Catherine said.

"But she pointed right!"

"That's what I said!" Stacy exclaimed.

Cody descended next, hand over hand, nice and quick. He still had the harness over his arms, but he made the journey on his own power with Darin holding the rope above as insurance.

"Whew! Now that was a whole rodeo in and of itself," Cody said as he reached the catwalk and jumped down. He took off the harness and tugged on the rope so Darin would know to pull it back up the shaft.

"You gonna be all right coming down on your own?" Matt asked Darin over the walkie-talkie.

"I'll be fine. I'll come down just like Cody did. Just gotta reconfigure this rope. I've got an idea on how to keep it."

"Keep it?" Matt asked.

"Yeah, I think if I loop it around the cabin's front posts, and you keep your end tied to the railing, I'll tie this end around me, take up all the slack, and lower myself down," Darin explained.

Matt agreed. "Then we can pull it to us. Like top-roping. Yeah. I learned that in Scouts. The rope would be great to have."

"Good thing you got a long rope," Darin said. "I'm reattaching it to the cabin, and I should be able to start sliding down here shortly."

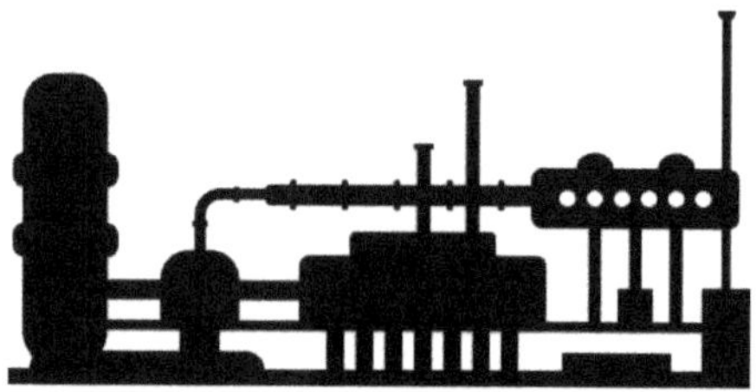

CHAPTER 9

Darin began his journey down the shaft with a joke over the walkie-talkie. "Hey, you guys!"

"Be careful!" Catherine cautioned.

The rope whipped back and forth as Darin made his way down, shouting, "Ruth! Ruth! Baby! Ruth!"

Catherine furrowed her brow. "Is he making *Goonies* references? Someone already used that a few days ago."

Matt shrugged. "Yeah, he hasn't seen as many movies as us. I think he's trying to fit in a little more."

"Stop messing around, and just get down here," Stacy shouted.

"I'm coming," Darin shouted back, no longer worrying about using the walkie-talkie. "I've just got to—"

Darin's legs slipped from around the rope, dumping all of his weight onto his hands as they gripped it. Sliding fast, his feet hit the metal railing, snapping the bars and sending him flying into the abyss.

Matt and Cody lunged, grabbing his arms and shirt to pull him up over the broken railing. Catherine took hold of the back of his pants to help hoist him over.

"We've got you!" Matt gasped as they yanked him back to the causeway. They all sighed in unison, relief evident on their faces.

"Are you hurt?" Catherine asked.

Darin shook his hands. "My hands." He opened and closed them, examining the raw palms.

"Did we bring Stacy's burn cream?" Matt asked.

"I did." Darin gestured to his backpack. "It's back there."

Catherine reached into his pack and pulled out the burn cream.

After applying it to Darin's hands, she gingerly wrapped them with gauze and athletic tape. "You're good to go. Kinda."

"I'll say. I won't be climbing back up that thing anytime soon." Darin squinted up at the rope.

"Well," Catherine said, "if we have to go back that way, we'll all pull you up like you let us down."

"I—I'm sorry. I didn't mean to let you down," Darin said.

"You know what I mean." She rolled her eyes.

Darin smiled.

Cody changed the subject. "You know, guys, this dang walkway is as rickety as the axle on my grandpa's tractor."

Matt grimaced. "Yeah. Let's get going. Get off of this section. A chunk of grating hit the whole thing when I came down too."

"Which way should we go?" Cody asked.

"I think east," Matt said.

"How can you know which way is east, chief?" Justin taunted.

Matt pointed to the catwalk. Spray painted in faint yellow paint were two arrows, followed by the word "east," with the letters stacked the length of the walkway.

Justin smiled. "Okay, smart-ass. I didn't see that."

Matt clapped Justin on the back. "It's okay, buddy."

"All right," Darin said. "Let's go that way. Bring the rope."

"Good idea," Cody chimed in.

Matt pulled the rope until all of it came tumbling down. He coiled it up and slung it over his shoulder.

"You ready to go, camp counselor?" Justin patted Darin on the shoulder.

Darin nodded, his lips drawn tight against his teeth as he clenched his bandaged hands.

They walked along the catwalk a quarter-mile, taking in the surreal metallic jungle. Every fifty yards or so was a cage-covered sconce or a pendulum light that seemed to flicker at inopportune times, so they would just hold the railing as their guide to the next flickering bulb. Just to the side of the railing and walkway, there were stiff cables bolted into the ceiling. Tubes of gurgling water big enough to be a waterslide wound through scaffolding. Rusted ductwork blew air down on them. They were in an industrialized maze.

"That must've been one big rooster to lay an egg that big." Cody pointed to a curious, rounded dome in the ceiling ahead.

Large glass bulbs, as big as a small house, hung down like clear eggs, containing dark soil and the curling roots of trees that poked through the subfloor above. Beyond, huge rock pillars with man-sized pipes bolted to them stood like sentinels every few hundred feet, holding up the roof of the underground base.

Justin's eyes bulged. "What the what? The forest floor is the ceiling!"

Cody whistled. "This is way bigger than I thought."

"What is this place?" Stacy asked.

"We are definitely not in Kansas anymore," Matt said.

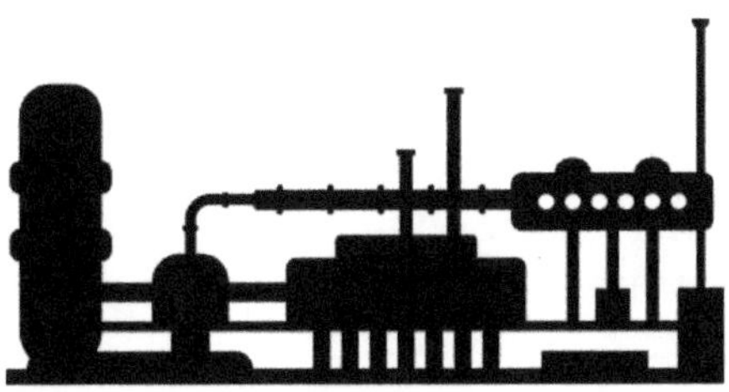

CHAPTER 10

"It looks like there's another, even bigger bulb up ahead," Cody said.

They moved a little faster, anxious to see what this unreal example of the underground world could be.

"That's not another tree in a pot." Darin pointed. "Look, it's like a sink basin, except we're seeing it from below. It's the lake!"

It, too, was made of clear glass or plastic. The higher shore had mud and rocks, but there were several spots without mud or sand where light shone through, as if the bottom was a dirty pool.

"It's all fake," Catherine gasped. "Nothing is real! Everything we thought about this world is man-made."

"Darin?" Matt questioned.

Darin narrowed his eyes, whispering, "I didn't know anything about this. I thought we were in the real world as much as you guys."

"What haven't you told me?" Matt pressed.

Stacy, standing beside Darin, stuck her tongue out at Matt.

Cody changed the subject. "There must be millions of yards of dirt above us to make a false forest."

"False everything," Catherine said bitterly.

"But how? Why?" Justin asked.

"*Why* is the best question." Darin craned his head around the incredibly huge perimeter beneath the lake.

Matt pointed at the collection of massive gears, huge tubes, and vents in the ceiling above them. "This reminds me of when my parents took us to the Universal Studios backlot tour. There were different movie scene places made to create atmosphere. Like we would go into a small South American city, and a flash flood would come racing toward the tour bus, but since it was fake, it never hit us. Then there was a subway area that simulated an earthquake, and a big fuel semitruck almost hits you, and the road collapses from above, and the fuel tanker slides toward you, and there's fire and water. But then everything resets."

"The tour has Jaws too, chief, so what?" Justin taunted.

"What I'm saying," Matt persisted, "is that this all reminds me of that. If everything here is a soundstage like for a movie, maybe that's how the cabins and trees reset after the avalanche. And how the water drained so quickly after the flood."

"It's not just a simulation, though. Our friends have died!" Catherine shouted, falling to her knees.

Stacy moved to help her up, but Catherine uncharacteristically pushed her away amidst sobs. "But why?" she cried. "Who is torturing us like this?!"

"I'd say Westbrook, but he's dead," Darin muttered.

"This has got to be bigger than just Westbrook," Matt said. "But if we keep going, we should find some answers." He leaned down and helped Catherine up, put his arms around her, and let her sob into his shoulder. "We'll get out of this, somehow."

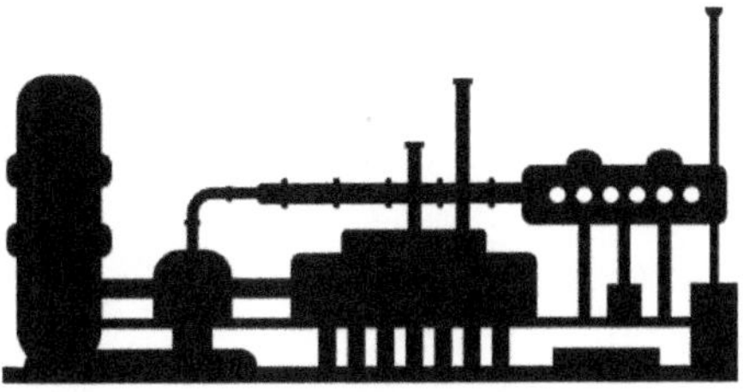

CHAPTER 11

The gloom of the humongous chamber was cast into further darkness as some of the dim light from the exposed sections of the lake basin above swirled and vanished.

"I think it's storming up there," Justin said. "Raining maybe."

"Or a hurricane," Stacy offered.

"Doubt that," Cody said.

"We're safe down here, for now," Darin assured her.

Catherine scowled. "It's all fake. Why would anyone do this to us?"

They watched the lake above cascade between bouts of moving water and glints of light from the surface.

Cody coughed, breaking the silence. "Matt, you said this is bigger than Westbrook. How can we know that?"

Matt held his hands out, gesturing to the massive volume of the underground facility. "Look at all this. Westbrook sure didn't do it by himself. He couldn't have. Plus, there was the apocalypse that had the government rallying to get people from everywhere cryogenically frozen to survive it all. This is so big, it had to have been built by hundreds, maybe thousands, of people, which took time and money."

"Lots of time," Darin said.

"Years and years." Justin nodded.

"How much money?" Stacy asked.

"Tons," Justin answered.

"So," Matt continued, "there have to be answers somewhere, and we have to find them."

"More than that." Catherine wiped at her tear-moistened face.

"All the crazy weather that's killed our friends, some of it must have come from inside here. Maybe there's an on and off switch."

Darin opened his mouth as if to speak, but then shut it and looked down at his feet.

"What is it, Darin?" Matt asked.

Darin shook his head. "I thought I might know something, but I really don't."

"Well, what are your thoughts? Since you knew Westbrook and the cryovault better than any of us ever will," Matt prodded.

Darin put his hand on his forehead, as if he could wipe away a memory, but came away just shaking his head again. "I really don't know. I thought I had an idea, but I lost it."

"Oh, Lance-Darin." Stacy ran her hands over his shoulders affectionately.

"I like the idea of there being an on and off switch," Matt said. "These are all machines running and creating a false world above. There must be a control room."

"And if there's a control room, there must be some answers!" Justin insisted. "I like where this is going, chief. Time for some payback!"

"There is no payback!" Catherine argued. "We just need to get out of here and find our families."

Matt stood between the two of them. "You're both right. We are going to get to the bottom of this mystery, find our parents, and hopefully get some justice."

"Where do we even start?" Stacy asked.

Cody looked up and down the causeway. "Well, we know what was back that way a good half mile or more. I say we see what farther down the line this way holds."

"I agree," Matt said. "I'm pretty sure this is taking us back the way we came in the truck when we all woke up. To the east."

"East? Are you sure?" Catherine asked.

"I sure think so. Besides, we're even deeper than the Sev here, so it makes sense that this might connect all the way to the mountain."

"Or it might not," Darin said. "I never saw anything like this back where I was with Westbrook. And we have no way of knowing for sure which way is east. Everything can get real mixed up down in a cave like this."

"But that doesn't mean it doesn't connect, either," Matt said.

"How can you know, Matt?" Catherine asked.

"I just have a good sense of direction."

"I trust you, Matt," Cody said.

"That's a big gamble," Justin said.

Matt closed his eyes and ran his hand over his short hair. "Every choice we have left is a gamble. This one seems safer than outside. I think if they built a warehouse in a cave, then the cave could be man-made as well. Just like this entire place we're seeing from a new perspective. We've already made the decision, so we need to carry on and go to the mountain."

"You're right," Darin relented. "I'm just not sure we'll be happy with any possible revelations we get from this place."

"Revelations? Like from the Bible?" Stacy asked.

"It *is* the apocalypse," Cody added with a wry grin.

"Oh geez, not with the Bible stuff again, cowboy," Justin said.

Darin looked at Stacy and pulled her close, his head over her shoulder.

"All right, you win, chief. We go the way you think the mountain is. You've been right about things so far." Justin gave Matt a warm slap on the back. "I'm trusting you about the man-made mountain inside the building. I guess the cave within a mountain must be man-made too."

"Thanks," Matt said, thinking the slap on the back was just a tad too hard to be sincere.

They walked on, water dripping somewhere in the dark, and rusted metal creaking under their feet.

"How old does this place look to you?" Matt asked Darin.

"I have no idea."

"It looks really old to me, like ancient history," Stacy said. "Maybe forty years."

There were cracks in some of the concrete pillars, along with mildew or algae growing along spots where it looked like water had leaked from above. The causeway had more rust, and the groaning of the metal became louder with each step.

"This does not sound good," Catherine said.

"We should probably space ourselves out a—" Cody's words were lost as the entire section of catwalk they were on collapsed.

Screams and curses echoed in the vast darkness.

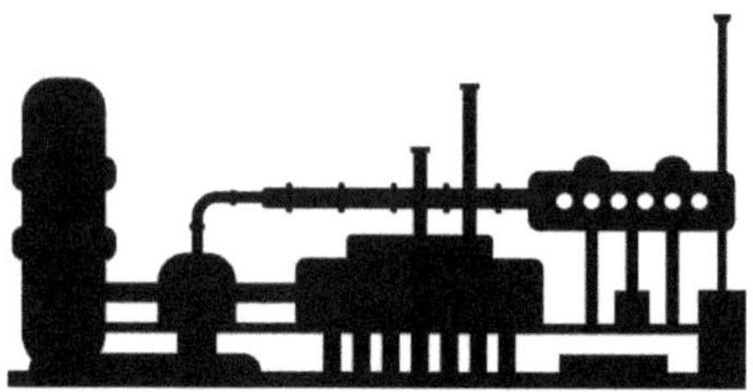

CHAPTER 12

The rusted catwalk slammed hard against another walkway below. Bodies spilled over the top of each other from the terrible impact, careening head over heels. Justin, Catherine, and Stacy flew forward into a rectangular hole. Stacy caught herself on the far edge and managed to avoid falling like the other two into yet another dark chamber.

Matt glanced at where the two had disappeared and rushed over to help. Darin sprang into action moments after him.

"What in the *Donkey Kong*?" Matt muttered.

"Are they . . ." Cody asked as he peered down into the hole.

"Is anyone hurt?" Matt asked.

"My heart about exploded," Stacy said. "But nothing is broken."

"Thanks to me," Justin grumbled. "What did we land in?"

Big metal gears with teeth the size of cars rose on either side of them.

"Catherine is looking dizzy. She might have hit her head. Get us out of here!" Justin shouted.

Matt slid the coiled rope from his shoulder.

"Hurry!"

"Stacy?" Darin asked.

"I'm all right, now that you're here. Help me get back over to that side with you," she said.

Darin stretched his arm out but wasn't even close to reaching Stacy on the far side of the hole. "I can't reach her." He glanced about for help.

"What about you, Darin?" Matt asked as he unwound the rope.

"Just some bumps and bruises," he answered.

"I bit my tongue," Cody said as he came forward to help. "But at least we landed on another walkway. Coulda been real bad if we hadn't."

"It will get real bad down here if you don't hurry up," Justin called.

As if responding to his warning, a motorized rumbling began in the distance.

"Something is starting up!" Justin cried.

With a slight jerk, the massive teeth of the gears vibrated. Catherine and Justin were trapped in a gear box between teeth that were about to move.

"Hold on!" Matt unwound another section of rope and tossed the end down. "Put this around you and Catherine, and we'll pull you up!"

"Not gonna work, chief. We'd be too heavy, and she's too out of it to hang on. I can't hold on to her and the rope."

"Then just you climb out!" Darin shouted amidst the growing cacophony of popping and buzzing as the machine continued to fire up. "We're running out of time!"

"I can't leave her!" Justin yelled.

Matt glanced about for what to do. Cody grabbed a broken section of railing and pulled on it. Matt guessed his intent and helped him yank on the rusted guard railing until it snapped from its housing.

Shaped almost like a piece of a ladder, they lowered it down to Justin, who caught the end and braced it against the top of a gear section. It was still a couple of feet short of the top, but if he stood on it, he could reach the others to climb out.

A loud hiss of steam blasted from a vent nearby.

"Hurry!" Stacy screamed.

Justin roused Catherine and guided her to the rickety, makeshift ladder. She seemed groggy, but followed his lead and climbed up the rungs one by one. When she got as high as she could, Matt and Darin reached down, took her by the wrists, and pulled her up.

A loud popping and a final snap indicated the gear was moving. The rickety, broken railing skittered as the gear moved beneath it. Justin raced up the rungs and caught the top of the box just as the gears forced the railing to drop between the teeth. The machinery chewed and pulled the twisted bit of metal until it vanished between the enormous gears like the final slurp through a straw. Justin launched himself up over the side, landing at the feet of the others.

He lay on the floor of the causeway, gulping in air. "I thought that was it," he panted.

"You're a good man," Cody said.

"Huh?"

"You saved Catherine." Matt extended a hand.

"Yeah," Justin said, getting to his feet. "Had to. We've only got each other now."

Matt nodded but said, "Our families are still out there. We'll find them."

They used another piece of railing to help Stacy cross over and reach the safety of the catwalk. She burrowed into Darin's chest, stifling her sobs. He wrapped his arms around her, holding her tight.

"Hand me a flashlight." Matt turned to Catherine. "Let me see your eyes."

"Why?" she asked.

"I want to see if you have a concussion."

"How can you tell?" She blinked as Matt shined the light in her face.

"Your pupils aren't different sizes, and they react to the light, so I think that means you don't have a concussion."

"Well, small miracles, I guess," she said.

"In this place, I'd call it a big miracle." Justin frowned.

"I think we can use this piece to get back up to our original catwalk." Cody ripped off another piece of railing and leaned it like a ladder up against the section above, across from where they'd been before it snapped.

"Like, what if it falls again?" Stacy asked.

"I think it was just this part that was worn through. The rest doesn't look nearly as rusted," Cody assured her.

"Let's try it out. We need to keep moving," Matt said.

Cody went first, then Matt and Justin.

"It seems solid enough," Matt said.

Catherine rubbed her forehead, still dazed. "I can make it. Just hold it steady please."

Darin held the bottom firmly, and she climbed up, assisted by Matt when she neared the top.

Finally, Darin held it for Stacy, who went up with only minor difficulty due to her injured foot. Then Darin ascended, and they were ready to continue on their path.

"From now on, we'd better look at our feet as often as around us," he said.

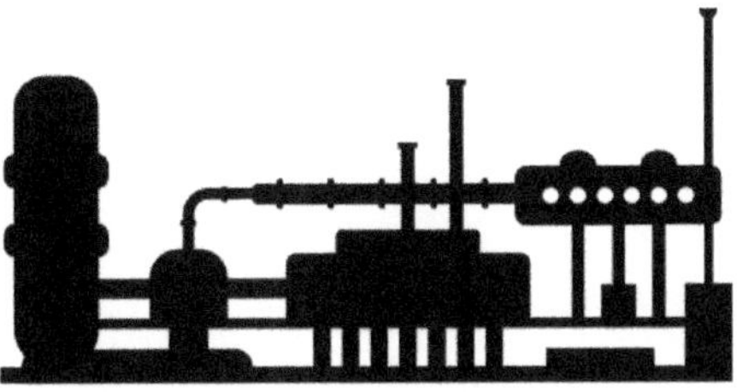

CHAPTER 13

They left the lake basin and broken section of the causeway far behind them. Along the way, they saw more bulb-like projections denoting the bigger trees, and even portions of rock used as natural pillars to hold up the great forest floor.

A few machines looked to be running smoothly—like water pumps or even what looked like giant furnaces and air conditioners. Once in a while, they would see a machine that was clearly broken or had scorch marks, as if it had caught on fire. One section of pipe had a split at an elbow and leaked gallons of water every second. The water fell into the dark below, splashing into whatever was down there.

Matt guessed they had walked almost a half-mile when something new in the distance caught his eyes.

"What is that?" Catherine asked.

"Might be some kind of turbine or big air-conditioning box," he suggested.

"I'll tell you what that is, chief," Justin said with a chuckle.

"What?" Matt asked, curious as to how he could possibly know.

"That, my friend, is what I used to call home."

"Home? Here?" Catherine and Matt asked at the same time.

Justin shook his head. "No. I grew up dirt poor. That is a single-wide trailer. Must be used here as an engineer's office or something. They're easy to move, so they always get used as office trailers on construction sites. When they were building all of this, they must have used that to keep blueprints and work orders and stuff in."

"That means it might have information for us! Maybe a map!" Matt's voice rose with excitement.

He and Justin started to run ahead. "Hey, remember we gotta

make sure the walkway isn't rusting out under our feet again!" Darin called to them.

They slowed and glanced at the causeway before deciding it was safe and rushing on.

The trailer was suspended on big cables attached to the ceiling. It was a single story, and except for this surreal location, it looked just as Justin had said, the perfect little portable office for a construction job site.

"Hang on, guys!" Darin called as he helped Stacy limp along, Catherine trailing slowly behind them. "Make sure those cables aren't rusted out."

Cody caught up to Matt and Justin and took it upon himself to investigate the far side of the trailer's support cables. "This side is good. No rust here at all."

"Not on this end either," Matt said.

"Well, let's go in. Anybody home?" Justin knocked on the door.

The thin metal door had a painted number four near the top. The doorknob was a standard silver, with a big keyhole taking up the center. Matt half expected it to be locked and was already wondering what they could use to break it open, when the handle turned easily in Justin's hand.

"It's dark," Cody said.

"Find the light switch," Matt said.

"It's over here, chief." Justin entered and flipped on the lights.

Matt and Cody cautiously followed him in. There were bookcases filled with rolled-up papers—probably blueprints—a pair of desks, a half-dozen chairs, a small fridge, and a wastepaper basket, all covered in a thick layer of dust.

Justin smiled. "Told you. There are lots of blueprints, kind of like back at the Sev."

Matt eyed the bookshelves. "Yeah, but a lot more."

They moved closer. The blueprints were marked "HZRD."

"That must mean that this is the HZRD site," Matt said.

Darin and the girls made it to the door. "I thought I asked you guys to wait up. We've gotta be careful."

"Just leave the injured one behind." Stacy crossed her arms and pushed her bottom lip out in a pout.

"Sorry," Matt said. "I just really wanted to see what was in here."

"Eager beaver," Catherine taunted.

"Look at these." Matt held out one of the blueprints for them all to see.

"Is that what I think it is?" Catherine asked. "It looks like the entire layout of the building. It's massive."

"More than massive. It's bigger than a city," he said.

Justin checked the fridge, grinning when he found a couple of cans of soda. He took one and reclined in one of the nicer chairs behind a desk. "Explain it to me, chief," he said, cracking open a can.

"Don't drink that. You don't know how old it is." Catherine screwed up her face in disgust.

Justin shook his head and lifted the can in salute. "Down the hatch."

"Is there any more?" Stacy asked.

Justin chugged the soda and pointed to the fridge. "Wow, that has a tang to it." He shivered as he swallowed again.

Darin and Matt looked at each other. "It can't be any older than the stuff in the Sev," Matt said.

"We don't know that," Catherine protested.

"Well, this should start giving us some answers." Matt pointed at marks on one of the blueprints.

"This is called the elevation of the blueprints of the building. So you can see what it looks like from the outside," Darin added.

Catherine pointed. "That enormous square looks like it has some little drawings of shrubs around a driveway to a door. What door?"

"To the outside—the *real* outside," Justin suggested with a hiccup.

"I was hoping we'd already reached the *real* outside, just in part of a big underground base," Cody said. "I mean, who in the world could make anything so dang big?"

"The government, apparently. But why?" Catherine said.

Darin pointed at different areas on the paper. "The blueprints have a bird's-eye view, which is typical. This shows both the ground level and the subfloor. That's where we are, down here. Over there, it shows the walkways, and over there is where the mountain is."

"So that's the cryovault where our parents are!" Matt almost shouted.

Darin kept going. "This shows a tram system and a track. Looks like a direct route to get there from here. You were right about wanting to come down here."

"Thank you," Matt said with a slight bow.

Catherine touched the blueprint. "Look! There's the forest, and next to it is Camp New Beginnings, and there's the Sev."

"Hang on a sec, I just found the size calculator for this thing," Matt said. There was a line and four hash marks in the lower part of the blueprint. His lips moved as he counted to himself and measured the diameter of the blueprint. "This is incredible. It's way bigger than I thought."

"How big?" Cody asked.

Matt held his arms out wide. "This thing is over forty-five miles in diameter."

"It's a fortress," Justin said.

"It's a city," Stacy added.

"It's bigger than a city." Darin shook his head.

"It's, like, bigger than Rhode Island!" Stacy shrugged. "I mean, probably!"

Catherine pointed to marks on the blueprint. "This shows where all the tram stations are. If the trams are running, we can ride to the mountain. No more walking for dizzy people or anyone with a bad foot." She put an arm around Stacy.

"Awww," Stacy cooed, embracing Catherine back.

"No more walking for anyone," Justin added with a smile as he cracked another can open.

"How about saving one for someone else?" Cody asked.

"I waited. Nobody else grabbed one." Justin took a gulp.

Matt took charge. "Guys. We know that the cryovault is B-35, but nothing is marked B-35 on this blueprint. But I think the mountain probably *is* the cryovault, isn't it?"

"I would think so," Darin said. "I saw it from the outside once."

"You did?" Stacy gasped.

Darin hung his head. "Yeah, but just once."

"I also think we need to find a way out of this place. These are all labeled HZRD, but nothing says B-35. What if it's not even in this giant building? What is the exit for a building this big?" Catherine asked.

"I think the tram stations will route us to exits. They had to have them when they built this place," Darin said.

"These marks on the edge look like exits to me." Matt gestured at the blueprint.

"We take the tram, find the mountain, and find an exit," Cody summarized.

"Exactly what I said," Justin proclaimed.

"So we're in agreement?" Matt asked. "We take the tram to the mountain, find our parents, and get out of here?" Everyone agreed with a nod. "All right, let's get moving!"

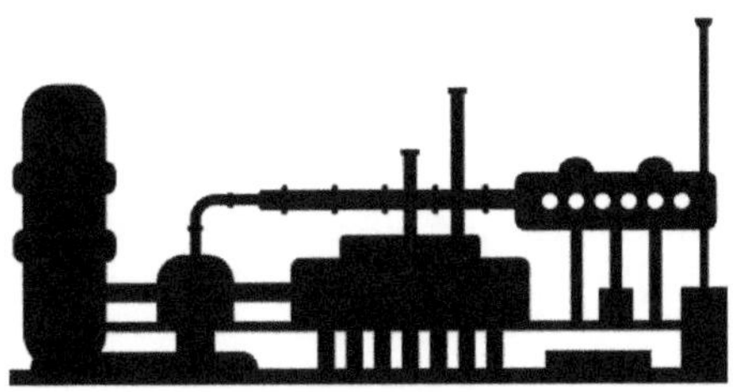

CHAPTER 14

"I'm taking these, since nobody has been here in ages." Matt rolled up the blueprints to put in his backpack.

"How long do you think it's been since someone has been here?" Stacy asked.

"Anyone who worked on this place is probably long since dead," Justin said.

"Morose much?" Catherine fixed him with her gaze.

"Hey, look at the dust in here. How long do *you* think it's been since anyone has been here?" Justin prodded. "Probably like twenty years or more."

"I'm sure I don't know," she answered. "How was your soda?"

"Good." Justin wiped his sleeve across his mouth for emphasis. "It's a dead man's soda. Who could ask for more? Don't run away. It's only me," he sang as he moved with arms outstretched, Frankenstein-like, toward Catherine.

"Stop it!" she said with a slight smile.

Matt was glad she seemed to be overcoming her breakdown from earlier.

"Wait, if this is like a map," Cody said, "how do we know where we are, though?"

"Already covered," Matt said. "This building is marked four on the door, and right in the dead center—"

"Don't say dead," Catherine cautioned as Justin continued his "dead man's soda" chant.

Matt shook his shoulders. "This trailer is labeled four, and I found a four on the blueprint right here in the middle. So the closest tram is just over here. Looks like less than a half-mile walk."

"I'm glad you understand that thing," Cody said.

"Do you think the tram still works?" Stacy asked. "I'm tired of walking like this."

"Lean on me." Darin put an arm around her shoulders.

They followed Matt as he pointed down one of several causeways leading in multiple directions.

Justin burped loudly, rather pleased with himself.

"Ugh, excuse you," Catherine said. "That echoed in my ears like a gong down here."

"That part wasn't me. There's some kind of banging up ahead," Justin said.

Along the causeway to their right, in the direction Matt had indicated, the noise grew. The ever-louder sounds rattled like an engine tugging against its support brackets to their left, and to the right, the noisy clanking of a vent banging against itself blasted their ears in stereo.

"That does not sound good," Catherine said.

"Sounds like they're still doing construction down here. I need earplugs." Stacy wrapped her hoodie around her head tight and covered her ears with her hands.

They passed by one of the vents slamming against itself. They could hardly hear each other speak, and Matt shouted for them to pick up the pace and get away from the noise.

Cody held his hands over his ears and tripped a little on a raised bar on the causeway, bumping into Matt. "Sorry."

"What?"

"I'm sorry."

Matt nodded as they covered their ears again.

Catherine tugged on Matt and shouted, "I'm beginning to think we went the wrong way!"

Matt shook his head and showed her the blueprints, shouting, "No, this is the right way. We're almost there!"

"What?"

"Just follow me!"

CHAPTER 15

They moved on and came to a walled section. Passing through the doorway, moving tubes came into view, and the constant drumming of machines pounded their ears.

"What are those?" Stacy asked.

"Looks like tubes?" Catherine answered.

The walkway curved like a big letter Z as it made its way through a section of massive pistons pumping up and down. Some of the larger ones were almost ten feet in diameter, and as tall as trees. Matt had never seen machines this big before, but considering the massive gears and other works down there, he wasn't surprised they existed. The noise eased slightly, but still pounded in his head.

"What the heck are these doing?" Stacy asked.

"They're pistons, like in a car engine," Cody said.

"Yeah, but what are they doing? Is this whole place moving somewhere now?" she asked.

Darin smiled at her. "Who knows? These must be pumping or powering something. I don't know what—maybe an air venting system or moving water from up above."

"It's an industrial forest of working trees," Cody said. "We have plenty of oil derricks out where I live, and these might be doing something similar to that."

"Like collecting the fuel to run this place?" Catherine asked.

"Maybe. This base is so big, it must take crazy amounts of gas to run everything—electric generators and water pumps, air vents, even sewage maybe." Cody shrugged.

"Nobody uses pistons to move sewage." Justin laughed. "Pistons power motors, but if you don't add oil, they seize up, and your engine blows."

"Well, I'm glad it looks like these are oiled, then," Catherine said.

"That one isn't moving." Stacy pointed to a single piston that remained still.

"You spoke too soon," Justin said. "Now we're in trouble."

The stalled piston shuddered as it struggled to move.

Stacy paused on the walkway, and Darin rushed to reassure her. "It looks like it's seized, but it's not gonna blow up. Just, this place is old, and some things don't work anymore. It's okay. Let's keep moving."

She shivered. "I don't like this place anymore. I want to get out of here and see the sun again."

"We haven't seen the sun for a long time," Justin answered.

"You're not helping," Catherine chided.

"We are getting out," Darin said calmly. "We're on our way to get out."

"So maybe those things power bad weather outside?" Stacy asked.

"Looks that way, and maybe if they aren't working anymore, weather will be better," Darin said.

"Well, I want all the way out of this madhouse." Justin gestured to their surroundings.

Matt broke in, trying to end the talk scaring Stacy. "We're on our way, guys. We'll get there."

The pistons continued their heartbeat-like action, and as they followed the walkway through the metal forest, someone dropped something. It skidded on the metal grating and then tumbled off the edge.

"What was that?" Matt asked.

"I dropped one of my snacks," Justin said. "I didn't hear it hit bottom."

Cody leaned over the side of the walkway and pumped his flashlight, aiming the beam of light below them. Matt moved in beside him to get a look too.

The pistons sunk way down into the ground, sliding up and down, with thick brown sludge around the junction of the compressing rod and the outer housing.

"We're higher up than I thought," Matt said.

"What do you mean?" Catherine asked.

"I thought the walkway here was like twenty feet off the floor, but I'd say we're more like over a hundred feet up."

"Are we still on the right path? I thought a tram station would be closer," she said.

"So did I," he lamented. "It's gotta be up here soon."

A hiss from far below echoed through the chamber, adding to the screeching of mechanical pumping. The sound was an ominous rhythm daring them to walk forward.

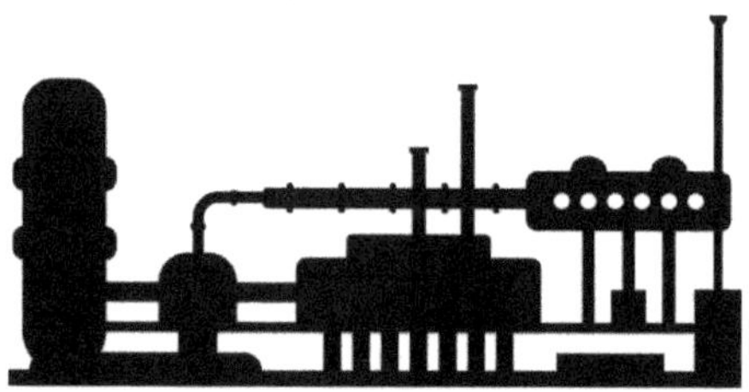

CHAPTER 16

"Maybe we took a wrong turn?" Catherine suggested.

Matt looked at the blueprint again. "I'm pretty sure I led us the right way. It shouldn't be much farther, but it does seem strange that there wasn't a more direct route to the tram from supervisors' section four."

"We all make mistakes, chief. You just make more," Justin joked.

"Thanks a lot for all your help." Matt gritted his teeth.

"You're welcome. So do we turn back or keep going?" Justin pressed.

"I still think we're on the right track to the nearest tram. I can't explain why they built it like this. Maybe they thought workmen would be running diagnostic checks on things as they walked between spots?" Matt suggested.

"That makes sense to me," Cody said. "You always gotta ride your fences to make sure things are on the up and up."

"Yeah, yeah, you two are always backing each other up." Justin glowered at them.

"It's not like that." Catherine moved to catch up to Justin, who was now in the lead moving down the walkway. Darin and Stacy followed after, while Matt paused a moment.

"Don't take none of that personal," Cody said. "We're all pushed to our limits down here."

Matt couldn't hear very well amidst the barrage of pistons pumping, but he could see Catherine talking to Justin as they walked ahead of the others. He was grateful she was such a good friend with a level head. Even after her breakdown earlier at the realization of their strange predicament, she seemed to be overcoming it for the good of all of them.

There was a loud pop, and Catherine screamed, racing back toward the others, Justin on her heels.

A black hose whipped back and forth, snakelike, spraying hot hydraulic fluid, drenching them all in the slick substance.

Matt struggled to cover the blueprints with his body, then stuffed them into his pack while getting sprayed.

"It's not stopping!" Catherine cried.

"We have to go that way. Let's run past it!" Matt shouted.

"No, let's find another way," Darin said.

"No other route was even close to this short," Matt protested.

"Can you run?" Darin asked Stacy.

She shook her head.

"I've got you." Darin picked her up and rushed to get past the spraying hose.

They all ducked and crawled and slipped their way past the angry, mindless guardian.

Twice, Matt's right foot slipped out from under him, and he slid dangerously close to losing his balance on the walkway. If it hadn't been for the stout guardrail, he would have gone over the side.

Just as they got past the spraying hose, it stopped flailing and went still. A few hot, pink drops fell from the detached end.

"Well, that's just great," Justin muttered.

"Is everyone all right?" Matt asked.

"I'm all right, just soaked in oil," Catherine said.

"Me too," Stacy echoed.

"Glad that's over." Cody wiped slime from his face.

A terrible grinding sound reverberated through the complex. Sparks shot from several of the pistons, and steam erupted from somewhere below, sending a wretched cloud up at them.

One of the closest pistons seized, buckled, and started swaying back and forth.

"It's gonna fall on the walkway. Run!" Matt shouted.

"We'll be trapped on the other side," Stacy cried.

"It's where we need to be! Let's run!" Matt insisted.

Catherine and Justin raced ahead. Darin helped Stacy move as Cody and Matt brought up the rear.

The piston, even though it was one of the smaller ones, was at least three feet in diameter. Like a falling tree, it rocked in place slowly then swooped down with incredible speed.

Covered in oil, everyone slipped and slid, ending up on their knees, where they crawled over the metal grate. Through torn pants, the sharp edges of the walkway cut into their knees. Their hands fared no better, as the metal railings had become too slick to hold on to. More pistons seized and fell like timber in the forest.

The one nearest them slammed against the walkway just a few feet ahead of Catherine. She screamed as it crunched and bent the metal railings, causing the walkway to bow like a melted cassette tape left on a car's dashboard in summertime.

"What do we do?" she gasped.

"We have to keep going. It's gonna snap this walkway!" Darin shouted.

He lifted Stacy over the top of the downed piston as Justin helped Catherine and then leapt over himself. Matt jumped, but only succeeded in sliding down the greasy side. He looked to Cody and Darin, both having the same trouble as him.

"Here." Matt cupped his hands. Cody did the same. "Darin, we'll boost you."

Darin stepped up, and they heaved him over.

"Thanks," Darin shouted. "Cody, you next, and Justin and I will pull Matt over!"

Matt closed his eyes and braced for Cody's weight pulling at his sore wrist. Once Cody was firmly on the other side, Matt took a few quick steps back and ran toward the piston. He jumped, reaching for the outstretched hands hanging over the top. His wrist slipped out of one of the boys' hands, but the other grabbed Matt's shirt and found purchase. Matt desperately kicked at the side of the metal in a futile attempt to find his way over.

"I got him!" Darin yelled.

Matt slid over the top, and both Darin and Justin helped him down. He nodded in thanks—no time for anything else.

The walkway bowed beneath Matt's feet. The metal groaned under the strain, threatening to snap in an instant. "Everybody! Keep going! Hurry!"

They struggled to make the last few yards to the end of the piston forest section. Oil smoked venomously somewhere behind them.

"Almost there. Keep going!" Matt urged, as a few of them had stopped to catch their breath and look back.

"We made it," Stacy gasped.

Another piston snapped from the ceiling and fell, crashing across the other.

The walkway collapsed at the impact, and the long strip of metal leading right to where they stood came apart like a zipper.

Screams filled the air.

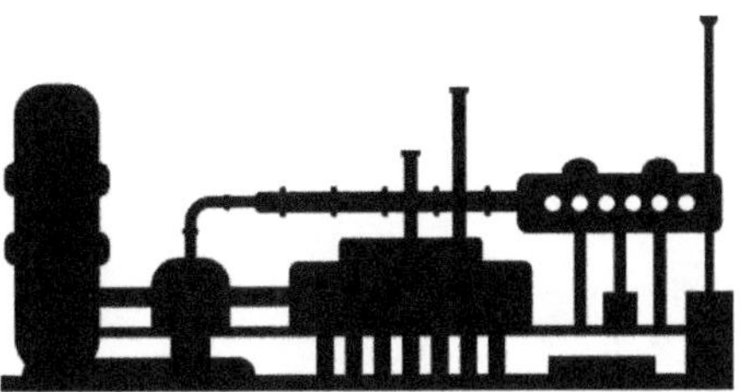

CHAPTER 17

The walkway toppled vertically just a few feet past Catherine, who was the farthest along the path.

Everyone managed to hold on to the railing as the causeway slipped and tumbled down. It hit something with force, sending a terrible shock like a thunderbolt back up the line.

"Guess we ain't going back that way," Justin said. He was only a few feet behind Catherine but had held on to the right side of the railing, while she was on the left.

Stacy crouched behind Catherine, Darin right behind her. Matt and Cody brought up the rear on the right side.

"I'm too greasy to climb!" Stacy wailed. She grasped the railing above her, but each time she tried to pull herself up, her fingers slipped.

"You don't have to do pull-ups on it," Darin said. "Treat it like a ladder. Nice and easy. One foot and then the other; your hands are just to keep you balanced. I won't let you fall." He spoke calmly and firmly.

"I can't," Stacy cried. "I keep slipping. I'll fall."

"I won't let you fall," Darin repeated.

His confidence gave Matt confidence. "We can do this, guys. Just take your time."

Cody reached up and grabbed ahold of the cross-section bar above him and climbed up. He made it look effortless—until he slipped.

CHAPTER 18

Matt's heart caught in his throat.

Cody's foot slid off a greasy rung, and he slipped down one section, two sections, three sections—Matt caught hold of his shirt.

"Don't you dare fall!" he shouted. Images of Kyle slipping out of his grasp and being drowned in a monster flood flashed through his mind.

"I ain't about to," Cody said as he scrambled to get back on the railing.

Matt's wrist ached. Luckily, Cody's shirt was made of a material that didn't let the hydraulic fluid make it too slippery.

Cody latched onto the railing beneath him, and Matt finally felt like he could let go.

"That was too close." Matt shook his twisted wrist.

"I hear you. Try being on the other end." Cody shook his head. "I know it ain't polite to say, but I might need to change my drawers."

"We can't afford to lose anyone," Matt declared. "Let's go slow and easy so nobody slips."

"Wipe your hands on your shirtsleeves or pants to get as much of the hydraulic fluid off as possible," Cody said.

"And let's be ready in case anyone else slips," Matt added.

Stacy whimpered. "I, like, can't do this. I'll fall just like Cody."

"I'm all right." Cody urged, "We've got to keep going."

The metal causeway groaned and moved a fraction of an inch.

Stacy screamed and clutched the railing all the tighter, her eyes clamped shut.

Darin looked at Matt. "I'm gonna need some help with her, and we gotta move."

Matt considered their options. The causeway was not wide, but he didn't dare jump from one side to the other since the grease could make him slip, not to mention a heavy jump might make the whole thing come tumbling down. Then it hit him. "I have the rope!"

"Toss it up to me, and I'll tie it off," Catherine said.

"Are you able to do that?" Cody asked.

"I'm almost to the top. Just hang on a minute," she answered.

Matt clenched his jaw, praying she wouldn't slip.

Catherine crawled her way up two more rungs to the top. She turned around on her belly and stretched her hands out to Matt. "I'm ready. Throw it to me."

He locked his legs around one of the rails and reached into the backpack with his left hand, still hooking the rail with his right. It was tricky, and he almost knocked the blueprint map out by accident, but he finally grasped the rope, took several loops in hand, and took a deep breath.

Under any other circumstances, it would have been easy to throw about twenty feet of rope ten feet up, but the slippery fluid changed everything. One wrong move could send him plummeting to his death.

Matt threw the rope too far out, and Catherine couldn't reach it.

"Stop playing around, chief," Justin said.

"Stop it. He's trying," Catherine said. "Again."

Matt looped the rope and tossed it one more time. Catherine caught it, but she didn't have a strong hold, and it fell from her grasp.

"Third time's the charm," Matt said as he looped it one last time and threw it.

Catherine caught it and edged backward out of sight. She pulled a good length of the rope from him, then called back, "I've got it as secure as I know how. I'm guessing that three big knots around an I-beam should do it."

"I'll double-check it." Justin climbed to the top and disappeared from sight for a moment before calling back, "It's good, chief!"

Matt tossed his end of the rope to Darin, who looped it around and under Stacy's arms. "You're going to have to let go of this railing and help climb. They've got you, and I'm here to be a backup."

Stacy still had her eyes shut. "I can't. I'll fall."

"No, you won't. You've got the rope, and Justin and Catherine are going to help pull you up. Just keep your hands on the railing and your feet on the rungs and help them get you up top."

"I can't." She shook her head. She still had not opened her eyes. "I'm going to totally die here!"

Matt looked at Darin, wondering what he could say to her that hadn't already been said. How could they get her to climb before it was too late? He was painfully aware of the stress on the metal and the continual light groan.

"Stacy!" Darin demanded.

Stacy cracked her eyes open to look at him. He leaned in and kissed her passionately on the mouth, and she melted into his arms.

"Now, help them get you up top, and I'll see you up there in a minute."

"Okay," she said softly. Catherine and Justin pulled on the rope, and she clambered up the railing.

Darin followed behind her, just a little bit slower, but completely free-hand in spite of the greasy surface.

Stacy crested the top. "I did it!"

The walkway shifted and dropped another couple of inches.

Darin, midstride between two railings, slipped but caught himself with one hand on the next rung down.

Stacy screamed. "Are you okay?" she called out.

Darin hung by one arm but strained and wrapped his legs around another rung. "I'm fine." He gasped for breath.

"Good thing she didn't see that," Cody whispered.

"Let's use the rope from now on," Matt said.

"Yeah." Darin nodded as he wiped beading sweat from his forehead.

We can't afford to lose anyone. Matt's own words echoed in his head.

CHAPTER 19

When everyone made it to the top, they moved farther down the walkway, where they didn't have to worry about it crashing underneath them anymore, and then took a good, long breather.

"Any good way to get all of this stuff off?" Catherine asked.

"We could use gas, if we had any," Cody said.

"You mean like unleaded?"

"Yeah, it works great. But then you gotta use soap and water after that," Cody continued.

"How would you even know that?" Stacy asked.

He shrugged. "We had to do that all the time on the ranch. If we ever got tar on us, or too much bag balm, gas gets 'er right off."

"Gross," Stacy said.

Matt glanced at the blueprint map, then down the walkway. "Guys, I think that's the tram station right there!"

They hurried the final hundred yards to the station. The tram was bigger than he had expected. Matt breathed a sigh of relief, having secretly been worried that the tram might be too small to fit all of them at the same time.

A small area jutted out right beside a suspended track. It wasn't anything elaborate, just a small bench and section where the tram was stopped. There were green and red lights on the side of the track, as if to signal when it was moving or coming to a stop. The track was a single suspended monorail. The tram hung below the track, reminding Matt of one of the rides at Disneyland. The tram itself consisted of three sections. Two pods looked like passenger cars, with plastic seats and more than enough room to carry all of them and have them stretch out, but the very back compartment was a platform. It was like the back of a flatbed truck. Attached to the platform was a robotic arm, folded up, and on the end was a big pincer. The pincer was about two feet long and looked very robust.

"Would you look at that? The robot claw!" Justin exclaimed.

"That's probably so they can load and unload construction stuff," Darin said. "Then they don't have to have a forklift for everything."

"They will when they move it," Catherine said.

"No, The Claw has the power to do all!" Justin fiddled with the control sticks at the rear of the robotic arm.

"Don't play with that. You don't know how to use it," Darin said.

"I'm just having fun is all," Justin argued as he jumped from the back of the flatcar to the walkway. "Someone has got to liven things up around here."

Stacy piped up. "Guys, the way things have been going, I don't know if we should even ride on that thing. Everything is falling apart. It's all dangerous. Let's just get out of here."

Matt looked to Darin and guessed he knew what he was thinking. As gently as he could, Matt said, "I get that, Stacy. We're all worried, and this building seems like it won't hold together very much longer, but the tram will be faster and more direct. It'll get us out of here a whole lot faster than walking."

"What if it falls?"

"Since the tram is used for hauling heavy equipment, it would be built a lot stronger than the walkways. Should be safer too," Darin said.

"So faster and safer?" she asked timidly.

"Yeah."

"Okay, let's, like, do the tram train, then." Stacy nodded, her frizzy hair bouncing a little.

Glancing at the red and green lights on the sides of the tram, Justin asked, "What do these even mean?"

"I think it's to show direction. That's my best guess," Matt said.

A shower of sparks rained down from overhead. Everyone dodged and ran for cover.

"What is with this deathtrap?!" Cody shouted.

The sparking stopped for the moment, but everyone looked about warily.

"You were saying?" Stacy said.

"All the more reason to get going out of here faster," Matt insisted.

"He's right." Darin stepped up on the flatcar. "Come on, give me your hand. Let's get moving."

Catherine and Justin followed, stepping up on the flatbed part of the tram. The whole tram swayed back and forth.

Justin again got behind the robotic arm and fiddled with the controls. "The Claw will show us the way out!" he proclaimed loudly. But as he moved a knob on the robotic arm, it elevated and swung, striking Catherine. She fell forward against the bench seats.

Justin froze, mouth open and eyes wide. Darin turned to face him, ducking to avoid getting hit by the flailing arm.

The tram hummed to life and zoomed down the track.

"Justin!" Darin yelled, trailing off into the distance.

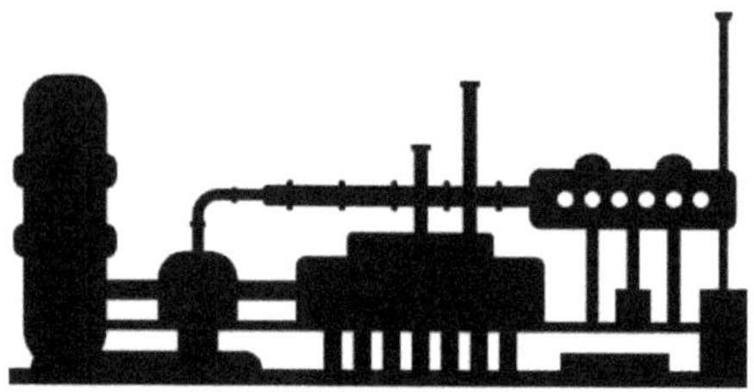

CHAPTER 20

"Guys! Stop it!" Matt screamed, running after the departing tram. He gauged it was moving at about fifteen miles per hour.

I've gotta catch up and stop the tram! Where are Justin and Darin? Why aren't they stopping it?

Matt ran as hard as he could. He kept up with it for a moment or two, but it slowly gained more and more ground on him and continued to get farther and farther away.

Red triangle lights on the back of the tram mocked his attempt at outrunning it. The lights turned a corner and disappeared into the dark.

Matt stopped, panting hard. He put his hands on his knees. He reached out for strength inside and yelled one more time, "No!"

He couldn't remember ever having a day in his life where he had such a workout—rappelling down into the shaft, climbing up a grease-covered fallen walkway, and finally running for all he was worth after his friends in the dark. He finally heard Cody calling to him over his own panting.

"You all, right?" Cody asked.

"Yeah, I couldn't catch them."

"I can see that. We gotta go back for Stacy. She can't move nearly as fast as us."

"Is she okay?"

"She ain't freaking out, if that's what you mean." Cody put a hand on Matt's shoulder and helped him up.

"They're gone," Matt said.

"I hope Catherine is all right." Cody shook his head. "But Darin and Justin will figure something out. It's got to stop sometime. We'll find 'em."

"You're right," Matt agreed. "They'll have the common sense to get off at the mountain."

"Yep," Cody said.

Matt looked at his feet, his shoulders slumped. He had tried so hard to hold them together and get through this way. He had been sure this would be safer than above ground, but now the group was torn in half. And he was scared.

"I know what you're thinking, and it's not your fault," Cody said. "Don't beat yourself up about it."

"I should have been in the pilot's seat for that thing. I should have stopped Justin from playing with that arm."

"Coulda, shoulda, woulda," Cody said. "Let's go get Stacy and get after them. We'll find them."

Matt nodded. "Thanks."

Stacy was hobbling down the track after them. "Not all of us can run, you guys."

"I'm sorry," Matt said. "I thought I could catch them and figure out how to stop it."

"I'm glad you didn't catch them. I'd rather it be three of us together than just two," she said. "If Darin can figure out how to stop it, he will."

"You're right. Let's keep following this track. We'll catch up to them soon enough, and we're still all heading toward the mountain," Matt said.

"Could you see them when you ran after them?" Stacy asked.

"I couldn't. They were all low on the floor. Catherine got hit in the head. Maybe Justin and Darin did too?" Cody said.

"We'll find our friends. It'll be okay." Matt's words were as much to convince himself as the others.

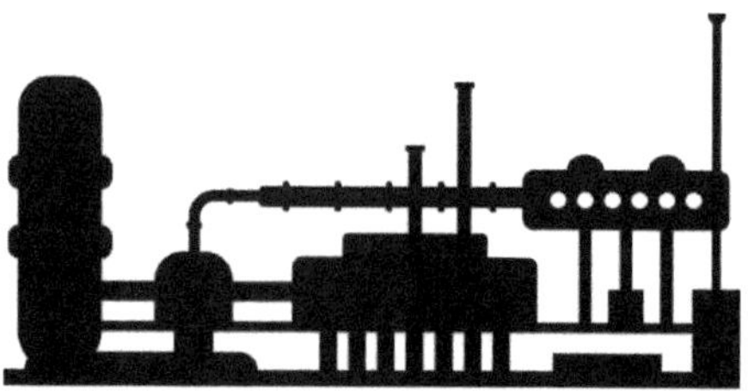

CHAPTER 21

"We better get moving if we're going to find them," Cody said.

"Do you think they're all right?" Stacy asked.

"Are *you* all right?" Matt put an arm around her.

"I think so. I mean, yes, I am. I just want to find them and get everyone back together—it's just . . . I'm holding you up."

"It's not your fault." Matt thought back to when Kim nearly got them all killed in the forest by refusing to walk. "It could have been any one of us that got hurt. We're not going to leave you behind."

"Guys." Cody spun about, already walking in the direction of the vanished tram.

"We're coming." Matt stayed close to Stacy, making sure she was walking as well as she could on her own. He was glad she was stepping up and not having any problems with Darin's being hit and speeding off on the tram. He squelched a bit of anger at Justin for messing with the robotic arm. He knew it hadn't been on purpose. Who could have known what this place would do? It was all falling apart. It seemed to be shaking itself to pieces from the very force of the crazy natural calamities it was trying to inflict on them topside. At least they were inside it now, where they were better protected.

Along the way, there were spots where the metal paneling was rusting and even starting to bend under stress fractures. Here and there, wires as big as Matt's thigh sparked as the lines were pushed and ripped out by the building falling apart. There were places where natural roots had grown and forced seams in the metal to snap.

"That looks just like where I've seen weeds growing in asphalt," Stacy said.

"Yeah, and even without the benefit of sunlight down here," Cody added.

"I guess even these flickering lights do enough to give them some kind of photosynthesis," Matt said.

Brighter light met them as they rounded a big bend on the tram and causeway. Another vent, open to the sky, allowed light to filter down from above, but this seemed a little different than the one they had first come down.

"Is it open all the way?" Stacy asked.

"I'm guessing it's a vent of some kind, like the one we came down before, but I think it's even bigger," Cody said.

"Almost, but it's vertical. There's no way up. Not that it matters. Our friends are still on the tram and went past this a long time ago," Matt said, taking a look up the shaft. "There used to be some flow vents, but they look broken, like they got blasted out."

"What?" Cody looked closer at the long scratch marks showing where terrific forces had pushed the vents out and scratched deep grooves into the metal siding.

"A vent for what?" Stacy asked.

"Maybe where the storms came from," Matt offered.

"I don't like the sound of that."

"You're gonna like this even less," Cody said.

Massive fans with blades as long as semitruck trailers came into view. There were six blades on each motor mount, pointing toward the shaft.

"So this thing makes tornados?" Stacy asked.

"It looks that way. They look kinda like the ones we saw in the junkyard," Cody said.

"Good thing they aren't on. We'd be blown away."

"Literally," Cody said warily.

"The air feels colder here, even though we just saw a little sunlight," Stacy noted.

"You're right, and it's not just the shadow," Matt said.

Cody shook his head. "I don't want to agree with y'all, but I'm gonna have to. This is downright chilly for my Texas blood."

Just past the giant fans, the air grew colder still, their breath puffing white clouds in front of them as they exhaled.

"We're at another door," Cody said. "It has frost on it."

"A freezer?" Stacy asked.

"Looks like. Awful big too." Cody tapped on it.

Matt frowned. "Our friends rode the tram through here, so we've gotta follow." He pushed the button, and the doors opened with a sci-fi-esque *swish*. A blast of even colder air hit them. The doors remained open, letting the cold out into the warmer chamber. On the far side of the walkway stood another open door.

"Whoa!" Cody gripped his shoulders at the cold.

Matt stepped forward to look inside, and the others followed.

Inside the freezer complex, lights covered with little black cages gave off just enough illumination for them to see that it was like a giant rectangular box lined with a multitude of pipes and what looked like fire extinguisher sprinklers.

"This is for making snow." Stacy smiled, then shrugged. "I told you I used to ski."

The walkway widened out inside the freezer to about thirty feet, then narrowed on the other side back to its normal width.

"This is weird," Cody said.

"Yeah, but at least it shows that it was made for people to be in here to do maintenance and whatnot, and we can keep going to follow the tram."

"I don't see the tram tracks in here," Cody said. "It must have gone around the backside of this freezer."

"Do we have to go in there?" Stacy asked.

"I don't see any other way." Matt replied.

He took a step forward and the walkway swayed. The large freezer had no bottom to it. The ice-covered grating gave Matt vertigo as he stared into the foggy abyss below.

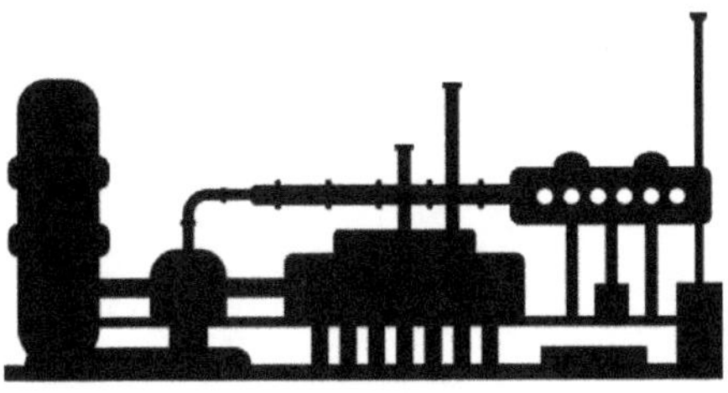

CHAPTER 22

Each step they took on the walkway caused chunks of ice to fall into the darkness below them. The box continued downward as far as they could see, all lined with the pipes and spigots. Extra pipes like the ones lining the walls lay on the walkway, along with a box of tools.

"Look at the size of this thing, all just to make it snow like crazy outside," Matt said. The ingenuity to create the fake climate outside was beyond the scope of anything he had ever seen before.

Cody, however, was more interested in the tools at their feet. "Can't believe they just left this stuff lying here."

"I guess they just didn't care enough to haul them out," Stacy said.

"Well, they should have. The cold can't be good for them," Cody explained.

"Maybe they knew they would need to get to them in a hurry to do repairs," Matt offered.

Cody shook his head. "They should have left them out of the cold. It will make them break easier."

"Speaking of 'break easier,' let's get out of here. My nose is freezing, and my hair is starting to get frosted highlights, and that's not a good thing," Stacy said with a laugh.

Ice crystals formed on Matt's nose from the sub-zero temperature. Everything in sight had a thick layer of frost. It was the biggest freezer he had ever seen. "All right, let's go." He crossed the stack of pipes and headed toward the open door on the far side of the box.

A tremor rocked the freezer, and the cold metal of the walkway twisted like a giant was playing jump rope.

They all held on to the railing, and just as soon as it had begun, it was over. The frigid cold metal inflamed their palms.

"What was that?" Stacy cried.

"This whole place is breaking down," Matt said. "Let's move!"

The doors behind them whisked shut with the tremor. They could just barely hear the *swish* of them shutting. The warmer temperature from the open chamber dissipated, and the room grew colder. The doors in front of them began to close too.

"Run!" Matt shouted, slipping on the frozen catwalk.

Cody raced ahead to catch the door while Stacy hobbled as fast as she could, but none of them were fast enough. The doors shut.

Cody pressed the round door-release button, but nothing happened. "It's not working!"

Stacy screamed as she reached the door. "This is too cold!"

"I'll go try the one we came in." Cody hurried back the other way.

Matt continued pressing the button to see if it might work after one, two, ten more tries. He jiggled the latch, but it wouldn't budge.

Cody returned. "I tried it like twenty times. It's not working. Like the quake broke it or made it lock or something."

"We're trapped." Matt slammed his fist against the door.

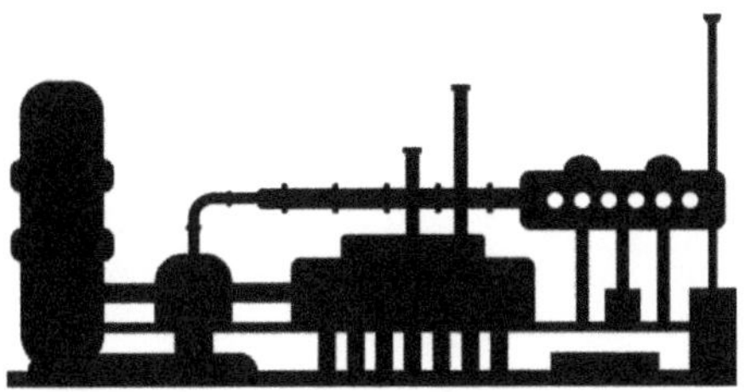

CHAPTER 23

"Get us out of here!" Stacy screamed.

"You've got to calm down. We'll figure this out," Matt said. They weren't dressed for this kind of cold. He knew they had to figure something out fast.

Looking over their heads, Matt realized he had missed something. There was a massive fan above them. Once it turned on and the spigots released water, this room would fill with snow that the fan would blast out and away. The blizzard. It had originated here. The avalanche. Nathan . . . He shook his head. He had to focus. He could only imagine how cold that fan would make things. As it was, he was afraid they wouldn't be able to last more than an hour in these temps.

Cody and Matt spoke at the same time. "The tools!"

Stacy crouched down on her heels and shivered while Matt and Cody raced to grab the tools from the middle of the walkway.

They pulled their shirtsleeves over their hands to hold the frozen tools—a big pipe wrench and a set of iron clamps. Racing back, they pounded on the door. But the thick steel held off their attempts like a backboard versus a basketball.

"We're not doing anything," Cody said.

"The latch," Matt suggested.

They took turns hitting the latch, oblivious to Stacy screaming at them to stop.

The latch snapped off and struck the walkway. It landed with a cold, cruel clank, knocking off another hint of frost that fell away into the darkness.

"I told you! But you lunkheads wouldn't listen!" Stacy shouted.

"This is all your fault. We shouldn't have come in here, and you shouldn't have let the door shut! And now we're all gonna die!"

"She ain't wrong," Cody said. "We gotta get out of here quick, or we'll be Popsicles."

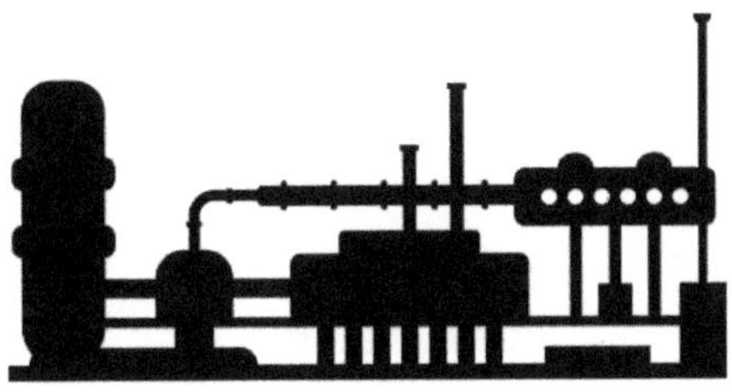

CHAPTER 24

Battering the door hadn't gotten them anywhere. Matt scanned what they had on hand and tried to think of a way to get out.

Monkey wrenches, iron clamps, big pipe wrenches, and all of the extra pipes lay on the walkway. He looked up at the fan and then at the caged lights.

Stacy had started to sob.

Cody put a hand on her shoulder. "Those tears will freeze on your face. You don't want that, do you?"

"It doesn't matter. We're gonna die in here," she said.

"No, we're not," Matt declared. "Cody, help me with one of those pipes and clamps. I've got an idea."

Matt stood on one of the railings of the walkway and stretched to reach one of the cage lights. He gauged how hard to hit and knocked one of the cages off from around the bulb without damaging the light.

Cody shivered. "I think I got an idea of what you're doing." He handed one of the clamps to Matt, then one of the pipes. It took two pipes to reach the door, but they spun them together and slammed it right up against the seam where the door opened.

"Hand me some ice," Matt said.

Cody used a wrench to break off a big chunk next to the door. He handed the piece to Matt, who held it up against the bulb. Water slowly trickled from his hand and ran through the pipe toward the door.

"Hold it right up against where the latch was. If the water freezes and expands there, maybe it will pop it open," Matt said.

It was slow, cold going. Matt's hands turned red and sore. Then before long, he couldn't even feel his hands from the cold of holding ice and cold water.

The water froze in the pipe, but enough of it kept running down that, slowly but surely, the lock and broken latch started expanding inside.

Matt's hands throbbed. The bulb burst, and a small section of the freezer dimmed.

"Now what?" Stacy asked.

"We keep trying with another bulb," Matt answered.

They moved the pipes to another bulb at the opposite side of the walkway and started over. Matt's sleeves, covered in ice, crunched with his movements. He knew hypothermia was setting in because he no longer shivered, but if he didn't keep going, they would all freeze to death. Matt closed his eyes, remembering his mom. Focusing all his efforts for just a mere second put him in a state his mom called Matt-itation. He instantly felt his heart rate slow, and the corners of his mouth tugged into a slight smile. Suddenly, he had the confidence that this part of the puzzle would be solved.

They watched intently as water slowly entered the crack in the door, and the freezing water forced it open a micron at a time.

It was now open almost a half-inch.

"It's a difference, but I don't know if that's enough to do anything." Cody's face was red and looked chapped.

Matt guessed his own must look the same. "We've got to keep trying."

A loud crack came from the door as they melted one more chunk into the broken latch. The expanding ice snapped and popped as it refroze. Another pop was followed by metal snapping.

Stacy took a monkey wrench and pounded on the door. "Open!" she cried, then dropped down, exasperated.

Another crack and pop of ice, and the door shifted, opening a bare two inches that seemed like a mile to the frozen teens.

Cody put the wrench into the gap and pried with all his strength. Matt slammed a pipe into the gap and joined in. The door gave up and slid open. The air outside the freezer felt like a tropical breeze compared to the icy hell they'd endured.

They said nothing as they took a long moment away from the freezer to warm up.

"I don't think I ever want to eat ice cream again," Stacy whispered.

"I don't ever want to leave Texas again," Cody said.

"Or Nevada." Matt blew into his hands to warm them up faster.

"I think I want to move somewhere even warmer than those places," Stacy said. "Maybe the sun."

After the feeling slunk painfully back into his hands, Matt said, "We gotta keep moving. They've got a huge lead on us."

Cody gave a brief sigh but stood up. He still looked awfully red, and Matt guessed the cold had been pretty hard on him.

"We'll take it easy, but we gotta get the blood flowing in our limbs."

"You're right," Cody agreed. "I don't think I've ever been this tired. Not even after a day of branding."

They made their way along the walkway. The tram tracks looped around the freezer and disappeared behind a massive pillar of rock. As they went around the big obstacle, they saw another building.

CHAPTER 25

The building hung beside the suspended tram track and walkway. A new track held big, bowl-like containers along the opposite side, hanging from the suspension system like enormous pots ready for a giant cook.

"What the heck are those, guys?" Stacy asked.

"I don't know." Matt shook his head.

"I bet Darin would know," she said quietly.

"They look almost like some of the big industrial vats I've seen that pour molten iron in the factory down the road from my old house," Cody answered.

As they got closer, they could see that the vats were full of a dark brown, sludge-type material.

"At least the air is warmer here," Cody offered.

"Yeah, but it smells like crap." Stacy made a gag-me sign. "Actual crap."

"At least we aren't freezing," Matt said.

Cody laughed. "That, little lady, is the smell of chemical fertilizer. Maybe that's what these vats do, fertilize all the trees and growing things in the whole complex."

"Gross." She pinched her nose.

As they got closer to the building, Matt pointed to a number fifteen on the door. He looked all around them, determined to be more cautious this time, and inspected the suspension area of what he assumed to be the control building for the vats of fertilizer. He didn't see any rust on the cables or anything else that looked like it might fall apart like some of the places they went past earlier.

"It looks safe enough." He patted the side of the trailer.

"That's what you said about the freezer," Stacy said.

"I don't think I said that."

"It looks okay to me too," Cody agreed. "Let's see if there's anything inside to help us figure out where we are."

They opened the standard door and went inside. This office was a little bit different from the earlier job-type trailer. There were botany illustrations on the wall and a small lab section with Erlenmeyer flasks and beakers with some dried chemical substances. There were bags of fertilizer in the corner. One of them was open and spilled out onto the floor. Everything was covered in dust.

"What's with the fertilizer? It's not like even those fifty-pound bags are enough to fill one of the vats," Stacy said.

"Probably just them working on formulas or somethin'," Cody said.

"Whoever it was, it looks like they left in a hurry. They couldn't even clean up the mess," Matt observed.

"The door said this is building fifteen. Let's look at your map and get our bearings straight," Cody suggested.

Matt pulled out the blueprints and spread them on the desk. "We're here." He pointed to the number fifteen on the blueprints. "Sub-level fifteen, fertilizer section."

"Kinda funny they kept the freezer next to the plant food," Stacy said.

"I don't understand any of the logic of this place." Cody wrinkled his brow. "Don't make a bit of sense."

"There's the mountain," Matt said. "But at this point, I think we need to put that on the backburner until we find the others."

"Agreed." Cody nodded.

"Definitely," Stacy chimed in.

Matt looked up at her. "You feeling better?"

"I'm always doing better when I'm not freezing to death," she said.

Matt shook his head. "So we're agreed. We find our friends, then worry about the mountain. Looks like the tram went around this bend and there's another stopping point here, so if we're lucky, maybe the tram came to a stop, and they were able to get off?"

"Let's go see," Cody said. "At least the tram track and our walkway stay together for a good long ways, instead of like that freezer split."

"Yeah." Matt's hands still hurt from holding the ice up to the light bulbs. *I hope I don't have frostbite.*

They left the building. The smell of fertilizer was so strong, Matt felt like it was permeating his clothes.

"Ugh, that smell," Stacy complained.

"At least it's warm," Cody joked.

"Yeah, but this?" She shook her head. "I need a shower just smelling it."

"That's why it's stronger now." Matt pointed at the vats under the walkway. They hung under a suspension track that could move whichever way the fertilizer line needed to send them, all over the complex. Matt peeked over an edge and screwed up his face at the brown slurry resembling gallons of raw sewage.

"Did you see that?" he asked.

"Looks like the bottom of an outhouse," Cody said.

Stacy held her nose. "Don't remind me. I had to use one at the county fair once. Second worst night of my life."

"And the first?"

"When I woke up here," she said.

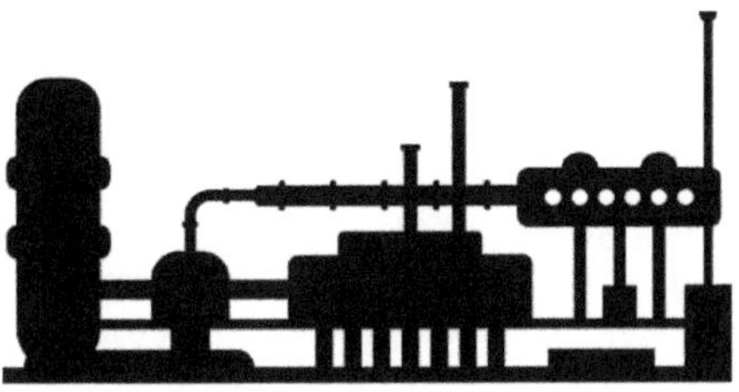

CHAPTER 26

The automation line suddenly hummed into a moving frenzy. Every single vat gave a loud clack as it moved down the conveyor belt, bumping along the suspension bridge. The sloppy sound of more fertilizer being dumped into the empty vats made Matt and Cody giggle.

"Boys and their potty humor. Lance-Darin wouldn't laugh at that. He's mature." Stacy groaned. "Let's get out of here."

"Hang on, let's see what it does before we just leave," Matt said.

"Why, so you can both make more fart jokes?"

"We never made any fart jokes." Cody chuckled.

Stacy rolled her eyes. Matt and Cody stifled laughter as the vats were filled, then moved down the line toward bulbs where tree roots dangled. The clear bulbs had hinges that opened wide, exposing the roots of the trees hanging down into the void. The moving vats, which were over eight feet wide in diameter and ten feet tall, hung on a special track, elevated by a chain system. Once in place, the roots were coated with the goopy fertilizer slurry. Within just a few seconds, the clear bulb would close over the roots again and fill with water from an automation system hidden somewhere inside the ceiling. They watched as the water and fertilizer mixed together.

"It's efficient," Matt said.

"I guess. Don't know why you couldn't just do it topside, though," Cody said. "I guarantee that would be cheaper."

"Not if you're worried about getting killed by volcanoes and blizzards," Stacy retorted.

"She's got a point," Matt said.

"I guess." Cody scratched his neck. "But I was just thinking about all of this and how much work it must be to mechanize every little thing, even caring for trees and fake lakes, and now no one is down here making sure the machines run smoothly. Everything has to be greased and managed, or it breaks down."

Matt stared at something in the distance. He stepped away from the others, much to their confusion.

"Matt? What did I say?" Cody asked.

Matt turned with a grin. "You said that the machines break down, and look at that!" He pointed down the track toward a tram car with their friends aboard. They could just make out Justin, Darin, and Catherine standing on the flatcar.

They rushed down the causeway, hooting and hollering in glee. "Darin! Catherine! Justin! Down here!"

They called back and waved, but Matt couldn't make out the words amidst the noise of the fertilizer vats and the groaning chains of the feeding system.

The causeway stretched way out, revealing a large, open space, wider than a football stadium, the boundaries lost in the darkness. Taking stock of the peculiar open area, Matt noticed massive fans in the ceiling. What could they be for? A wind tunnel in a basement? "Do you see that, Cody?"

"Yeah, must be a place where they make the non-frozen windstorms and tornados. The people that dreamt this stuff up are real creeps."

"Hold on, guys! I can't run as fast as you, remember?" Stacy called.

They slowed to wait for her despite being anxious to talk to their friends again. "Why do you think they stopped out in this wide-open space?" Cody asked.

"Maybe they finally figured out how to stop it, and it's just good luck that it was kinda close by." Matt shrugged.

A sprinkle of dirt hit Matt's shoulder, and he moved forward, dodging the falling particles. One of the plastic bulb covers opened, jammed with roots dangling outward. The fertilizer vat spread its goo, but as it started to move on, it struck the bulb, breaking it. The water mixture sprayed, but without the plastic bulb to hold the slurry, the earth and water fell to the causeway below in a muddy heap. The dirt around the tree was washed away by the automatic watering cables, and the tree slipped. Matt stared in horror as the tree slammed into the walkway with a great crash—separating him, Cody, and Stacy.

Matt raced ahead, while Stacy and Cody jumped back toward the fertilizer building.

The causeway groaned under the strain of the enormous tree, and metal girders snapped with loud pings.

Matt slid as the causeway tore away from its supports. His friends on the tram screamed, but they could do nothing to stop the terrible tug of gravity.

Matt grabbed the edge of the railing as the causeway bent nearly vertical.

Straining to hold on, he glanced up at Stacy and Cody. "Oh no!" he cried. "Guys!"

Cody and Stacy fell into one of the vats covered in the fertilizer slurry as it jerked along on the chain-driven link to feed the artificial forest.

Darin, Catherine, and Justin shouted Matt's name. He could barely make it out above the din of the machinery.

The causeway bent and rumbled, spurring Matt to act before the entire section fell with the tree into the dark abyss below.

The vat containing the goo-covered Cody and Stacy bumped along below him and farther back along the way they'd come.

"Matt! Drop into the next vat!" Darin called.

What? That was crazy. Then he would be as stuck as Cody and Stacy.

"The walkway is collapsing!" Justin shouted. "Hurry!"

"The vat will go right under us!" Catherine cried. "We've got you. Just jump in!"

Understanding dawned, and with a groan, Matt dropped into the horrid-looking brown mass. It felt like a massive, thick mud pie. He was grateful that it only went to his knees and not over his head. With some difficulty, he could almost get a leg out, but the other stuck farther down. This was gonna be tricky.

The walls of the vat were high enough that Matt couldn't see much of anything except those ominous fans in the ceiling and more sunlight now. Why was that? Oh yeah, there was a big, exposed hole from where the tree fell inside. *Built to last,* he mused.

"Matt, we're right behind you," Cody called. "Looks like we'll get to the tram, just a little dirty for wear."

"This is so gross!" Stacy shouted.

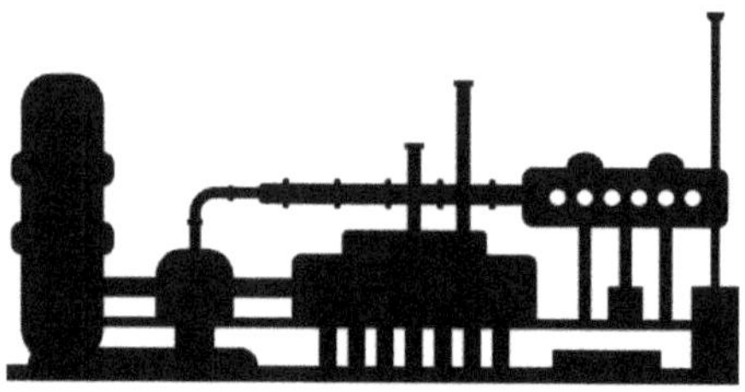

CHAPTER 27

"Matt, are you okay?" Catherine called.

"Never better. Oh wait, except that I'm stuck up to my knees in this muck!" he shouted back.

"At least it's not in your hair," Stacy answered from the next vat over. "I fell in, and Cody landed on top of me!"

"Not my fault when trees are falling from the sky." Cody laughed.

"We'll get you out with the robot arm," Darin shouted. "I think I've got the hang of it."

"I sure hope so," Matt said. "I don't want to get pressed into tree fertilizer."

The fertilizer vat line ran just a few feet beneath the tram track. Matt knew he couldn't reach the tram line on his own unless maybe he was able to climb on top of the vat, but he was stuck in the fertilizer goo like a rat in a cage.

"So long as the tram battery is on, we're good," Darin answered. "I'm gonna reach down to get you as soon as you get here. Should be in about one minute."

"What about us?" Stacy cried.

"I'll get you too," Darin said firmly. "We can time it right so long as everyone keeps cool. Can you keep cool?"

"I can keep cool," Stacy whimpered.

"It's all right," Cody said. "I'm here to help you."

"Oh crap," Justin said.

"What's 'oh crap'?" Matt called.

"Justin bumped against the ignition switch, and it broke off. We'll get it," Darin answered.

"I don't want to die," Stacy whined.

"You're not gonna die," Darin shouted. "I'll get you."

The clanking of the vats on the chain drive kept a malevolent beat like one of those German industrial bands. Matt did his best to extricate himself from the morass of sticky fertilizer, but it was hard going. Again, he thought that if he could climb to the rim of the vat, he wouldn't be dependent on the robotic arm. But climbing was not as easy as thinking about it.

"I think I can hot-wire it," Justin said.

"Hurry!" Catherine said.

"I'm trying," he grunted.

"Coming up quick, Matt. Be ready," Darin called.

"Is the arm working?" Matt asked.

"Not yet, but I'll pull you up if I have to hang upside down like a monkey."

"No, Lance-Darin, don't risk it. Save yourself!" Stacy shouted.

"It's gonna be okay. Almost here," Darin shouted. "Get ready, Matt!"

The vat banged along the track, keeping a rock-steady beat as the chain thumped like a drum machine.

Matt finally caught a glimpse of the tram and Darin leaning far over the edge, ready to lunge and grab him. The look of frustration on his sweaty face made it clear that the distance was farther than he had hoped.

"Got it!" Justin shouted as the tram engine crackled to life.

Darin manipulated the arm down into the vat. Matt grabbed hold, and the arm lifted him out of the muck and up onto the flatbed of the tram just before the vat, continuing its rhythmic beat down the track, traveled out of reach.

"We're gonna have to be really quick to get two people out. I barely made it with Matt," Darin alerted Cody and Stacy as the vat they were in neared the tram.

"I've got my rope. You get Stacy with the arm, and Cody, grab the rope!" Matt shouted.

"I'll be ready," Cody answered.

Matt unwound the rope and tossed it into the vat before Darin could even maneuver the arm down.

Cody helped Stacy climb onto the robot arm and only then took hold of the rope. Darin lifted Stacy to safety just before the vat ducked under the tram track.

Matt moved along the side of the tram flatcar. "Cody, I've got you. Let's pull you out." He heaved backward with Catherine and Justin's help.

"I'm having a hard time holding on. I'm slick with this slime," Cody said. "It got all over my hands and clothes."

"Wrap it around yourself," Matt answered.

"I'll try, but I'm running out of rope while this thing is moving," Cody said.

"Pull!" Matt shouted.

They pulled and pulled, and Cody came up out of the vat but dangled alongside the big bowl. He gradually slid back down the rope, only holding onto it with his goo-covered hands.

"Can you move the arm over there?" Matt asked.

"It won't reach that far," Darin answered.

"Come on, Cody, hang on till I can reach you," Matt grunted. "Guys take the rope; I'll reach for him."

Darin took Matt's place pulling the rope, while Matt bent down at the edge of the tram to reach for Cody's hand.

Cody slipped farther down the rope. Each tug only seemed to steal more line from his grasp.

Matt watched in horror as he strained to reach his friend. Visions of Kyle slipping away flashed, haunting him. This time, it wasn't turbulent waters that would carry his friend away, but the all-encompassing darkness below.

"I'm slipping." Cody's eyes widened.

Matt stretched as far as he could, but Cody's hand was still inches away, then farther as he slipped again, as if in slow motion.

Cody reached the end of the rope—and plunged into oblivion.

"No!" Matt screamed as Cody disappeared into shadow.

"What? No!" Catherine cried. "No! He didn't fall. He *couldn't*!" Justin took her in his arms.

"Is he . . . dead?" Stacy asked.

Darin nodded, and she buried her face into his chest.

Matt remained prostrate on the flatcar, staring into darkness. "I failed again," he muttered as he pushed himself to his knees. He stared straight ahead at nothing, fists clenched at his sides and teeth clamped together, willing himself not to lose it as pressure built up in his eyes.

A terrific crash brought daylight streaming down a few yards away. Another tree fell in a shower of dirt and debris as yet another mechanical mishap caused the ceiling and fertilizer units to break down.

"If you can get the tram running, get us out of here," Matt ordered.

"What about Cody?" Justin argued.

"He's gone, and if we don't get moving, we'll be joining him. Get us out of here."

Fifty yards away, another bulb and tree broke through, and a huge piece of the ceiling fell, ripping a massive gash in the artificial world above. This brought in a burst of light, changing what had been perpetual twilight below into midday.

A beam of light revealed a large reservoir beneath them. The banging of the metal fertilizer vats and chain drive had hidden the sound of the trees and dirt splashing into the gigantic lake below.

They all glanced down and shouted in joy.

Cody was alive and treading water.

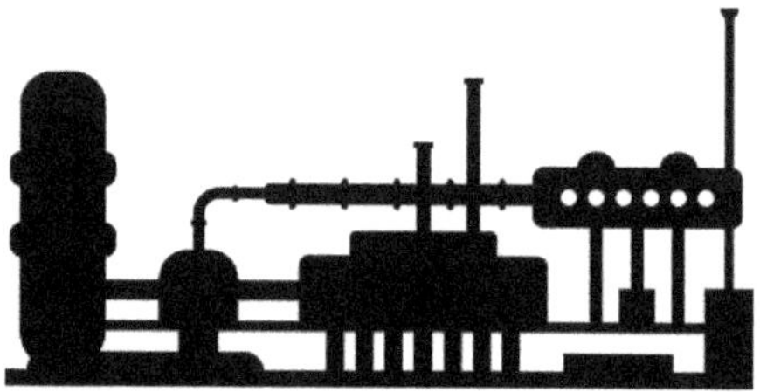

CHAPTER 28

The boundaries of the enormous reservoir stretched farther into the shadows than they could see.

"Is there anything we can throw him?" Justin asked. "Like a life preserver?"

"There's nothing like that on the tram," Darin answered.

"He could swim to a tree to float," Stacy offered.

"Can your rope reach him?" Catherine asked. "Maybe now he won't be as slippery."

"Yeah, he's had a bath the hard way!" Justin said with a nervous laugh.

"Cody! Can you hear us?" Matt called.

Cody swam toward a tree far below.

Another crash behind them rocked the tram's rail as a falling section of the ceiling slammed against it. Brighter sunlight revealed more of the reservoir and beyond.

"Matt was right. If we don't move, we're all going down with Cody," Darin shouted.

"Let's move and figure out how to help him when we're away from this crashing," Catherine agreed.

Justin stepped to the controls and started the tram gliding along. As they moved and more light shined down, an empty concrete canal and spillway revealed itself. Because of the direction of the sunlight, the back of the reservoir was still hard to see. The light didn't reach that far. The large fans slowly turned above them. More sections of the roof and forest collapsed around them.

"Go faster!" Stacy shouted.

"I can only do so much; it won't let me go any faster!" Justin yelled back.

"Hurry!" Catherine cried.

A bulb burst beside them, showering plastic and dirt down on them and the tram track, causing the tram to bump hard and almost derail. It moved another thirty feet and came to a screeching halt.

"Did we hit something?" Stacy asked.

"No." Justin glanced over the controls. "We lost power."

"Get us moving!" Darin barked.

Another chunk of the ceiling fell just a few yards away to their right.

Catherine looked down. "I can't see Cody anymore. I hope he didn't get hit with something."

"He's there." Matt pointed back to where he could see his friend dog-paddling amidst the dirty, swollen reservoir.

"The tram car can't go anywhere. It's stopped because of sporadic power surges. But there's an onboard battery that charged when the tram was running," Justin said.

"Can you get it going again?" Darin asked.

"For a fourth time now? Yeah, I think so."

Justin pulled out wires from a speaker system. He thumbed through the different wires and terminals underneath the control panel. Matt anxiously watched him while keeping an eye on Cody. Justin took a pair of long red and black wires from the speakers and connected them to the spare battery. Sparks jumped from exposed wires.

"Be careful," Catherine cautioned.

"Trust me," Justin said with a smirk.

More of the roof caved in a short distance away, but for the moment, their position was untouched.

Matt watched Cody swimming along. "He's getting closer. My rope could probably reach him now."

"I've got an idea as soon as someone gets the power back on," Darin said.

"Working on it!" Justin hollered in response.

"Throw your rope to Cody and tell him to make a seat. If this gets some power, I think we won't need to muscle him all the way up," Darin explained.

Matt nodded in appreciation and shouted, "Cody! I'm gonna toss you the rope. Make a seat, and we'll get you up!" He couldn't hear Cody's response, but he could see a big thumbs-up. Matt couldn't believe Cody had survived that horrific fall, but he was so thankful. He tossed the rope down. It took most of the length to reach all the way down to the reservoir. Cody must have fallen almost a hundred feet. It was incredible, but the Texan was sure tough.

Darin took the end of the rope and attached it firmly to the robotic arm's pincer.

"What's that gonna do?" Stacy asked. "It can't lift him all the way up here."

"Just wait," Darin said. "This arm has got some neat tricks. Do you have power yet?"

"Almost," Justin answered as another big shower of sparks shot from the control panel. "Got it!"

"Is Cody to the rope yet?" Darin asked.

"Yeah, he gave me another thumbs-up. He must have made a seat for himself," Matt answered.

"Watch this." Darin flipped a switch on the robotic arm's control panel. The pincer spun incredibly fast, looping the rope around itself, and brought Cody zooming up. "Just let me know when he gets close so I can slow it down. Don't want him slamming his head against the rail."

"Bitchin'!" Stacy yelled. "I totally knew you'd save us, Lance-Darin!"

"I'm watching," Matt said, ignoring her.

Cody zipped up into the air as the robotic arm grew fatter and fatter with the looped rope.

"Slow it down. He's almost here," Matt said.

Darin slowed the spinning pincer.

"Okay, stop," Matt said.

Darin stopped the arm as Matt sighed. "We've got him." He helped Cody climb over the side.

Cody breathed hard as water dripped from his hair and clothes. "Talk about one heckuva swimmin' lesson. I never want to do that again."

Catherine hugged him, and then Cody tromped into the nearest covered tram car and collapsed onto one of the sofas.

Justin was finishing his rewiring job when Matt noticed a screen with a small menu and a list of numbers. They corresponded to those on the blueprint map and to different tram stations. Some of the stations were near maintenance buildings, and other stations were just junctions. The screen itself was black, and the writing on the menu was in green DOS-style text. Matt looked at the blueprints and the next stations, and in his mind, he used these station markers as breadcrumb-style points on a map.

"The next station is twenty-three. But if we skip it, we can go right to the mountain, thirty-six," Matt said.

"How do we do that?" Catherine asked.

"Right here, it shows a way to program it where you want to go, but you can't really type on this, so I'm not sure how to bypass the other stops."

Catherine smiled. "It's simple. I guess you never took accounting?"

"No, I didn't."

"Use the down arrow and scroll to thirty-six." She moved the cursor and hit the enter button. The tram took off with just a few more bumps from debris on the tracks.

"Good work, brainiac!" Stacy said. "You must have been in one of those AP groups."

"Thanks." Catherine blushed.

Justin smiled at her. "Maybe you want to help me drive?"

"Sure." Catherine sat beside him in the front seat of the first car. The crimson shade her face had turned deepened.

Matt's stomach churned with a touch of jealousy as he watched them.

Stacy lounged on the back seat of the first car while Matt and Cody spread out on the middle passenger car's front seat. Darin remained on the flatcar, working the robot arm, carefully unwinding the rope into a neat coil on the floor.

The tram zoomed forward for another few hundred yards, then slowed to a stop.

"Out of power again. Are you kidding me?" Darin shouted.

"Maybe you used all the juice with your rope trick," Justin shot back.

"That's not fair. We had to get Cody," Catherine said.

"I'm grateful y'all got me out of the drink, but can we get moving again?" Cody said.

Sparks blasted Justin in the face. "Ouch!" He jerked back and rubbed his eyes. "Those suckers have a lot of power."

"Did you fry the whole system?" Stacy asked.

"I dunno." Justin returned to getting the tram going.

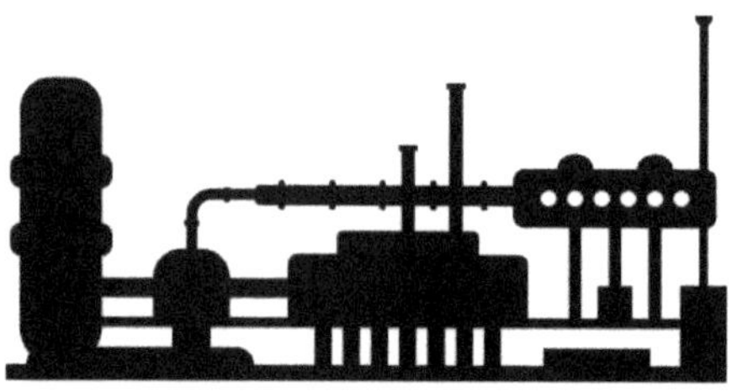

CHAPTER 29

Justin messed with the power and disconnected the wires, wiping the ends down on his shirt then reconnecting them again. The tram moved forward ten feet. "Yes!" Justin shouted.

The tram stopped again. "No!"

He repeated the process and was able to make it go again, but each time it only seemed to have enough power to move the same ten feet, jarring everyone each time it came to a stop.

"Do you need help?" Darin asked as he finished spooling the rope and lugged it back over to Matt.

"I got it. There must be a short in the line," Justin answered angrily.

"Just get it figured out!"

"I will," he muttered. "I think I liked your leadership approach better, chief."

Matt shrugged and stuffed the rope into his pack.

The vats on the chain system continued lifting their payloads of slurry beside the stuck tram, doing their programmed feeding routine despite the ceiling caving in around them.

Matt noticed a missing section of roof that the vats were approaching. "That won't end well," he said, pointing it out to Cody.

The line of vats continued on until they had almost reached the broken section of ceiling. A great rip and popping sounded, like buttons on a fat man's shirt snapping, as the support bolts for the chain drive fell and the vats began dropping. This made the ceiling break apart more.

Almost a full football field away, a few trees in the forest above began to bend and sway, then fell into the reservoir below. It was like the forest was all jumping in for a swim. Vats continued to lift as the column moved along, but the strain was too much for the failing ceiling. Trees and plastic bulbs crashed down, hitting a massive spinning fan. The huge fan blade, as long as a tractor trailer, snapped and plunged onto the track like a knife, slicing the track cleanly in half. The tram shook like an earthquake. It swung to and fro, reminding Matt of trying to balance on top of a barbed-wire fence. Without the stability of a solid track, the high-strung tramline was just a long piece of metal waving in the wind.

"Everybody, hold on!" Darin cried.

"I think I got the power back!" Justin said excitedly.

"You missed it," Catherine said. "We can't go forward anymore."

"Why not?" he asked, incredulous.

"It's gone. The track's gone."

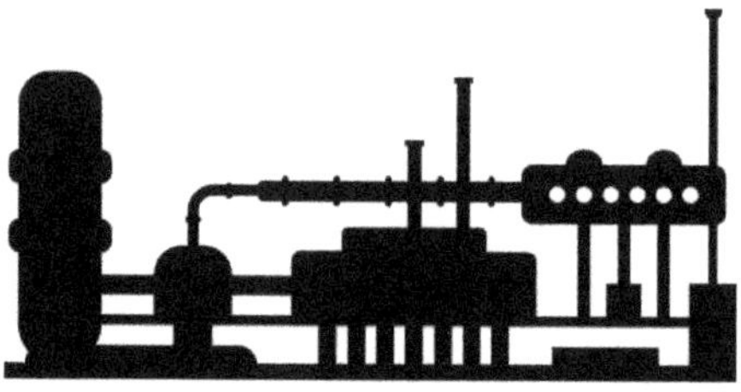

CHAPTER 30

Everything was caving in. Dirt, trees, bushes, rocks, fans, metal, and grates showered down, covering them in their weak shelter inside the tram cars. The beating on the roof sounded like *The Gong Show* gone wild, while a multitude of dents magically appeared in the ceiling. The suspended track swayed, wobbled, and began to tip lower.

"I got a bad feeling about this," Justin murmured.

"I don't like this!" Stacy shrieked.

They were all thrown forward, as if heading down a very steep hill.

Stacy and Catherine screamed. Justin swore. Matt realized he was screaming too, but Cody, who had so recently taken a high dive, remained silent.

"Everyone, hold on!" Darin shouted again.

The tram slid toward the end of the line, which dipped sharply down into the dark waters of the reservoir.

Darin swung the robot pincer arm around to grab hold of the track above and behind them, bringing their descent to an abrupt stop, at least for the moment.

"How does that still have power?" Justin asked as he hugged the front control panel.

"I don't know, but even if it loses power, I've got all the force I could get gripping the track. So long as the hydraulics hold out, we're okay. Besides, the last place we want to go is forward."

"What if the track doesn't hold out?" Stacy asked.

"I can't fix that." Darin shook his head.

"Can we walk back down the track?" Catherine asked.

"It will be tricky, but I think it's our only choice," Matt answered.

"Not with all that stuff falling out there, we'll be killed," Stacy whined.

"We can't stay here, Stace," Darin said.

"Is that really going to hold?" Matt tipped his chin at the robot arm.

"I think the pincer itself has an independent battery. It can keep us here, but that's it," Darin explained.

"So we need to get out and climb up onto the track and balance-walk our way back," Matt said.

"Or pull a Cody and swim our way to safety," Justin offered.

"I don't want to do that again," Cody said. "Rocks and dirt were hitting me. I almost got my clock cleaned by a boulder as big as my head."

"Neither choice is great," Darin growled.

The track shook and pitched them forward toward the reservoir. But the tram cars remained hooked together. Everyone braced themselves to stay upright.

One by one, each securing cable or metal support that hooked the track into the ceiling popped like corks out of champagne bottles.

The vat line had done the same thing under stress, and Matt knew how that had ended. "We can't go back. There isn't time," he said.

The track leaned more deeply toward the reservoir, while the track behind them slanted up to where it was still attached to the ceiling. It might have seemed like a roller coaster if it wasn't so deadly.

"We're stopped," Darin assured them. "The robotic arm is holding our position. We've got to figure out the best way down."

"Maybe we slide down my rope to the water?" Matt suggested. "Better than jumping for it from this height."

"Can you shut up about your rope for a minute!" Stacy huffed, then buried her face in Darin's chest. "It's no use!"

"How about the causeway?" Cody suggested. "I'm done swimming."

"I know it looks bad, but it can't get any worse," Darin said.

The support points holding the track pinged and broke. The entire tram line pitched, and everyone was thrown forward as the tram hung straight up and down. Catherine and Justin slammed against the windshield. Stacy's back pressed against the front seats. Cody and Matt were thrown forward, leaning against the front doorway of the middle passenger car. Darin hung above them, holding onto the robot arm.

CHAPTER 31

Somehow, with the strength of the robot arm and the grooves of the tram itself, they were still attached to the track.

"You were saying?" Justin coughed.

"Are we dead?" Stacy squeaked.

"No." Darin's voice came out a little strained as he clung to the robot arm. "Like I said, it's holding. For now."

"Can we move?" Catherine turned her head to look out the windshield she was pressed up against.

"We're going to have to at some point," Matt said.

Darin nodded, frowning.

"Is everyone okay? That was quite the tumble," Cody said.

Justin and Catherine moved with care, lowering themselves closer to the front of the tram car, backs against the front wall. Stacy remained pressed up against the back of the front row of seats.

"It looks like it's attached firmly to the track, and thanks to Darin's quick work with the arm, I think we're stuck here good," Matt said.

"Like a tick on a hound," Cody added.

"Why aren't you scared?" Stacy peered around the seat to look at the Texan.

Cody smirked. "Maybe cuz I already thought I was a goner twice today. I'm feeling numb to this roller coaster ride. Heck, I like 'em."

"Not me," she responded.

"I don't either," Catherine agreed. "If we ever get out of this, I'll never go on another one."

Darin released his grip on the robotic arm and landed spryly on the back end of the passenger car. Matt and Cody were ten feet below him and the others another ten feet beyond that. There was little they could use to climb up to his position.

"Everybody, take some deep breaths; we're going to have to get out of here one way or another, and soon," Darin said. "We'll need that rope again, champ. If there's one thing I'm glad about, it's that we decided to bring it along."

Matt nodded at him. "Thanks."

Catherine twisted around and glanced straight down the almost vertical track line. The swirling waters below moved, almost hypnotic, with the currents caused by the falling debris.

"Oh no." She gulped.

"I told you not to look down," Justin said.

"No, you did not!" she shot back.

"We're so high up." Stacy shivered and shut her eyes.

Matt withdrew the rope and looked through the windows for the walkway. It was much too far away.

"What are we gonna do?" Stacy's voice quivered.

"We'll figure it out," Darin said.

"How?" she whined.

"Shut up." Justin ground his teeth.

"Don't talk to her like that," Darin snapped.

"Everybody, take it easy," Matt said firmly. "We aren't gonna sit here forever, are we?"

"Maybe," Justin muttered.

Matt ignored him. "We'll figure it out. Let's all think on it and throw out some ideas. No wrong answers while you're brainstorming."

Darin looked back at the robotic arm. "If I release the arm's grip, we'll slide down into the reservoir. We'll all get down together, and then we can swim for that canal and spillway we saw."

"We'll be killed. Genius idea, *champ*," Justin spat.

Darin glared at him.

"Hey!" Matt snapped. "I said we were just brainstorming. Take it easy, we're all just trying to figure things out. This situation is too dire for us to start fighting amongst ourselves."

"*Dire?*" Justin mouthed mockingly. Catherine hit him in the shoulder.

Matt did his best to ignore the combative attitude. "I was wondering if we could toss my rope to the walkway."

"It's way too far," Darin said.

"What about with the robotic arm?" Matt looked up at him.

Darin shook his head. "It doesn't have that kind of kinetic force. It can lift great, but—"

"And spin," Stacy interrupted.

"And spin a rope, but it can't throw with any skill," Darin finished, nodding his head appreciatively at Stacy.

"I was thinking if it could spin things fast enough, we could wind it up and then have it throw a line with a weight attached," Matt suggested.

Darin nodded. "If we had the time, we could try and experiment, and maybe we could send a weighted line like you're saying, sure, but—and this is the big 'but' right now—as soon as the arm releases the track, we are falling down to the reservoir. We can't use the arm to throw anything."

"Then what are we gonna do?" Stacy asked with a dramatic shrug.

"Looks like all we can do is go down to the water and swim for it," Justin said.

"I don't have gloves anymore. I don't want to slide down the rope and burn my hands up and then try and swim," Catherine said.

"I could try and ease it down, then at least we're not plunged into the water," Darin said.

"Like easing your toes into a cold pool?" Matt asked.

"Well, more like jumping into the kiddie pool before you go into the deep end," Darin admitted.

"Ewww, kids, like, pee in the kiddie pool." Stacy winced.

"There's worse than that down there already," Cody reminded her.

Matt took charge again. "Let's have everyone buckle up as best they can and try your idea. Maybe let's attach a rope to you since you can't buckle at all while you're manipulating the arm."

Darin shook his head. "I don't know what will happen, but I'd rather not get hung up on a rope if we go down fast. I'd rather take my chances jumping clear than being tied to the tram when it hits water. We don't know how deep it is, do we, Cody?"

"No idea," he answered. "I sure never touched bottom, not even when I fell a hundred feet. I must have gone under at least twenty feet, too."

"Guys, this is too dangerous," Catherine argued.

"We're out of choices, Catherine. We've got to try something before the roof right above our heads comes down on us. We have a ticking time bomb right now," Matt said as a handful of dirt fell amongst them.

"Okay," she said softly.

"Everyone, buckle up," Matt ordered.

Darin climbed back up the robotic arm, so he sat astride the base and control panel. "Everybody ready?"

"We're ready," Matt answered.

"We're ready! *Gajong*!" Justin waved his arms as if he were playing a guitar, mimicking the beginning of a Van Halen song.

Darin wiped sweat from his forehead and gingerly put his hands on the control toggle that both opened and moved the claw. He pressed lightly, and nothing happened.

He took a deep breath and repeated the motion.

"Everything good back there?" Matt asked.

The claw sprung open, and they raced down the track.

"Oh crap!!!" Darin hung on for all he was worth, desperately trying to get the claw to grasp the track again, but now they were falling straight down, and the claw could not get a grip. Instead, sparks and metal from the track flew behind them like a comet's tail.

Someone screamed.

The tram slammed to a stop, and Darin faceplanted into the control panel.

"You did it! Are you all right?" Matt asked.

"Am I bleeding?" Darin mumbled, staring down at his wet shoes. His hands shook from the force of holding the toggle and panel's switches during the plummet.

"No, we're in the water—and we're horizontal again! We might have to start swimming, though." Matt splashed at the water with his feet.

"Oh, Lance-Darin, you're a hero!" Stacy squealed. She slogged over to him and threw her arms around his neck.

"Good," Darin whoofed.

"It's a boat now." Stacy smiled.

They all looked about. They were upright and floating on the reservoir, while behind them, more pieces of the roof dropped into the water, causing waves and swirling eddies, which made them bob across the deep-green waters like a cork.

"Are we sinking?" Darin asked.

Cody shook his head. "Not yet, anyway. It's almost like it was designed to float like a raft."

"Now, if we just had a way to move this tub," Justin said.

"We'll find a way. We always do," Catherine said with a big smile of relief on her face.

"That's right," Matt agreed.

"Smooth sailing from here on out, eh, chief?" Justin slapped Matt on the back.

"I hope so," he answered.

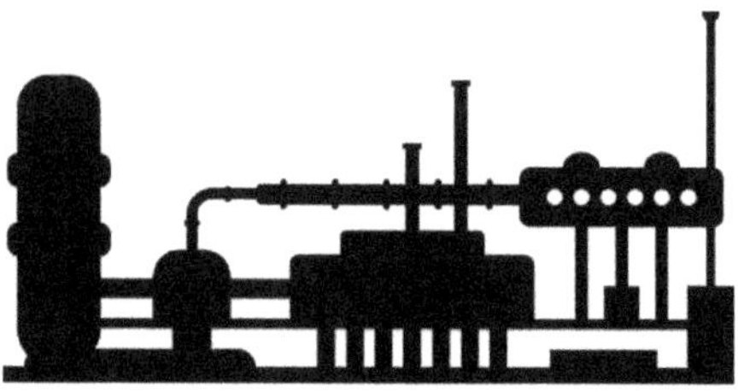

CHAPTER 32

A long piece of tin crashed into the roof of the tram pod connected to the flatcar where they stood, admiring their luck at floating over the waves. They all dashed for the enclosed pod.

As Cody ran for cover, a splash of earth-covered tree roots doused the floating pod, blinding him. Stumbling back, he tripped on the sidewall of the flatcar. "Matt!" he yelled as he fell overboard.

Somehow, over the din, Matt heard him and raced headlong through the showering dirt and debris to extend a hand to Cody.

"We've got to get out from under this!" Darin shouted as he glanced about for a way to paddle the pod-turned-raft. "Stacy, grab that broom!"

They rushed back outside the pod to help Matt and Cody.

A girder splashed down not far behind them, sending a wave that pushed them away from the most dangerous of the falling debris.

Matt grasped Cody's hand, braced himself against the edge of the pod's plastic wall, and pulled him to safety.

Mud ran down the side of Cody's face, mingling with the blood from a cut to his jaw.

Matt gripped Cody's shoulders. "You all right?"

"Let's just say I don't feel like taking another bath just yet. But this ain't my first rodeo. I'll be okay." He grinned.

"Let's try and move this heap," Justin scowled, "before the rest of the roof lands on top of us!"

Without a means to paddle beyond the broom Stacy found, they reached their hands in and stroked in unison.

"This isn't working!" Stacy cried.

"Maybe we can use the robotic arm . . . if it still works?" Justin suggested.

"It's dead." Darin looked back at it. "Coming down that roller coaster almost tore it out of its housing."

Matt glanced about and pointed at the spillway. "If we can get to that canal's edge, we can climb down the spillway."

"To where then, Einstein?" Justin complained.

"Well, we can't stay here. Besides, it looks like the only way out of here," Matt said.

"He's right," Darin confirmed. "The rest of this is just a service basin. People weren't meant to be down here."

"If we're gonna move this, we have to work together," Catherine shouted over the chaos. "Half of us stroke together on this side and the other half on the other side. Hopefully, that will give us some kind of uniform force to move this thing."

They paddled as in sync as they could manage toward the man-made spillway and the empty canal. It was slow going, since the pod floated but was not designed to be a streamlined boat at all. As they neared the edge of the concrete bank, Matt cursed under his breath. The sides were much steeper than they'd looked from afar.

"If I jumped out to that, I think I'd tumble right back into the boat," Cody said.

"Maybe with good climbing shoes, I could Spider-Man up that," Justin answered.

"Yeah, but you're not wearing good climbing shoes, are you?" Catherine glared at the concrete wall.

"Nope."

As they paddled, more debris fell from above. A heavy piece of metal, big as an engine, splashed water over the top of them, sending another chaotic wave that turned the pod about in the dizzying lake.

"Guys! Faster! It's gonna get bad," Darin shouted as he paddled furiously.

A big fan blade whirled down, slowly spinning as the last of its inertia failed.

Stacy screamed.

"Paddle! Everyone together!" Matt ordered.

They grunted and gulped in air as they paddled in unison in the other direction, but the sloshing reservoir waters made them spin almost in place.

Narrowly missing them, a careening fan blade landed like a giant's sword stroke on the edge of the reservoir, cutting into the concrete. Cracks formed where the blade hit, and water flowed over and through the damaged spillway, slowly at first, until the cracked barrier could no longer hold the water pressure back. Chunks of broken concrete flushed away in an instant, and the gouge grew larger as they watched.

"Look at that force. This must be a lot bigger reservoir than we can see," Darin said.

"Guys, I think we should get away from that," Catherine yelled, just before it ripped open like a deafening zipper.

Powerless to do much else, they all held on as the tram car raft was yanked toward the gaping wound in the reservoir.

"Paddle harder! All together!" Matt shouted.

They dipped their arms into the cold, dark water and stroked for all they were worth, but were pulled inexorably toward the open fissure. The gap widened as more pieces of concrete fell with the force of the water. Chunks battered and slid down the newly formed canal.

"This must be like how the Grand Canyon was formed," Justin said.

"Not now," Cody muttered, shaking his head.

The cascade of water swept them toward the spillway. The tram car slammed against the edge, held there for now, as it was still too wide to fit sidelong through the breach.

"Should we jump?" Catherine asked.

"It's too steep. Stacy couldn't make it!" Darin answered.

"Save yourselves," Stacy cried. "I'll love you forever, Lance-Darin!"

"I'm not leaving you. We have nowhere to run to yet, and this whole spillway is breaking up."

"You're breaking up with me?" Stacy gasped.

"What? No!" Darin shouted.

"Don't yell at me!" She broke into tears.

More cracks beside the spillway caused a full-on flood out into the canal, toward the open pipes on an opposite wall.

Matt turned to Darin. "We're stuck. Can the arm push us off or anything?"

Darin shook his head with a scowl. "I told you the arm is broken!"

"Can you just try it?" Matt asked, a note of desperation in his voice.

Darin rolled his eyes but took the controls and tried to move the arm. Sparks flew from the lower base, but the arm swung in spasmodic jerks and grabbed the side of the spillway. "It worked!"

The pincer of the arm held onto a piece of concrete connected to a protruding section of rebar.

"Now what?" Justin asked.

The concrete crumbled, and the tram cars whipped forward and slipped off the edge. They slid down at a forty-five-degree angle into a canal. They zoomed along, screaming as dirty water gushed over the top of the tram car, soaking them. The tram shuddered as debris slammed into the front of it and scraped underneath it.

"Hold on! It's gonna get worse!" Matt cried.

"What is it?" Catherine shouted.

"Duck low and hold on!" Darin dropped to the floor, abandoning his station at the arm.

A fan blade stretched across the canal. The tram cars slammed into the waiting blade, and the roof peeled back with a screech. Glass, plastic, and metal fragments covered the group.

A rending groan and thump sounded behind them.

"What was that?" Stacy asked.

"The arm!" Darin answered.

"What?"

"It's gone!"

The water, carrying them with it, rushed toward massive tubes sucking the water up. "That has to be where water goes to feed the floods or something," Matt said.

"Then we don't want to go there!" Darin grimaced.

"What should we do?" Catherine asked.

"I've got an idea," Matt said. "This canal is about as wide as the tram cars. Maybe if we all go to the back, hold on, and jump up and down, it'll drag us sideways and wedge us."

"Or it might just flip us over." Justin eyed the approaching tubes.

"Would we be any worse off?" Matt asked.

"No. Let's try it," Justin agreed.

They all crowded to the back of the flatcar. The bottom scraped against the concrete beneath with the added weight.

"Now, let's jump in place," Matt said.

They jumped, and as they landed in unison, the pod slammed against the bottom of the canal, forcing the car to catch on the bottom edge. The front-end car whipped about and wedged against the other side of the canal. The water hitting it sideways tilted the tram, nearly flipping it over into the turbulent water.

"That was risky," Justin said.

"Quick! Everyone out!" Matt ordered.

They scrambled out onto a concrete bank. Darin went last. He crouched to leap, and the tram car flipped, throwing him into the murky water.

"Lance-Darin!" Stacy screamed.

He spun end-over-end in the brown water. He righted himself and, with desperate strokes, tried to swim against the strong current to no avail. The unforgiving deluge carried him toward the big, open pipes.

Matt rushed forward, working to make a lasso with his rope, inwardly cursing himself for his dangerous plan to get them to shore, potentially costing his friend his life, and wishing he could be as good with a lasso as he guessed Cody was. But there was no time. His hands shook as he formed a loop in the rope and glanced up at the massive open pipes that gulped down thousands of gallons of water every second.

Matt tossed the looped end to Darin, who was spitting out mouthfuls of dirty brown water. Darin caught the rope, and it stretched taut as he vanished beneath the churning waters into the gaping black hole.

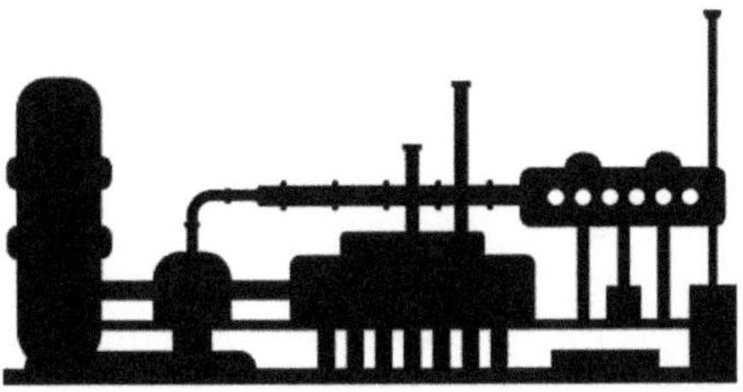

CHAPTER 33

"Lance-Darin!" Stacy cried. "No!"

"As long as he holds on, we've got him!" Catherine tried to comfort Stacy, who was awash in tears once more.

"Chill, it's going to be fine." Justin grabbed onto the rope behind Matt.

Catherine narrowed her eyes at Justin but said nothing as she rubbed Stacy's shoulders.

Matt, Cody, and Justin pulled the rope hand-over-hand against the flow of the water. Darin broke the surface with a sputter—alive and conscious, but coughing, gasping for breath, and almost drowned. As they pulled him onto the edge of the concrete bank, Stacy struggled to reach him.

"Hold on, give him some room to breathe." Catherine held her back.

Darin coughed up a gut-full of water.

"You all right?" Matt asked.

Darin nodded and coughed up another mouthful before finally answering. "That was a ride I never want to go on again. The pipes look like they flow on this level, but they don't. That was a sheer drop down. Never would have gotten back if you guys hadn't pulled me up."

"Oh, Lance-Darin, don't scare me like that!" Stacy broke away from Catherine and threw her arms around his neck.

Darin struggled to draw a breath, but he didn't bother to make Stacy let go. His face flushed a little with the moment.

"Let me get just a little more of a breather, huh?" he finally said.

Stacy stepped back to give him space, but she beamed.

As Darin lay on the edge of the concrete bank, Matt glanced around at their new surroundings. There hadn't been much of a chance while they'd been riding the floating tram or fishing Darin out of the pipe.

Matt's eyes widened, and he pointed at two green steel doors, one on each side of the canal.

Darin's gaze followed the trajectory of his pointing fingers. "Maybe I was wrong, and people were meant to be down here to check on things."

"Two doors." Stacy looked back and forth between them. "Which one should we take?"

"The only one we can without swimming," Darin answered. "Besides, they probably connect together on the other side of the wall anyway."

"So the maintenance people could have gone everywhere down here," Catherine agreed.

"If maintenance people had been around doing their jobs, this thing wouldn't be falling apart," Justin seethed. "I mean, how long have we been frozen for all of this to be in this condition?"

"Decades," Darin answered somberly.

There was a hint of gloom that hung over them at the thought. Matt gave himself a mental shake. "Let's go bust open that door and keep moving."

Justin raced ahead and kicked the door to no effect. Cody ran and tried the same maneuver, but the door held up to his assault too.

"Let me." Darin threw his full shoulder against the door. It didn't even budge.

Stacy raised an eyebrow at the boys, put her hand on the knob, and turned it. The door swung open on creaking hinges.

"I can't believe we didn't try that in the first place." Cody laughed.

"I just thought it would be locked." Justin shrugged. "Who knew it would be so easy?"

"I totally did." Stacy gestured at herself with a thumb.

A rare moment of laughter broke the tension.

"Come on, guys, let's check it out." Matt led them through the doorway.

Pipes of varying sizes covered the walls inside. Running water echoed through the massive plumbing system, and leaking water dripped from a few of the more rusted pipes. One spit a pin-sized leak at them like a squirt gun. The wall stretched the entire height of the subfloor. Dim lights shone at a wide doorway far ahead. Matt led them toward that light. They passed by ladders and scaffolding showing where workmen could climb up to check gauges and other apparatus among the multitude of pipes. Streams of water pooled on the ground and ran into musty-smelling grates.

Once they had walked the length of a basketball court, they passed through the brighter doorway into another walled-off section. The doorway was thick, and the passage extended almost twenty feet through a solid rock wall. None of the water pipes came to this side. This section housed an open bay with towers and different construction vehicles on different lift systems. It reminded Matt of a toy shop for a giant, with full-sized toy trucks on the shelves, just waiting for a gargantuan child to come and take them down.

The veritable lattice of vehicles reached close to the top of the sub-floor, back up by the walkway.

"I can't hear the water anymore," Catherine said.

"I think all of that damage is behind us," Justin answered.

"Good riddance," Stacy said.

Matt nodded, looking up. "I think it's because we're on the other side of a big rock wall dividing the collapsing reservoir side from this garage. This area had to be built strong to hold all these vehicles."

"Stronger than holding a lake-sized reservoir?" Justin teased.

"You know what I mean."

Catherine broke in. "Guys, at least the building isn't coming down on us at this point."

"Should I be scared that I don't, like, think we're going to die right this second?" Stacy piped up. "I mean, is it a bad sign that nothing is happening to us right now?"

Darin held her close. "It's all right. There doesn't have to be something horrible every moment."

Matt looked at the trucks and elevators. "I think we're as far down as anyone is supposed to be."

"The basement?" Cody asked.

"Looks like, since this is the lowest the elevators go."

"So we can only go up from here," Catherine said with a smile.

"Exactly." Matt smiled back at her. "The walkway is way up there, but as long as these lifts are working, we can get up there and keep moving."

"Maybe we can even get one of these trucks working, and we can drive our way out of here," Justin said.

"Hot dog, that's a good idea!" Cody slapped his hands together. "Let's see what we can get running!"

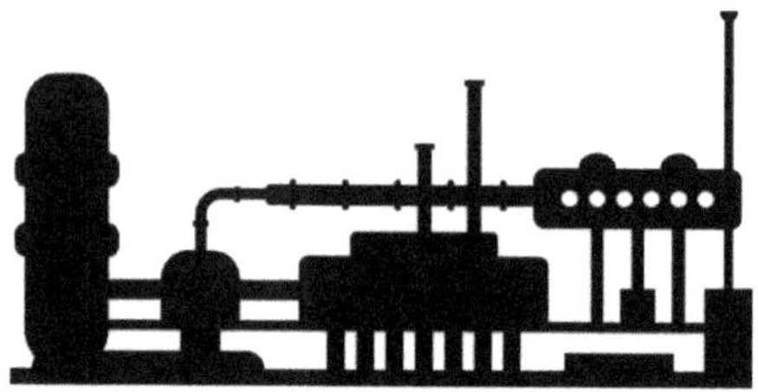

CHAPTER 34

"Well, let's check them out!" Darin raced forward to look over a Humvee.

Stacy followed, giddy at the idea. "I've never ridden in one of these before."

"We gotta see if we can get it started first." He smiled down at her.

Several of the vehicles on the ground floor had their hoods open, as if someone had been working on them and then just walked away, never to return.

Catherine tried the door of a small pickup. "This one is locked."

"Break the window!" Justin said.

"I'm not gonna break and enter." She put a hand on her hip.

"Like anyone here will care," he responded.

Cody looked under the hood of the first truck he came to. "This one is missing a battery."

"So is this one," Matt announced. "It's almost like somebody took them and hurried away. Why would they do that?"

"Maybe they were expecting an EMP and wanted to have extras in the shelter," Matt suggested.

"Like, what's an EMP?" Stacy asked.

"An electromagnetic pulse—it happens with nukes and maybe space stuff, like a flare from the sun. There was something I read about once called the Carrington Event. It happened back in like 1859. It fried all the telegraph wires."

"What?" Justin gasped. "No way, man."

"Really," Matt insisted, in all seriousness. "For all we know, that could be part of what this apocalypse is caused by."

Catherine had not broken into the locked truck, but moved on to another and announced, "There's no battery in this one, either."

"Let's keep trying," Matt shouted. "I don't think they could have taken all of them."

"Don't be so sure, chief," Justin said. "Every single one I've checked is missing a battery."

"As long as we can get even a hint of a spark, we can get them running," Darin responded.

"Don't even need the keys. I can hot-wire any of these." Justin laughed.

"Dang it!" Cody said.

"What?" Matt looked at his friend.

"I keep forgetting the time we've lost," Cody responded.

"So?"

Cody scratched at the back of his neck. "The gas has evaporated, and where would we drive to anyway?"

"B-35," Darin said soberly.

"It's been so dang long that any gas left in these has probably long since gone bad. The tram only worked cuz it was electric," Cody continued.

"We've gotta try," Matt said. "Doesn't diesel last longer?"

"Maybe. But without batteries, we're never gonna get any of these started and drive them anywhere."

"Plan B, then," Matt said.

"Which is what?" Justin asked with more than a hint of disdain.

"We climb up the tower of shelved vehicles as high as we can go. Back to a regular walkway, hopefully without any pitfalls and roofs falling in, and we keep going to B-35. We've got to do it with or without a ride."

Justin slammed the hood down on the truck he was looking at. "You're right, chief. If we can't drive, we might as well start walking."

"Climbing." Catherine pointed at the ladder and scaffolding.

"Ugh, why can't the elevators work?"

"The way things have been going, they'd probably drop us," Stacy said.

"I've still got the blueprints, and the walkway that leads to the mountain is right up over there." Matt lifted his chin to indicate the walkway.

"You sure about that, chief?" Justin asked.

Matt studied the blueprints he'd laid out on the hood of a truck. "There's another tram up there. I say we stay on mission, find the mountain—and our parents."

"Do you think that's a good idea?" Stacy asked. "The tram, I mean?"

"If the roof isn't falling in, and we keep Justin away from the robotic arm, it will be fine," Darin answered.

"Hey!" Justin muttered.

"I'm kidding."

Matt folded the blueprints and shoved them back in his backpack. "Let's head up here." He led them past other abandoned vehicles, dump trucks, backhoes, and dozers. Reaching the ladder, they slowly ascended. Climbing was tiring but pretty efficient. There were landings on every story, and they could rest, even though their destination was almost forty stories up.

Halfway up, Stacy looked down the ladder and gasped.

Darin was right behind her and put a hand on her calf. "Don't look down. I'm right behind you, and we can do this, no sweat."

"I'm already sweating like it's the Fourth of July. Wait, does anyone know what day it is?"

"It doesn't matter anymore." Darin chuckled.

"Don't laugh at me," she snapped.

"I'm not laughing *at* you. I'm laughing *near* you. It was just funny to think about how days don't matter anymore, just right now."

"That makes sense," Stacy said as she continued her ascent up the ladder.

"This reminds me of climbing the radio tower on the top of U Hill back where I grew up," Justin said.

They reached the top row of vehicles and looked over toward the walkway. "I thought you said this would connect?" Justin complained.

The long climb had not brought them to the walkway. Instead, they were parallel to it, separated by almost twenty feet. Twenty feet that stretched out over the gap, including a drop of more than two hundred feet. There was a collective sigh. Matt had promised them a simple walk, and now they were faced with a crevasse.

"Hang on, guys, I think we can get over there," he said.

"How?" Stacy cocked her head to the side and tapped her toes on her good foot, as if he had just told her they would have to walk home from the mall.

"I've got my rope," he said cheerily.

"You and your damn rope," Justin scoffed.

"It saved my life." Darin narrowed his eyes at him.

"Yeah, but—" Justin stammered.

"Yeah, but what? Hear the man out," Darin insisted.

"Thanks." Matt lifted his chin toward Darin. "Anyway, if I can find something to use as a grappling hook, I think I could shimmy over. We all could."

"Not me," Stacy said. "I might as well start climbing back down now. Come on, Darin."

"No, he's onto something. Besides, we don't know what way down there would get us back to the walkway. I didn't see any other stairs or anything."

"This is the only way," Matt said, glancing around the back of a suspended truck that was parked on the side of the vehicular elevator. "This will work," he proclaimed, holding up a vehicle jack.

"Don't tell me. This one has a battery?" Justin asked, still teasing the concept.

Cody shook his head. "Gas would still be bad, even if there was one."

Justin frowned.

Matt ignored the discussion. He really wanted this to work. He hated the idea of making everyone climb all the way back down just to hunt for another route to the walkway and farther on to the mountain, where their parents lay in frozen slumber. This had to work.

He tied the end of the rope to the heavy jack, hoping it would function like a grappling hook. He threw the jack like a shot-put over the railing, hoping it would snag and wrap around the walkway. A loud clang echoed throughout the massive garage when the jack connected with the metal. But it did not hook around the railing like he'd hoped, and it pulled loose. He pulled the rope to him, preparing to try again. Justin sighed loudly, and Stacy rolled her eyes so aggressively, Matt swore he *heard* it.

It took a few attempts before he got the jack to snag on the railing and the support structure. He tugged on it hard to be sure it held tight. He tied his end to the frame of the shelving. It was almost even and straight across. Matt laughed to himself. *Finished my Eagle Scout badge forty-something years ago. Guess it really stuck with me.*

"Looks good, boss," Darin said.

Matt pulled on the rope one more time to test its hold. "Here she goes," he muttered. He grasped it with both hands, then kicked his legs up over the rope. He hung there for a moment as they all waited, holding their breath.

"You okay?" Catherine asked.

"Yeah, just making sure that if it went slack and dropped, I'd still be right next to you guys," he said.

"Well, next time, give us a warning, huh?"

"Sure," Matt said.

The rope bowed a little bit, and the metal railing made a slight creak, but the jack held true. Matt pulled himself, hand-over-hand.

He was about halfway when the jack slipped a little, and the rope dropped a couple of inches.

Catherine gasped.

"It's okay. It's holding fine," Matt assured her. He looked down. He dangled over the open-air bay of vehicles. The drop was greater than when he had come down the air shaft, but then it had been dark. Now everything was all lit up, and he could see the gray concrete floor as plain as day. It disturbed him more than the dark had. He lost focus, and his legs slipped off the rope. He dangled by just his hands.

"Matt!" Cody yelled.

"I'm fine. I wasn't paying attention." Matt grunted as he readjusted his grip.

"Focus, man," Darin boomed.

Catherine held her hand to her mouth and looked away.

"Idiot," Justin muttered.

Matt breathed heavily. This was a little more difficult than he thought. It had been a hard day, and they were all pushing themselves to extremes. It took a few attempts, but he got his legs over the rope again.

"Don't scare us like that," Cody shouted.

"Sorry," Matt answered. The coarse rope burned the back of his calves. But he kept going until his hand finally touched the cold metal of the railing. He made it. Matt breathed a sigh of relief and awkwardly climbed onto the walkway.

"You did it. Good job," Darin shouted.

"Thanks!" Matt made sure the end of the rope with the jack handle was secure and tight. "All right, you saw me do it. We can all do it and keep going."

Stacy folded her arms. "I can't do that. You're stronger than I am, and you almost fell!"

Matt shook his head. "Stacy! I quit paying attention for a second and let myself slip. It was dumb, but I'm okay, and guess what? We've been doing these amazing things on our journey to find our parents all day. You have done awesome things all day, and you can do this too! I know you can. I believe in you. Darin believes in you. We all do!"

"You really think so?" she asked.

"I know so. You climbed down the elevator shaft. You got out of the fertilizer vat. You helped us in the freezer. You can do anything you set your mind to."

"You promise?"

"I absolutely do!" His stomach twisted a little. *I hope.* Doubt crept in. *What if we lose someone else because of one of my ideas?*

"Okay, I'll try," she said.

Darin helped her get on the rope and looped a short safety line to her to give her a little more confidence. She went hand-over-hand and slid her ankles along the line until Matt could reach her and help her down to the walkway.

"See? I told you, you were amazing." The tightness in his chest eased just a bit.

"I don't remember you saying that." She blushed.

"Well, you are," Matt said.

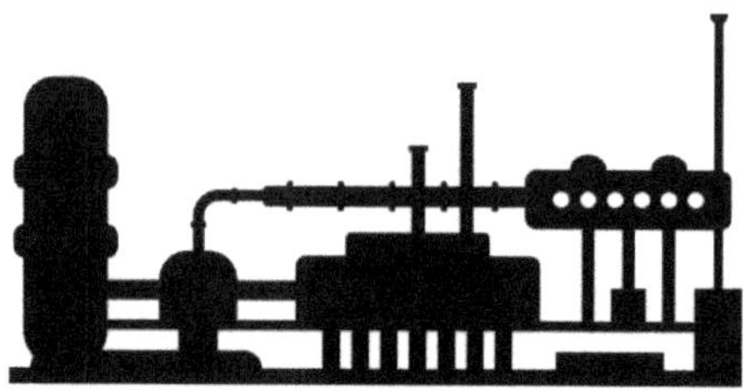

CHAPTER 35

Darin was last and looped the rope about through the railing on the other side and attached it to himself as a safety line, so once he got to the other side, they could unravel the loops and keep the useful line. This was one tool that was too valuable to leave behind.

"Everyone good?" Matt asked after they had all rested from their climb for a few minutes.

"I'm great! Amazing even!" Stacy beamed.

"I think we're good to go," Catherine said.

"All right." Matt wiped sweat from his forehead. "The blueprints say we should go this way, and we should be close to another section where we can find a tram and get to the mountain."

They joked together as they walked; all of their moods improved. The causeway curved in an easy arc several blocks long and took them away from the reservoir and solid rock wall that helped retain it.

Justin, walking in front with Catherine, suddenly stopped. "No way."

"What?" Catherine asked.

"Look at that!" He pointed.

A hundred yards in front of them stood an elevator.

"What's the problem?" Darin asked.

"Another elevator. Where the tram was supposed to be. Chief here isn't interpreting the blueprints right," Justin accused.

"There's a long platform. For sure the tram would have stopped here," Matt countered.

Darin glanced over the prints. "Maybe because it's a long ride up?"

"Guys," Catherine interrupted. "Let's not fight. Let's just see if it works and keep moving." She pushed the button. Motors groaned on the other side of the doors. From behind the steel doors came the tell-tale whine of cables operating.

"It's moving," Cody mused, "but why isn't the door opening?"

After a couple of minutes, Stacy suggested, "Maybe it's broken."

"Then let's find another way," Catherine said. "Let's look at the blueprints again."

Darin studied them. "There's another junction back the other way past the wall we walked through earlier, so we could go check that out."

"Isn't that where the roof fell in?" Justin said.

"Maybe not as far as we floated and walked," Catherine said. "When the tram finally went down, we could see far on the opposite wall that the track was still there, along with other doors and things."

"Well, if the door isn't opening, we better go another way." Matt's shoulders slumped a little. He felt a lot of pressure to be the voice of reason and try to keep everyone's spirits up, but leading them to false starts was not the way to do that. He rolled up the blueprints, thankful they didn't get so wet as to ruin them, and put them safely in the backpack.

Just as they began to walk away from the elevator, the doors moved apart with a screech of metal-on-metal and a pressured *whoosh*.

"I'm so tired of hearing metal grind," Catherine said. "What's happening now?"

They all turned in unison. The elevator doors were partly open, beckoning them to enter.

Cody rushed forward to keep them from closing.

One of the doors stuck halfway, so Justin pushed it open the rest of the way.

"Is it safe, though?" Stacy asked. "I mean, why did it take so long to open?"

"Maybe it had a long way to go to get here; the blueprints did make it look as long as a tram track," Matt guessed.

Darin looked inside. "I think it's old, but I don't see any water damage."

"What about the parts you can't see?" Justin asked.

Cody scanned everything he could as well. "Old, but looks solid and clean."

"Let's go, then," Catherine said.

"We've got to keep moving," Matt agreed. They all crowded inside.

"Look at that. It's almost like a window." Stacy observed a clear plexiglass side that revealed a concrete wall beyond.

The doors slowly closed, and the elevator jerked and started to rise.

"Did someone hit a button?" Catherine asked.

"I didn't see one," Darin said. "Must only go between two floors?"

The elevator rose, and through the plexiglass, they watched as they moved beyond the ceiling of the subfloor. They saw a floor grate with several feet of dirt above it.

Stacy cupped her hands around her eyes and pressed them up against the scratched, foggy window to try and see more of the world outside while the elevator rose. "This is like the Steamtown Mall, where you can look down on the food court four levels down," she said. "But where is the top?"

Almost in answer, they passed by massive metal beams and I-beam roof trusses, then multiple cables and pipes hidden inside a dark outer housing.

"This is the mountain," Matt said as he pointed at the blueprints. "We're almost there!"

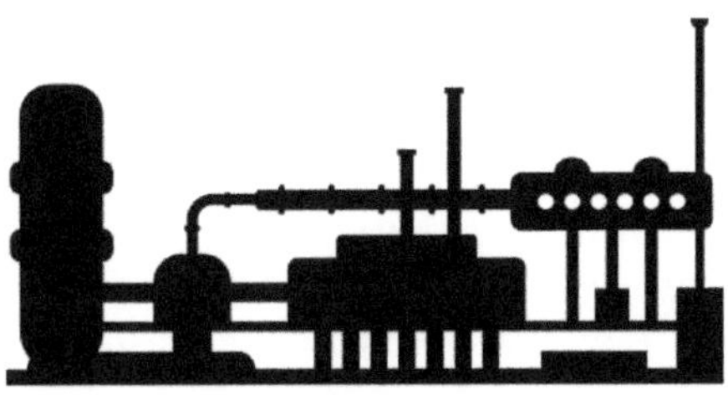

CHAPTER 36

The elevator bumped along slowly.

Matt grinned and grabbed Catherine's arm. "We're getting close!"

"You really think this might be B-35?" she asked.

"Yes." Matt let his hand linger on her arm, enjoying the flush of warmth it brought him.

"Everything is so fake," Justin complained. "Why here?"

Matt shrugged. "It's all man-made. This could be an extension of HZRD. This could be the cavern. We've traveled a long way from where we were topside, past the trucks, and where Nathan . . ."

"I know what you mean," Catherine interrupted, taking his hand.

Justin slowly nodded. "Sorry, chief. I sure hope you're right."

The elevator continued rising, and the tension and excitement of where it might stop had all of them glancing about anxiously.

"Can't wait to see my folks again," Cody said with an *aw shucks* grin.

"We're almost there," Stacy squealed, taking Darin's hand. "I'm going to introduce you to my parents!"

Darin was the only one who seemed devoid of excitement.

The elevator slowed and came to a stop. The doors crept open onto a large room.

Matt raced out ahead of everyone, shouting, "Mom, Dad, I'm here!" He ran halfway across the room, then slowed and looked back at the others.

"What is this?" Stacy asked.

"Looks like a control room," Darin said.

There were panels with dials and pressure gauges. Red, yellow, and green buttons blinked off and on in different sequences.

Matt raced about, searching in every direction, but it was apparent there was no cave, and that this was not where anyone was cryogenically frozen.

The room had windows all the way around, granting a view of the valley beyond. A multitude of computer screens and empty chairs revealed that at one time, a lot of people had worked there. But everything was covered with a thick film of dust.

"I wanted to believe you were right, Matt, but this is worse than not knowing where they are!" Catherine shouted. "Giving me hope and then taking it away is breaking me!" She covered her face, awash in tears.

Some of the computers were broken. Cracked and broken switches sparked occasionally. Old lab coats hung on the backs of swivel chairs and hooks on the wall and had the logo for Demo Trench sewn onto the left breast pocket. Two parallel lines with a sphere in the lower third. A single slanted line on the right side of the double lines. Underneath the logo were the letters "HZRD."

Matt slid his thumb over the frayed threads of the logo patch. "What is going on here?"

No one answered.

Levers labeled for each of the disasters resided on a panel in front of one of the windows. The room was painted a sickly light yellow. Clocks, tickers, gauges, and dials were embedded in machines labeled: "Blizzard," "Flood," "Heat Wave," "Tornado," and on and on.

Matt had rushed to the hallway across the room, opening and closing the doors all along the walls, only glimpsing inside the rooms long enough to see there were no cryopods within. At each room, he yelled frantically, "Mom? Dad?"

"They're not here!" Darin shouted. "And even if they were, they couldn't hear you!"

"Mom! Dad!" Matt raced to the next room down the hallway.

Stacy tugged on Darin's arm. "Somebody has to stop him. He's losing it."

"Dude! Stop! Take a breather!" Darin shouted. "This isn't the vault!"

Matt came back to the main room and stopped. Tears streaked down his face. He glowered at the machines. "They made all this just to torture us!" He kicked the nearest one until the exterior paneling fell off and the mechanical guts were revealed. He tore at colored wires, then picked up a chair and slammed the legs into the machine. Sparks showered the floor. The panel snapped and popped. Matt covered his eyes with his arm.

"Please, stop before you hurt yourself or one of us!" Catherine cried.

Matt looked at her, his chest heaving in anger. He threw the chair and dropped to his knees.

"They were supposed to be here!" Matt cried. "Argh!" He screamed and seized another chair and threw it against a window. The glass splintered into an ugly, spiderweb-like pattern but didn't break all the way through.

"Matt! Please, stop. We're here for you!" Stacy cried. "You're, like, amazing too!" She rushed toward him, and the others followed.

Stacy and Catherine wrapped their arms around him as he fought to hold back the tears.

"They were supposed to be here," he murmured.

"They're still out there somewhere. We just got to keep looking." Darin put a hand on Matt's shoulder.

After a few silent moments, Cody said, "Let's take stock of what's in here and go from there."

"You're right." Matt looked his now oldest friend in the eye. "Thanks, Cody. Thanks, everyone. I'm sorry."

"It's okay. I'm sorry too." Catherine hugged him tighter. "It's hard for all of us."

Darin sighed. "I agree with Cody. Let's see what we can find out in here. There's a lot to look over. There's a big bookshelf, and maybe we can log into one of these computers and read some files or something."

The bookshelf sagged under the weight of dozens of drab-green three-ring binders labeled with things like: "The Mission of Site HZRD," "Motion Sensor Diagram," "Demo Trench Emergency Operations," "Ecological Simulations," "Manual Overrides," and "Environmental Maintenance."

"Maybe these can tell us more about what's out there." Matt pulled down the manual that had "Emergency Operations" written on the spine.

Darin, Matt, and Cody looked through the manuals while Justin, Stacy, and Catherine stared out the windows.

"We're really high up here," Catherine said. "No wonder the elevator took so long. It's like you can see our whole world from here."

Stacy shouted with glee as she looked out the window, "Guys, I think I can see Camp New Beginnings! Over there!" She tapped her finger repeatedly against the glass until everyone came to look. In the distance, they recognized the camp.

"Over there is the junkyard," Matt said.

"Look at all the holes in the ground! We came through that!"
Cody said.

"Under that, you mean," Justin corrected.

"I think this is telling me how to turn it all off." Matt thumbed
through the manual.

"It can't be that simple," Darin argued.

Matt gave him a grin and strode over to a control panel. "It says
that there's a lever that has to be pulled back once, pushed forward,
then back again to cause an emergency shutdown of systems. I think
it's this one." He laid a finger on a big lever marked with "DO NOT
TOUCH" and "Emergency Shutdown."

"How do we know that won't make things worse?" Justin asked.

"What could be worse than what we've already gone through?"
Matt asked in return.

"Good point, chief, give it a whirl!"

Matt followed the instructions, pulling the lever back from its
middle position, then forward, then back once more. He had to put
quite a bit of muscle into it, using both arms. It sure didn't feel like it
had ever been done before.

The sound of gears that had been just vague white noise before
suddenly became apparent as they ground down to a halt, and the
general mechanical hum went silent. The mountain shuddered once
and went still.

Stacy gasped. "Please tell me we aren't dealing with earthquakes
up here."

"I think it's just part of it all shutting down," Darin assured her.

"Wait a minute," Matt said as he skimmed through the manuals.

"What is it?" Darin asked.

"More tricks," he lamented.

"What do you mean?"

"This." Matt pointed to a spot in one of the manuals denoting the
mountain.

"What?" Darin asked again. "I don't know what you're saying."

"How high do you think we are on this mountain?"

"I don't know, looks really high up. I'm not great with distances,
but I'd say a half mile or so?"

"I was guessing something like that."

"Okay, so?" Darin asked.

"Well, it's more tricks. They've built this place with forced perspective, and here is the proof. It says the mountain is only two thousand feet tall," Matt explained.

Darin squinted at him. "I don't follow."

"Amusement parks do this all the time, like Disney's Matterhorn.

They all use this forced perspective. It's all part of the trick of how this place is made up. Now I just need to find something that tells us how big this park, or whatever it is, is!"

"I think I understand you now," Darin said. "There must be some kind of limit to how big an area they can control, but it is pretty big."

"Guys, what is that?!" Stacy called out.

"What?" Matt asked.

"Something is falling from the sky. Out there in the forest."

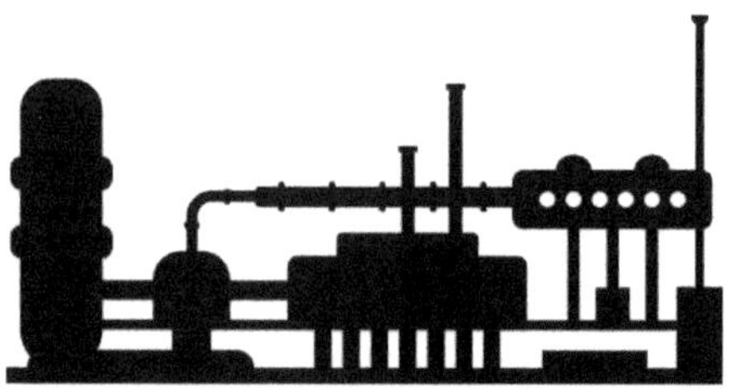

CHAPTER 37

"That was weird," Justin said. "What the heck could that have been?"

"I don't know," Matt answered, "but I know where we can get some answers."

"Don't tell me. The Bible," Justin said with more than a hint of sarcasm.

"Manuals actually." Matt handed him one that was labeled "Motion Sensor Diagrams."

"Thanks," Justin muttered, reluctantly taking the manual and flipping it open in the middle. Darin and Cody started looking through other manuals.

"I'm hungry. We're going to look in these other rooms for some food or something to drink," Stacy said.

"Be careful," Darin called.

"We will," Catherine said.

"Listen to this." Matt read aloud. "'This mountain command structure is HZRD. It's not A-67 or B-35. The mission of this area of this building is to evaluate and train personnel to survive an artificial apocalypse in anticipation of a real event.'"

Justin guffawed. "I'd call bull crap, except for everything we've already been through. This is totally unbelievable. There is no way my parents knew we were getting signed up for this garbage."

"I think you're right," Matt said. "But listen, there's more weird stuff. Remember when they tried to slow the apocalypse by detonating a bomb in the Mariana Trench? It didn't work, obviously. It says here that the world government built multiple buildings like HZRD. There are three within the vicinity. The idea was to train families to eventually survive the apocalypse, since it wasn't just going away. The think tanks figured that if they could train people with all the skills they needed to survive super-bad, man-made disasters, then they could survive the real apocalypse."

"That's messed up," Justin said. "Everything we've been going through was a training mission?"

"No, it wasn't," Darin snapped. "We weren't supposed to do anything like that. Westbrook is the mad scientist that dumped us in this hellhole."

Matt interrupted them to continue reading. "This says that, at first, they brought in soldiers and other specialists to survive inside HZRD and learn to adapt through all possible outcomes. Soldiers came in, it worked okay, most survived, but some died. There're notes about those that died."

"That's awful. How could they think this was a good idea?" Cody asked.

"Power corrupts. Some egghead in a lab coat talks and holds a clipboard, and then everyone else just goes along with it because they think they can trust the expert," Darin said bitterly. "Follow the leader if he has 'authority.'" He held up his fingers for air quotes.

"Nailed it." Justin nodded.

"I've got the handwritten logbook here," Cody said. "The last page says that this HZRD site was abandoned. The operation was to be forgotten, and they wanted to move to the second phase, plan B, which was to get everyone into cryosleep and into the cryovault. That's what was recommended by the team of scientists running this. It was called the 'Save the Population' project."

"Crazy," Justin said.

"They all lied," Darin snarled.

"Our parents didn't lie," Matt said. "They just believed what everyone was telling them: 'For the good of the world.' I think so many people were working on this, some had good intentions."

"Good intentions will get us killed," Darin snapped. "Men like Westbrook built this place, and it's all a big lie designed to kill people just to satisfy their—"

"Easy," Matt said. "Take a breather if you need to. We're all friends here, just trying to figure it out."

Darin nodded, snapped his book shut, and sat on the floor with his back against the wall.

Matt read on. "'Power to the vault and HZRD complex is all geothermal, from natural volcanoes on account of the bomb messing the land up.'"

"Molten energy," Cody said. "Interesting."

Matt shrugged. "Weird; I figured everything must be solar-powered here, but I guess not."

Justin broke in. "Okay, it's my turn. I've got the manual on motion sensors. There's a big diagram showing all the motion sensors. They're everywhere, to keep an eye on where people are and then make things happen! Some even look like tree branches just so you can't see them. But that's what triggers all the crazy weather."

"This is messed up," Darin said from where he squatted.

"What did you find, Cody?" Matt asked.

"I found a lot on how to fix and maintain all the inner workings of the machines and stuff," Cody answered.

"Last thing we want to do is fix any of that crap!" Justin said.

Stacy and Catherine came back with a handful of dried food and a few cans. "I even found some warm soda." Catherine held up a can. "Did you guys find anything out?"

"We did. We got an idea on where we are and what this is all for," Matt said.

"We've got to figure out where to go now and what to do," Justin said.

"Is there anywhere safe?" Stacy asked.

Justin pushed the manual away from him. "The Sev was safe, and it had no motion sensors."

"Motion sensors?"

"Yeah, they're everywhere, waiting for us to trigger the crazy weather."

"Which is all turned off now, we hope." Darin took a granola bar from Stacy's outstretched hand.

"Maybe going back to the Sev to live is the best plan?" Catherine said.

"I don't want to stay here. I want to go find my parents." Matt studied the book in his hands without really seeing it.

"You know that's not what I meant." Catherine touched his arm. "Just . . . we need to get some good rest and be safe and then go on to wherever it is we have to go. I don't know if you've taken the time to think about it, but we've had a very rough last twenty-four hours and really need some good sleep before we keep pushing ourselves so hard, or we're all gonna drop."

"Was it that long?" Stacy asked.

"I have no idea how long we were in the subfloor," Catherine said. "I was guessing."

Matt looked at her. "You're right, we have been pushing ourselves really hard, and we need to be safe when we rest. Maybe the Sev is our best bet."

"We had one heck of a party there." Justin chuckled.

Cody nodded toward a window. "It's getting dark now. Maybe it's been two days."

"You ever gone two days without sleep before?" Darin asked.

"I ain't never had two days like this before," Cody said.

"You guys have been reading all these books to figure this stuff out?" Stacy asked.

"Yeah?" Matt raised an eyebrow in her direction.

She held up one of the manuals. "Well, this one explains the sun."

"What?" Darin exclaimed. "The sun?"

"Yeah, it's always cloudy but has never looked right. It says here that there are just a bunch of lights hung up high everywhere that are on a timer. It's nighttime, so it's dimming down like at my friend Wanda's house. They had lights on a dimmer switch in the living room."

"No way." Darin stood and looked over her shoulder at the manual.

"This says the timer is right over there." Stacy pointed at one of the control panels. A red digital clock read "dusk." "Like, let's see what happens if I turn the knob."

"This will be good," Justin said.

Before anyone could tell her to stop, Stacy twisted a big red knob, and as the readout turned back to "afternoon" in digital letters, the lights outside brightened as if she had turned the sun back up to full.

"I'm the queen of summer!" She laughed.

"This place is a madhouse." Darin groaned as he gave himself a facepalm.

Catherine unwrapped a dehydrated fruit package. "This place doesn't seem to be the most comfortable. There's food and stuff, but it doesn't feel as homey as the Sev did."

"What else did you two find?" Matt asked.

Stacy's eye widened. "There's a room with lots of guns!"

"Guns?" Cody asked.

"Yeah, and bio-hazard suits and gas masks," Stacy added.

"There's a kitchen or cafeteria with food. Mostly cans is all that's left—the Sev had a better variety." Catherine shrugged. "There's a mechanics shop that smells like oil, but it has tools, and then there are sleeping quarters, and the last thing we found at the very end of the hall is another elevator."

"Why didn't you tell us about that?" Justin snapped.

"I thought you would rather eat first," Catherine replied sharply.

"Well, you're right," he said, half apologetically.

Matt popped open a soda can. "Let's stay the night here and resupply. We can figure out where to go in the morning."

"I could make it morning now, if you want." Stacy gestured, queen-like, to the digital clock.

"No!" came the collective response.

"Jeez, guys, like, take a joke from your queen of summer," Stacy said, kicking her toe at the floor.

"I want to go back to the Sev," Catherine said.

"It's late, and you said we need rest," Justin reminded her.

"Yeah, but I don't feel safe here. At least there I could relax."

"I want to get out of here entirely. If it's just a big complex with halogen lights for a sun and fake weather, I want out, period." Darin scowled, looking out the windows.

"Maybe we should vote on it," Cody suggested.

"What do you think, chief?" Justin asked.

Matt hadn't been expecting that. He was wrapped up in all the terrible revelations of the last hour. He had been wrong about so much. This mountain was not where their parents were. He had risked all of their lives for what? To play with a fake sun?

"Guys," he said, his voice cracking just a little, "I don't want to sway you in either direction. I've been wrong, and we didn't find our parents. We almost got killed multiple times. I've failed you all. Someone else should take charge of the situation."

"We'll vote on it," Darin said. "Everyone write down your vote, and we'll tally it all in the morning after we've slept."

"So vote for Matt to keep being the leader and get us out of here?" Stacy whispered a little too loudly.

Darin shook his head. "Elevator or Sev, Matt stays the leader."

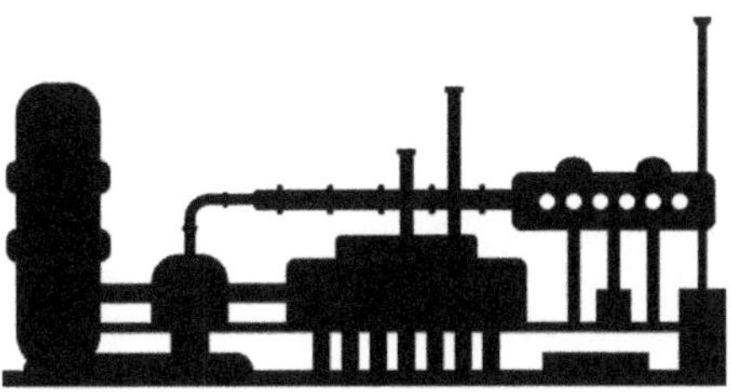

CHAPTER 38

They went to sleep in the barracks area of the control center. And while there were no windows and they slept as late and long as they felt like, there wasn't a general feeling of rest once they all awoke and got up for a breakfast of canned dry oatmeal and peaches.

Catherine handed Matt a can containing everyone's votes from the night before. "Here you go."

"Thanks, Catherine, but I don't need to be the one to decide anything."

"You're not. We voted, and we didn't vote about you leading us." She shrugged. "Honestly, you and Darin have been awesome down here, but you're the one who found this place. You got us here. It's unanimous. You're the head counselor."

Matt paused for a moment. Counselor. Arriving at Camp New Beginnings felt like a lifetime ago. So much had changed in just a few short days. "Unanimous? Even Justin?"

"He looks up to you more than you know. He's just prickly sometimes."

"All right, I'll count the votes now, everyone," he said louder to all those gathered about the table.

Darin and Stacy stood close by. "This is anonymous, right?" she asked.

"It is if you didn't sign it," Darin said.

"Yeah, but wait. Matt, can you, like, recognize our handwriting?"

"Not yet," he answered.

"Okay then, the queen of summer says you may proceed."

Darin laughed at Stacy's antics and gave her a peck on the cheek.

Matt counted the votes. "First one says: 'Go down the elevator.' Second one says: 'Go to the Sev.' Third: 'Elevator.' Fourth: 'R&D.'"

"R&D?" Justin asked.

"It's the Sev," Stacy explained.

"Oh yeah." Justin shrugged

Matt continued. "Fifth: 'Elevator.' Last one: 'Elevator.' So it's two to four, elevator, and I guess that means continuing our search for our parents instead of waiting it out at the Sev."

Catherine hugged herself and slumped against the back of the chair. Matt knew she'd voted to go back to R&D, but wasn't sure who else had voted that way—maybe Justin?

"Well, regardless of where we all wanted to go, we need to get gear and backpacks," Darin said. "And anything else that will come in handy for the apocalypse."

"Guns?" Stacy asked.

"Sure," Darin said. "Even if I don't know how to shoot, I figure one of you all do, right?"

"I've shot guns." Catherine folded her arms. "Though I don't know how shooting at the rain will help."

"Loads of times." Cody nodded. "Gophers on the ranch will break a horse's leg."

"Once," Matt said sheepishly.

"I never have, but I want to," Stacy said.

Justin stayed silent, revealing well enough that he had never shot a gun either.

They grabbed green army-style backpacks and filled them with dried foods from the cafeteria, as well as any other useful supplies they could find.

Cody found full-face oxygen masks and oxygen tanks in the bio-hazard area. "These are like what firemen use."

"You think we might need those?" Stacy's eyebrows scrunched together.

"It's a crazy world out there," Cody answered.

"True." She nodded, her red hair bouncing.

Matt reminded them as they loaded blankets and food into the packs, "Leave any cans that even hint at bulging. That means they're bad, as in poisonous."

"We know, chief."

Fully stocked up and ready, they rounded the corner and pushed the button to the elevator.

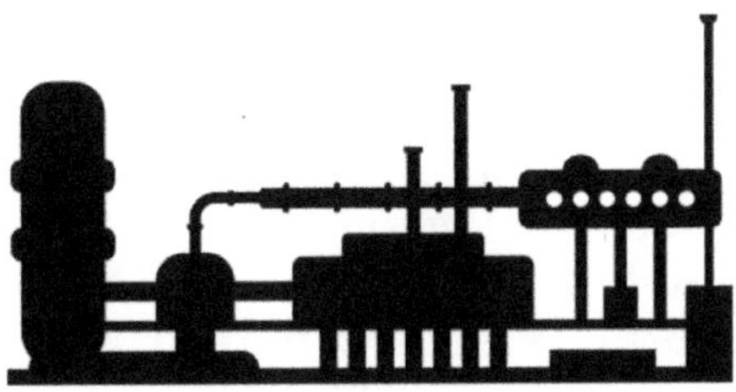

CHAPTER 39

The elevator buzzed like a microwave, as if it were powering up. The doors swiftly opened, functioning much better than the other elevator.

"Sounds like we should have ridden this one up in the first place," Justin said.

"Well, I didn't see it when we got in the other one," Catherine said.

They crowded into the elevator. With their stuffed backpacks, extra oxygen tanks, tools, and guns, the small space was rather squished. It was quite a bit different than when they had come up.

"Are there any buttons?" Matt asked.

"I don't see any," Darin said. "But the other one didn't have any either. Single destination lines, I guess."

"Maybe we should take the one we know, since we don't really know where this one goes." Catherine bit her bottom lip.

But it was too late. The doors slid closed, and to their surprise, the elevator shot off sideways, slamming them into the side and each other.

"How is it doing this?" Justin pushed off the metal wall and regained his balance.

"I don't know. I've never heard of anything like it. Darin?" Matt asked.

Darin shook his head, steadying himself with a hand pressed against a waist-high handrail.

"It must be on a track like a tram instead of cable—but why not just have a tram?" Cody questioned.

"I knew we shouldn't have got on this thing." Catherine dropped to her knees. "Make it go back."

"It's all right, Catherine. It's running smoothly." Matt crouched and gently rubbed her back. "I don't think we're in any danger of it falling apart or anything. It's a much smoother ride than yesterday's elevator."

Matt picked at a hangnail and felt a small bubble of panic creeping into his thoughts. He stared at the back of Catherine's shoulder, the burned skin peeking out the top of her shirt. Focused on the rippled skin, he counted slowly to ten and back. His Matt-itation. He felt his breathing and heart rate return to normal. He couldn't wait to tell his mom how helpful it'd been. Tell her in person.

"How much longer? This feels like it's been–"

"It's been ten minutes," Darin said. "I found a watch." He held up his left wrist, a black-banded watch encircling it.

"I thought you said it didn't matter, like, what day it is. Just *right now* matters, silly," Stacy reminded him.

"Yeah, but when I found a watch, I wanted it. Just had to wind it, and it worked. Now I can keep track of how long it takes us between destinations."

"Elevator rides should not be this long." Catherine wrapped her arms around her abdomen. "I'm getting sick."

"Probably those canned peaches," Justin said.

"More like the oatmeal, ack." Stacy poked a finger into her mouth. "I mean, gag me with a spoon."

"Stacy, please," Catherine choked.

"Sorry."

The sideways elevator traveled for over an hour. They couldn't see out, and pressing any of the irregular buttons inside the service panel did nothing to slow its humming speed.

"Maybe we're not even moving, and we're still right beside the hallway, but this thing is broken and just vibrating to make us think we're going sideways, because we all know elevators totally don't do that." Stacy's eyes widened.

"It sure feels like it's moving sideways to me," Cody said.

"It's doing more than just vibrating." Darin placed his palm on the wall.

Stacy shrugged.

"I am tired of this!" Catherine shouted.

"It is weird," Darin said. "Maybe we should try and open the door."

Matt looked to Cody. "You've got a crowbar, right?"

"Yep." Cody took his pack off and reached for the tool. They tried to get it between the doors, but to no avail. The seal was too tight.

"What about the ceiling? I've seen people in movies escape elevators by climbing out the ceiling," Justin said.

"It's worth a shot." Matt shrugged.

They pried at the ceiling panels but only succeeded in taking off a decorative tile, revealing a solid steel roof to the elevator.

"Well, that's that. We're trapped," Cody lamented.

"Can we tear apart the control panel?" Justin asked.

"We might end up trapped inside in the middle of a long tunnel," Darin said. "Whoever made this meant for people to get whisked around long distances. I think we need to just wait it out. Everyone get comfortable. Who knows how much longer this will be."

"How long has it been?" Stacy asked.

"One hour and twenty-seven minutes."

Catherine cried into her sleeve.

"Well, let's get comfy," Matt said.

He spread his gear out over the floor, and everyone followed suit, trying to make themselves comfortable. Cody turned his pack into a chair, but Matt couldn't get his to sit right.

"What if it just keeps going forever?" Stacy asked.

Darin hushed her as Catherine started to cry softly again. Matt put an arm around her and pulled her against him.

The elevator slowed, then dropped for a couple of seconds before coming to a dead stop.

"It's done?" Stacy looked wildly back and forth from Matt to Darin.

"Let's hope." Matt removed his arm from around Catherine and rubbed his hand over his buzzcut.

"Be ready for anything," Cody said as he cocked his gun.

Matt gripped his own gun but wasn't ready to cock it.

CHAPTER 40

They waited for what seemed an eternity, but it was just a few seconds until the doors slid open to yet another small control room, only ten feet wide by thirty feet long. The walls were padded, off-white, and cracked with age.

"What is this place?" Justin asked. "A looney bin?"

"I have no idea," Matt answered.

"There's a window back there." Cody slowly moved forward, his gun at the ready.

As they entered the room, the elevator door closed behind them with another *swish*, and then an airlock door closed, and the loud hissing sound of forced air echoed in the room.

"It's a trap! Get the masks on!" Matt ordered.

They struggled to get the masks and air tanks on—several were not connected, and Stacy panicked as she tried to get hers to snap closed over her face and hair. Darin assisted her and then stroked her hair to calm her, since their voices were muffled by the masks.

"Is there poison gas in the room?" Catherine asked.

"Don't know, let's look around," Cody said.

The room remained as it had been when the elevator opened.

Cody signaled them forward toward the window. Only Matt joined him.

He reached the circular window and peeked out. General fogginess greeted their view upon a bleak landscape. A meteor way off in the distance plummeted to Earth and sent black soil flying into the sky. Matt's heart raced. Actual snow fell in the fog, and an even stronger blizzard raged off to their left, while dark gray ash fell to the right. Hot and cold. Barren landscape . . . red and scorched.

Matt shook his head. "We're in the middle of a frying pan that's in the deep freeze."

Cody went back to the air ducts and examined them and the outer door that was sealed shut. He took his gas mask off.

"You sure that's smart?" Justin asked.

Cody nodded. "I think this was just ventin' because we came out of the elevator, and it was adjusting for the pressure differentiation. Probably need the masks again if we open that door that goes outside, though. I'm guessin' that's why all that apparatus turned on in the first place."

"Well, what's outside, then?" Catherine asked.

"Take a look," Cody offered.

"Out of the fire and into the freezer that's on fire," Justin said.

"What do we do?" Stacy asked.

Darin shook his head.

"We should have just gone back to the Sev," Catherine said.

"You want to get back in that elevator?" Justin taunted.

"I didn't say that," she snapped. "I said we never should have got on that *hellevator*!"

"Nice," he snapped back.

"Guys, take it easy," Matt said. "It's important that we know everything we can about where we are and what's out there as we try to find our parents. Darin, is this like what you said you had to drive through to get to Camp New Beginnings?"

Darin shook his head. "It was bad, but this is really different."

"Well, we either need to go on or just go back to the Sev and sit on our hands. But I think we need to keep going and get out of this place."

Catherine put her hands on her hips. "Tell me I'm wrong all you want, but I've always stood by you, Matt Voorhees, and I'm telling you I want to survive. And if that means making the best of what we do know is safe—R&D—then I think that's what we should do!"

"I'm not saying you're wrong for wanting to be safe, Catherine, but we can't sit back and keep eating old food. If we're gonna get out of here and rescue our parents, we need to keep moving."

"We could go back to the control room," Justin offered. "At least we know that's just an hour-and-half ride away."

"The Sev *was* pretty dang comfy," Cody said.

Stacy raised her hand. "R&D."

"We don't even know if we can survive out there." Catherine folded her arms like she had won the debate.

"You're right," Matt said. "We don't know. But I've got to find out. Hang on a minute, okay?"

Darin nodded.

Matt put on a gas mask and waited for the others to do the same before he opened the exterior doors. Again, the air venting system kicked on and blasted all of them inside with fresh air as Matt stepped outside.

The ground was black and caked with ash. Far behind the new control room and doors where his friends crowded against the glass to watch him, he could see the false mountain. His feet dragged in a tar-like substance near a wavy yellow line. Asphalt and potholes led to another mountain in the far east. The road had been severely damaged by volcanic action, or maybe from the falling asteroids—the real adversary of the Earth. The real apocalypse.

Matt hurried back inside, allowing the vents to do their work before he lifted his gas mask up. "I'm going to find my parents or die trying. Who's in?"

TO BE CONCLUDED . . .

APOCALYPSE SPRING

Tyler H. Jolley
Holli Anderson

I dedicate this to all the cassette and VHS tapes of the '80s.

CHAPTER 1

Matt stared at his remaining friends gathered around the circular, portal-like window. It reminded him of the submarine ride at Disneyland, and he wondered briefly if the amusement park was even still standing. He'd just reentered the air-lock room after taking a short walk outside through the black, tar-like substance that covered every surface.

So much had happened in a matter of days. When Kyle had slipped from Matt's hands into the raging flash flood, it had nearly broken him. He'd never seen someone die. And it wouldn't be his last. The tall, lanky boy from Utah was the next victim. Crushed. Victoria's and Rhett's deaths marked the most gruesome demise he could have imagined. That was until what happened to Kim. He shuddered. Her melting face would haunt him for the rest of his life—which at this rate, might not be very long.

But he was proud of the last twenty-four hours. They'd made it out of that man-made hellscape, and without losing anyone else.

He set his gas mask on the padded floor. "Well? Who's with me? Who's going with me to find our families?" His gaze lingered on Catherine longer than the others. He really hoped she'd overcome her fear and come with him.

"I don't know, man." Justin gestured to the window. "This is . . . it's crazy out there."

Matt stepped closer, peering out at the raging, schizophrenic weather.

Stacy, closest to the window, started to narrate what was going on outside, completely ignoring Matt's question. "Look, it's snowing.

Like, real snow, not the man-made stuff like at Camp New Beginnings." She gasped. "Is that a meteor?"

A fiery red orb with a flaming tail shot across the darkened sky, disappearing somewhere in the distant fog.

"That, little lady, is indeed a meteor," Cody said. "That's the second one I've seen since that crazy elevator dropped us off here."

Catherine shuddered at the mention of the elevator. Her face was just starting to return to its natural color after the long, nauseating ride.

Stacy continued to stare out the window. "Snow stopped. Now it's raining." The rain splattered straight down onto the ground for a minute or two, splashing into the black dirt, before there was a sudden change in direction. "The wind must be blowing, like, really hard all of a sudden. Look, the rain is falling *sideways* now!"

Darin stepped closer to her and rested his hand on the small of her back. She smiled up at him.

"We should decide what we're going to do." Catherine frowned, not taking her eyes off the ash-colored whirlwinds dancing around like miniature tornados from hell. "I don't want to stay here. It's so . . . eerie."

"Maybe we should just go back to the control room and think on it for the night," Justin said.

Stacy looked at Catherine and smirked. "You up for another hour-and-a-half ride on the *hellivator*?"

Catherine's face paled, and she wrapped an arm around her abdomen. "No. But I don't know which is worse: the elevator or this creepy room."

"It's not that creepy," Matt said, looking around at the cracked yellow padding of the walls. He pointed at one of the many panels with broken gumdrop buttons and small indicator lights, the covers of which were milky with age. He smiled. "It reminds me of the hallways in the Millennium Falcon. Or the med bay in *Alien*."

"Yeah." Cody nodded. "And you're Han Solo, and Justin is Chewbacca—because he's tall, ya know? And hairy."

"And no one understands him when he talks," Darin added with a chuckle.

Justin rolled his eyes. "You guys are real hilarious. You're just jealous of my studly physique and gorgeous locks." He ran his fingers through his sandy-blond hair, then flexed his arms so his biceps popped out.

Yeah, Matt thought as he eyed Justin's bulging muscles, *maybe just a little.*

"Besides," Justin said, "it's Texas here who no one can understand, with his Southern drawl, and 'y'alls' and 'ma'ams.'" He nudged Cody with his shoulder.

The small group laughed, which relieved some pressure from Matt's chest. That's what he'd been aiming for, to defuse some of the building tension in his friends.

The building shuddered, followed closely by a groan from deep in the earth. Catherine and Stacy screamed, and Stacy buried her face in Darin's chest. "Was that an earthquake, Lance-Darin?" The words came out muffled against his shirt.

"I . . ." His voice was a higher pitch than normal. He cleared his throat and put his arms around her. "I don't know. Maybe."

Catherine looked out the window. "Look, it's hailing out there. I've never seen hail that big before." Her voice quivered a little, and her eyes were wide as she turned to look at Matt.

He moved closer to her and put his arm around her shoulders.

"This really sucks." She swiped angrily at a tear trickling down her cheek. "The whole purpose for the cryopods and the vault and the decades-long forced sleep was so we'd miss this! So we'd wake up when this crap was all over and done with! And instead, we're stuck right smack in the middle of the apocalypse." She jerked away from Matt and scrubbed the tears from her face with both hands. "I can't watch it anymore." She staggered to the back of the air lock and slumped against the wall next to the horizontal elevator door.

They all followed her, trudging silently, mouths turned down in defeated frowns. All but Matt, who stayed by the portal window, staring out into the gloom. His thoughts turned back to his parents. He had to find them, even if he had to go it alone—but he really hoped he wouldn't have to.

A football-sized chunk of frozen ice slammed into the upper edge of the round window. Matt flinched, his heart leaping into his throat, nearly choking him. He took a deep breath and ran a hand across the short hair of his buzz cut before walking, shoulders drooping, to the back of the room to join his friends.

CHAPTER 2

Indicator lights around the room blinked off and on. Some of them were static, flickering slightly, but the light waxed and waned, like the bulb or electricity was failing. Matt slumped to the floor next to Catherine, his back resting against the cracked padding of the yellowed wall—it reminded him of the padded rooms in *One Flew Over the Cuckoo's Nest*, a '70s movie his parents rented at the local video store. Catherine sniffed and turned her face away from him, wiping again at her cheeks.

He wanted to comfort her, but he wasn't sure if her anger was directed toward him or the continuing apocalypse. He needed to bring up the idea of leaving this place again, but he didn't want to make things worse—seeing Catherine cry made his guts churn uncomfortably.

Cody saved him from having to decide. "This is as serious as a heart attack. We need to talk about our next steps. What the heck are we gonna do now?"

"First," Stacy said, "I think we should, like, list our options so we know what our choices are."

As far as Matt was concerned, there was only one choice. "Leaving what's behind us *behind us* and going to find our parents. Finding Vault B-35."

Justin rolled his eyes. "Yeah, Matt, we all know what you want to do. You haven't shut up about it."

Matt stiffened, but before he could defend his position, Catherine spoke up. "Cool it, Justin! He's just starting the list. What do *you* think we should do?"

"I don't know . . . I'd like to hear what Darin thinks. He's the only one who knows what the vault was like when we left."

Darin rubbed the back of his neck and flicked his eyes up at Justin, then down, not making eye contact with anyone. He cleared his throat. "I . . . I don't want to go to the vault. I think we should go back."

"Why?" Matt asked, frustration making his voice come out louder than he intended. "We almost died multiple times in that underground death trap! That place was falling apart around us."

"I know . . ." Darin closed his eyes and took a deep breath. "But so was the vault, last time I was there. When he woke me the second time . . . the carbon foam doesn't last forever."

"Are you talking about the meteor strike?"

Darin looked away again. "Yeah, the meteor strike." He rubbed his neck again, then wiped his hand on his pants. "It was . . . bad. It did a lot of damage. It's why your column started to fail. And like I said, the fix was only temporary, I think."

Stacy laid a hand on his arm. "It must have been awful."

"It was." He shook his head. "When the fifteen-year-olds all died . . . Westbrook . . . he lost it. He thought he'd fixed the damage, at least that's what he told me. He made me go outside with a gas mask to try to seal the cracks in the rock. But things got worse."

"So he decided to start moving us," Cody said.

Darin nodded, still not looking at anyone. "I don't want to go back there."

Matt clenched his fists. "But that's where our parents are!"

"And my brothers and sisters," Stacy whispered.

Darin looked up at her. "We don't . . . we don't even know—"

"No. We don't know," Matt interrupted. "Which is why we *have* to try to find them. We have to save them if we can." He thought of the last time he'd seen his parents. Right before they were separated to be put into suspended animation inside the cryopods. His mom's frightened tears. His dad's assurances that it was going to be okay, that they'd all be together again soon.

"I'm with Matt," Cody said. "Besides wanting to check on my folks, I *do not* want to go back down in that crumblin' cesspool."

"We don't have to go back down there," Justin argued. "We can take the elevator back to the control room, then walk, aboveground, back to the Sev."

"I love the Sev," Stacy said.

Darin continued, "We at least know it's safe there, and there's food."

"And beer," Justin added.

"But *is* it safe?" Catherine's whisper was low, and Matt had to lean closer to hear her. "That whole area is on top of the underground 'soundstage' system. The roof was caving in on us just hours ago. The roof that is the grounds of Camp New Beginnings."

"I thought you didn't want to go out into the apocalypse, Catherine? That you were on our side." Justin nodded at Darin.

"Ugh!" Catherine growled. "I don't know what I want! Nowhere is safe."

"Exactly." Matt softened his tone and took her hand in his, worried she might pull away. But she didn't. Instead, she grasped his hand like it was a lifeline. "Nowhere is completely safe. So we should go find our parents." He looked at Stacy. "And siblings. If there's even a small chance we can save them, we need to try."

"Welp, you already know I agree with Matt," Cody said. "So how do we decide?"

"Maybe we should just go our separate ways." Justin crossed his arms and scowled.

"No," Cody said. "We need to stick together. It took all y'all to save me from the stinkin' reservoir. And Darin—no way just one of us could have pulled him out of the swirling water down there."

"What should we do, Matt?" Stacy asked. "Like, how do we decide?"

Matt's stomach twisted into a knot. He looked around, racking his brain for an idea. His gaze landed on Darin, nervously picking at a small rip in the padded wall, pulling on some thick threads dangling from the edge of the tear.

Matt sat up straighter. "Everyone pick a thread from one of the tears in the padded walls. Only one thread each. We'll pull them out at the same time. The person with the longest thread will decide where we go."

Catherine nodded. "Like drawing straws."

"Exactly. When everyone has a hold of a thread, let me know."

When all six of them had chosen their threads, Matt said, "Okay. Pull on three. One, two, three." He winced at the short strand he now held pinched between his thumb and index finger.

The friends compared.

"Stacy wins," Matt announced, trying not to sound disappointed. She would for sure choose what "Lance-Darin" wanted.

CHAPTER 3

Darin grinned, his eyes sparkling as he looked at Stacy. But she avoided his gaze, instead staring at the six strings lying side-by-side on the dirty tile floor. She twisted her mouth, biting on her bottom lip.

Stacy exhaled loudly, then looked up at Darin, touching a hand to his chest. Her eyes glistened with newly formed tears, not yet fallen, and her voice quivered a little as she looked around the circle of friends. "Lance-Darin, I'm sorry, but . . . I think Matt's right. We need to move forward. I want to see my family too."

Darin's shoulders slumped and Justin scowled. But neither of them voiced an argument to her decision.

Releasing the breath he'd been holding, Matt's head spun a little from lack of oxygen. *Glad I wasn't standing up*, he thought. "Okay. When do we leave?"

"No time like the present," Cody said.

Stacy nodded. "Like, I don't know about you guys, but this place is so totally not rad. I agree that we should leave now."

"Yeah," Catherine said. "We slept good last night, and it's still pretty early in the day. I definitely do not want to spend the night in this creepy air lock anymore."

"Darin? Justin?" Matt forced himself to get their input even though every nerve and muscle in his body screamed to get moving.

Darin nodded. "Yeah, okay, but what about your foot?" He turned to Stacy.

Gritting her teeth and wincing, she slowly pulled her shoe off. They all looked at the damage. "I'll be okay," she said.

"We can change the wrapping before we go," Matt said.

Stacy nodded and tugged at the corner of a piece of athletic tape holding the gauze on. She winced as she freed the bandage completely and replaced it.

"Justin?" Matt asked.

"Whatever," Justin said. He pushed himself up from the floor and walked over to the small window. "Now's as good a time as ever—looks like the weather has calmed down for a minute."

They grabbed their backpacks, full of the supplies they'd collected from the control room, and gathered near the door. "Make sure our gas masks fit good before we open this door," Darin said. "The air's toxic out there."

Having been outside, brief as it was, Matt had to agree. He was glad Darin had insisted they bring them when they'd found the stash in the barracks of the control room.

Everyone fitted the full-faced masks over their heads. Darin helped Stacy by holding her strawberry-blonde hair out of the way so the mask would get a good seal, then he tightened the straps on the back of her head before putting his own mask on. Matt turned to see if Catherine needed help with her hair, too, but her dark curls were pulled back into a ponytail, and she was already pulling the straps taut on the mask.

Matt tightened his, then took a couple of deep breaths in and out to make sure the seal was good. "Ready?" He spoke loudly to be understood through the sound-muffling apparatus.

The others nodded, and Justin, who stood closest to the door, pushed it open with a whoosh. They were met with a blast of snow that immediately melted with a wave of hot air that washed over them.

Catherine grabbed Matt's hand in a death grip. Her eyes were wide and her chest rose and fell at a too-rapid rate. He smiled, squeezed her hand, and laced his fingers through hers. "It's going to be okay."

She nodded, and they ventured into the raging apocalypse.

"Which way, fearless leader?" Cody yelled.

Matt's racing heart and sudden cold sweats belied the "fearless" part as massive lightning strikes lit up the ashen sky nearby. He pointed to a foggy mountain range in the distance—to the east, he thought.

"Look at that," Cody said, gesturing.

The small group stood within a stone's throw to a narrow asphalt road. Or what was left of it. The broken blacktop had pieces of it rising up like it had boiled from intense heat. Cracks and fissures spiderwebbed throughout, parts of the asphalt fractured into dozens of smaller pieces.

"Let's follow this . . . road." Matt shrugged. "Or what's left of it."

Stepping past the group with Catherine in tow, he led the way, walking down the middle, halfway between two faded yellow lines on each shoulder of the road. There was no way two average-sized vehicles could pass each other going in opposite directions—and the absence of a middle line agreed with his assessment. The surrounding land was desolate and sandy, with outcroppings of pock-marked lava rock sticking up all over.

The wind kicked up, bringing with it frigid temperatures. Matt hunched his shoulders and dipped his head to try to block the freezing air from penetrating the bare skin of his arms. Catherine pulled her hand out of his, to his dismay, and crossed her arms over her chest, pinning her hands in the warmth of her armpits. Dark clouds rolled in with the speed of a bullet train, obscuring the red sun as it feebly tried to shine through.

Gooseflesh popped up on Matt's arms, and he wondered if it would be worth it to get a blanket out of his pack. Lightning streaked from the dark clouds, hitting the ground so close to them that the boom of thunder came almost simultaneously, rattling their eardrums. Catherine screamed, as did at least one person behind them, probably Stacy.

Catherine stepped closer to Matt, her shoulder rubbing against his, and pointed with a trembling finger at scorch marks on the ground all around them. "That's from lightning, isn't it?" Her hysterical voice barely carried through the powerful wind.

Matt nodded and pulled her to him in a one-armed hug.

"This is too dangerous!" Catherine looked behind them at the others, then at the barely visible building they'd left behind.

Matt's gaze followed hers back even as his feet continued to plod forward on the fractured road. *Maybe we should go back.* The thought ripped a hole in his chest and he faced forward again, toward the mountain he could no longer see in the distance. He couldn't abandon his parents. He *knew* they were there, and they needed his help.

Lightning pounded into the road ahead of them like Thor's hammer. Catherine screamed again and buried her head in Matt's chest, trembling sobs rippling through her body.

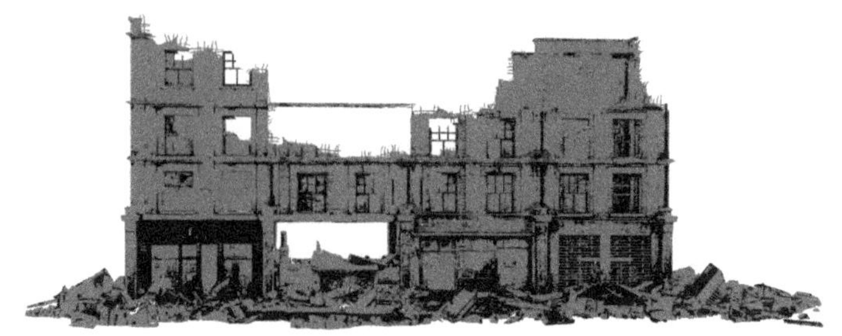

CHAPTER 4

As if the last bolt of electricity had hit a switch, the wind stopped, and the lightning strikes moved farther away until they could no longer hear the accompanying thunder.

Darin rushed up to Matt, Stacy hanging on to his arm as tears streaked down her face beneath the clear cover of her mask. "This is crazy, Matt!" he said. "It's too dangerous, we need to go back!"

Steam rose from the ground as the stifling heat returned. Matt readied himself for an argument, even though he knew Darin was right.

"Hey!" Cody yelled. "Look at this." He'd passed them as they prepared to face off and stood a couple of feet to the side of the pavement, his shoes almost swallowed up in the black sand.

Justin reached him first. "What the hell?"

Catherine straightened up and sniffed as she adjusted her gas mask. She, Matt, Darin, and Stacy joined Cody and Justin as they stared down at the ground.

Justin kicked at something in the sand. "It's hard, like glass."

Cody bent down and touched the rough surface of the tube-like object, the same color as the ash-stained sand surrounding it. "It *is* glass, sort of."

Catherine leaned in closer. "The lightning caused it. Intense heat turns sand into glass. It's called fulgurite, I think."

"How do you know that, genius?" Justin teased.

"My mom." Her voice hitched, and she swallowed and started again. "My mom and I took a girls' trip to Palm Springs over spring break when I was thirteen. They sell it in a lot of the little tourist shops there."

"They're all over here," Stacy said as she pointed out several within twenty yards of them. Her eyes were wide when she turned to look at Matt. "Wait . . . that means there's a lot of lightning strikes out here."

"Which is one of the many reasons why we should give up on this crazy expedition and go back to where we know we're safe. Relatively," Darin said.

Matt's stomach dropped. Darin was right; they were sitting ducks out here. Matt bent over, resting his hands on his knees as the world spun around him. "I can't—" He closed his eyes and fell back on his butt, hiding his head in his arms, folded on top of his bent knees. He barely registered the gas mask digging into his forehead. He started counting slowly—Matt-itation, his mom had called the familiar exercise—to try to stop the anxiety building in his chest.

"Matt! What's wrong?" Catherine crouched on the ground right next to him.

He hadn't even noticed her arm wrapped around his back until she spoke.

"Are you okay?"

"Give me a minute," he choked out.

She rubbed his back while he silently finished counting to ten, then back down to one. He took a deep breath and raised his head, staring out into the distance. "I can't give up on them," he whispered. "*We* can't give up on them."

"I know." She squeezed his shoulders. "But we need to find a better, safer way to get there."

Matt pushed himself to his feet and faced his friends. "You guys head back to the air lock. I'm going to keep going a little farther. You know, try to scout some things out. Maybe it gets better up ahead."

Catherine tried to hold him there, but he shrugged her off and started walking back to the road.

"Matt, buddy." Cody caught up to him in a couple of steps. "You know this is crazy, right? It ain't gonna get better up ahead. It's the apocalypse. It's the whole world."

He did know. He knew, but he didn't care. "I have to try."

They stepped back onto the pavement, and Matt's gait picked up speed. He narrowed his eyes—the road looked different a little ways in the distance. He started jogging, leaving Cody to catch up or go back, he didn't care which. Matt skidded to a stop, his toes inches from the lip of a large, ragged-edged hole in the asphalt. He dropped to his knees and peered into the opening.

He yelled over his shoulder, "Hey, guys! Get over here! I think I found a better way!"

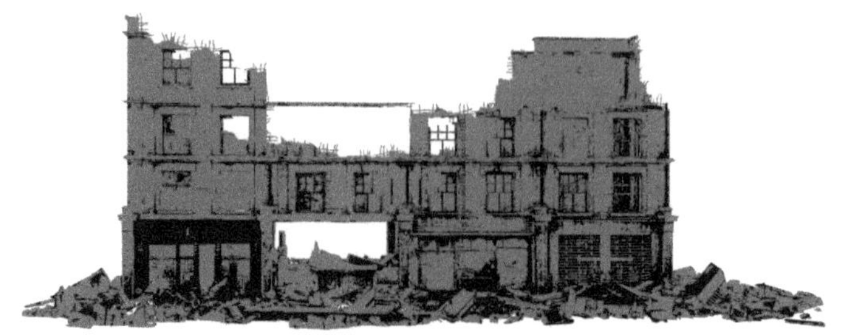

CHAPTER 5

The road looked like it had been blasted apart where Matt stood—like a meteor had struck there, or lava had melted the asphalt and underlying ground away. He smiled. A slightly unhinged-sounding laugh bubbled up into his throat.

"There's a tunnel down here!" he yelled.

A tunnel ran directly under the road as far as Matt could see. He dropped his backpack and knelt down to unzip it as Cody, and then the rest of the group, made their way to him.

"Holy cow patties," Cody said as he came to a halt at Matt's side.

Matt pulled a flashlight from his pack and cranked the handle to energize it before shining it down into the pit. Just as he'd hoped, the beam landed on a damaged concrete walkway running parallel to the road about ten or fifteen feet down. "What do you think?" he asked Cody.

"It'll get us out of the weather."

"Well, let's get down there before the lightning, or something worse, starts up again," Catherine said from behind Matt.

He looked up at her, smiling, and nodded. He shoved the flashlight into a side pocket of his backpack so he could reach it easily once they were in the tunnel. He stood and, in an act of spontaneous relief, hugged Catherine, the sides of their gas masks clinking together. He was glad when she hugged him back, and flooded with warmth when she squeezed harder before releasing her embrace.

"Okay, it looks like we can just climb down that pile of rubble. We'll have to hang from the edge to reach it with our feet. We can use the rope as a safety harness." Matt pulled it out of his bag and worked on tying a rope harness like he'd learned to do in Scouts. "Justin, since you're the tallest, you go first so you can reach up and help the girls if they need you to."

Justin nodded.

"Then Darin, you go next for the same reason—the two tallest at the bottom to give the rest of us a hand." Matt was no shrimp at six foot one, but Justin and Darin were taller. "Cody and I will hold on to the rope up here, since there's nothing to tie it to. The girls can go next, then Cody, and I'll climb down last."

"Sounds like a good plan," Cody said. "And at least it isn't a hundred-foot drop like the last thing we climbed down into. This'll be easy compared to that."

"Cody!" Stacy slapped him on the shoulder. "Don't jinx us!"

Justin waved Matt off when he offered him the rope harness. "Nah, chief," he said, finding a good place for a handhold. "I'll be good."

Matt watched him tug on a horizontal piece of rebar where the asphalt wasn't crumbling as much. He swung himself down feet first, hanging on with his fingers. He did a couple of chin-ups for good measure, his large biceps bulging. "That was for you, girls!" he yelled as he dropped down after the second chin-up. He easily found footing on the rubble and scrambled the last eight or nine feet down to the pathway.

Catherine rolled her eyes, and Stacy clapped at his bigheaded display of strength.

Darin, not to be outdone by Justin, refused the safety harness too. He swung down and then pulled himself up like Justin had, only his fingers slipped on the rebar, and he lost his grip with one hand.

"Lance-Darin!" Stacy yelled, clambering to her knees to look into the hole.

"I'm fine," he shouted up. His feet rested on the top of the pile, and he let go of the lip completely. It took him a little longer than Justin to climb down to the bottom; a couple of curse words broke free from his mouth as he slid the last few feet to the ground.

"All right, Stacy is coming down next." Matt helped her get into the makeshift safety harness. "Hold on to the rope with one hand, or you might tip upside down," he warned.

Stacy nodded, mouth set in a determined line. She lay down on her stomach on the cracked pavement and scooted backward until her legs dangled over the edge. She took a deep breath and looked back into the hole. "Lance-Darin, don't let me fall!"

"Never!" he replied.

The rope rested against her chest and to the side of her face. Matt and Cody pulled it tight and braced themselves to lower her down.

Stacy let out a little squeak as she lost contact with the road, but the rope harness held her firm. They lowered her down to the rubble heap, then kept the rope taut as she climbed her way down into Darin's waiting arms.

The process was repeated with Catherine—except Justin helped her the rest of the way down.

"You next, Cody." Matt held out the loops of the rope harness. "I'll keep you steady as you descend."

Cody looked unsure. "I don't know, Matt. I'm pretty solid. I weigh more than I look."

"No kidding, dude. Your shoulders are as broad as a prize bull's. I'm not going to try to lower you down like we did the girls. You'll have to hang from the edge and drop to the heap. I'll just keep the rope tight so you don't go tumbling all the way down."

"I used to think five ten was an okay height . . . until I met all you six-foot-plus giants," Cody grumbled.

Matt wasn't worried. He figured Cody could probably out-bench all of them, including jock Justin.

Cody's descent went smoothly, and Matt pulled the rope back up and coiled it before returning it to his backpack. He scraped his arm on the edge of the road as he lowered himself into the hole, but other than that, it seemed like it would be an easy climb down. And it would have been if something hard hadn't sailed past his head and splattered up chunks of rubble at his legs.

CHAPTER 6

Matt hurried the rest of the way while working to avoid being hit. Golf ball-sized hail pounded through the opening, bouncing off the pile of debris. The group of teens skirted down the pathway away from the onslaught, in the direction they'd been traveling above.

"Looks like you found this tunnel just in time, Matt," Catherine said.

"Yeah." He looked back. "Getting pelted by those giant ice balls would not have been good."

Cody took his gas mask off and drew in a breath.

"What are you doing?!" Darin asked.

"Don't worry, it's fine," Cody said. "The air up there is bad because of the ash blowing around as thick as flies on a pile of manure, but down here it's pretty clean."

All but Darin took off their masks.

Catherine used the bottom of her T-shirt to wipe her face. Matt nearly choked on his own spit at the sight of her bare midriff. "I don't recommend crying while wearing a full-faced gas mask," she said.

"Totally," Stacy agreed.

The pathway looked like an extra-wide sidewalk—one that had been attacked by an army of rogue jackhammers in spots. Matt peered down the dim tunnel, grateful to realize that enough light filtered through the broken spots above that they wouldn't have to use the hand-cranked flashlights much.

As the others stowed their gas masks in their packs, Darin examined them, his face drawn tight with concern. Stacy sidled up to him and trailed a finger down the bare skin of his arm. "Lance-Darin, take that mask off so I can kiss you."

His face turned red as he glanced up at the others, then down at Stacy. Her pouty lips must have convinced him. He slowly loosened the straps around his head, then held his breath as he peeled the mask off.

"Don't be a chicken," Justin said. "Take a breath." He stepped forward and punched Darin in the gut—not hard, just with enough oomph to force him to take a breath.

Darin sucked in a lungful of the stale air and moved to shove Justin, who easily dodged out of his reach. Stacy hopped between them like a skilled cheerleader and turned Darin's face to her with a hand to each cheek. "Kiss, Lance-Darin," she reminded him.

Catherine rolled her eyes. "Uhh, we'll leave you two alone."

"But not too long," Matt said. "We aren't going to wait for you. You'll have to catch up." As they walked down the path, dodging the more jagged pieces of concrete, he wondered if Catherine might want some time alone with him . . .

Her arm brushed against his as they walked, and he smiled down at her. "Feeling better?"

She nodded. "Yeah. Sorry I freaked out a little. I'd ask if you're feeling better, but I can see that you are by the bounce in your step."

Matt laughed. "I prefer to call it a swagger. 'Bounce' sounds too bunny-like."

The swagger may have briefly turned to a bounce when Catherine slipped her hand in his, interlacing their fingers. She sighed. "I do feel a lot safer down here."

They were able to walk four abreast on the walkway, and Cody wondered aloud, "What do y'all s'pose this was built for? I mean, it's bigger than a sidewalk, but not wide enough to be a road. There aren't any tram tracks or anything."

Stacy spoke up from behind them. "It reminds me of, like, the path for a golf cart. It's about the same width, except that most of those are made out of asphalt."

"Glad you two could join us," Justin said. "You didn't spend much time playing tonsil tag."

"Ooh, barf!" Stacy said. "That makes it sound gross."

"If it's gross, then you're doing it wrong."

Darin stiffened. "She didn't say it was gross. She said the way you described it is gross."

"Relax, dude. I'm just joking."

Cody looked up through a hole big enough to see out of. "Looks like it stopped hailing."

"Way to change the subject," Catherine whispered as she followed his gaze.

"It's a gift." He shrugged.

They walked on for about an hour, occasionally having to dodge rubble that had fallen from above or what looked like hardened lava that had seeped into the tunnel. The path ahead brightened more than at their starting point, and as they got closer, it became hard to breathe. Ash swirled in the light from above. Catherine coughed and pulled her shirt collar up over her mouth and nose.

"Time to put the masks back on," Darin said, being the only adult in the group.

Stacy sighed, but they all stopped to put them on before moving closer to the area.

Matt inspected the large cave-in. Dirt, asphalt, and cement blocked the whole tunnel. "What do you think did this?"

"My guess would be a meteor," Darin said, his face turning pale.

"Yeah," Matt agreed, "that seems about right. This hole is huge. And look at the scorch marks."

"We're gonna have to go topside again," Cody said. "At least until we find another spot to climb down."

Catherine stared up into the red sky and hugged her arms around her chest. "At least there isn't lightning at the moment." She turned wide, fearful eyes to Matt.

He touched her arm. "It'll be okay. We'll get past this blockage and find another way down in no time."

"I hope so." She turned and climbed up out of the tunnel, Matt close behind her, no rope needed this time. Twisted rebar stuck out from the walls, and they used it like a warped ladder to reach the surface.

Matt was glad to see that his theory was correct: The underground tunnel followed right beneath the road.

The landscape hadn't changed much, except for the increased number of pits in the earth from falling meteors. Catherine bit her lip and looked up. "Let's hurry and find a way back in before the world decides to attack us again."

CHAPTER 7

A light wind swirled around them, kicking up the ash and dust. The air was cool, but not cold enough to be uncomfortable—at the moment. Matt searched the ground ahead of them, walking at a fast pace, determined to find a way back down to the tunnel before something else fell from the sky. He looked back at Catherine. She seemed to be doing okay, other than her eyes darting back and forth, up and down, as she watched for something ominous to occur.

The wind picked up, blowing straight at them, the temperature turning icy. The ash blowing in his face made it hard for Matt to see more than a few steps ahead, so he slowed his pace. He didn't want to fall into an open pit.

Matt breathed a sigh of relief, fogging up his mask, when he stepped to the edge of another hole big enough to climb back down into the tunnel. He turned to Catherine, who was only steps behind him. "We can go down here. It looks like less of a decline than the first one. I'm going to go down first to make sure. I'll yell up to you if it's safe."

Catherine nodded, hugging herself as she shivered. She twisted to relay the message to the others as they caught up in a group.

The hill of debris was situated almost like someone had intentionally used it to lay stairs in that spot. Even so, Matt stepped carefully in the dim light; he didn't want to twist an ankle with a misstep. He stepped onto the concrete pathway and hollered up to the others, "This one's easy, just watch your step."

Catherine started down first and took Matt's proffered hand as he helped her down the last few steps. When the group was all assembled, they walked away from the breach in the tunnel and removed their masks as soon as the air cleared.

"It would really have been nice if we would have known to wear layers for this ever-changing weather." Catherine rubbed her bare arms as they walked.

"For sure," Stacy agreed.

Catherine removed the elastic from her hair and shook it out before pulling it all back into a tight ponytail again. "I really need a shower. A *warm* shower, with clean water—not an apocalyptic rain shower full of ash and radioactive dust."

Matt looked down at his own black-streaked clothing and skin. "Yeah. We could all use a good spray down."

"Yep, you all smell like someone's gym shorts," Justin said as he jogged ahead of them.

"Well, you smell like gym shorts rolled in chicken crap," Cody yelled after him. "Chicken crap is the most foul-smelling of all the smells on a farm," he explained with a grin.

"Really?" Darin asked. "Why is that? I would think that pigs would be the worst."

Cody shook his head. "Pigs get a bad rap; they aren't nearly as smelly as chickens. Chicken poop stinks because it's high in ammonia. It's real bad when it gets wet."

They stopped and looked up to where Justin's lower body dangled from an opening in the ceiling, just big enough to fit his head and shoulders through. He dropped back down to the short pile of rubble he'd climbed up on to reach the hole. He jumped down to the pathway and shook the ash out of his sandy-blond hair.

"What were you doing up there?" Stacy asked.

"Just looking around. I kinda want to know if anything changes out there."

Stacy wrinkled up her face. "Like what? We already know that, like, the weather changes all the time."

Justin shrugged. "More like if the terrain changes or something. I don't know. Or if there's a bigfoot or aliens or something out there."

"As if." Stacy rolled her eyes.

"I used to think bigfoot was real," Darin confessed with a self-deprecating smile.

"Oh, Lance-Darin! That's so cute!"

"And who says aliens aren't real?" Matt chimed in. "What about Area 51?"

"You believe those conspiracy theories?" Catherine bumped him with her shoulder and smirked.

Matt smiled. "I believe in the possibility of those conspiracy theories."

"I had a neighbor who swore he was abducted by aliens in nineteen eighty-two," Cody said. "But then again, he also said his sheep talked to him and that he could predict the future by examining patterns in cow manure."

They all laughed as they continued along the pathway. Now that Justin had done it, they all took turns peeking out of any of the breaches in the ceiling that were big enough to poke a head through—at least for the ones that had rubble to climb up.

Matt figured they'd walked several miles, maybe more. The sore muscles in his legs told him probably more. He reached the next ceiling hole before the others, but there wasn't much of a pile to climb up on. "Hey, Justin, give me a boost."

Justin held his hands, fingers laced together, at Matt's knees. He put his foot in Justin's hands and Justin lifted him to where he could reach the edge with his own hands. Matt pulled himself up through the hole until his chest lay against the side. He held his breath as he looked around. The wind had died down and the sun was making a rare, though muted, appearance. Matt almost gasped, but remembered in time that he shouldn't breathe in the contaminated air. In the distance, through the haze, was a building. The first they'd seen since leaving the air lock.

CHAPTER 8

"Help me back down," Matt yelled when his head and torso were back inside the tunnel. He hung by his fingers, a little too far for him to just let go and drop to the pavement below. Justin wrapped his hands around Matt's right calf, and another pair of hands grasped his left calf. They lowered him down by walking their hands up his legs until his butt landed on one each of their shoulders. He wobbled and used their heads to hold on to for balance, then he dropped to the ground.

Stacy laughed. "You guys could totally be cheerleaders. Not."

"Guys." Matt ignored her jab. "I saw a building! It's in the direction we're heading."

Five questions came at him at once.

"What kind of building?"

"How far away?"

"Did it look occupied?"

"Is it damaged?"

"Do you think there's food there? Or beer?" That one, of course, was Justin.

Matt held up his hands, palms forward. "Whoa, whoa. One at a time. It was really too far away to see much, other than it looks to be a ways away and it's a few stories tall."

"Now that Justin mentioned food, I'm hungry," Cody said as the group moved away from the opening.

"Now's as good a time as any to stop and eat," Matt said.

They dropped their packs on the dusty floor of the tunnel and dug out some of the dried food they'd scavenged from the control room before beginning the ridiculously long elevator ride to the air lock.

"Who has the can opener?" Justin asked, holding up a can of peaches.

"Here." Stacy handed it to him.

"So, seriously," Catherine said, "what do you all think the building is? Best guess."

They discussed as they ate, sitting on the dirty cement, backs against the tunnel walls.

"Did you guys see *Day of the Dead*?" Matt asked. "Maybe it's a house full of zombies."

"Not funny, Matt!" Stacy shrieked.

"Yeah, man." Justin scowled. "We have no idea how the apocalypse affected people who weren't in cryopods! Don't say stuff like that!"

"Okay, okay! I was just joking," Matt said.

"I hope it's a shopping center." Stacy's eyes grew glassy.

"Seriously?" Justin snorted. "Just what we need—makeup and perfume. Maybe some accessories for our fancy clothes." He waved his hands around his ears like a jewelry model.

"Rude! You know we could all use some different clothes. Like, at least a rain jacket or something."

"As much as I'd like it to be a store—full of food *and* clothes—I think that's really unlikely," Catherine said. "Why would something like that be here? I mean, so far, everything has been centered around the cryo experiment and prepping for the apocalypse. It's not like this is some sort of destination resort."

Cody shoved the wrapper from his dried fruit into his backpack. "Maybe it's just another control building or something. Hopefully it's like the Sev, though—a place where we can get some food and rest."

"And beer," Justin added.

"What do you think it is, Darin?" Matt asked.

He shrugged. "I have no idea. Probably an empty, bombed-out shell."

"Way to be a downer, dude." Justin gulped water from his canteen.

"Well, no matter what kind of building it is, I think we should try to make it there before nightfall." Matt stood and positioned his backpack straps across his shoulders, signaling the others that it was time to get moving again.

They walked in silence for a while. Matt watched for another place where he could peek outside again. He was pretty sure the road and tunnel would take them right past the building, but he wanted to confirm that with his vision. Plus, as they got closer, he was hoping to get some idea of what the building was and if it would be a good place to shelter for the night.

Stacy broke the silence. "So, umm, like, do you really think there might be zombies out there, Matt?"

He laughed. "No way. Zombies are just fiction. The reanimation of a corpse is biologically impossible."

"Maybe that is impossible," Justin chimed in. "But there are other things that can turn living people into brainless monsters."

"Like what?" Catherine asked.

"Like drugs that make you mental. Or diseases, brain infections that mess with your personality. Maybe radiation." Justin's voice rose in pitch with each theory.

"You forgot to mention alien probes inserted into your brain," Cody joked.

Matt laughed. "Yeah, by way of your anus."

"This isn't funny, Matt!" Stacy's eyes bulged. She was well on her way to hysteria. "You're the one who told us that aliens are real!"

"Relax, Stacy. I said that I think it's *possible* that they exist, not that they *do* exist."

Her chin trembled and her voice wavered. "But . . . what if there's something like that in that building?" She stopped, her body going rigid. "What if there's something like that down here?!"

"Shit, Stacy," Justin said. "Now you have me freaking out."

Darin put an arm around Stacy. She buried her head in his chest, and he urged her forward, guiding her down the path.

"Don't worry, little lady," Cody said. "Me and Matt will check it out before you all go in. We'll make sure it's safe."

"And what are you two going to do?" Justin's voice rose. "Lull them to sleep talking about stupid movies and your idiot theories?"

"Whoa, Justin, not cool," Catherine said. "I don't know why you two are so worked up about this, but being a jerk isn't going to help anything."

Before he could respond, a large segment of the ceiling fell from above, bringing with it a rush of dirt, ash, and asphalt. Matt and Catherine were knocked to the side in a plume of fine dust, barely avoiding getting smashed in the head. Cody skidded to a stop and covered his face with his arms as the chunk of cement landed just inches from the toes of his shoes and burst, fragments and dust flying everywhere. Stacy screamed. Within moments, it was all over.

Matt coughed. "Everybody okay?!"

Catherine dusted herself off and helped him up.

"Yeah," Cody answered.

"We're okay," Stacy said through sobs.

"Justin?" Matt asked.

There was no answer.

Matt rushed to the center of the tunnel. Chunks of asphalt and dirt formed a new obstacle.

"Justin?!" Stacy screamed. "Justin, where are you?"

Matt's heart pounded in his rib cage, and it was hard to swallow. He knelt down and looked under the bigger chunks of road.

"Justin!" Catherine yelled. "Can you hear us?"

The teenage jock emerged around an older pile from a previous cave-in. "Yeah, yeah I'm here."

"What the freak!" Stacy rushed to him and pounded her balled fists on his chest.

"What?" he asked.

"Why didn't you answer?" Matt asked. "We were getting worried."

"I was taking a leak and didn't want to get stage fright."

"Dude," Cody said. "Not cool. Not cool at all!"

"Maybe it isn't what's in that building we need to worry about," Darin said.

"Yeah," Matt agreed. "We might actually be safer up on the surface." He glanced at Catherine. Her face had gone white and she shook her head as she stared up at the fractured ceiling.

CHAPTER 9

Matt examined his forearms, where small rivulets of blood seeped out of nicks and cuts caused by the fragments of broken cement that went flying as the slab crashed onto the pathway. He glanced up and then at Cody. "We should keep moving. Some of those slabs of cement hanging from rebar up there don't look too stable."

"Right," Cody said. "Giddyap."

After walking in silence for about a hundred yards, Catherine pulled on Matt's arm to stop him, and the others came to a halt behind them. "We should clean up Matt's cuts real quick," she said.

She lowered her pack to the ground and dug out an old first-aid kit. The iodine was mostly dried up, so she poured a little water on a gauze pad and wiped the blood and dirt off as well as she could. She examined her work and sighed. "That'll have to do for now, but you should definitely clean them up better when you get a chance. None of them are too deep or gaping or anything, so that's good."

"Thank you." Matt held his arms out as she wrapped them in gauze. "That feels much better."

"We should probably check out Stacy's foot too," Darin suggested.

"Good idea," Catherine agreed. She gathered up the first-aid kit items, then went to sit by her. "Let me take a look."

Stacy removed her shoe. "It doesn't hurt as bad as before."

"That's good to know." Catherine swabbed what little iodine was left onto her foot. "Remind me and I can do this for you a few times a day."

Stacy nodded and let Catherine do her work.

"There you go," Catherine said.

"Thanks," Stacy said. "Remember those suckers you'd get from the doctor?"

"Yeah," Cody said.

"What I would give to have a Tootsie Pop right now," Matt said.

"I always liked the root beer Dum Dums," Stacy said.

They all reminisced on all the suckers that they missed. From the chalky Smarties lollies to Whistle Pops, they all agreed that they missed their old lives, even the doctor's office.

The group trudged on for another hour and a half before coming to another opening in the ceiling. Matt climbed up and held his breath as he peered out. He couldn't hold back a big smile as he descended, using the exposed rebar as a ladder. He dropped the last few feet. "We're almost there! I think we should go the rest of the way up top in case there aren't any more good holes to climb out of."

"Did you see any . . . activity?" Stacy asked, nervously tugging on a strand of frizzy hair.

Matt shook his head. "Nothing, but it's still hard to see details because of how hazy the air is."

"All right," Darin said, "let's get our masks on and get this trek over with."

Matt was surprised no one argued—especially Stacy. The cave-in must have taken the fight out of her. Or she'd just resigned herself to the fact that danger lurked everywhere, so no one place was any safer than another.

They climbed out and kept going. As the building drew nearer, a nervous energy cascaded through Matt's body, and he couldn't help but walk faster. "It looks like half of it was still under construction," he yelled back at the others. "Looks like a hotel, maybe." He jogged the rest of the way to the pitted circular drive in front of the three-story building. He'd been right—it was a hotel. Well, half of one anyway.

"In the middle of, like, nowhere? This remote?" Stacy asked. "It's either going to be creeptastic, or it was built for the ultra-wealthy."

Matt's lungs burned as he sucked in air through the mask, then forced it out again. Maybe jogging hadn't been such a good idea under the current conditions. He stood looking up at the lavishly carved columns holding up the awning across the drop-off area and the entrance to the hotel while his friends caught up to him.

"Is that, like, the ocean?" Stacy asked, staring out past the building.

"The ocean?" Matt turned to look in the direction she faced.

As if of one mind, the group walked toward the black sand of the litter-strewn beach. A slight chill ran down Matt's back as he took in the sight. The water churned and bubbled instead of lapping at the shore in waves like the ocean should. Or like it used to.

Catherine stepped up beside him, their arms brushing. "It's so . . . sad. All the dead fish on the shore and floating in the water. Garbage. Parts of buildings."

Matt nodded as his eyes took in a large section of a roof, a couple of windows still attached, half in the churning water and half on the beach. Chunks of plastic, garbage, plywood, and other detritus floated among the tons of dead fish.

"The water . . ." Justin blinked and shook his head. "It's like a continuous megaplume."

"What's a megaplume?" Darin asked.

"A big one was discovered right before we went into the deep freeze. I was fascinated by it; I watched every news story about it. It was in a place in the Pacific called the Juan de Fuca Ridge. It's like, I don't know, boiling water. They thought it was from a hydrothermal vent forming that released a bunch of hot water at once." He ran a hand over his head, dislodging some of his hair from beneath the straps of his gas mask. "This is crazy."

"Yeah," Catherine agreed. "It's like the tide is just . . . gone. Like the Earth is so off-kilter that it messed up even the tides."

"I used to love the ocean," Stacy said quietly. "But not this one. It looks so dangerous . . . and, like, filthy."

Cody turned in a slow circle, then stopped, facing the churning, white-capped water. "Do y'all reckon we're on an island?"

The dried fruit he'd eaten in the tunnel suddenly felt like lead in Matt's stomach. Yeah, he did reckon there was a good chance they were on an island. A real good chance. But where?

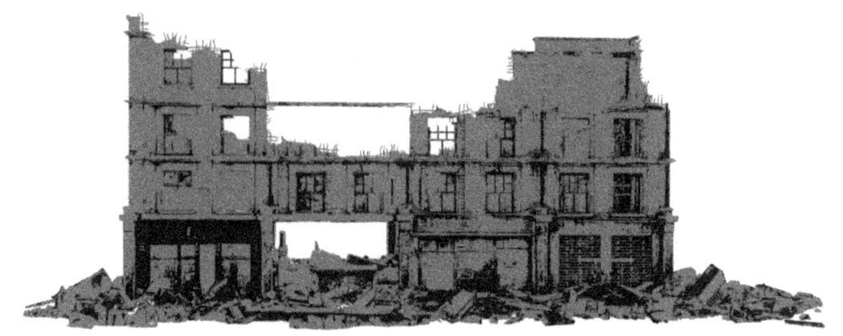

CHAPTER 10

Matt led the disheartened group back to the entrance and climbed through the broken glass of the first of two sets of doors leading into the lobby of the once-lavish hotel. He pushed open the second set of doors, glass still intact, and stepped onto a dust-covered marble floor with a large crack running down the center.

"Umm, like, wow. I was right! Ultra-wealthy." Stacy stared up at a huge crystal chandelier, hanging crookedly a few feet from a large hole in the ceiling. "Looks like we've moved up in the world. Five-star accommodations for the A-Team!" She pumped a fist in the air.

Matt smiled even as he followed an imaginary diagonal line from the hole above to a deep hole in the floor, plunging down at least a couple of stories. No escape from meteorites here.

"Yeah!" Justin high-fived Stacy. "*A-Team* is rad! I'm Mr. T." He ran a few steps and jumped over the back of a velvet-like couch, landing on the cushions in a giant plume of dust. He waved his hands in front of his face, coughing like a three-pack-a-day smoker.

"Y'all, look at this." Cody stood in front of a large painting hanging in a gold-embossed frame next to the fireplace.

The others joined him, Justin still hacking up a lung.

"Pangea . . ." Matt read out loud. "You were right, Cody, we are on an island. An island named Pangea."

"Pangea?" Catherine asked. "I've never heard of an island with that name."

"I'm sure there's a lot of islands out there you've never heard of," Justin said.

"That's true," Catherine said. "But what if it's a fake? Like the soundstage? Like HZRD?"

"Good point," Matt said. "Let's keep our guard up. Not that it ever went down. I mean, we know what kinda crap the government has been pulling, so just watch out for signs. I hope it's not fake."

Cody nodded and pointed to a building labeled "Hotel Isla Pangea" near the beach. "This is where we are."

"At least it isn't *Hotel California*," Catherine said. She looked around at her friends. "You know, like the Eagles song?"

"More like *Island* California," Matt whispered, "where you can never leave."

A small company logo painted in the bottom left corner read "Demo Trench."

"Look at all the hotels." Catherine pointed to several of the extravagant buildings in the painting. "And neighborhoods? Stores? Are these all really here, on this island?"

Darin shook his head. "I think this is more of a design plan, like this is what it would have looked like if they'd been able to finish everything."

"Know what I ain't seein'?" Cody asked. "Anything resembling a cryovault."

"Yeah." Matt scratched his neck. "That HZRD building isn't on here either, though."

"That's all top-secret government stuff. This looks more like they were planning a resort," Darin said.

"Crazy." Justin shook his head, then slapped Darin on the back. "But I'm hungry. Think there's any food in this place?"

Matt looked around at the lavish furnishings of the lobby. "Probably caviar and expensive wine."

"Mmm." Stacy rubbed her stomach. "Caviar."

"Ain't that just fish eggs?" Cody asked, smirking. "That's what we in Texas call fish bait."

Stacy rolled her eyes. "I wouldn't expect someone as uncultured as you to have any taste for the finer things in life." She stuck her nose in the air, but couldn't keep up her charade and started laughing.

Cody joined in her laughter. "I will never understand rich people."

Justin wandered over to the front desk, exploring behind it. He flipped a light switch and said, "Whoa," in surprise when some of the lights in the lobby turned on. "How in the hell is there electricity here?"

"Yeah, I didn't see any powerlines or anything," Catherine said.

"Like, the underground had power," Stacy pointed out.

"And the vaults," Darin said.

"True," Matt agreed. "But remember the instruction manual in the control room? That whole area, as well as the vaults, is powered with geothermal energy from volcanoes. Do you think it could be the same here?"

"That's the only logical explanation," Catherine said. "Right?"

Darin frowned. "I do remember Westbrook saying something about natural volcanoes and geothermal something or other. I wasn't really listening to the psycho at that point."

Matt cringed. He mostly trusted Darin's story about Dr. Westbrook not being the hero he'd portrayed himself as in the videos he'd left them, but once in a while, the initial doubt he'd had about Darin crept back in. "Well, whether or not that's the source of power, I'm just glad to have it. I say we spend the night here. Who wants to explore a little?"

"I'm all in with that," Justin said.

The others nodded. Matt pushed off the front desk counter he'd been leaning against. "Okay. Let's just keep the exploring to this general area for now, stay within shouting distance of each other." If there was one thing this place had taught him, it was that even if something seemed completely safe in the moment, it could turn deadly in a heartbeat.

"For sure, chief." Justin saluted him.

Matt followed Catherine toward a couple of doors next to a small dining area just off the lobby. She looked at him before trying the knob, and smiled when it turned. Inside was a small pantry area, the shelves filled with large cans of food. Restaurant-sized cans. And not just the usual fare they'd been eating for days, like canned fruit.

Catherine's eyes lit up as she grabbed a large, unopened can of dehydrated mashed potatoes, and she let out an adorable squeak when she saw the dehydrated eggs next to it. Even the canned vegetables looked good: green beans, corn, peas, carrots. "We can have a three-course meal tonight with these!"

Matt laughed at her enthusiasm and reached past her to grab a can of cherry pie filling. "Four courses. Don't forget about dessert."

"Now we just need water, pans, and a heat source."

"Hey, guys!" Cody yelled. "Look what I found!"

They put the food back on the shelves and hurried down a short hallway, where Cody stood in front of a set of double doors. When they all got to him, he grinned and flung open the doors with a flourish, gesturing inside with a "ta-da!"

CHAPTER 11

The sounds that escaped the throats of the assembled group ranged from squeals of delight to whoops of joy. Matt reached out to touch one of the large mattresses—still in the plastic cover it had arrived in. He did a quick count: fifteen. Perfect.

"Let's pull these out and line them up in the open corner by the map," he said. "I'm going to sleep like a king tonight!"

"Slumber party!" Stacy yelled.

"Oh yeah!" Catherine high-fived her.

They doubled up and carried the mattresses to the corner, arranging them near each other before ripping the plastic off. Cody turned so his back faced one of the mattresses, his heels next to its side. "I'm takin' the Nestea plunge!" He fell straight back, bouncing up a few inches as his body hit the springy surface.

The others laughed. "I love those commercials!" Catherine said.

"Now I'm thirsty," Stacy whined.

"Well, you're in luck," Matt said. "Catherine and I found a pantry full of treasure, including multiple six-packs of soda."

"Well, why didn't you say so?" Justin asked, already heading in the direction of the pantry.

Each of them grabbed a can out of the armload Justin brought back with him.

Darin and Stacy wandered off, soon disappearing from sight, and Justin and Cody resumed their exploration of the spacious lobby and connected hallways.

Matt and Catherine sat on a mattress, talking and sipping the flat, room-temperature soda. Matt retrieved his Trapper Keeper out of his backpack, pulled out a notebook and mechanical pencil, and started to draw the island, looking up at the painting of the map for reference every couple of minutes.

"You're pretty good at that." Catherine scooted closer to him, so their legs touched.

He shrugged and smiled. He momentarily lost control of his hand as the warmth of her thigh, pressed so close to his, reached his nervous system, shorting everything out for a heartbeat. The pencil lead snapped as he pushed it too hard against the paper. "Thanks." He looked up at her. Catherine's face was only inches from his; her breath smelled like stale cola as she exhaled. He was held hostage by her eyes, mesmerized. He dropped the pencil and notebook to his lap and touched her arm as they both leaned in a fraction of an inch. Matt licked his lips, his heart doing the fifty-yard dash around his chest.

"Come see what we found!" Justin yelled, breaking the spell.

"Damn it," Matt whispered as he and Catherine jerked away from each other. He hadn't meant to say it out loud, and his face flushed as he dared a peek at her.

She smiled, eyes shining, and let out a short laugh.

Matt set his notebook on the mattress and stood, offering his hand to help her up. She took it and got up, and instead of letting go of it, entwined her fingers through his. He gave her hand a slight squeeze and smiled down at her, hoping they'd finish later what they'd almost started before being interrupted.

Justin and Cody waved them over to the area behind the front desk. As they got closer, Matt could see an open door down the short hallway behind them. "What did you find, Cody?" he said. "And it'd better be good."

Cody raised an eyebrow at his friend. "A security room with monitors. Most of the cameras are still working."

"Really?" Matt picked up his pace, and he and Catherine followed Cody inside the small room, Justin at their heels. The nine-inch CCTV monitors flickered as they cycled through the different cameras placed throughout the building. Each time the picture changed to a new location, a label appeared at the bottom of the screen: "Elevator South Side," "East Hallway," etc.

"I wish there was a radio in here," Matt said. "I'd love to try to get in contact with the vault, if we could."

"Yeah, I don't see one," Cody said. "Plus, who knows how to use one."

"I don't," Matt said.

"Me neither," Catherine said.

The four of them watched the monitors for a few minutes in silence. Matt was acutely aware of Catherine's hand in his, their arms pressed together in the small, dark room, and wished it were just the two of them in there, maybe playing seven minutes in heaven . . .

"What are you guys doing in here?" Stacy's too-loud voice made all four of them jump.

Before any of them could answer, she squealed and pushed her way between Justin and Cody to grab a black-and-silver tape recorder off the desk. "This is just like the one I have at home."

"*Had* at home," Justin corrected.

She rolled her eyes. "Whatever." She pushed the "eject" button, and the top of the cassette recorder popped open to reveal an empty tape slot. "We should totally record ourselves."

"What would we record?" Darin asked. "Besides, I doubt it has batteries, and if it does, they'll have died long ago."

"No duh." Stacy flipped the tape player over, popped open a small compartment, and pulled out an AC adapter. "I think we should record an account of our journey so far and leave it for someone to find in the future."

Matt nodded. "Great idea. Plug it in, let's see if it works." He held a cassette tape still in its plastic that he had retrieved from the shelf to his left.

CHAPTER 12

Stacy pressed the "play" and "record" buttons at the same time, and the tape in the cassette started spinning. She smiled. "Testing. Testing. The apocalypse has arrived." She pressed "stop," and the two previously depressed buttons popped up and the tape stopped. After rewinding it, she hit the "play" button and her voice came back to her, repeating her test message.

"Awesome. How do we want to do this?" Matt asked.

Catherine flipped a light on in the dim room. "First, I think we need to bring some chairs in here, this might take a while. Then I think Cody should start, since he was the first one out of his pod."

"Actually," Stacy said, "Lance-Darin was the first one out of his pod."

Darin smiled but shook his head. "Yeah, I was out, but I was unconscious for two days. Cody should start, and we can all chime in as the story moves along. Just like we're having a conversation, instead of some official-sounding log."

They gathered up some chairs from the dining area and jammed them into the room—a couple of them half-in and half-out of the doorway. It wasn't a perfect setup, but it got everyone as close as they could be to the cassette recorder that sat on the desk. Cody scooted closer to the table, and Stacy counted to three, then pushed the "record" and "play" buttons.

"Hey, y'all. This here's Cody Anderson from the great state of Texas."

Justin snickered.

Cody ignored him and continued. "I don't really reckon I know how many days it's been, maybe a couple of weeks, maybe more, maybe less. I ain't rightly sure. But I woke up when Dr. Westbrook opened the cryopod I'd been in for . . . well, I don't know that either, just that it was a long time. Decades." He looked up at Darin and cocked an eyebrow.

Darin shrugged and shook his head.

"Anyhow," Cody went on, "Westbrook opened my pod and woke me up. He was frantic and said somethin' along the lines of 'we have to get them out.' Before I even had a chance to decipher what he meant, the other pods slipped off the back of the truck and Dr. Westbrook . . . he was smashed underneath them.

"I was disoriented and confused, but I knew I needed help to get those pods off him. The only problem—I didn't know how to open them. Matt's was closest, so I grabbed a tree branch and started pounding on the plexiglass covering the top half of the cryopod. Matt woke up and pounded from the inside, yelling for me to get him out." Cody nodded to him.

Sweat popped out on Matt's forehead as he remembered the ordeal. He leaned closer to the recorder. "Yeah, all I can remember is Cody puking all over the glass, my feeding tube ripping out of my stomach, and feeling like I couldn't breathe. It sucked. Cody finally busted through and pulled me out. Then I puked."

"We couldn't lift the pods with people still in them. They were too heavy," Cody said. "Plus, Catherine woke up and was pounding on hers and crying. So we got her out next."

Catherine smiled at Matt. "And Matt called me Cher, as if I wasn't already confused enough."

Matt's face reddened. "Your hair . . . just . . . reminded me of hers."

She laughed. "We worked together to get Justin out, then the boys slid his pod off the doctor." Her tone turned serious. "He was dead. There was nothing we could do."

"Yep," Cody said. "His whole face was smashed in. He'd lost as much blood as a butchered hog."

"Eww! Gag me with a spoon!" Stacy covered her mouth.

"Sorry," Cody apologized. "While we worked on getting someone else out the hard way, Catherine used her brain and searched Westbrook for a key. Next thing I knew, she'd unlocked the rest of the pods."

Matt scrunched up his face. "She was covered in his blood. I thought for a minute she'd been injured, but"—he looked at her and smiled—"she was just showing her bravery and smarts."

Catherine squeezed his hand. "When we opened the last one . . ."

Matt finished for her. "It was a girl—number seven was on her uniform. She hadn't made it through the crash. Oh yeah, the army truck we were in had crashed."

The group was silent for a few seconds.

Matt started again. "So everyone was out of their pods except Kim—"

Justin let out a single, harsh laugh and pointed at him. "She took one look at your blood-soaked tank top and refused to let you help her with her feeding tube."

"Yeah." Stacy's voice turned sad. "She only wanted Rhett to do it."

"Remember how he walked over to her and just kissed her?" Cody shook his head, a sad smile tickling his lips.

"Those two and their PDA was disgusting," Justin said. "But Rhett was cool."

He and Justin had hit it off right away. Like jocks just instinctively gravitated to each other. Matt nodded. "Yeah, Rhett was cool."

Catherine wiped at a tear trickling down her face. "There were ten of us, eleven counting the dead girl whose name we never knew. This was before we discovered Darin in the cab of the truck." She named all of them, speaking toward the recorder. "So besides me, Matt, Cody, Justin, and Stacy, our group consisted of Kim, Rhett, Victoria, Kyle, and Nathan."

"There are only six of us left," Stacy said softly, "and that *includes* Lance-Darin."

"Five of us are gone." Catherine's voice cracked and more tears plunged from her eyes.

"Let's take a break for a few minutes." Matt reached over and hit "stop."

CHAPTER 13

Catherine leaned her head on Matt's shoulder and he put his arm around her. "Let's go for a short walk," he suggested.

"Okay." She wiped her face and stood.

"We'll be back in five minutes," Matt said. "Then we can start recording again." They walked to the front of the lobby and gazed out at the debris-strewn beach through the glass doors.

Catherine sighed and turned to face him, wrapping her arms around his waist in a tight hug. He returned her embrace and laid his cheek against the top of her head, enjoying the warmth of her body pressed against his.

"I hope this is the end of it," she whispered. "The death. I can't bear to lose another friend."

Matt didn't respond with words, just pulled her closer. He was afraid his voice would betray his jumbled emotions. He'd been hit hard by the deaths in their group. He blamed himself for most, if not all, of them. As the reluctant leader, it was his job to keep them all safe. And mixed in with the guilt and pain was hope—hope that he was closer than ever to finding his parents, and hope in the growing feelings he had for Catherine. His heart raced at the thought, and he gripped her tighter to him.

"Five minutes are up!" Justin yelled.

Sighing, Matt gave Catherine one last gentle squeeze and released his embrace. They walked back to the security room hand in hand.

Catherine put her mouth next to his ear and whispered, "Thank you."

Her warm breath against his neck gave him a chill—the good kind—and he nodded in response.

When they all got situated around the cassette recorder again, Stacy said, "I get to tell this part—the Lance-Darin part." She started the recording. "And now for the best part. We found Lance-Darin passed out in the cab of the big truck."

"Actually, Catherine found him," Justin butted in. "And you said he was gross and wanted to leave him there."

"You said that?" Darin raised an eyebrow at Stacy, half smiling.

"Well"—Stacy stroked his arm and stuck out her lip in a pout—"you were totally filthy. And, like, you had on that lame big belt thingy."

Darin spoke through clenched teeth. "Yeah, the belt with explosives strapped to it, courtesy of the loony, Westbrook."

"That was messed up." Cody shook his head.

"Like, yeah, totally messed up," Stacy said. "But anyway, we named you Lance and put you in one of the empty pods so we could drag you with us to Camp New Beginnings. You and the two dead bodies. Barf."

"We just wanted to give them a proper burial," Matt said.

"You're such a Boy Scout, chief." Justin punched Matt's shoulder.

"It just . . . seemed like the right thing to do."

Catherine gave his arm a squeeze. "It was, Matt."

"And don't forget the damn video tapes," Justin said. "You were obsessed with those. You had to haul them with us to the cabins."

They talked about their first night at Camp New Beginnings. About the generator powered by riding a stationary bike, finding a VCR and TV, watching Dr. Westbrook's videos, swimming in the lake, and exploring the cabins and finding food and clothes.

"Darin was still out cold on day two," Matt said. "I was afraid he wasn't going to wake up and we'd have another body to bury."

Justin snorted. "Yeah, like that worked out so well for the mad scientist and the nameless girl. Shallow graves and a flash flood don't go good together."

Mention of the flash flood darkened Matt's mood. He bowed his head and spoke solemnly. "At that point, I just wanted to go find my parents. I knew there was no one back at the vault taking care of the thousands of people in the cryopods." He swallowed. "So a group of us decided to go back to the truck to see if we could get it running and follow the tracks back to the vault."

"That turned out to be an epic bad idea," Stacy said.

Catherine stiffened. "No one could have known what would happen. That whole place was like one giant booby trap, but we didn't know that yet. We didn't find that out until much later. What happened was no one's fault."

Matt appreciated her loyalty, but guilt still filled his chest, suffocating him at times. He took a deep breath and blew it out slowly. "Me, Cody, Catherine, and . . . Kyle headed out. The flash flood hit after we'd reached the truck and were trying to fix a flat tire." He ran his hand over his face and buzz-cut hair and whispered, "I had him. I had a hold of him. But the water was too strong, like a raging river—it ripped his hand right out of my grip."

"It slammed that big truck into the trees, remember?" Catherine said quietly. "There was no way you—or anyone else—could have held on to him."

Cody took the reins to finish out this part of the journey. "When we got back to camp, we could see that everything had been flooded. But everyone there had survived."

"Darin finally woke up on day three." Matt glanced up at Darin, then back down at the marble floor. "You had zero helpful information, though. And I thought you were lying about who you were because Dr. Westbrook said in one of the videos that you'd died."

"Freaking crazy bastard," Darin muttered.

"You were frantic to get that belt off." Catherine shook her head. "We had no idea it contained explosives."

"Good thing you kept that key ring you filched off the dead scientist," Justin said.

Everyone nodded.

"And then the snow started," Stacy said.

CHAPTER 14

The tape continued to turn, recording the silence as the group sat, each lost for a moment in their own recollections.

Matt sniffed and rubbed his nose.

Stacy sighed loudly. "Just think, if we would have had winter clothing, we could have built the world's biggest snowman!"

"Or had a mega snowball fight," Justin said. "We wasted all of those snow days moping around, watching stupid videos of some crazy dude."

"Y'all act like this was just a normal, pre-apocalyptic snowstorm." Cody glared at the two of them. "It wasn't. Remember the avalanche?"

Matt dug his fingernails into his hands. Someone else would have to tell this part of the story. He couldn't do it.

"Poor Nathan," Catherine said. "That avalanche happened so fast . . . and he just . . . panicked."

"He was kind of a wimpy dude," Justin remarked.

"Shut up, Justin!" Catherine glared at him. "He was really nice."

Matt stared blankly at the floor, seeing the collapsing walls of the cabin, the huge beam swinging down, bashing into Nathan, the snow burying him. Pulling his dead body out from under it all in the silence of the aftermath. The intense heat that followed, melting all the snow so fast.

"Remember how the trees the avalanche knocked down just popped back up afterward? Like they had springs on them," Matt murmured, still looking at nothing with his glazed-over eyes. "Too bad Nathan couldn't have done the same."

"Ooh, like, he would have been like a zombie. Gag me!" Stacy said.

Matt looked up then, his eyes boring into hers. "Stacy, if you can't take this seriously, maybe you shouldn't be adding to the recording. Joking about the dead is not cool."

She rolled her eyes. "Whatever. Just trying to lighten the mood."

Matt shook his head and resumed staring at the floor. Catherine rubbed his back with slow, steady strokes. Her touch revived him, reminded him that they had survived together and were closer than ever to finding the vault . . . and his parents. "We found the Sev right after that—"

"The R and D," Stacy corrected him.

"Call it what you want," Matt said. "I prefer the Sev."

"Me and you and Catherine found it when we went to look for Kyle's body," Cody added.

Now it was Justin's turn to feel the weight of the deaths taking its toll on his psyche. He slumped down in his chair. "We deserved that party in the Sev after what happened when you guys got back to camp."

"You want to record that part, Justin?" Catherine asked.

"No. But I will anyway." He jumped to his feet and paced in the small space as he talked. "We took you guys out to see the big junkyard, or giant chem lab thing we found. And while we were dinking around, the sky turned black, and tornados—huge ones—came out of nowhere. Texas Boy told us to find shelter and get low, and we all dove behind one of the big gears stuck in the ground. All of us but Victoria—she huddled up under a tree." Justin wiped his hands over his face. "She saw us and tried to get to us . . . but . . . but a huge piece of glass or something cut her leg. And Rhett, the big idiot—" His voice faltered. "He ran out in the middle of the flying glass and metal and . . . and *trees* for hell's sake! And tried to help her."

Matt's head filled with images from that day. The surrealness of those enormous trucks and gears and glass beakers that seemed like they belonged in the land of giants from a sci-fi book or something. He crushed his eyes shut, but that made it worse. Black tornados swirled on the backs of his eyelids. He held his breath as Justin continued.

"She crawled toward Rhett. But before he could reach her, the wind picked up a truck, and he ducked when it flew at them, but she didn't. It . . . it . . ." Justin closed his eyes and shook his head.

Cody stood and put a hand on Justin's shoulder. "It killed her. That's all we need to say."

If only that was all Matt's internal movie projector would say. But instead, he saw her head, black hair flying all over, as it rolled toward them.

Justin's eyes were vacant as he nodded. "Yeah. It killed her. Then a big piece of metal blew into Rhett as he tried to make his way back to us. He was still alive, but as he crawled—" His voice hitched again. He and Rhett had been tight. "A tornado snatched him up . . . and he was gone."

Stacy sighed. "Kim went all kinds of crazy. When the storm ended, she just wanted to stay there."

"Maybe we should have let her," Catherine whispered. "The way she died was . . . brutal."

"She was my friend, I'll tell this part," Stacy said. "As we got back to camp, a volcano erupted and started shooting, like, hot lava blobs all over. Almost all of us got burned. My foot almost got burned off! Lance-Darin had to carry me." She looked over at him lovingly. "Everyone jumped in the lake except me and him. We stayed on the shore and I put my foot in. The lava started falling like crazy into the lake, so everyone got out . . . except Kim. She was being a stubborn baby."

Stacy wiped her cheeks with her arm. "A big chunk hit her right in the face. Her face, like, *melted*. Like, she looked like Sloth from *Goonies*." What started as a laugh turned to a sob, and she blubbered out, "She died!"

"Like I said," Justin added as he sat back down, "we deserved that beer party at the Sev that night."

"When some of us came back to camp the next morning, we found the underground," Matt said. "And I'm tired of talking, so to make a long story short, it was crazy. The whole area—all the disasters, weather, night and day—were controlled in that enormous underground. We almost lost Cody and Darin. We found out it was the HZRD Westbrook had talked about in his tapes. All fake. A training ground for the apocalypse."

Catherine picked up from there. "We found blueprints and made our way to where we thought we could get closer to the vault—and our parents. We took a long and wild elevator ride—sideways—to an air-lock room, then made our way here, to the Hotel Isla Pangea."

Matt sat up straight and leaned forward, focusing his eyes on one of the security monitors. "What's that?"

He pointed to the monitor that said "Kitchen" on the bottom, showing what looked like the prep kitchen. A big lump, indistinguishable in the fuzzy picture, lay right in the middle.

"I don't like the looks of that," Darin said.

"Me either," Matt agreed.

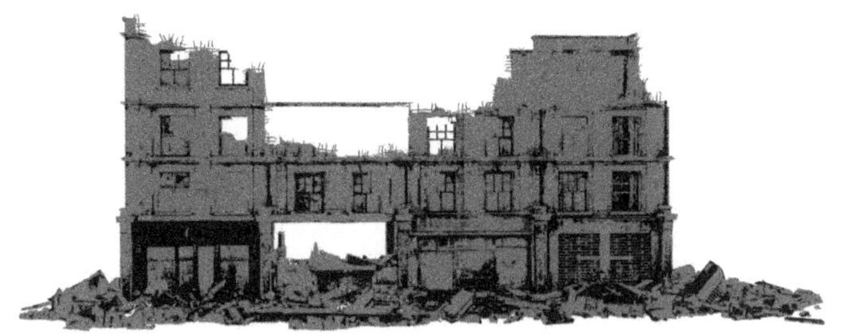

CHAPTER 15

Stacy stopped the recording. "What *is* that?"

They all moved closer to the monitor. Matt squinted, trying to make out the lump. He shook his head. "I can't tell what it is. But I think we should go check it out; I don't think I'll be able to sleep without knowing if it's something that could be dangerous."

"I agree," Darin said.

"Let's go explorin', then," Cody said.

With the memories of death so fresh in his mind, Matt frowned. "We need to stay together, though."

No one argued, not even Justin.

"I thought we'd done a pretty thorough search of the first level, but I guess we missed something," Cody said.

"Yeah, a *big* something." Stacy bounced on the balls of her feet, leading the way down a wide hallway.

Catherine came to an abrupt halt. "Stop. It can't be back there. These are guest rooms. No way they'd have a loud kitchen next to the rooms."

Stacy continued forward. "Trust me, I *know* luxury hotels."

Matt looked back and forth between Catherine and Stacy, but before he could say anything, Darin made the decision for him.

"Come on, guys, we gotta search the whole first floor again anyway. Does it really matter where we start?"

"True." Matt turned to Catherine. "You okay with this?"

"Sure." She smiled at him. "We better catch up. Stacy took off."

Matt and Catherine jogged to catch up with the group a short distance away. He thought of taking Catherine's hand, but held off.

"Found it!" Stacy shrieked. She'd passed all of the guest rooms and stood at the entrance of a narrow hallway. "Not only am I the Queen of Summer, but I'm also the Heiress of Hotels!"

"Nice goin'," Cody said.

"Another title?" Justin groaned. "Chief, why don't you lead the charge and give the Heiress of Summer a break."

"Hotels," Stacy corrected him.

"You sure?" Matt asked. "You found it."

"No way," Stacy said. "I've done my part, right, Lance-Darin?"

Darin pulled her close and kissed her on the top of her head. "For sure."

Matt brushed past them and led the way down the hallway, entering the kitchen. Off to the right was the doorway to a prep kitchen. A wide piece of athletic tape with "JW's Laboratory" written on it in black marker was stuck to the wall next to it. "JW. Jim Westbrook?" Matt asked.

"Dude, seriously?" Justin smirked. "You are so obsessed with Westbrook and the mountain vault, you see him everywhere."

"Yeah, like, what would he have been doing here?" Stacy's laugh was a pitch higher than normal, which made Matt think she might be just as nervous as him.

"Besides," Catherine said, "it's just a kitchen, right? Not a laboratory." She gestured around her at the stoves, ovens, cupboards, and large refrigerator.

Matt shrugged, annoyed at the teasing, and pushed the swinging doors to the prep area open, stepping inside. "Aah!" He couldn't stop the short, girly scream from forcing its way out of his throat. Someone bumped into him from behind.

"What the hell?" Justin looked over Matt's shoulder.

"What is it?" Catherine asked.

Matt stepped closer and decided it was safe. "Come see for yourself."

As the others filtered in, gasping at the sight, he slowly walked around the large exoskeleton. It appeared to be some kind of insect, but Matt had never seen a bug this big before, not even on *Mutual of Omaha's Wild Kingdom*. The whole insect was almost as tall as him. The organs inside were shriveled and completely desiccated. Matt couldn't tell which organ was which. Someone had clearly been dissecting this specimen. For what reasons, no one would ever know. He shuddered at the thought of this thing living, walking around . . . hunting with its claw-like pincers.

"Eww! Disgusting!" Stacy shrieked. "Is that, like, a brain or something?" She pointed to a large jar with some sort of organ floating in clear liquid.

Matt joined her where she stood in front of a column of shelves with different-sized jars sitting on them. Each jar contained a strange organ or insectile body part suspended in liquid. He shook his head in disbelief. "Westbrook really was a psycho mad scientist."

"No duh!" Darin said. "I've been saying that from day one. You just refused to believe me."

"I believed you all along," Stacy said.

Catherine had a hand over her mouth, her face pale. "What on Earth do you think he was doing with all this?"

"Mad-scientist stuff," Justin said. "Probably building a giant-insect army so he could take over the world." He cackled like an unholy combination of Young Frankenstein and the Wicked Witch of the West.

"Seriously, Justin. That wouldn't surprise me," Darin said.

Cody wandered over to a corner of the kitchen, keeping a wide berth around the exoskeleton. "Do any of y'all know how to work a computer? Maybe this thing will give us some answers." He pointed his thumb at a table that had an Apple II computer, a stack of floppy disks, and a printer sitting on it.

"Oh! *I* know how to work a computer." Stacy hurried over to Cody. "I had one of these in my room at home." She reached behind it and flipped a switch to turn it on, then hit the "on" switch on top of the monitor. She clapped her hands when it powered up.

Matt had thought she'd been lying, or at least exaggerating, when she said her family was rich, thought she'd just been trying to one-up Kim, but maybe she really was rich. She'd definitely used a computer before, and only rich people could afford to have home computers. The cost of those things was outrageous.

Stacy flipped through the floppy disks. "What kind of information are we looking for?"

"I don't really know," Matt admitted. "What are those disks labeled?"

She started reading off the labels. "Lab Notes, Schematics, Record—"

"Let's start with the lab notes," Catherine interrupted.

Stacy dropped the pile in her hand with an annoyed exhalation. She inserted the disk labeled "Lab Notes" into the drive and smiled when it started to make a whirring sound. She opened the first file and scooted over so Catherine could see it.

Matt looked through the other floppy disks while the girls read through Westbrook's notes. The monitor was too small for all of them to crowd around it.

"This is crazy," Catherine said, pointing at the screen.

Matt stopped flipping through the disks. "What?"

"He was seriously trying to create monster insects! He was messing around with DNA. He keeps mentioning research done by someone named 'Sanger.'"

"This is totally warped." Justin looked around the kitchen/laboratory and shook his head.

"Yeah," Matt agreed. He looked down at the disk he still held in his hand, and a jolt of excitement stabbed through his chest. "Stacy, put this one in." He shoved it at her.

"What is it?" she asked.

"It says 'Topographic Map.'"

"You and your obsession with maps," Catherine teased.

Matt smiled and shrugged as Stacy swapped the disks out.

CHAPTER 16

A folder labeled "Formative Stages of Pangea" caught Matt's eye. "Open that one." He leaned in.

It was just a word processor document. Matt put his hand on the mouse and scrolled quickly.

"What does it say?" Stacy asked.

Matt shook his head. "It looks like Pangea was formed when the bomb went off in the Mariana Trench. Seems to suggest the ocean floor pushed upward, causing this land mass. No one knew about it except for the top brass of all the world. Weird." He stood and shrugged. "Okay, Stacy, go to the map."

"Ay, ay, captain," she said, clicking on the folder that said "Map."

A pixelated portion of the island filled the monitor. Matt grew even more excited when he saw that everything was labeled. He pointed to a place marked "J-75 Vault."

"J? How many vaults can there be on this island?" he asked.

Stacy hit the right arrow key and another section of the map came up. "There are, like, six pages to this map."

"Is there a way we can see the whole thing at once?"

"Not on this tiny screen." Stacy looked over at the printer. "Maybe if we can print it out, you can lay the pages out to form one big map."

"Brilliant idea," Matt said.

Stacy turned the printer on—Matt let out a breath he'd been holding when it actually powered up—and checked to make sure the holes on the sides of the paper already inserted in the printer were lined up with the sprockets on either side. The paper already threaded in the printer was connected to a pile of fan-folded continuous paper sitting on the table behind it.

Matt crossed his fingers, hiding the gesture from the others by putting his hand under his opposite arm. Stacy clicked some keys on the computer like an expert, and the printer whirred to life, noisily pulling the paper in through the back and spitting it out slowly from the top as the printing mechanism glided back and forth.

As the images formed on the paper at a snail's pace, Matt thought about Stacy's computer knowledge. He could have taken a computer science class at school, but chose weightlifting instead. He figured computers would never be something he'd need to worry about—they were only for rich people and maybe the government. The closest he'd come to actually using one was his friend's Atari—and that was just a bunch of games. You didn't need to know how to do more than turn it on, insert the game cartridge, and maneuver the joystick to play. Matt was the master of *Space Invaders*. He smiled at the memory.

The printer stopped, ejecting the last page of the map out far enough to tear it from the blank piece of paper behind it along the tiny perforations. Stacy handed the small stack of papers to Matt. "Here you go, Map Boss."

"Can we get out of this creepy room now?" Catherine asked.

"Yes, of course," Matt said. "Let's go back to the dining area so I can lay these all out on a table."

Back in the dining area, they gathered around a table. They all helped Matt remove the sides of the paper where the holes for the printer were so he could lay the sections of the map side by side. Like a puzzle, it took him a few minutes to get all the pieces lined up in the right spots to form a pixelated picture of the entire island.

Cody pointed to a section. "There's the HZRD site."

"And there are a few more soundstage buildings like it." Darin pointed them out on opposite areas of the island. "DSTR, CTRPHE, THRT, and PTFLL."

Matt didn't care about the soundstages—he never wanted to get near one of them again. He searched the map until he was sure he'd found all of the vaults, amazed to count ten of them, labeled A-67 to J-75. He did the math in his head, assuming there were five thousand people in each vault as there were in B-35. "There could be close to fifty thousand people on this island still in cryosleep!" he exclaimed.

"What?" Justin scoffed. "How do you figure that?"

"Look." He pointed at each vault as he counted to ten. "Ten vaults, five thousand people in cryosleep per vault, equals fifty thousand."

Cody whistled. "That's crazy."

"Maybe not all of the vaults have the same number of pods," Catherine said.

"That's possible," Matt agreed. "But still . . ."

Darin stared at the map. "Yeah. That's a lot of people."

"Who cares?" Stacy put her hands on her hips. "We only care about one of those vaults—the one where *our* families are."

"That's harsh," Cody said, adding softly, "Those people have families too."

"Again, who cares?" Stacy said. "We obviously can't help all of them, so the priority has to be our families."

Catherine exhaled slowly. "I understand what you're saying, Stacy. Our choice has to be our own families, but we can still care about those other people's lives."

"Whatever." The slight quiver in Stacy's voice gave her away as she crossed her arms and turned her back on them.

She cared. The aloofness was all an act. Matt was convinced of it.

"Listen," he said, "those other vaults have someone in charge. They didn't have a Westbrook. I'm sure their vaults are fine and running well."

"That's true," Cody said.

Catherine and Stacy nodded in agreement.

Matt turned back to the map and put a finger on the building labeled "B-35," and a finger from his other hand on the hotel they now stood in. "Look, guys. There's a road that leads right to B-35 from here." He traced it for emphasis and noticed that it went near several small circles, each labeled "Geothermal Access Point."

Justin bounced from foot to foot. "I say we head there as soon as we're rested up."

"I'm good with that," Matt said. "But maybe we should check out the rest of the hotel? See what else we can find."

"No way!" Stacy said. "I've done enough today. I'm ready to relax."

"Come on, Stacy," Darin prodded. "Maybe there are some really nice bathrobes in the rooms. Or maybe even a change of clothes."

With this, Stacy's whole mood brightened.

"So it's settled," Matt confirmed. "The search continues."

The others nodded, smiles breaking through on most of their faces. Matt gathered up the pages of the map—excitement building at the possibility that he could see his parents within the next couple of days—and put them in the "Maps" section of his Trapper Keeper.

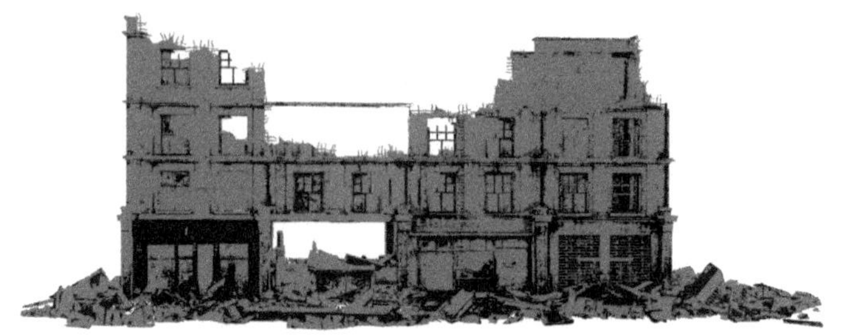

CHAPTER 17

They'd already seen almost everything on the first level, so they headed for the elevators. Stacy, suddenly renewed with enthusiasm, lunged in front of everyone to push the button. Only one of the elevators came to life; the other sat silent. The doors whooshed open and the group stepped in—Catherine with hesitation.

Matt put a hand on the small of her back and whispered, "This is just a normal elevator, nothing to worry about." He figured she was thinking about the one-and-a-half-hour horizontal elevator trip from the HZRD underground to the air-lock room. She came very close to hurling her guts out toward the end of that ride.

She turned her head and smiled shakily at him, nodding.

"Let's go floor by floor, start low and work our way up," Cody suggested.

He reached to press the second-floor button, but Stacy beat him to it with a smirk on her face. "Ha! Beat you!"

"Why are you acting like a child?" Catherine asked.

"Hey!" Darin scowled at her.

Stacy's smile faltered a little. "It's just something we used to do, my brothers and sisters and me. We always raced to see who could push the button first." She ran her fingers down the buttons, careful not to push any as the elevator ascended. "I was the baby, and I beat them there more times than I didn't. I think they let me win." She wiped at her eyes.

"I'm sorry, Stacy," Catherine said. "I didn't mean to snap at you. That's cool about you and your siblings."

Stacy sniffed and stood straighter, nose in the air. "Of course, the hotels we stayed at had, like, a zillion more floors than this. And we usually stayed in the penthouse."

The elevator came to a stop and the door opened with a warbling ding. They stepped out into a carpeted foyer with hallways running perpendicular to it on both sides.

Matt touched the textured golden wallpaper, tracing the white velvet floral pattern with a finger. The gold trim around the elevators, windows, and built-in shelves was flaking off in places. He bounced on his toes, enjoying the cushion the plush carpet provided. "It's been a long time since we've actually stood on carpet."

Catherine and Stacy looked at each other and grinned, both dropping to the floor to remove their boots so they could walk on it barefooted.

"Girls are so weird," Justin said.

"How does it feel?" Darin asked.

"Soft and cushy." Catherine skipped across the foyer to one of the hallways.

Stacy sniffed and wrinkled her nose. "This carpet smells like mildew, though." She stood and shrugged. "But it still feels good to walk on it. Gives my sore foot a break from my shoe."

The girls put their boots back on, and the group explored the second floor. Some of the guest rooms were fully furnished, but most of them were empty. The only other thing on the floor was a small housekeeping closet with a fully stocked, wheeled cart inside.

"Do you think this place actually had guests stay here?" Catherine asked.

"I doubt it. They wouldn't let people stay here until the construction was finished," Darin said.

"Some of the rooms look like they've been used, though."

Matt nodded. "I noticed that. I bet the construction workers and architects stayed in these rooms. I mean, where else would they have stayed?"

"That makes sense," Cody said. "Hey, do ya'll suppose the showers work? And the toilets?"

Both Catherine's and Stacy's eyes widened and they bumped into each other trying to get through the nearest room's door. Matt smiled as the familiar sound of a toilet flushing met his ears. Stacy whooped when she twisted the faucet and water sprayed from the showerhead.

Stacy poked her head out of the bathroom. "Why don't you boys go finish searching the rest of the floors? I'm going to take a shower!"

"No way," Matt said. "We aren't splitting up."

She cocked her hip and fluttered her lashes. "You just want to watch, huh, Matt?"

His face turned as red as the carpet, and he sputtered, "No . . . I . . . of course not." He could not even look at Catherine.

"I'll watch," Justin offered. "Hell, I'll even help." He raised his eyebrows.

Darin puffed up his chest and stepped toward him.

"Just joking! Don't go all ape on me, dude. I'm a perfect gentleman, for real."

Matt had to get control of this conversation before chaos broke out. He looked to Cody for help.

"How about we finish our search, just to make sure there ain't no monsters lurking about, and then we can stand outside the rooms while y'all shower. Heck, we all need to shower." Cody looked down at his dirt-and ash-covered clothes and exposed skin. "We can take turns."

Stacy's smile faded, but she agreed. "Okay. But let's get on with it. I'm not going to wait all night."

After a brief argument, they decided to check out the third floor before going back down.

"It seems like we're just going to find more guest rooms up here," Darin grumbled as the elevator doors closed. "Why waste time looking at identical floors?"

Matt actually agreed, but he wanted to explore every inch before going back down. They'd missed the kitchen upon first search. He didn't want to make the same mistake twice. He rounded a corner, and his gut instinct was correct. Matt smiled. In front of them was a partially wallpapered area, and the uncarpeted floor was covered with painter's plastic. He peered down the hallway at bare boards and construction materials strewn about. He walked toward a pile of lumber, the others following behind him. "Jackpot!" he exclaimed as he walked faster.

"What?" Cody asked.

"Blueprints!" Matt picked up the stack of papers that had been draped across a couple of sawhorses. He spread them out on the pile of lumber, flipping through and skipping over the areas they'd already explored.

"There's a lot more to this place than we thought," he said.

CHAPTER 18

Matt had to admit that a warm shower felt amazing. He laughed again as he thought about the cry of joy that had come from Catherine when actual hot water had sprayed from the showerhead. He and Cody had been standing just outside the bathroom, and laughed as Catherine explained through the door what her excitement was about.

Justin and Darin stood guard in the room next door as Stacy showered—for twice as long as Catherine.

"I wish we had clean clothes to put on," Catherine said as the freshly washed friends took the elevator back to the first floor.

Matt couldn't take his eyes off the glowing pink skin of her face; her happy, sparkling eyes; her long, wet curls bouncing down her back from one side of her head, the other being shaved from the burn. Then there were her perfect lips . . .

She smiled a smirky smile, and Matt knew he'd been caught. He licked his lips as warmth rushed up his neck into his face. He met her playfully glinting eyes, shrugged one shoulder, and smiled back.

Back in the lobby, Cody and Catherine volunteered to go to the kitchen and cook some of the dehydrated food they'd found. Darin and Stacy had disappeared again. Justin stayed with Matt, who spread the map out on his mattress so he could double check the route they'd need to take to the vault. If it were up to him, they'd leave first thing in the morning, but the others had voted to spend one more day at the hotel, getting some much-needed rest and preparing supplies.

A rattling noise came from the hallway leading to the kitchen. Matt and Justin looked up to see Cody and Catherine pushing a two-tiered metal cart loaded with freshly cooked food.

Justin sniffed the air and jumped to his feet with a big grin. "Whatever you guys made smells bitchin'!" He rushed to help them push the cart over to the mattress corner.

Matt stuffed the papers back into his Keeper and stowed it in his backpack. "It really does smell fantastic."

The wafting odor of hot food brought the lovebirds from wherever they'd been hiding. "Do I smell eggs?" Darin asked.

"Why, yes, you do," Cody answered with a smile.

Catherine handed out plates and forks to everyone. "Serve yourselves." She removed the lid from a pot full of mashed potatoes and handed a serving spoon to Justin, who was, of course, first in line. Then she lifted the lid off of a large, deep frying pan full to the brim with scrambled eggs and handed a big spoon to Matt.

"Eww. Like, mashed potatoes and eggs do *not* go together," Stacy said.

"Then don't eat them," Catherine responded.

Stacy stuck her bottom lip out in a pout. "I never said I wasn't going to eat them. I just said they don't go together." She bumped Catherine's hip with hers. "But it smells totally rad. Thank you for cooking."

The tension in Catherine's jaw softened and she smiled at Stacy. "You're welcome. And there's cherry pie without the crust for dessert."

Matt laughed. "The filling is the best part anyway." He and Catherine filled their plates, then sat together on his mattress to eat.

Even without gravy or a big blob of butter, the potatoes were the best Matt had ever eaten. By the time he finished a pie's worth of cherry filling, his stomach was more than full, and his abs hurt from laughing with Catherine as they talked about their high school experiences before being frozen.

Catherine's hair was now dry and lay in shiny black curls over one shoulder as she lounged on one elbow on the mattress. She pushed a strand out of her face, sat up, and removed the elastic hairband from around her wrist. As she reached up to pull her hair back, Matt stopped her with a hand on her arm.

"No. Leave it down, please. I like it." He moved his hand from her arm up to tuck her hair behind her ear, brushing his fingers across her cheek in the process. "And . . . I like you. A lot."

She put the hairband back on her wrist and smiled, scooting closer to him. "I like you too. A lot."

Matt's stomach flipped and he looked around quickly. Cody and Justin had taken the cart back to the kitchen, and Stacy and Darin lay on a mattress away from Matt's, lost in their own world. Looking back into Catherine's dark eyes, he readjusted to face her more fully.

He swallowed and almost went into cardiac arrest when she licked her lips, then parted them slightly. He wove his fingers through her hair and rested the palms of his hands on the sides of her face, pulling her gently to him. He tilted his head and closed his eyes as their lips touched. Then he was lost. Everything forgotten except the sensation of her lips responding to his, her soft hair tangled in his fingers, and her hand resting against his chest.

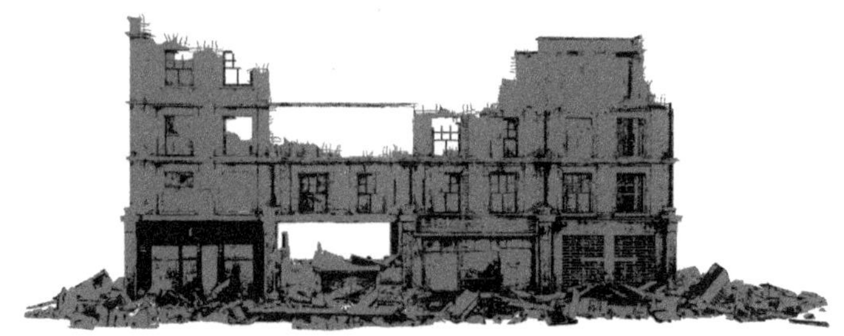

CHAPTER 19

With the mattresses all pushed together into one giant "mega-bed," as Stacy called it, they settled in for the night, everyone on their own mattress. The only light came from a small lamp on the front desk across the room.

"Are you guys sure we need to stay here another day?" Matt asked as he stared up at the ceiling. "I think we should head out to the mountain tomorrow, to the vault."

Stacy sighed. "After knowing how wonderful these mattresses feel against my battered body, like, I'm especially certain we need to stay another day—at least."

Matt propped himself up on his elbows. "One day—maximum." No way was he going to stay here any longer than that, not with his parents so close.

"Chill, Matt, I was just joking. Mostly," Stacy said.

The mattresses were amazing, he had to admit. Matt rolled to his side and smiled at Catherine, who lay facing him on her own mattress. She smiled back and winked. He wasn't sure how to respond to that, so he just laughed and winked back. He didn't have much experience with girls. The girls in his high school tended to go for the jocks, and he was more of a nerd with jock potential—except he really didn't like to play sports. He did know that the kiss he and Catherine had shared was mind-blowing, at least for him. And he couldn't wait to be alone with her and do it again. He flopped onto his back and sighed. His thoughts were interrupted by Cody.

"Why do y'all suppose there's so many hotels on this island?"

"Good question," Darin said. "Do you think any of the others are finished? Maybe the people who were in training for the apocalypse stayed there."

"Yeah, maybe," Cody conceded. "I was also wonderin' why we never heard about this island. You'd a thought at least a fisherman or two would have seen it, that the news would have investigated it."

Justin yawned. "I bet the Navy controlled the water all around it, so nobody could get close enough to see what was going on."

Catherine nodded. "That sounds legit. Wouldn't the Navy have had to bring all the supplies to build everything, anyway? I mean, how else would the government have gotten everything here?"

"Like, those aircraft carriers are mega huge," Stacy said. "They could've brought all the giant equipment we've seen."

"I think you're right." Darin smiled at her. "I don't see how else it could have been done. This place took a lot of mobilization and man-power to create."

Justin yawned again, and they all quieted down. Matt fell asleep with thoughts of Catherine floating around in his head.

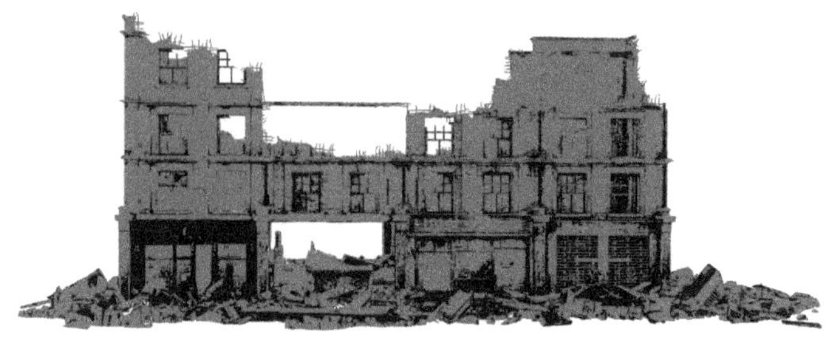

CHAPTER 20

The first thing Matt did the next morning was get the folded-up blue-prints out of his Trapper Keeper. "I thought I saw something interesting on here before I got distracted by the kitchen." He flipped through the pages and pulled one out. "Here."

"What is it?" Catherine put her hands on his shoulders and leaned over him as he kneeled in front of his mattress.

He touched one of her hands with his and smiled up at her. "It's an outbuilding. A big one. It's labeled 'Emergency Supply Storage,' and it looks like we can get to it without being outside longer than a few seconds. It's only steps away from the back employee entrance. Wanna go check it out with me?"

"Of course." She smiled.

After putting the blueprints away, Matt stood and, taking Catherine's hand, walked toward the back of the hotel.

"Where y'all headed?" Cody caught up and walked beside him.

"To check something out that I saw on the blueprints."

Matt's disappointment at the interruption must have shown on his face. With a wink and a grin, Cody did what any good friend would do in such an instance. "Well, you two have fun. I'll get the rest of us organized to go search for supplies . . . away from where you guys are 'checking something out.'"

"Thanks, Cody."

"Yep." He loped off to intercept the others.

Matt squeezed Catherine's hand and smiled to himself, his worry about Vault B-35 taking a back seat to the chance to be alone with her for a short time. Guilt at these thoughts caused a pressure in his chest, but he pushed it aside by telling himself that they were going to the storage building to find stuff for the trip to the vault—being alone with Catherine was just an added bonus.

They found the employee entrance down a back hallway near the kitchen and held their breath as they pushed the door open, hoping the adjacent building would be unlocked. It was only about ten yards away, with a regular-sized door facing them. They hurried to it, still holding their breath in the ash-filled morning air, and Matt grasped the rusted doorknob and twisted it. Unlocked!

Air rushed out of his lungs and he hurried to refill them after he shut the door.

Catherine flipped a light switch on the wall. "This place is huge!"

Matt could only nod as his eyes took in the numerous shelving units, all stacked to the top with supplies. He wandered down the aisle between two rows of shelves, Catherine at his heels, and choked on his own saliva when he got to the end and saw a most beautiful sight—a vehicle that appeared to be in prime condition.

After he coughed so much his face turned red, Catherine patting his back, he grabbed her hand again and headed straight for the Jeep Wagoneer. They slowly circled the forest-green Jeep, Matt stopping to admire the big black grille guard with attached winch. The round KC lights affixed to a bar on top reminded him of his cousin's pickup truck they used to take out mudding on the rare occasions it rained in their small Nevada town. Looking at the tires, he thought that maybe the Jeep was lifted even higher than that truck—which had been nearly illegal.

"Do you think it runs?" Catherine asked, looking into the driver's side window.

"I sure hope so. Can you imagine how much faster we could get to the vault if it does? We should go get Cody before we try it; he knows the most about engines and stuff."

"But last time, all the batteries were gone," Catherine said.

"Good point. Let's look under the hood," Matt suggested.

He opened the driver's side door. "That's weird looking."

"Yeah, like something seventies sci-fi."

The instrument panel was not like the Jeeps he was used to—instead there were strange screens and toggles unlike anything Matt had seen.

"Um, I don't see the hood latch in here." He stood.

Catherine shrugged. "I don't know either."

"Let's let Cody take a crack at it."

"Ye-ah." Catherine looked at him, her eyes glinting. "But we should explore a little, *alone*, first."

The emphasis she put on the word "alone" made his knees go

weak. Matt focused intently on the shape of her lips. He knew he was staring, but he couldn't tear his eyes away. His mind fuzzy, he had trouble forming words. "Uhh . . . umm . . ." He nodded instead and smiled, finally moving his gaze from her mouth to her eyes.

She laughed and led him away from the big garage doors by the Jeep, over to an area with a leather couch, a couple of chairs, and a throw rug covering a small section of the cement floor. They sat next to each other on the couch, Matt hyperaware of every miniscule nerve fiber firing off at once in the areas of his arm and leg that came into contact with hers. Holy cow, he liked her so much. Maybe even loved her . . .

He twisted to face her and put his arms around her waist, pulling her closer as her arms wrapped around his neck. Their lips collided. As they kissed—his hands pressed into her back, one of her hands stroking the back of his head and neck—he knew. He was in love with Catherine. And that scared him worse than anything he'd encountered up to this point in his life.

CHAPTER 21

The air outside the storage building had gone from windblown ash to eerily still when Matt and Catherine hurried back to the employee entrance of the hotel. Matt glanced up at the sky behind them, and his body turned cold at the sight of the blood-colored sun. He wished they could have stayed on that couch, tucked safely away from the world outside, for the rest of their lives.

The smirk on Justin's face as they joined the group in the lobby told Matt that his and Catherine's secret wasn't much of a secret.

"How was the make-out session, lovebirds?" Justin asked.

While Matt's face turned red, Catherine shot right back with, "Jealous much, Justin?"

His teasing grin turned to a scowl. "As if," he grumbled.

Catherine nodded. "That's what I thought."

Cody, master of subject changes, asked, "Did you guys find anything?"

Matt perked up, remembering the good news he had to tell them. "Yes! There's a storage building behind the hotel. It's huge. And . . ." He paused for effect. "There's a battle-ready Jeep Wagoneer in there!"

"And a ton of other stuff. Shelves full of food and supplies," Catherine added.

"What kind of supplies?" Stacy asked.

Catherine shrugged. They hadn't really explored much after finding the Jeep . . . and the couch. "Doomsday prepper stuff."

"Let's go check it out," Darin said. "All we found were a few painter's tarps and construction tools, besides the food pantry we already knew about."

Matt and Catherine led the way to the supply building.

"This is so wicked!" Justin walked slowly down the nearest aisle, calling out the items on the shelves. "There must be thousands of MREs on this row alone, boxes and boxes of them stacked to the ceiling. And canned food, good stuff—they even have SPAM!" He grabbed a box from the shelf and ripped it open, grabbing one of the ten or so tins of the processed meat.

"Eww." Stacy wrinkled her nose. "Like, barf me out. Who eats that stuff?"

"Poor people," Justin said. "I don't expect a snob like you to understand, but this stuff was like the filet mignon of the trailer court."

"Do you think it's still good?" Catherine asked. "It's probably been in here a while."

"Only one way to find out." Justin pulled the key off the bottom of the rectangular can and slid it over the little tab near the top before twisting it all the way around the can to roll up the top section of metal.

"Is it supposed to smell like that?" Stacy plugged her nose.

"Smells like home," Justin said. He turned it upside down and plopped the whole chunk of processed meat and accompanying blob of gel onto his hand.

"Did you make sure the can wasn't dented or swollen before you opened it?" Cody asked.

"Duh, yeah." Justin bit into the SPAM, tearing a huge piece off. He closed his eyes and chewed.

"Well?" Darin asked.

Justin swallowed. "A little stale, but not bad."

"Why don't we all grab something to eat while we're right here?" Matt said. "Then we can eat while we take inventory and mess with the Jeep." He pulled a random box of MREs off the nearest shelf and opened it. He read off the contents of the freeze-dried, airtight packages as he rummaged through them. "Beef stew."

"Dibs!" Justin grabbed it from his hand, having just finished off the whole can of SPAM.

Matt shook his head. "Frankfurters. Diced turkey."

"That one's mine." Stacy held her hand out.

Matt handed the diced-turkey package to her and continued pulling the packets out of the box. "Beef patty. Beef slices in barbecue. Diced beef with gravy." He looked up at Cody, Catherine and Darin with a raised eyebrow.

"I'll take the diced beef with gravy" Cody said. "Sounds like something my mom would have made."

"I'm waiting to see what all the choices are before I decide," Catherine said.

"Me too," Darin agreed.

"Pork patty, ham and chicken loaf—that sounds like SPAM, want it, Justin?" he teased.

"No thanks." Justin rubbed his stomach. "The last one isn't sitting so well." Which hadn't stopped him from ripping open the beef stew package and warming up the main dish with the heating unit that came with it.

Laughing, Matt continued. "Chicken à la king. Ground beef with spiced sauce. That's it for this box. I'll take the ground beef." He looked from Catherine to Darin. "What do you two want?"

"I'll take the barbecue one, I guess," Catherine said.

"Frankfurter for me." Darin held out his hand to accept the MRE.

Catherine watched her friends struggle to open and prepare the food while standing in the aisle between shelves and suggested they all go sit down. She led them past the Jeep to the couch area.

Spirits high, they ate and talked—mostly about the Jeep.

"Do you think it runs?" Darin asked.

Matt looked to Cody, who answered, "Soon as I'm done with this here gourmet meal, I'm gonna find out."

Justin finished before everyone else and walked back to the shelves, a different aisle this time, calling out what he found. "Duffel bags—big ones, like the military uses. A whole slew of canvas tents. Flashlights." He turned down another row. "Hey, there's some walkie-talkies back here."

"Bring some of those for sure," Matt said.

"Toilet paper! Tons of it! And blue tarps!" Justin yelled.

Cody looked at Matt and grinned. "He sounds pretty excited about the TP."

"Well," Stacy said, "I, for one, do not ever want to run out of it."

Licking barbecue sauce off her fingers, Catherine nodded. "Same here."

Justin jogged up to the group, two boxes in his hands. One small and one medium sized. He opened the small cardboard box first. "Swiss Army knives for everyone!" He tossed one to each of them. "And there's a whole section with guns and ammo."

"What's in the other box?" Catherine asked between bites.

Justin opened the flaps. "Oh, these are the radios."

Matt stood. "No, these are *ham* radios." He took a brand-new one still in its packaging. "Yaesu FT-350R." He traced the name and model number on the box. "Does anyone know how to work one of these?"

Matt looked at everyone in the group one at a time, but they all shook their heads no.

There was no way to contact B-35 or the other vaults. Cody put his head down like he had let someone down. "Sorry, Matt."

Matt sat back down to his food and set the radio next to his Swiss Army knife. "It's not a problem. I'll take one with me. Let's just stay the course for now. We know where we need to go."

Cody stood, wiping his hands on his pants. "Let's go check out this Wagoneer."

"We couldn't find the hood release," Matt said, following him. "I checked near the doorjamb under the steering wheel."

"See, that's where they were put years later," Cody said, "but this latch is just above the grille." He went to the front of the vehicle and pulled a hidden lever just between the hood and the grille. A low, thudding click echoed through the storage room and he lifted the hood.

His eyes went wide, and he whistled. "What the heck? This ain't no normal engine."

Matt moved next to him and gazed down, his eyes drawn to a glowing cylinder where the carburetor should have been. "Is that . . ." He looked at Cody. "Is that *nuclear*?"

CHAPTER 22

Stacy stepped back, away from the Jeep. "Nuclear? Like, isn't that radioactive?"

"Well, yeah." Matt looked at Cody nervously, then back at the futuristic engine. "But I'm sure it's shielded—the radioactive part anyway."

"Don't look at me," Cody said. "If it ain't got a gas tank and a carburetor, I don't know anything about it."

"Those batteries are huge." Matt continued to stare under the raised hood. "And why so many of them?"

Cody shrugged.

Matt looked around at the others. All but Catherine returned his look with blank stares or a shake of the head.

Catherine sighed. "The batteries are probably to store the excess energy the nuclear fission makes. You can't turn it off, so it has to go somewhere."

They all gaped at her.

She crossed her arms. "What? I did a science project about nuclear power when I was in junior high."

"So, Matt, your girlfriend's a genius," Justin teased.

Matt's eyes swiveled to Catherine's, and he couldn't help but smile when she didn't correct Justin's use of the title "girlfriend."

"Should we see if it runs?" Cody shut the hood.

"Sure," Matt said.

"You do the honors, Matt, since y'all are the ones who found it."

Matt climbed into the driver's seat and wiped his sweaty palms on his pants. He looked on both sides of the steering column for keys, but there wasn't even a place for a key to go. The dashboard looked more like it came from a spaceship than the local Jeep dealership. He studied the toggle switches and chose the one labeled "Engage Motor" on top and "Disengage" on the bottom, where the toggle was now positioned. He flipped it up, disappointed when the Wagoneer didn't roar to life.

A rap on the window next to him made him jump. *Just Catherine.* He rolled down the window, a little embarrassed by his reaction.

"If you're waiting to hear the engine rumble, that isn't going to happen. Just put it in gear and try pushing on the gas pedal—gently," she said.

"Yeah . . . that makes sense." He pulled the gearshift on the steering column down into Drive, then pushed on the gas pedal, barely. The big vehicle moved forward, toward the garage doors. Matt hit the brakes and put it back in Park as his friends cheered. Finally, something had gone their way!

They spent the rest of the afternoon and into the evening in the supply building. They each packed a duffel bag with supplies.

"How much food should we bring?" Matt asked. "I mean, should we plan on taking enough for whoever might be awake at the vault?"

"We have no idea how many people are awake," Darin said.

Catherine folded and then rolled up a blue tarp as small as she could get it, then stuffed it in her duffel bag. "How about we take some extra, just in case, knowing we can always come back for more."

"What about the other vaults?" Matt asked.

"You are, like, so obsessed, Matthew. Give it a rest." Stacy flopped down on the couch, her duffel only about half full.

"My name is not Matthew."

Cody looked at Stacy with narrowed eyes that said *not one more word, young lady!* To Matt, he said, "We can check them out later, after we see what's going on at B-35. Heck, now that we have transportation, traveling around the island will be a snap."

"What do you think we're going to find at the vault?" Catherine bit her bottom lip, her forehead creased with worry.

"Hopefully our families . . . alive," Matt said.

Darin sat on the carpet near the couch, shoving MREs into every segment of his bag where he could fit one. "I hope so, too, Matt. But . . . I don't know. Me and Westbrook were the only ones there to run things. Alarms were going off day and night." He closed his eyes and slumped against the couch. "With no one there to address the alarms . . ." He shook his head.

Eyes still closed, voice barely above a whisper, Darin said, "I don't want to go back there. I mean, I know *he* isn't there anymore. I saw his body float by when the camp flooded. But . . ." He put his face in his hands, and his voice became a little wobbly. "The memories are there. How he basically held me captive. Ordered me around. Yelled at me. Threw things."

"Oh, Lance-Darin!" Stacy dropped down next to him on the floor and rubbed his back.

"It must have been so hard for you," Catherine said. "Especially when you were younger."

Darin sat up straight again and ran his hands over his hair. He cleared his throat. "Yeah. It was. All I wanted was my parents. I plotted ways I could sneak into their section and wake them up. But Westbrook never allowed me to go anywhere near them."

The group sat in silence for a few minutes, huddled around Darin. Then Matt shrugged at Cody and followed him toward the back to finish filling their duffel bags. Stacy shot them both an angry glance.

"Guess we ain't being sensitive enough to Darin," Cody muttered. "I've never been good with feelings."

"He has Stacy and the rest of the group," Matt said. "Honestly, I feel like a jerk now for questioning him so much before."

"We can hear you!" Stacy shouted. "Maybe you should apologize to Darin, *Matthew*."

Matt's spine stiffened. He would have preferred to do this in private, but this seemed fitting since he *had* called Darin out in front of everyone. "Look, man, I'm sorry. I really am."

"I . . . it's fine." Darin released a deep breath. "Come on, guys. Let's help Matt and Cody."

The tension in the room slowly dissipated, and they continued filling the bags. After fastening the top of his, Matt picked it up and lugged it to the Wagoneer, even more grateful for the Jeep, so he wouldn't have to try to carry the heavily loaded bag. "Everyone, bring your bags here and we'll get them all squeezed in. Then I think we should go back to the lobby and make one last recording. Sort of a 'last night at the hotel' send-off."

"Last night at Hotel Spectacula," Stacy said.

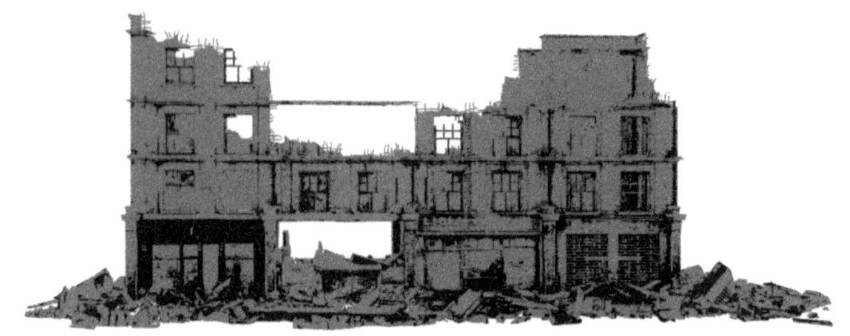

CHAPTER 23

"Matt Voorhees here. This will be our last recording here at the Hotel Isla Pangea—at least for the time being."

Stacy busted up laughing. "You're so Captain Kirk sounding! Do you think this is your captain's log?"

Matt glared at her. He'd had enough of her offhand remarks and rudeness. "Stacy, I'd like for you to leave this room and let me record this last little bit without your comments, please."

"Fine. Lance-Darin and I have better things to do anyway." She grabbed Darin's hand and flounced out of the security office.

After Matt finished, he decided it might be a good idea to have each of them record one last short thought. Catherine went to find Darin and Stacy while Justin started.

"Justin here. Not sure what to say except it was bad enough when Darin and Stacy started sneaking off together, but me 'n Cody are the lone bros now that the chief and Catherine are a thing. All I can say is there'd better be some cute chicks at the vault."

Matt rolled his eyes but didn't say anything. He pointed to Cody.

"This is Cody," the Texan said into the recorder. "It's sure been nice to sleep on a fancy mattress here—I felt like a hog with a brand-spankin' new mud puddle to wallow in!"

Justin and Matt laughed, and Matt paused the recording as Stacy, Darin, and Catherine returned. "You go next, Stacy," he said. He reached for the recorder, but Stacy beat him to it and unpaused it.

"Like, Stacy, giving my last will and testament." She snickered at her own wittiness. "Totally joking! Anyway, this hotel is totally rad— maybe Lance-Darin and I can come back for our honeymoon." She ended by making kissy noises right into the microphone.

Darin blushed and cleared his throat. "Uhh . . . hon . . . honey-moon? But seriously, best two days of this whole messed-up adventure. I wish we were just staying here."

Matt signaled to Catherine that it was her turn.

Staring right at Matt as she bounced a little in her chair, she said, "I'm hopeful to see what the future holds for us. It's gotta be better than . . . I just know we're going to make it." She looked around the room and added, "The six musketeers!"

The others gave a short, spontaneous cheer before Matt took his turn. "This has been a nice break from the horrors we've faced. I will definitely never forget our time here." He looked at Catherine, a small, nervous smile touching his lips. "Tomorrow—on to the vault and our families!"

Matt stopped the recorder. "That's a wrap. We should get some sleep now so we can leave first thing in the morning." With everything ready to go, the Jeep as transportation, and a full belly, he could finally relax. He waited for everyone to get settled on their mattresses and turned off all the lights except the small desk lamp they'd left on the night before.

As he crawled onto his mattress, he smiled over at where Catherine sat on hers. He reclined and put his hands under his head, with his elbows bent out to the sides. Though he was tired and content, the excitement of their journey ahead and the anticipation of finally being reunited with his parents wouldn't allow his mind to rest.

Apparently, Matt wasn't alone in this.

Darin sat up on his mattress and blurted, "I have something I need to tell you guys."

Matt propped himself up on his elbows. "Okay, go for it."

Looking down at his lap, Darin drew in a deep breath. "I . . . I want to tell you what really happened at the cryovault. I haven't been . . . well, completely honest about some things. Matt, you didn't need to apologize earlier."

Stacy gasped.

Matt sat up and scooted so his back rested against the wall. He'd had suspicions all along that Darin wasn't telling the whole truth, and his stomach churned to think what he might have lied about. "Like?"

Everyone waited in silence, the movement of breath going in and out of the room's occupants the only sound for several moments.

Darin swallowed. "The damage . . . from the meteor strike . . . it wasn't really caused by a meteor. Westbrook made me go outside the vault." He shook his head and ran his fingers through his hair. "He made me climb up on the rocks on top of the vault and plant some dynamite, then I set it off when I got back down to the ground."

"What?!" Matt yelled, standing and stomping off the end of his mattress. "*You* are the one who caused the damage that made our column fail?"

Justin stood, too, his eyes shooting daggers at Darin. "The one that *killed* all of the fifteen-year-olds, including Rhett's sister?"

Darin held his hands out, palms forward, and shrunk into himself. "It wasn't my fault! Westbrook made me do it!"

"Why?" Catherine asked. "Why would Westbrook make you do that?"

Bitterness seeped into Darin's voice. "So he could fix it, of course, and be the freaking *hero*. I didn't . . . I didn't know anything about explosives. I was just a kid! I just did what he told me to do. The blast was bigger than Westbrook thought it would be. It caused more damage, and we were able to eventually fix it with his carbon-foam invention. But it caused other issues—ones we couldn't see. And sometime later, after I was put back into cryosleep, the fifteen-year-olds' column failed. The column wasn't supposed to fail. They weren't supposed to die."

"Oh, Lance-Darin." Stacy's voice was quiet, almost a whisper. "You were just a kid. You said you didn't know! Why didn't you tell me?"

Matt clenched his hands into fists. His heart pummeled his chest from the inside.

Darin wiped at the tears now free-falling from his eyes. "He threatened my family, said he'd pull their plugs and make me watch them die."

Catherine put a hand to her chest. "That's awful. What kind of person . . ." Her voice trailed off as she shook her head.

"A freakin' crazy one!" Darin's voice shook and the tears fell harder. "I'm sorry. I'm sorry I lied and sorry I did what he told me to do. But damn it! Like Stacy said, I was just a kid—a child—scared and alone and afraid for my family."

Unclenching his hands, Matt drew in a few deep breaths. Darin was right. He'd been just a kid. Matt probably would have done the same. And it was tearing Darin up inside—he could see that now.

"Darin," he said, "Westbrook used you. You were just a pawn in his demented plan, just like everyone else. I can see that clearly now. It wasn't your fault. Any kid would have done the same."

Darin looked up at him, his face splotchy from crying. "Thank you, Matt. I'm sorry. I really am."

CHAPTER 24

Sometime during the night, Catherine had rolled to the very edge of her mattress, closer to Matt. Close enough that when he awoke, he found her warm hand entwined with his, and they lay facing each other, only a couple of feet apart. As much as he yearned to get started on their trek to the cryovault, he wanted to savor this moment a little longer. He watched Catherine sleep, her dark curls spread out around her face, her breathing slow and steady.

"Let's get this party started!" Justin yelled as he arched his back in a big stretch.

The magical moment shattered. Catherine pulled her hand away with a start at the loud exclamation. She sat up and ran her fingers through her hair, trying to tame the bedhead, and smiled at Matt. "How long do you think it'll take to get to the vault?" she asked as she wrapped her hair elastic around the ponytail she'd just fashioned.

"If I'm reading the map's scale right, we should be there before nightfall." Anticipation welled up in his chest, and he reached over and grasped her hand. "We're so close. I can't wait."

She squeezed his hand.

Matt's heart skipped. He stood, then helped her up and pulled her close in an embrace full of so many emotions, he thought he might burst. "Catherine, I—" He stopped himself from blurting out his feelings for her. He'd tell her later, when they were alone. Maybe after they reached the vault. "I think we should get going," he finished lamely, still holding her tight against him.

"Okay," Catherine whispered next to his ear. She tightened her hold on him for a too-brief second before letting go and stepping back. "To the Jeep!" She flung her arm, fingers all pressed together, in the direction of the supply building.

"What about breakfast?" Justin whined. "I'm starving."

"We can eat on the road," Matt said. "It's probably going to be an all-day trip. Like twelve to fourteen hours."

"Make sure you have your gas masks!" Darin yelled so they could all hear him.

Everyone grabbed their backpacks that had made the trip all the way from the control room with them.

When they got to the Jeep, Matt went to the front passenger-side door. "Darin, why don't you drive so I can navigate?"

"Okay." Darin climbed into the driver's seat, an excited grin plastered on his face.

Matt opened the door and gestured for Catherine to sit in the middle of the front bench seat, then he jumped in after her. He pulled his Trapper Keeper out of the backpack he'd shoved on the floor between his feet and opened it to the "Maps" section. "The seals on the Jeep's doors seem pretty good. I don't think we'll need our gas masks in here."

Darin agreed. He flipped the toggle switch to engage the motor, pushed the button on the garage door opener hanging on the visor in front of him, and put the Wagoneer in gear as the garage door slowly opened.

Matt gazed out the windshield. The devastation before him came as sort of a shock after spending two days of relative safety inside the hotel. He'd pushed reality to the back of his mind, and now it flooded into the forefront. Darin followed a road heading in the direction of the mountain, dodging meteors and cracks in the ground. The going was slow, but Darin was doing a good job of navigating around the many hazards.

"Watch out for that meteor!" Catherine shouted.

CHAPTER 25

Catherine pointed to a small ball of flame falling near the road ahead.

Darin pushed the brake pedal until the Wagoneer barely crept along as they waited for the impact to hit in front of them several hundred yards. A flash of light at ground level and a rumble in the ground beneath them verified the meteor had touched down. Through the ashen sky, the red sun could be seen, but its light was dimmed to an eternal dusk.

"We should be coming up to a fork in the road ahead," Matt said. "Take the left one."

Nodding, Darin dodged a large crevice in the center of the road. The tires bounced over chunks of asphalt and clods of dirt.

"Try driving on the shoulder next to the road," Catherine suggested. "It looks a little smoother."

"Yeah, okay." Darin maneuvered the Jeep to the dirt beside the broken asphalt.

Catherine was right. It was a less jarring ride for a while. It was slow going, with all the debris and cracked earth they had to dodge.

"Maybe we should, like, turn on the radio," Stacy suggested.

"We can try," Matt mumbled, looking up from his maps long enough to turn the knob. "But I doubt it'll play anything."

They listened to the static as Catherine spun the dial, trying to find a functioning station. After only getting static on every channel, she turned it off. "I guess we won't be listening to any Wolfman Jack on this trip."

"Ahh, man! I love that dude!" Justin said.

"Who's Wolfman Jack?" Cody asked.

"You're joking, right?" Justin's voice held a note of incredulity.

"Uhh, not really, no."

Justin leaned forward and stared at him around Stacy. "What did you listen to on the radio? Did you even have a radio? Or electronics of any kind in backwoods Texas?"

Cody laughed. "Country-western music, of course. *American Country Countdown* and *Live From Gilley's*—those were the best!"

Justin threw himself back against the seat and shook his head. "Country music? I just . . . I just can't."

"Oh, it's hard to be humble . . ." Cody sang loudly, his Texas twang coming on strong.

Justin and Stacy plugged their ears and moaned while Darin, Matt, and Catherine laughed.

"More like, 'Mamas, don't let yer babies grow up to be cowboys.'" Justin's fake, exaggerated Southern accent made them all buckle over with laughter.

"What kind of music did you listen to?" Cody asked him.

"Dude, the good stuff. Rock and roll! AC/DC, Def Leppard, Black Sabbath, Aerosmith! So much great music."

"Umm, like, yuck." Stacy wrinkled her nose.

"Yuck?" Justin said. "What music do you like?"

"New wave all the way, and pop, definitely pop."

"Favorite bands?" Catherine asked her.

"Tears for Fears, for sure the best. The Cure. And A Flock of Seagulls—"

Darin snorted. "Is that for real? A real band?"

"Yeah," Justin laughed, "it was named after the lead singer's hair!"

Stacy slapped his leg. "Shut up! 'I Ran' was, like, my fave song!"

Justin dug around in his backpack and pulled out a can of pork and beans. "Who has the can opener?"

Catherine retrieved it from an outside pocket of her pack and handed it back to him. He snatched it from her before she realized what he wanted to open with it. "Really, Justin? Do you think that's a good thing to eat when we're all crammed in this small, poorly ventilated space for who knows how long?"

He smiled as he cranked the can opener around the rim of the can, the odor of bargain beans wafting through the Jeep. "What's wrong with beans?" He tipped the now-opened can to his mouth like he was drinking a soda. The Jeep rolled over a large chunk of asphalt at the same time, and sauce-slathered beans and bits of pork plopped onto his face and chest. "Son of a . . . Darin! You did that on purpose!"

Darin shook his head, but only laughed along with the others.

Licking sauce and beans off his fingers, Justin joined them. He wiped his face with the hem of his T-shirt, then finished off what was left in the can.

The group quieted down while they all found something to eat from their backpacks. Catherine handed some dried fruit to Darin so he could eat while he drove.

After a few minutes, Darin slowed the Jeep to a crawl and squinted at the road ahead. "Is that a tunnel?"

Matt looked up from opening his MRE and smiled. "Yes! I know where that is." He handed his packaged meal to Catherine and sorted through the maps in his folder. He picked up one of the papers and nodded, bouncing in his seat a little. "Go through the tunnel. We are totally on the right track."

"Are you sure you're reading that map right?" Justin asked.

"Of course I'm sure." Matt took his meal back from Catherine. "I got a merit badge in Scouts for orienteering."

"Orien-*what*-ing?" Justin asked

"It's, like, knowing how to read a map and stuff," Stacy said.

"And a compass," Matt added. "Though, we don't have one of those that works."

"What did y'all have to do to earn that badge?" Cody asked.

"Well, I don't know if it's officially approved by the Boy Scouts to do it this way, but it was kinda like what your dad did for you to learn how to survive. My dad dropped me off in the middle of nowhere with a canteen full of water, a day-pack, a map, and a compass, and said, 'See you in a few hours at the rendezvous point.' It only took me two hours. You should have seen my dad's face when he pulled up and saw that I'd beat him there!"

"That's crazy!" Catherine said. "What if you'd gotten lost?"

Matt shrugged and shoved his MRE wrappers in his pack. "I wasn't too worried about it. I'd had a lot of practice with my dad and my scout troop. But I suppose if I'd got lost, my mom would have called in the Army, Navy, Air Force, and Marines to find me."

"Moms are like that," Catherine said.

Justin grunted. "Ha. My mom wouldn't have bothered to call anyone. She probably wouldn't have even noticed I'd gone missing."

Catherine frowned. "That really sucks, Justin. I'm sorry."

He shrugged. "No biggie. I survived just fine without their 'care.'" He made air quotes with his fingers.

"We're getting close to the tunnel." Cody pointed ahead. "How long do you think it is?"

"I'm not sure, it's hard to tell from the map," Matt said. "But you should turn the headlights on, seems dark in there."

"Oh!" Stacy leaned forward to stare over Catherine's shoulder. "We should, like, totally hold our breath when we drive through!"

"Why?" Darin asked.

"To prevent bad luck, duh, silly. If you can hold your breath all the way through, it protects you from bad luck."

"In that case," Cody said, "hopefully it isn't too long."

Stacy clapped as the tunnel neared. "When I say go, everyone hold your breath until we come out the other end."

As the front of the Jeep entered the tunnel, Stacy yelled, "Go!" And they all played along, holding their breath.

The tunnel was long. Matt could barely see the dim light coming from the exit. About twenty yards from the end, Justin lifted up his right butt cheek and emitted a loud fart.

"Justin! Seriously?" Darin said, releasing his held breath.

Catherine laughed, inhaling just before they reached the tunnel's exit.

Stacy, Matt, Cody, and Justin breathed in as soon as the muted sunlight hit the windshield, and Stacy smacked Justin's shoulder. "Barf me out, Justin!" She plugged her nose and continued to give him the evil eye.

"Well, Stacy," Darin said, "I guess we're cursed with bad luck."

CHAPTER 26

Coming out of the tunnel was like landing on a foreign planet. The terrain went from dirt and ash, rocks and hardened lava to a lush, thick, humid jungle. Matt fanned his T-shirt in and out as sweat broke out on his chest and armpits. "Justin, you reek—and this sudden blast of humidity makes your odor even worse."

"Have any of you ever seen plants like these before?" Catherine asked, fanning a hand in front of her face.

"No," Cody answered. "But then again, I ain't never been to a jungle."

"Well, I have," Stacy said. "We went to Belize for a family vacation once. But these plants don't look the same as they did there."

Darin dodged a huge chunk of asphalt ripped out of the middle of the road. "Maybe it just looks different because of the large holes burned into the leaves from lava dropping on them."

Maybe that was part of it, but Matt thought the huge green leaves looked waxy, almost like they were made of plastic. He looked up at the trees encroaching on the battered road. Broken branches and scorch marks indicated where lightning strikes had hit. "I'm not sure why the terrain is so different here, but it definitely hasn't escaped the apocalypse." He gazed out the window at a tree tipped at an odd angle, half of its roots dangling into a wide crevasse slicing through the earth.

They drove in and out of large patches of jungle, the beat-up road winding through. Darin had to dodge plants and small trees that had grown up through the broken asphalt.

The Jeep bumped over an uneven surface where the asphalt transitioned to a dirt road. Soon, there were no tracks at all to follow, and

Darin stopped the Jeep atop the lush greenery. "Where to now?" he asked Matt.

"I'm not sure." Matt rifled through his maps, finding the one that showed this side of the tunnel. "I think there used to be a road here, a dirt road at least. But it's been overgrown." He shook his head. "I'm going to get out and look around for a minute to see which way we should go." He grabbed his gas mask out of the top of his backpack.

"I'm going with you," Catherine said.

"Me too, I need to stretch my legs," Cody said.

They all decided they needed a break from sitting, so after donning their gas masks, they got out of the Jeep. Matt held Catherine's hand and smiled at her, wishing they didn't have to wear the stupid masks so they could sneak behind a tree and kiss.

Suddenly, he stopped.

Up ahead was a large, rusted tube extending up about six feet from where it sprouted from the ground. Drab olive-green paint had flaked off, littering the ground around it. Corroding rivets held the whole cylinder together. It reminded Matt of the pipes Mario always had to jump on or over or into in the *Super Mario Bros.* video game that came out just before his family was chosen for the cryovault.

He and Catherine walked far enough to determine which route was clear enough to take the Jeep through, then met the others back at the vehicle.

They drove slowly, winding between plants with large leaves, still dodging chunks of lava here and there. Through the trees, Matt noticed another of the tubes coming up out of the ground, and then another.

"What are those tubes?" Darin asked.

"I don't know," Matt said. "We saw one when we got out."

"Look." Catherine pointed to one that was closer to the Jeep than the others had been. "They have ladders hanging from the side. Weird."

"I say we go check it out," Justin said, leaning over Stacy to look out Cody's window.

"Get off me, you dumb jock." Stacy pushed Justin back toward his side of the seat.

"I wasn't on you, bimbo," Justin shot back. "I was leaning *over* you. You just wish I was on you."

Darin stomped on the brakes, jolting them all forward.

"Okay," Matt said, "let's go check out these tubes. Then maybe switch seats when we get back." He looked back at Justin and Stacy.

The ladder wasn't long on the outside—the tube only extended about six feet above the ground—but Matt climbed the first few rungs so he could peer inside the open top of the tube. Blue and green wires as thick as his leg followed the ladder down into the cylinder. They each took a turn climbing up to look inside, but none of them really had any ideas what the tubes and wires were for.

Matt wiped sweat off his brow with his arm, anxious to get moving again. Without a road to follow, it was going to take them longer to get to the vault. A barely perceptible buzzing sound caught his attention, and he looked up in the direction of the Jeep. A swarm of winged bugs flew toward them. Matt's eyes widened. They were huge bugs that he shouldn't be able to see individually at this distance. "Umm, guys." He didn't take his eyes off the large swarm. "We should, uh, get back to the Jeep now."

The others followed his gaze.

"What in the french toast . . ." Cody stared.

"Come on," Catherine urged. "Let's go!"

When they got to the Jeep, Matt and Catherine climbed in back with Justin, and Stacy and Cody sat in the front seat with Darin. Stacy curled up to Darin, her left hand wrapped around his bicep and her right hand resting on his thigh. "This is much better," she purred.

Darin smiled and cleared his throat. "Yes. It sure is."

Stacy laid her head on his shoulder and sighed. "Oh, Lance-Darin."

Twisting in his seat so he could look up at the sky, Matt reached for Catherine's hand and squeezed. "Let's get moving!"

Darin pushed on the gas pedal, and they advanced a little faster.

"Whoa, stop, Darin," Cody said.

Darin hit the brakes. The teens watched as a large group of crawling bugs with segmented bodies passed slowly in front of them.

"Dang." Cody leaned forward, hand pressed against the dash. "Those things are bigger than my mama's English setter."

CHAPTER 27

"They're huge! Like prehistoric bugs or something." Matt put his arm around Catherine's back as she leaned over him to watch the slow procession out his window. She pressed her shoulder into his chest and tilted her head back to smile at him. He bent his head toward her, forgetting about the prehistoric bugs for an instant, not even caring that they weren't alone in the Jeep. All he could think about in that moment was kissing her. His heart sped up as his lips neared hers.

"What's going on? Why did they speed up?" The alarm in Cody's voice broke the hypnotic spell Catherine's lips held on Matt, and he jerked his head around to look out the window.

The bugs, which had been moving at the speed of a teenager on his way to do the dishes, now scurried across the terrain in front of and under the Wagoneer.

"Holy shit!" Justin had his forehead pressed against the window on his side of the Jeep.

Gigantic bugs, the size of a German shepherd or maybe even a Great Dane, rushed forward on long, spindly legs. The first one to reach the straggler of the crawling insects clamped its wide mouth over the smaller bug's midsection, whipped it in the air, and swallowed it whole. Then it turned into a melee as the wide-mouthed giants hunted and dined on their smaller prey.

"I've never seen insects like this before," Matt whispered.

"No duh, dork," Stacy said. "Like, none of us have. I mean aside from the dead one at the hotel. I honestly thought it was fake."

Matt rolled his eyes at her. "What I mean is, they don't look like any of the insects from before. They aren't just normal bugs that have been enlarged for some reason. They're just . . . different from any-thing I've ever seen."

"You got that right," Cody agreed. "I say we move on out of here while those big 'uns are still distracted."

Darin pulled the Jeep slowly away from the onslaught. The strange beasts ignored them, intent on either escape or dinner, depending on whether they fell under the guise of predator or prey.

The front tires bounced over a segmented bug corpse and its guts that were spread out around it. The back tires spun in the goo before catching traction and moving forward. They drove past as one of the bigger insects dragged itself into the jungle, several of its spindly legs broken and hanging limp.

"Eww." Stacy hid her face in Darin's shoulder as a big bug bit into its prey, spraying dark-colored ichor from the thing's shredded body.

An odor of fermented grass clippings and animal feces wafted into the Jeep. Catherine gagged. "What is that smell?"

Matt covered his nose. "Bug guts."

Darin pressed harder on the gas pedal, but the Wagoneer struggled to drive forward over the slippery mess.

"Someone needs to get out and lock the hubs into four-wheel drive," Cody said.

Darin stopped and put the Jeep in neutral. "Who's going to do it? I don't have a clue how to, so I can't."

"I'll do the front driver's side," Matt volunteered.

"And I'll do the passenger's side," Cody said.

Everyone remained silent, watching the big-and-bigger bug parade and slaughter. The insects paid no attention to the humans in the Jeep, too intent on their meal.

Matt sighed. "All right, Cody. Let's get this over with."

Quietly, they each pried their door open in slow motion. Like synchronized swimmers, they ducked down to the slimy ground and crawled to the front tires. Matt twisted the lock on the hub that would secure it into four-wheel drive. Cody did the same on his side.

As they climbed back in and shut the doors, a couple of the bigger bugs noticed them and ambled toward the vehicle curiously. One of them, about the size of a cow and at least as tall as the lifted Jeep, bumped lightly into the front fender purposely, as if it were testing to see if they were a threat.

Darin stomped on the gas pedal as more bugs ran to and bumped into the Jeep. The girls screamed.

"They're chasing us!" Cody yelled.

The large bugs that caught up to them crashed into the vehicle, thrashing it with their chitinous jaws and front pincers. The Wagoneer shuddered with each slamming insect.

"They think we're prey because we're running from them!" Matt yelled.

The Jeep hit a pile of bug guts and spun out of control. It jerked to a stop facing the oncoming herd of bugs.

"Turn around!" Justin yelled.

Darin cranked the wheel and hit the gas with adrenaline-fueled strength. The Jeep fishtailed, spraying dirt and guts from the tires. He slammed his fist on the steering wheel. "Damn it! Go!" The tires spun, digging a bumper-high trench with the left rear tire. "We're stuck! What should I do?"

Several bugs jumped onto the hood and roof of the Jeep. Catherine screamed and ducked down as the roof dented in toward her with the weight of the huge insects. Matt pressed his hand against the roof in a desperate attempt to keep it from caving in on them. More bugs piled on, skittering forth and jumping onto the collapsing vehicle.

The side windows all shattered at once as the Jeep rocked back and forth. Even the boys were screaming now.

CHAPTER 28

Matt's chest hurt, his heart pounding within it, as more of the giant bugs slammed into the Jeep. No light penetrated the mass of insects now glomming on to the Wagoneer. The screech of armor-like carapace against metal penetrated his ears, stabbing into his brain.

A tire popped and air hissed out, eliciting another round of terror-filled screams from the Jeep's occupants.

"Listen! Everyone listen to me!" Matt yelled. Five pairs of terrified eyes looked at him. "We need to make a plan. We can't just sit here and wait to be devoured."

"What should we do?" Catherine asked, tears streaking her dirty face.

Matt turned in his seat, looking for a way out. The rear window was still intact, and he spotted one of the tubes sticking out of the ground nearby. "Look, most of the bugs seem to be attracted to the heat of the engine, so they're up front. We can crawl out the back and run to that tube"—he pointed—"and hide inside until they leave. Then we can come back and see if the Jeep will still run."

Stacy screamed as a spiky leg stabbed through the busted front windshield and into the dash. "Fine! Let's go!" She climbed over the front seat, pushing Catherine to the side on the back seat, then climbed over that one and into the cargo area where all their supplies were.

"Catherine, go!" Matt yelled.

She scrambled over the seat and huddled down next to Stacy, their arms wrapped around each other. Darin and Cody climbed back next as more legs gouged the steering wheel and dash just inches from where they'd been sitting.

"Someone needs to open this window!" Cody searched the back panel for a switch of some kind.

"There's a toggle switch on the instrument board," Darin said. "Someone's going to have to go up there."

Justin took one look at the damaged steering wheel and dash and shook his head. He joined the others in the back, now squished together like cattle going to the slaughterhouse.

"I'll do it," Matt said.

He climbed to the front seat and dodged to the side as a spiked leg stabbed toward him. He hunkered down, trying to avoid the serrated, sword-like appendages using the front seat as a pin cushion. He pulled the toggle switch down and the back window opened less than an inch before stopping. Catherine slapped the palm of her hand against the glass and tried to force it down as the little motor whined uselessly. "It's stuck!" she yelled.

"Hurry up!" Stacy shrieked.

"I'm trying!" Matt toggled the switch up and down to try to get the window moving.

A spike-covered leg hit him in the arm, throwing him back and pinning his shirt sleeve to the seat. Blood trickled down his arm where the barbs grazed it. He struggled, pulling on his sleeve to free himself.

"Matt, what's wrong?!" Catherine cried. "Get back here!"

"I'm stuck! My shirt is pinned to the seat." He grunted with the effort of trying to free himself. Between the stress, intense heat, and high humidity, Matt was slick with sweat.

"I'm coming!" Darin climbed to the front and kicked the monster's leg at a joint. A jet of pale-yellow insect blood sprayed from the amputated limb, covering both him and Matt.

The bug backed away with a high-pitched scream. Matt grabbed the lower part of the leg, still pinning him, and wiggled it out of the seat. He dropped it to the floor, then tried the switch one more time. But the window was stuck.

A jarring crash hit the roof as another giant insect jumped on. The back window shattered from the added weight. The pillars holding up the Jeep's roof finally gave up and started to bend under the pressure. The roof crushed down inch by inch.

"Go!" Darin, already back with the others, pushed Stacy and Catherine out.

"What about the packs?!" Cody yelled over his shoulder as Darin prodded him out the window.

"I'll get them. Justin, go!"

Matt leaned over the back seat into the cargo compartment. "You go, Darin. I'll get these."

Darin nodded and dove out the narrowing space where the window had been. Matt climbed over the seat and pushed the packs out one at a time into Darin's waiting hands.

CHAPTER 29

Darin held a hand over his mouth and nose. "What about the gas masks?"

Shaking his head as he climbed to the back of the Jeep, Matt yelled, "No time!" He rolled out the window, grabbed a pack, and ran toward the pipe, gesturing for the others to follow.

A bug the size of a small dog nipped at Matt's leg, and he sent it flying with a kick. Cody stomped on one next to him. The horde of insects turned to them, homing in on their prey.

"We need to get to the pipe!" Matt yelled.

He and Cody reached it first. Matt kicked and stomped as the horde tried to take bites out of them. He followed Cody up the ladder and over the lip of the tube, both waiting there to help Catherine, and then Stacy, climb over first.

After they descended farther down to a walkway that coiled around another tube to make room for Justin and Darin, the four of them looked up. It looked like Matt and Cody were the only ones who grabbed a pack.

Stacy screamed, swatting at a smaller bug that followed them down the tube. Another dog-sized bug crawled over the lip of the pipe, its insectile eyes darting from target to target. A huge bug snatched the smaller one and swallowed it whole.

"Hurry!" Matt yelled, glancing briefly down at the girls, then back up as the giant insect clambered over the lip of the pipe, trying to crawl inside.

The girls scrambled down the tube, staring up and screaming as the bugzilla, too big to enter the tube fully, chomped its giant maw in their direction. Drops of spittle the size of golf balls rained down on them.

Matt stared, frozen in a temporary state of shock as slimy extensions shot from its open mouth toward them. A scream caught in his throat as one of the mouth tentacles snagged Darin and jerked him from the tube.

Screaming, Stacy leaped for Darin, grabbing at his leg. "Lance-Darin! No!" She sobbed and screamed while Catherine pulled her down and hovered over her, protecting her from the insect and from her own impulsive actions as she clawed at the tube, trying to get to Darin even after he had disappeared over the rim.

Matt rushed back to the top of the tube.

Darin roared and kicked at the giant insect as it dragged him away.

"No!" Matt screamed, his mind fragmented into a million simultaneous thoughts. He lifted himself just over the lip of the pipe. A shadow darkened the ground below him, and he ducked just as a flying bug swooped down, dagger-like jaws clamping shut mere centimeters from his head. If his buzz cut had been any longer, it would have gotten away with a clump of his hair.

"Matt!" Catherine shrieked among the screams and yells of Justin and Cody.

He ignored their pleas and stuck his head above the rim again, desperation tearing at his insides like a woodchipper. He caught one last glimpse of Darin's feet, now dragging limply, his blood painting the bug-entrail-covered ground red as the giant predator dragged his friend into the jungle foliage. Smaller bugs scurried all around, many of them following the successful hunter, likely hoping to score the leftovers. Matt's stomach lurched as the thought of his friend being torn to bits, consumed by the abhorrent creatures, forced itself into his mind like a fast-growing tumor.

"Matt! Get down here!" Catherine's frantic voice broke through, and with one last look at the smashed Jeep, covered in bugs, plumes of smoke rising from the crushed engine, he ducked back inside.

When he reached them, Stacy looked up at him, her face a mess of snot and tears, her eyes still carrying a trace of hope.

Hope that Matt crumpled with the shake of his head. "He's gone."

"Are you sure?" Justin asked. "Maybe we should—"

"I'm sure." Matt spat the words. His anger at losing another friend, another life, boiled over. His voice shook. "He's gone." He glared at Justin. "And going back out there—" His voice broke, and he slammed his fist into the wall of the tube. "They're everywhere. Thousands of them. Like they came just to get us."

"C'mon, then." Cody urged Matt onward with a hand on his shoulder. "There's only one way to go for now."

"But . . . no!" Stacy cried. "He can't. This is a nightmare. A nightmare! I just need to wake up!"

"I know," Catherine said, her eyes full of unspilled tears. "I'm so sorry, Stacy. I can't believe this. But we have to move. Remember how Kim almost got us all killed in that forest after Rhett? We can't do that again. Please. We can cry, *all* of us can cry together, when we're safe."

"We'll never be safe." Stacy reluctantly resumed climbing down the tube.

The tube changed from a solid green material to clear, see-through material as they descended below ground level. The large tube shifted over at this point, and began a slow twist around a huge column made of rock. Lights were embedded in the tube above them every ten yards or so. The blue and green wires, each at least six-inches in diameter, continued on inside the tube. Except for the small protrusions every couple of feet along the mild slope, it reminded Matt of a waterslide as it slowly wrapped around and down the rock column. It was easier at this point to sit down and scoot along. Even though the slope was gentle, it was an odd angle to try to stand and walk at.

"What in the . . ." Cody stopped, staring out into a foreign, underwater world.

CHAPTER 30

Like humans in a reverse fish bowl, they were surrounded by water. Strange-looking fish swam by, barely giving the humans a glance inside their tubular air aquarium. Matt gazed out at multiple columns of rock that seemed to go from just beneath the island down to the floor of the ocean. *Like a multi-stalked mushroom cloud*, he thought. Like the columns were what held the island above the water.

Each of the rock pillars had a similar clear tube wrapping around it and cross sections that traveled from one twisting tube to the next, so you could get from one to another without going back up to the island.

Matt swiped his arm across his forehead, now dripping with sweat.

"It looks like a double-helix DNA strand," Stacy whispered.

Matt nodded, not taking his eyes from the alien sight.

"A double what?" Justin asked.

Even in her period of deep mourning, Stacy was able to roll her bloodshot eyes. "Freshman biology, ditz."

Justin stiffened. "Yeah, well, the cheerleaders took turns doing my homework for me so I could concentrate on football."

Cody changed the subject. "It's hotter than a Texas July in here."

Matt turned to examine the column their tube wrapped around. His gaze followed the thick wires down a couple of feet to where they entered the column through an airtight, watertight conduit. The wires returned to the clear tube in the same manner about a foot later. "Do you think these rock columns are full of lava or something? Like that's where the island is getting its power?"

Catherine squinted out at the forest of identical pillars. "Didn't one of the manuals we looked at say something about geothermal power?"

"Yeah. I remember something about that," Justin said.

Cody slapped Matt on the shoulder. "I think you're right, boss. And that explains why it's hotter than Hades in here."

"I think these columns are holding the island up too," Matt said. "I mean, how else would you explain the physics of this thing? Islands don't just float on top of the ocean. They grow out of the ocean floor like mountains."

"Curiouser and curiouser," Stacy whispered.

The boys looked at her like she was speaking a foreign language, but Catherine smiled slightly. "*Alice in Wonderland*. One of my favorites."

"Mine too," Stacy murmured. "And very fitting for this whole ridiculous situation." She wiped tears from her face with both hands.

"So where's the lava coming from?" Justin asked.

"Deep ocean volcanoes," Matt answered. "They're all over the place. They were even before the apocalypse. And they constantly emit energy."

Catherine scooted up to where Matt sat staring out into the ocean and laid her head on his shoulder. "The ocean has always been like a whole different planet . . . but this . . ." She shook her head against him. "It's like a whole different universe. Maybe it explains what we saw above. Like some sort of pocket of heat and humidity that, I dunno, makes a perfect environment for giant plants and bugs. Matt said it himself—they were like prehistoric bugs. Seems like the right climate anyway."

Matt nodded as a gigantic mutant creature swam around one of the distant pillars. It sort of resembled a whale, but with tumor-like protrusions growing on its body, each emitting spurts of small bubbles at different times. Beneath them, in the deep water, a creature resembling an octopus glowed in the dark. An old, rusty barrel floated by. As Matt watched, the cephalopod wrapped an incandescent limb around the steel barrel and collapsed it like it was made of paper.

The tumultuous white caps they'd seen from the beach near the hotel presented below as fast-moving water funnels—like underwater tornados, with releases of air in large bubbles boiling from the sea floor, and a constant motion whipping smaller fish to and fro on its turbulent current.

"There are an awful lot of wrecked ships down there." Cody pressed his forehead against the tube.

"What do you think these tubes were made for?" Catherine asked.

Matt readjusted so he could put his arm around her and pull her closer. He needed human contact. Not just any human, but Catherine. Having her next to him, even in the heat radiating from the stone column so near to them, was the only thing keeping him together. The only thing keeping him from losing it as his mind wandered to thoughts of Darin being ripped apart by those demonic insects. Eaten alive. He shuddered.

"Matt?" Catherine whispered. "Don't think about it right now. Think about my question. The mystery."

She knew. Of course she knew where his mind kept taking him. He kissed the top of her head and thought about her question for a few seconds. "Maintenance. I bet the tubes are for maintenance of the wires."

She nodded, running her hand up and down his arm. "I bet you're right. That makes sense."

"So what's the plan, man?" Justin asked. "I can't just sit here." He rubbed his face like it was crawling with lice. "I need to keep moving."

Matt shrugged, no longer willing to be the decision maker.

"Let's keep going down," Cody suggested. "I'd like to see what else is swimming around down here. Plus it's going to be a while before it'll be safe for us to surface again."

Stacy stared forlornly out into the murky water. "It will never be safe for us."

"C'mon, let's keep moving." Cody scooted down the tube, disappearing from sight as it curved around the rock column.

The others followed him, Matt and Catherine bringing up the rear.

As they rounded the curve, Catherine bumped into Justin. "Hold still," he whispered.

"Why? What's . . ." Catherine clutched Matt's arm.

An enormous creature glided toward them at an incredible speed.

"Not again," Matt murmured.

CHAPTER 31

"What is that thing? It can't get us in here, can it?" Stacy whimpered.

Cody shook his head. "Some kind of mutated alligator-saber-toothed-shark monster."

Matt stared, eyes wide, as the creature circled around the column and tube, disappearing behind them, then reappearing in seconds. Cody had summed it up almost perfectly. Its resemblance to an alligator ended with its shape, though. "Its skin is like a shark's." Matt followed the monster with his eyes. "How many eyes does it have?" He tried to count the row of eyes that started on one side of its elongated snout, ran up over it, and ended on the other side.

"Seven, I think," Catherine answered.

The monster turned away from them and swam off a distance.

"Let's get moving while that thing is over there!" Justin didn't wait for the others. He moved quickly down the tube.

"It's coming back!" Stacy shrieked.

"Justin, stop moving!" Cody shouted.

The creature spread its jaws wide—the sabertooth-like canines protruding from the top were the length of Rambo's survival knife and as thick as Matt's wrists. The tube shuddered as the creature's jaws snapped onto it. They all screamed as the monster pulled on it, jostling them back and forth.

Justin punched the wall of the tube near the creature's head and shouted, "Go away! Get the hell out of here!"

Stacy grabbed his arm and yelled, "What are you doing? Don't provoke it!"

The sabertoothed alligator shark shook its head, rattling the teens further. A crack appeared in the tube, spreading out from one of the giant canine teeth.

"Duck!" Matt yelled. The tooth pierced the tube, missing Justin by just an inch, and water flooded in through the breach. The deluge of salt water turned the pipe into a true waterslide, and they each grabbed on to the wires to keep from being flushed away.

"We have to go back up!" Matt shouted as the tube filled with water. "Go!" He pushed Catherine and Stacy ahead of him and looked frantically around for the monster as the water closed over his head.

He scrambled to catch up to the others and gulped in a breath when his head surfaced. He continued to climb, making it to where his feet were above the water. But the water kept rising. Cody lost his footing and missed as he reached for the wires. He fell, sliding past Matt like a waterslide rider. Matt's attempt to grab him failed, and his mind flashed back to Kyle—his hand slipping out of Matt's grip, lost in the flash flood while he watched, helpless to intervene.

"Cody!" Stacy and Catherine screamed.

"I'm okay!" Cody yelled.

Matt had never been so happy to hear that Southern drawl. He looked behind him, continuing the climb up the pipe. Cody's head appeared around the curve. He dog-paddled as the churning water rose, bringing him with it. A huge weight lifted from Matt's chest. Cody was okay.

"Let's cross over," Justin said. "That tube across from us isn't filling as fast." He didn't wait for the others to concur as he pushed himself into the horizontal pipe connecting to another twisting tube.

They reached the other column and neared the ladder leading straight up through the island. Matt was last to reach the ladder, the water churning below him, rising faster than before. The monster creature torpedoed through the sea directly below Matt and slammed into the tube, biting into it and shaking its head as it tried to dislodge the tube from the column. The jar of the collision shook the teens, and they screamed as they held tight to the rungs of the ladder.

Matt, only clinging to the bottom rung with one hand, slipped and fell into the raging water. His heart pounded against his ribs, and he flailed, unsure what direction he faced. His lungs burned as he kicked his feet and flapped his arms in a panicked attempt to find which way was up—and air. His head broke the surface just long enough for him to gulp for air, only partially succeeding as the rushing water followed the air into his lungs. Black spots floated in his vision. His lungs burned and his chest felt like it was being crushed by an anaconda. He was going to die. His brain pushed against his skull. He squeezed his eyes shut against the pressure—it was going to explode.

Something latched on to his arms, his shirt. For a terrifying moment, he thought it was the creature. It pulled him upward. His friends. They pulled him onto the ladder, out of the reach of the water—and the creature. His first attempt to breathe failed as his lungs spasmed, expelling seawater all over Justin's face.

"Dude!" Justin snorted.

Matt drew in enough breath to elicit a coughing fit. Catherine pounded on his back. When the hacking subsided, Matt leaned his forehead against the rung he gripped with all his might, sucking air into his battered lungs. Again, his thoughts turned to Kyle. What he'd felt as he drowned. Matt knew now. Guilt tore through him and he sobbed, so grateful and relieved that his friends saved him, but still devastated that he wasn't able to save Kyle.

Catherine put an arm around him, holding on to the ladder with her other hand, and laid her head on his shoulder. "It's okay, Matt. You're okay."

He nodded and took a shuddering breath before lifting his head. "Thank you. All of you."

"Well, o' course, buddy." Cody slapped him on the shoulder. "Heck, you've saved all of us enough times—figured we owed you."

Matt shook his head, the emotions and guilt welling up again. He swallowed it down. "Let's get out of here."

CHAPTER 32

The climb out of the tube was silent except for the rushing water slapping against the broken tube below them. Matt's lungs burned and he coughed every time he tried to take a deep breath. He pulled himself over the lip of the tube after the others and lowered himself to the muddy ground with a grunt.

"Wow," Catherine whispered.

He looked at her, her eyes wide with wonder, then looked around and gasped. They'd emerged in a new area of the island after crossing to the other tube. "The mountain. We made it." Matt's hoarse voice sounded more like Shaggy from *Scooby Doo* than himself, but he didn't care. They'd made it to the base of the mountain.

"And no dinosaur bugs," Stacy said.

"Or underwater mutant creatures." Cody smiled.

"Yeah," Justin chimed in. "And what is it with you and water, Texas? You fell in the reservoir under the control room thing and then you fell in again today. What a dip."

"Hey!" Cody objected. "Matt fell in today too."

"Naw. He was pulled in by the water monster shaking the tube. You just fell."

Cody laughed. "I guess you're right. The shower I took yesterday just didn't get me clean enough, so I decided to seize on the opportunity to take a swim."

"Did any of our packs make it out?" Matt asked, unable to take his eyes off the mountain he'd been trying to get to since the day he awoke from cryosleep.

"Yep." Cody dropped a soaking-wet backpack to the ground. "I dropped mine when I was trying not to drown in the waterslide, but I yanked yours off your back when we pulled you out."

Matt knelt down and opened the pack, exclaiming, "Found it!" as his hand came out gripping a pair of binoculars. He put them to his eyes and looked toward the mountain. "One lens is cracked, but I can see just fine through the other one." He adjusted the focus and grinned.

"What do you see?" Catherine asked.

"Take a look for yourself." He handed her the binoculars.

"It's a huge door." She passed the binoculars to Cody. "Like a vault door—and it says B-35 on it! How far away do you think it is?"

"Maybe a mile." Matt smiled down at her, and she threw her arms around his neck and kissed him hard on the mouth.

"We're so close," she whispered.

"Umm, like, could you two *not*." Stacy turned away from them and wiped at her cheeks.

Again, guilt welled up in Matt's stomach, and he pulled away from Catherine's embrace. Seeing them together like that was probably like rubbing salt in a fresh, new wound for Stacy. He still couldn't believe they'd lost Darin—especially the way they did. He didn't think he could handle it if he lost Catherine. He looked back at her and smiled. "Hopefully today's the day you meet my parents."

"There's the rockslide from where Darin was forced to blow up the side of the mountain to fake a meteor strike," Cody said, binoculars still pressed to his face.

"Let's see." Justin took the binoculars from him.

"Poor Lance-Darin." Stacy sniffed. "I can't believe what that evil man put him through. He survived all that just to get eaten by a stupid giant bug!" She broke down in sobs and Catherine wrapped her up in a hug.

"Yeah." Justin sighed. "I was just starting to like him too."

"I know it won't make missing Darin any better, Stacy," Catherine said, "but maybe you'll get to see your family today."

Stacy sniffed and lifted her head from Catherine's shoulder. "That would be bitchin'."

"Let's get going!" Matt's initial excitement returned.

A meteor streaked across the sky and slammed into the side of the mountain. Chunks of rock and ash flew from the impact, and dust and smaller rocks pelted the group. They dived for cover behind the pipe they'd just crawled from.

"Shit!" Justin spit dirt from his mouth.

"We need to hurry and get there." Matt's heart pumped at triple speed. "We need to make sure they're all okay, our families and everyone else."

"And we need to get somewhere safer," Cody added.

As soon as the falling debris subsided, Matt motioned to the group and grabbed his backpack from where he'd left it on the ground. "Let's go!" He ran up a single-lane road and stopped after turning a corner around a clump of trees.

"Why'd you stop?" Catherine asked, coming to a halt beside him. "Oh."

Justin, Cody, and Stacy joined them, all staring at a group of dump trucks and pickups parked askew. Matt walked closer, examining burn marks, broken windows, and dents on the nearest dump truck. He laid his hand on the winch affixed to the front guard and gazed down at the attached cable on the ground, unraveled several yards in front of the truck.

"Whoever was camping out here must have left in a big hurry," Cody said. He walked slowly in the vegetation at the side of the road, winding around broken-down army vehicles and abandoned tents that had definitely seen better days. He kicked the tall grasses aside. "They appear to have left everything right where it was. O2 tanks. There's at least five fifty-gallon barrels tipped over out here—looks like they had gas or oil in them."

Matt pointed out some newer-looking tire tracks skirting around a rockslide area. "This must be where Westbrook drove to get out of the vault."

"All this equipment, the trucks and everything, has Demo Trench symbols on it." Catherine ran her fingers over a symbol plastered to the side of a dump truck.

Matt studied the image on the pickup he'd walked back over to. He recognized it from some of the manuals back at the control center. Two parallel lines with a sphere in the lower third. A single slanted line on the right side of the double lines.

Something whizzed past Matt's head and slammed into the side of the vehicle. He glanced up, then covered his head with his arms as fireballs and ice chunks flew at him from the dark gray clouds above. "Take shelter!" He ripped the door open and jumped into the cab of the truck as hellfire rained down all around.

CHAPTER 33

Justin dived in the other side and slammed the door.

"Where are the others?" Matt twisted back and forth on the seat, frantic to find Catherine. She waved from the cab of the dump truck, where Cody and Stacy hovered on each side of her. Matt blew out a breath. "They're safe."

Large chunks of hail fell amongst frozen snowballs that must have been full of methane or some other flammable gas that caused flames to engulf them as they plummeted to the ground. As Matt stared at one such ball of ice and fire as it sizzled out on the hood of the truck, the island quaked. He tried to steady himself by grabbing the dashboard and the seat back, but the tremor rocked the truck back and forth, up and down, slamming him and Justin into each other.

A fissure opened up in the ground between the pickup and the dump truck. As it expanded rapidly, the trucks slid toward the widening crevasse. Matt and Justin scrambled out of the pickup just before it disappeared and ran to more solid ground. Matt skidded to a stop and turned back toward the unfolding disaster, panic rising in his throat, choking him as he tried to draw in a breath.

Cody and Stacy appeared to be a safe distance away, but Catherine was still inside the tipping dump truck, climbing almost vertically across the seat. The door Cody and Stacy had exited from slammed shut with the shifting of the truck, and Catherine struggled to open it against gravity.

Matt's feet froze to the ground as he watched, his mind numb with terror.

With a guttural scream, Catherine forced the door open enough to slide out and jump to the ground. She ran toward Cody and Stacy as the dump truck tipped over the edge of the newly formed preci-pice. Matt felt a split second of relief before his eyes caught on the unspooled cable still attached to the winch of the falling truck. The cable whipped around Catherine's leg and pulled her. She fell to the ground, face first. Cody dove for her as she slid toward the widening hole. Catherine futilely pawed at the ground, desperate to find pur-chase.

"No!" Stacy pushed her hands against her ears and squeezed her eyes shut. "No, no, no!"

The cable tightened more. Catherine smiled at Matt. He knew her fate. She knew her fate. Everything slowed around him and his ears rang. He had the urge to puke but didn't. Catherine reached out to him as the cable became taut. Matt moved to her, but she plummeted over the edge of the chasm before he could reach her.

A split second later, everything sped up again. The sound of rocks and metal smashing emerged from the maw that swallowed Cather-ine. Dust formed a mushroom cloud above the crevasse. He didn't know where anyone was. He only wanted Catherine. He fought the urge to dive into the fissure to save her, to be with her.

In an instant of pure insanity, Matt ran, his mind engulfed in horror, blinding him. Justin ran beside him and pulled him to a stop just inches away from the edge. Cody and Stacy reached his side as he peered over into the chasm. The dump truck was wedged into the crack, front side facing up. Catherine lay on the grille with the heavy cable piled on top of her, one of her legs twisted at an unnatural angle.

"Catherine!" Matt yelled. Was she breathing? She was uncon-scious. He dropped his backpack and continued to yell down to her as he pulled the rope out.

Stacy, Justin, and Cody joined him, yelling, "Catherine! Wake up!"

Her eyes fluttered and she moaned. She rolled to her back with a grimace, then smiled up at them. She looked around her. The side of her head was plastered with blood, and she cried out as she tried to move her twisted leg. The truck dropped a foot, wedging itself even more.

"Ah!" Catherine screamed.

Matt swung the rope and threw it down to her, his heart trying to claw its way out of his chest. Catherine rolled to her side to grab the lifeline. She caught it, but the movement was too much. The dump truck dislodged, disappearing into the abyss, taking Catherine with it.

The line snapped taut, nearly taking Matt over the edge with it, but he held true.

"Help me!" He dug in his heels.

Cody and Justin stood behind him, pulling. Stacy peered over the edge.

"Can you see her?" Matt asked.

And then the line went slack. He fell backward in a heap onto Cody and Justin.

"No!" Matt screamed. He crawled to the edge once more. Nothing but dark and dust. He pounded the dirt and let out another guttural scream as he arched his back to the sky, throwing fistfuls of dirt into the air. Tears poured from his eyes and he screamed again. "Catherine! No!" He couldn't breathe. His face was a mess of dirt and never-ending tears; his chest tightened like a vise around his lungs. He sobbed, saying her name over and over, as he mechanically pulled the rope up.

The island shook again. Matt barely registered the movement or the danger it posed. Justin and Cody each grabbed him by an arm and dragged him to his feet. They led him at a run toward the vault door.

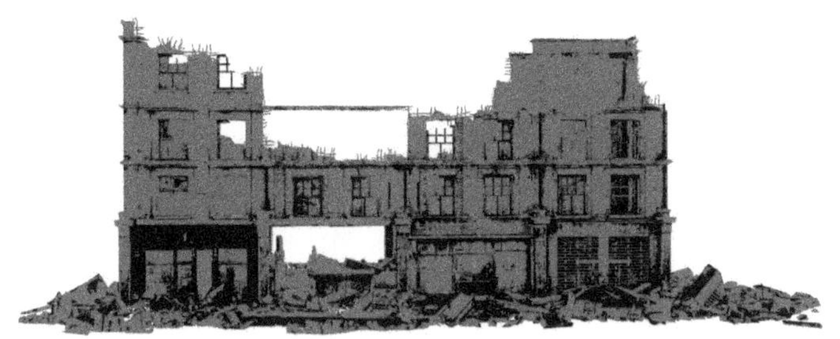

CHAPTER 34

The clouds grew even darker as Matt's friends half-dragged him toward the vault. He stumbled multiple times and would have fallen on his face if he hadn't been held up by Cody and Justin. The world was a blur, and his body wasn't performing as it should. It just wanted to shut down. *He* just wanted to shut down. Everything was numb except his heart—the part he wished would go numb the most.

Stacy reached the door first, pounded on the center of the "B-35" stenciled there, then turned back to the boys. "How do we open it? Darin would have known." The whites of her panicked-looking eyes shone through the storm's darkness.

Another barrage of fire-hail pelted the ground around them, this time accompanied by lightning. The four of them scattered, ducking for cover wherever they could find it. The rumbling thunder moved farther away, and the fire-and-ice balls grew smaller and less numerous.

Matt rubbed his face, shook his head, and set his jaw. Heartbroken though he was, he needed to find his parents. He got up and approached the door, searching it for any latches or openings. Of course it would have to be difficult—no doorknob to twist or doorbell to ring.

"Could that be the way to open it?" Cody asked from beside him, causing Matt to jump at the sound of his voice. He'd forgotten anyone else existed at the moment.

Matt examined the area Cody pointed to while Stacy and Justin leaned in for a look. A circular depression about ten inches in diameter was sunk into the thick metal door. Inside the circle was another depression, this one in the shape of a triangle about the size of his fist.

A lone sphere of hail fire shot down next to Matt, and he jumped to the side to avoid it. *Clank.* He looked down to where his feet had landed on something hard.

Kneeling, Matt brushed the dirt, mud, and ash off to reveal a large, trunk-sized metal box. The dented lid had a Demo Trench symbol emblazoned on it. Matt found the lip of the lid with his fingertips and pulled up on it. It didn't budge. He stood, crouching down to hold on to it, and used the strength of his legs to try to pry it open. He growled. "Someone find something to pry this open with. Maybe it's a way to get in, like a trapdoor to a tunnel under the vault door or something."

Cody and Justin went in different directions to search for something to use as a pry bar, while Stacy stood and stared up at the mountain before them. Matt tried again to force the box open, but ended up slumping to his butt with a grunt, hitting the ground hard and not caring. He folded his arms across his bent knees and hid his face in them. He tried to think of anything but what had just happened to Catherine—but his shocked mind wasn't in the mood to cooperate. Like flipping through a photo album, recent images of Catherine flashed one after another. Her Hulk-like strength when she forced the heavy door of the dump truck open. Her determined face as she ran for safety. The cable wrapping around her leg, pulling her to the ground, then into the pit, like a Kraken from the depths of hell.

Matt shook his head violently within the confines of his folded arms, squeezing his eyes shut against the nonstop images playing out in his head. But they wouldn't stop. Catherine, lying lifeless on the grille of the dump truck. Her twisted leg. The blood on her head. Her dark curls spread out around her. Her smile when she regained consciousness and realized she'd survived. The flash of terror in her eyes when the truck shifted. Matt being a fraction of a second late with the rope. Renewed hope when he realized she'd be able to grab the rope. Then utter devastation as the rope went slack.

An involuntary wail ripped through his throat. Then someone was beside him, arms wrapped tight around his trembling shoulders, sobbing right along with him. Stacy's fuzzy strawberry-blonde curls tickled his neck, but he barely registered it. Matt had no idea how long they sat like that—it could have been seconds or it could have been hours. But it was long enough for his energy to be spent and his tears to dry up.

Matt slowly raised his head. Cody and Justin stood a few feet away, a crowbar in Cody's hand, silently waiting. Matt patted Stacy's arm and whispered in a raw voice, "Thank you, Stacy."

She nodded and gave his shoulder one more hug before standing and wiping her face. She tucked her hair behind her ears and held out a hand to help him up. "Come on. Let's get this thing open."

Matt nodded and took her offered hand, careful not to pull his petite friend over as he stood.

Cody stepped forward and handed the crowbar to him with a sad smile. "Found it over by the fifty-gallon barrels."

"Perfect." Matt positioned the hooked end of the bar under the lip of the metal lid, wiped his face on his shoulder, then pried the lid up with a screech of rusted hinges. He dropped the pry bar to the ground and bent down to look inside the box.

"What's in there?" Justin asked, moving to stand beside him.

"It's some kind of tool." Matt lifted it out with both hands. "Or maybe a weapon." He raised the red-colored device to his shoulder, fitting it there like the butt of a shotgun. A cord trailed from just behind the "trigger" down into the metal box.

"I ain't never seen a gun or tool like that before," Cody said.

"Me either," Matt agreed. "Must be custom built." He moved it away from his shoulder and held it in front of him with both hands.

"Custom built for what?" Justin examined the tip. "Looks like a jackhammer or a drill."

"Umm, boys?" Stacy sidled over to Justin. "Notice anything about the tip of this thing?"

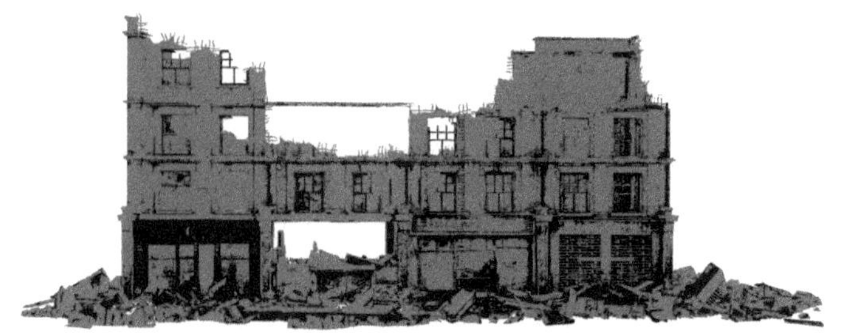

CHAPTER 35

Matt examined the end Stacy referred to. It reminded him of a drill bit, but not in a shape he'd ever seen before. A triangle drill bit. He snapped his head up and looked at the vault door. "A triangle drill bit." He side-stepped to better align the tool with the depressions in the door, dragging the cord with him.

Justin eyed the cord, following it into the metal box. "Pull the trigger thing. See if it even works before trying it in the door."

The drill vibrated in Matt's hands when he pulled back on the trigger, and the triangle-shaped drill bit spun counterclockwise. "It must be using the volcanic power from below the island for its energy."

Stacy sighed and rolled her eyes. "Who cares, you nerds? Just shove it in that keyhole and, like, get the door open before something else tries to burn, eat, or kill us."

Anger flashed in Matt's gut, quickly replaced with equal parts guilt and fear. Stacy was right. He nodded and attempted to fit the drill bit into the triangle keyhole. It clanked against the metal, refusing to go in. "Help me get the trajectory right. It's freakin' hard with the length of this thing."

Cody grabbed the drill near the tip and guided it toward the matching keyhole. After a couple of adjustments, it clicked in with a solid fit. "You're all set, boss."

Gripping the gun-like drill with both hands, Matt pulled the trigger. The drill, the triangle, and the inside of the circle in which it resided turned slowly. Matt leaned into it, using his body weight and shoulder to keep the thing in place and to keep it from spinning in his hands. Sweat broke out on his forehead. "Could use a little help here," he grunted.

Cody and Justin grabbed on and helped him hold it in place. The lock stopped with a jolt, and Matt released the trigger before they all lost their grip or the drill broke. Stacy stood behind them, looking up at the mountain again, in the direction of the man-made rockslide.

Matt wiped the sweat off his face and took a couple of deep breaths. He looked at Justin and Cody. "Ready?"

They nodded, and he leaned in and pulled the trigger. The lock moved another quarter of a turn, then seized up again. Matt stopped the drill, wiped his hands on his pants, got a better grip, then nodded to his friends and pulled the trigger again. It turned a little more. The sound of gears grinding and metal popping caused a spike in Matt's adrenaline. He released the trigger and pulled the drill out of the lock and out of Justin's and Cody's hands. He looked side to side, turned in a circle to take in his surroundings with eyes darting around like hummingbirds, then looked up at the sky—fully expecting to see a catastrophic event bearing down on them. Nothing happened. In fact, the sky was clearer than it had been all day.

Matt turned to his friends. They all seemed to have experienced similar symptoms of PTSD, staring back at him with wide eyes, their faces a shade paler than a moment before.

"It was just the door," Cody said. "We aren't in the HZRD zone anymore."

"No." Stacy chewed on her dirty fingernails. "But we're still in danger. Like, get on with it!"

Shaky hands made it even more difficult than before to fit the drill bit into the triangle lock. Justin and Cody helped guide it back in, and the three boys braced themselves before Matt pulled the trigger.

The lock turned at a snail's pace, but Matt was encouraged—it felt different this time. With each degree of movement, the mechanism inside the door clicked. The lock was disengaging bit by bit. Matt tilted his head back and closed his eyes. "Come on already, just open," he said through gritted teeth.

Almost a full minute later, and likely after taking years off Matt's life, the final click sounded, and he removed the drill from the lock as the door slowly slid open.

A rush of stale air blew by them, the stench of death riding its currents. Matt's stomach heaved. The four teens looked at each other, color draining from their faces.

Stacy shook her head, her mess of curls whipping about her face in furious denial. "I can't look. I can't . . . I can't go in there."

Matt couldn't blame her. What if they were all dead? That odor . . . it could be nothing else. He pulled the neck of his T-shirt over his nose and mouth and, fighting the dread welling up inside him, he trudged through the doorway.

CHAPTER 36

Rows of bodies lined the way inside, the dead leading him down to the unknown hell they had just entered. Matt's legs were first to surrender, first to declare that it was all too much and he was done. His knees gave and he sank to the floor of the cavern.

"Hey, buddy." Cody's soft voice sounded distant, worlds away. "I know this looks bad, but they're all covered. Someone had to do that for them."

Matt blinked, some of the fuzziness leaving his sight. He looked at the bodies on each side of him. Cody was right. They'd been laid in neat rows, each one covered with a plastic tarp or a wool army blanket. *Someone* was alive. Probably more than one person. The bodies had to be moved here and covered by someone.

"Yeah . . . yeah, you're right. We need to keep going." Matt stood and looked behind Cody. "Where are Justin and Stacy?"

Cody hooked a thumb toward the vault door. "Justin's trying to get Stacy to come inside."

"Pick her up and carry her, Justin!" Matt yelled. "I need to get out of here."

"Okay, chief!" Justin sounded all too eager to do this bit of Matt's bidding.

"Oh no, you don't!" Stacy's voice rose on the last word and ended with a loud grunt of expelled air.

At any other time before, Matt would have laughed at the sight of Stacy slung over Justin's broad shoulder, her fists pounding into his back, his grin spread wide as he clamped his arms around her struggling legs. But not now. Maybe not ever again. A flash image of Catherine falling into the dark chasm slammed into him, choking off his air. Nope. He probably wouldn't ever laugh again. He rubbed his eyes with the heels of his hands, pressing hard enough to render him blind for a few seconds afterward.

"C'mon," Cody urged. "There's a door in the rock wall up ahead. Let's head for that."

Matt nodded, and they trudged toward it. He looked back to make sure Justin followed them. Stacy had stopped struggling. She hung limply over Justin's shoulder, with her hands clamped over her eyes and nose.

Cody reached the wide door first and opened it without a problem. They stepped into the warehouse inside the cavern. Matt trailed his fingers along the side of the bus they'd come in on so many years ago as he slowly walked down its length. The overhead lights flickered. Matt pulled his hand away from the bus, his fingers covered in dust. He looked around him. Everything in there was covered in dust.

At some point since entering the warehouse, Justin had set Stacy back on her own feet. One of them had shut the door out to where the dead lay, decaying in their eternal slumber.

"I remember this place," Justin said. "I woke up as the bus was pulling in here."

"Me too." Matt pointed at a large industrial-strength double door. "That's where they took us to put us in the cryopods."

He looked each of his remaining friends in the eye, took a deep breath, and twisted the handle on the big door. It turned easily, and Matt swung the door open.

A short, blond-haired man rushed toward them.

CHAPTER 37

A group of people, both adults and children, gathered around them as they stepped through the door. The blond man reached them first and eyed them a bit warily, mouth turned down into a slight frown. "Who are you? Where'd you come from?"

"I'm Matt Voorhees. This is Cody, Justin, and Stacy." He pointed to each of them. "We came from this vault. Westbrook, the guy in charge of taking care of everything here, took us out, in our pods." Matt shook his head. "Look, it's a long story, and we've had a long and terrible day. We've been looking for this vault,"—he glanced around at the gathering crowd—"for you all, pretty much ever since we woke up."

A kind-faced woman gave the blond man a narrow-eyed look, then smiled at Matt. "I'm Suzanne. We're so glad you made it back. Come in. Have a seat. We'll get you something to eat and drink."

She led them to a seating area, but none of them sat at first. Matt searched the crowd of people for a familiar face. They all wore the same Save the Population Project uniforms—tan tank tops and tan shorts, a number over the left breast that corresponded to the number on the pod they'd been in. Not seeing his mom or dad in the group, Matt's eyes flicked to the columns. Row upon row of occupied cryo-pods as far as he could see into the vault.

A wall full of windows faced the columns. The opposite wall was full of small control panels, many of them with blinking lights. Multiple computers were set up haphazardly on one desk. Cody nudged him with his shoulder and pointed to a room. A bed and a cluttered desk were the only furnishings in it. "That must have been West-brook's sleeping quarters," Cody whispered.

"Yes," Suzanne answered. She glanced at the four filthy, bedraggled teens and pursed her lips. "Is he . . . is Westbrook . . . with you?"

"No," Stacy said sharply. "He's dead. Thankfully."

Suzanne raised an eyebrow.

Matt was surprised that no one in the group seemed to be too surprised at her words. "He . . . uhh . . . he died right at the outset when a bunch of our pods fell on top of him."

Suzanne sighed. "Not to speak ill of the dead, but I'm afraid, from the looks of some of his journal entries, he'd gone rather loopy over the last decade. Plus, he recorded himself a bunch." She pointed to a toppled pile of black plastic VHS tapes. "All of those are him recording something about saving humanity and being the savior of the human race. He was trying to get everyone out to some place called HZRD, and then he was going to wake everyone up and immediately put himself in charge of saving the world from all of the disasters."

Matt nodded, and Suzanne turned to him. "Do you know of this HZRD place?" she asked.

"Oh yeah," Justin said. "And you don't want to go there."

"I can tell you all about it sometime," Matt said. "But we can tell you Westbrook was nuts. Grade A certifiably crazy."

"We are lucky to be alive." Stacy bowed her head and tried to hold back tears. Matt put his arm around her.

"Do you guys have a radio?" Matt asked. "There's some other vaults, and we could call to them. Maybe they have a lead scientist like Westbrook who could help."

A man pulled a box from below Westbrook's desk. Matt's shoulders slumped at the sight. The box was full of radio parts, clearly smashed by someone.

"He must've destroyed it before he left," he said. "We couldn't call out to anyone."

Matt had his answer. Broken radio, no emergency call. These people couldn't call out. They were stuck. No one came for them besides the four teens who were there now.

"Well, that sucks," Matt said.

"I kept the parts," the man continued, "just in case someone can jerry-rig it back together."

A little girl no older than ten brought each of the four newcomers a can of soda and some dehydrated apple slices. They sat in the uncomfortable folding chairs nearest them and nibbled on the fruit.

"How are all y'all out of your pods?" Cody asked, popping the top of his soda.

Suzanne and most of the others moved chairs around to face the teens in an informal semicircle. "Well, Westbrook woke Dave and me up just before he left in a truck loaded down with your cryo-pods." She nodded toward a tall man wearing eyeglasses whom Matt assumed was Dave. "He gave us a thirty-second tutorial—after we finished vomiting—about how to keep the columns from failing, told us to stay inside until he got back, and left."

"Yes," Dave said, pushing his glasses back up the bridge of his nose. "It was a highly stressful situation to leave us in. Alarms blaring. Lights blinking." He shook his head. "I was terrified we were going to lose everyone."

"But ya didn't." A man with a deeper Southern accent than Cody slapped him on the back. "Ya did a real fine job, Dave."

Dave blushed, but a small smile peaked at the corner of his mouth. "Thanks, Robby. I could not have done it without Suzanne."

"We figured things out as best as we could," Suzanne said. "We decided on day two to wake up a few more people to help, but we knew we couldn't wake everyone up because we have such limited resources."

Looking down at his hands, Dave spoke with a solemn voice. "We were not able to keep all of the cryogenic pods going, though." He removed his glasses and wiped them with the hem of his tank top before putting them back on. "Power had been lost to parts of some of the columns before Dr. Westbrook even woke us up."

The blond man, Eric, who had rushed up to them at the door said, "You saw the dead, I'm sure. You'd a had to come through there to get to the warehouse."

Matt nodded.

"We didn't know what else to do with 'em. We didn't dare go out-side, because of Westbrook's warning *and* because he didn't return. We had no idea what was out there. I mean, we thought maybe he just erupted into a pile of ash as soon as he pulled out into the apoc-alypse." He shrugged. "So we designated the cavern area as a sort of crypt, and we piled them all up there, covered 'em up."

A tall, skinny man and a thin woman whose head came to his shoulder hurried up from one of the rows of columns. They held hands and wore hopeful smiles. Their smiles faded a little more as their gazes slipped from Matt to Cody to Stacy, and finally to Justin.

"I-i-is Nathan with you?" the man asked. "Nathan Moore?"

Matt dropped his hand to his lap, still holding a slice of dried apple, no longer hungry. He twisted the soda can around on top of his thigh as he dropped his gaze, hoping one of the others would answer. But after a prolonged awkward silence, Matt met the couple's eyes, already void of the hope he'd seen in them as they'd rushed up. They already knew by his reaction. He just needed to say the words. Matt cleared his inflamed throat, then swallowed a sudden well of emotion. Nathan had seemed like a really great kid. "He, umm, he didn't make it. I'm so sorry." Not knowing what else to say, he added, "Nathan was a good friend."

The woman, Nathan's mom, nodded and touched Matt's arm. "Thank you. He was a good boy." She buried her face in her husband's chest and sobbed quietly. The tall man with Nathan's build and eye color hugged her close as silent tears rolled down his cheeks.

CHAPTER 38

The grieving couple excused themselves, and as Matt watched them walk away, he realized he hadn't even looked for his parents yet. He'd been inside the cryovault for at least ten minutes. He'd been so obsessed with finding them since the minute he woke up. He shook his head. His traumatized brain wasn't functioning at full capacity.

"Hey . . ." He paused, suddenly afraid to learn the answer. "Do any of you know my parents? Or know where they are? Dan and Pat Voorhees?"

The adults in the room looked at each other and shook their heads.

"They for sure aren't among those of us who are awake," Suzanne said.

But that didn't mean anything, did it? They could just be in their columns. Anxiety welled up, flooding Matt's entire being. The few apple chips he had eaten churned in his stomach. He dropped the remaining chips to the floor and set the soda down with a shaky hand. He bent at the waist, putting his head between his knees to keep from spewing everywhere.

The nausea was going to win. Matt panted, his breath coming in short, shallow gasps. His lips tingled.

"Hey, I'm, like, really good at computer stuff. Which one should I use?" Stacy's voice declared her annoyance. "Or, like, a list of where everyone is?"

Matt assumed the hand on his back belonged to Stacy, since she was sitting right next to him. It reminded him of when his mom had taught him how to Matt-itate. He counted slowly in his head, matching his breathing to the cadence.

Dave answered Stacy. "There is a computer. It's in Westbrook's sleeping quarters over there. I've had to use it from time to time to check on things. Do you know how to use it?"

Stacy nodded, standing abruptly. "Come on, Matthew." She pulled on his arm. "Quit hyperventilating, and let's go find our families."

"It's *Matt*," he mumbled. He took two more measured breaths and slowly raised his head.

Stacy pulled on him again. Cody and Justin stood. As soon as Matt was confident he wasn't going to vomit, he stood and followed his friends into the monster's lair. Stacy powered up the Apple II taking up a good chunk of the messy desk as Cody flipped through a pile of floppy disks.

"Here, try this one." Cody handed the square disk to Stacy. "It says 'Column Schematics.'"

She popped it into the slit on the front of the computer and it whirred to life. Stacy hit a few keys and arrow buttons. Matt watched the screen go from showing numbered rows and columns to a list of names.

"Voorhees," Stacy whispered as she scrolled down the long, alphabetized list. "You *would* have a name that's at the end of the alphabet."

"There!" Matt pointed as he spotted his and his parents' names on the list. "Pod locations forty-two twelve six and forty-two fifteen nine." He scribbled the numbers on a notepad. "Go back to the schematics."

Stacy sighed. "Fine. But then I'm going to find my own family."

"And ours," Justin said, pointing to himself, then Cody.

Keys clicked as Stacy's fingers flew over them, and soon the diagram of pod locations flashed onto the screen. Matt studied it for a few minutes. "Okay. I think I get it. The first number is the column that corresponds with age, the second number is the row top to bottom, and the third number must be the pod's position in the column front to back."

Justin scratched his head as he studied the blueprint-like diagram. "I thought there were, like, five thousand people-cicles in here. How many rows and columns are there?"

Matt pointed to a legend in the corner of the screen. "There are twenty rows with twenty-five columns per row."

"That just don't seem to add up to five thousand people to me," Justin said, shaking his head.

"Like, do the math, Justin," Stacy said. "Twenty rows times twenty-five columns equals five hundred columns; ten pods per column equals five thousand pods."

Matt was impressed with her quick calculations. He'd underestimated Stacy's intelligence too many times. The whole "valley girl" act was deceiving. He ripped the paper from the Garfield-shaped notepad he'd written on and headed out of the little room to go find his parents.

He walked along the rows, looking down at the floor, where the numbers were stenciled onto the cement.

"Whatcha doin'?" a tiny voice asked.

A young boy looked up at him as he answered, "I'm looking for my parents."

"Cool. Can I come with you?"

Matt looked around for an adult or someone that might be supervising this kid. "Umm . . . I guess so."

"Cool. I'm Jake." The kid turned back to face the open area where the chairs were and yelled, "Hey, Mom! I'm goin' with this guy to find his parents!"

Suzanne looked up and smiled at the boy, then walked toward them. "How about I come, too, Jakey? To make sure you stay out of Matt's way."

Matt nodded his appreciation to her. His nerves were already raw and functioning just below panic mode. He didn't need to be responsible for a kid right now.

The odd trio walked to column forty-two. His parents' age. Matt took in a deep breath and headed down the row, again looking at the floor where numbers were stenciled in front of the fifty-foot-tall columns. He stopped in front of the number twelve and looked up at the pods stacked on the shelves of the column. Squinting, he counted to pod six. That should be where his mom was. "Is there a ladder somewhere?" he asked without looking away.

Suzanne gestured to the side of the column, where a ladder was built into it. Matt wasted no more time as he started his climb to reach the sixth pod. He glanced over toward where his dad should be, three columns up, and noticed that a bunch of the pods in that direction were cracked open and didn't appear to have anyone in them. His heart sunk and he clung to the ladder, taking shallow breaths, as his mind wandered to what that could mean. "Come on, Matt," he whispered to himself. "Mom first."

He finished his twenty-five-foot or so climb up to the sixth pod, squeezed his eyes shut for a minute, then looked into the clear cover—his mom, a peaceful look on her face as she slept in suspended animation. She was alive.

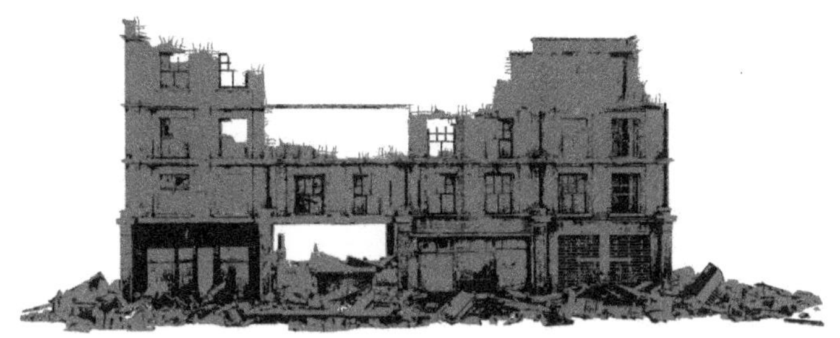

CHAPTER 39

A few more people had joined Suzanne and Jake at the bottom of the ladder. Suzanne looked at Matt with a raised eyebrow as he stepped off the bottom rung.

"She's alive," he said, as some of the tension released from around his chest.

Suzanne gave him a quick hug. "I'm so glad."

"My dad should be up and over here." Matt walked to the base of row fifteen. The lower pods were intact and doing their jobs at keeping the occupants alive. It gave him some hope as he climbed the ladder, yet his heart still pounded out of control. The fifth pod up was cracked open. And the sixth. He hurried past the next two pods to reach his dad's, the ninth one. He wasn't there. His pod was empty.

Matt looked down at the group of people below him. "What does it mean if the pod is open and he isn't in it?"

A couple of the people far below just bowed their heads. Suzanne shook hers.

His dad was dead. That's what it meant.

Devastation crashed into him. His knees gave, and he almost lost his hold on the ladder—and he didn't even care in that moment. A forty-foot plunge to the cement might be a blessing. But as the tears came flooding out of his eyes, he remembered his mom. He wrapped his arm around a rung of the ladder and held tight as he sobbed, not caring who heard his cries.

The weight of everything that had happened since a frantic Cody had freed him from his cryopod by smashing the cover with a tree branch came crashing down on him. All the death. His friends. Catherine. All his fault. Even this one, his dad's death. If he'd only gotten here sooner, maybe . . . He slammed a fist into the empty pod, barely registering the sharp pain that shot through his hand.

Matt cried himself to exhaustion. He had no idea how long he'd been up on that ladder next to the pod where his dad had died. Long enough that his muscles ached and felt as weak as a newborn kitten's. His tears had all dried up, but his throat still hitched every few breaths as he continued to press his forehead against a rung.

The ladder vibrated as someone climbed it beneath him. Matt didn't even look to see who it was. After a few minutes, a hand gripped the side next to him and the person touched him on the back.

"Matt, buddy." Cody's voice was soft, for his ears only. "I'm so sorry about your dad." He let that hang there for a couple of minutes, his hand still pressed against Matt's back in support.

Finally, Matt responded, still not lifting his head. "Thanks. If I could have gotten here sooner—"

"No way I'm gonna let y'all blame yourself. You heard 'em say that some of the people were dead before Westbrook even woke Suzanne and Dave. And heck, ain't no one who tried harder to get here than you. You ain't responsible for this whacked-out place or all the crazy things out there hell-bent on killin' us, Matt. The way I see it, we're all just lucky to be alive."

Matt didn't think "lucky" was a word that fit this situation. But maybe Cody was right about it not being his fault. Westbrook had done this. He murdered Matt's dad. For what? To stroke his own hubris? What about all the others? Jim Westbrook was a mass murderer!

He sighed and lifted his head away from the ladder, swaying a little as a wave of dizziness swept over him. Cody's strong arm tightened across his back as his hand locked on to the other side of the ladder. His friend's support warmed Matt's heart a little.

"Y'all okay?" Cody asked.

Nodding, Matt replied, "Yeah. Just a little dizzy."

"I reckon we should be climbing back down soon before Stacy and Justin decide to come up here and rescue us. You ready?"

"Yeah." Matt tested his strength by bending his knees one at a time while standing in place on the ladder. "But maybe you ought to stick close to me, just in case. I think my body has had enough and might just decide to fail me at any moment."

"I've got ya, buddy."

"I know." Matt realized in that moment that he did know. And that was reason enough to toughen up and keep going.

They made it to the bottom, where Matt realized most, if not all, of the vault's conscious inhabitants had gathered.

Stacy grabbed him around the waist in a fierce hug. "I'm sorry, Matt," she whispered.

He hugged her back. He and Stacy had their differences, but she really was a good friend. He pulled away, realizing that in his grief, he hadn't even asked his friends about their own families. "What did you guys find out about your families?"

"We just wrote down their numbers," Justin said. He put a hand on Matt's shoulder. "We saw the commotion down here and wanted to make sure you were okay. Well, as okay as you can be in this crappy situation."

Now Matt really felt like a jerk. He'd been so pushy, so intent on finding his parents—not just today, but this whole time—he'd frequently forgotten the other kids had loved ones here too. "Well"—he looked at the three of them—"let's go find them."

CHAPTER 40

Stacy handed Matt a page from the notebook with two numbers written on it. "I found Catherine's parents' locations. I figure we should try to find all the other kids' families, too, like Kim and Rhett. But I wanted to start with Catherine."

Matt took the paper, again surprised by Stacy's thoughtfulness.

"Did you say Catherine?" A burly man he hadn't seen earlier made his way through the small crowd. "Would that be Catherine Turner?"

That's where she got her dark, curly hair from, Matt thought as he met the man's eyes. "Yes, sir. Catherine was . . . she was with us."

Matt's use of the past tense hit the man squarely in the gut.

He doubled over, hugging himself around the middle. "My little girl." It took him a few moments to regain his composure. He straightened up, wiped his face, and nodded as he looked at Matt. "What happened?"

Matt couldn't do this. Her terrified face flashed in his mind, and he closed his eyes as he spoke. "She was with us . . . She made it . . . almost made it . . ." He shook his head and turned away. He'd thought he was too tired to cry anymore. He was wrong.

Cody told Catherine's dad what happened to her, then said, "She was an amazing girl, sir. Strong and level-headed. Loyal."

"Thank you, young man. All four of you." His voice hitched. "It's probably a blessing that her mom is no longer here to feel this . . . this heartbreak. But in my selfishness, I wish she were. I wish she were here to share with me—the grief, the memories, everything."

Matt looked down at the paper in his hand, crinkling it as Catherine's dad walked away.

"Come on, guys," Suzanne said to the small group of survivors.

"Let's go get some work done while these young people find their families."

Cody handed Matt a paper with a list of names and numbers written on it. "Here's all of our families. You choose where to start."

He really didn't want to do this. Exhaustion, both physical and emotional, tugged at his eyelids, begging him to go curl up in a corner and sleep for a week. But these were his friends. They'd survived together. He needed to help them. "Okay. Justin's parents are close by, so let's start there."

Justin's parents were both still asleep. As much as he'd bad-mouthed them, as awful as his life with them had been, relief still showed when he hugged the pods, finding them alive. Matt looked back at the paper. "That's it? No brothers or sisters?"

"That's it. Once you've been given the perfect child, no need to have any more." Justin flexed his muscles with a grin.

Stacy rolled her eyes.

The columns where Cody's parents were supposed to be were closer than Stacy's family—who were kind of spread all over—so the four of them went there next. Cody's shoulders relaxed a little to see them, still breathing in animated suspension.

Matt squeezed Cody's shoulder, then looked at Stacy. "You ready? We'll check your parents next."

"I'm ready," she answered.

Her parents remained safely frozen in their pods. They looked quite a bit older than Matt's parents, but he guessed that was to be expected since Stacy was the youngest of five kids. As they traipsed from row to row, column to column to find her four older siblings, Matt asked, "How in the world did all of you guys get picked in the lottery? I mean, parents and minor children were a package deal, but your brothers and sisters are all adults, and each of them would have had to be chosen separately . . ."

As Stacy shrugged, Justin tapped a finger on his chin sarcastically. "Hmm, I don't know . . . maybe because they're *rich* and bought their way in?"

Stacy stopped short, hands on her hips. "How dare you say that, Justin! My parents would never . . . I mean, like, they couldn't have . . . They wouldn't have been able . . ." She turned and looked at Matt. "Would they have been able to?"

"I don't know," he answered.

"Does it really matter at this point?" Cody rubbed his face. "I mean, we're all here. We all made it. Let's go find the rest of Stacy's family. I'm ready to sit for a spell."

All four of Stacy's siblings were safely tucked away in their pods.

Some people get all the luck, Matt thought. But he was too tired to feel bitter. He *was* happy for her. And he had to give her credit— her usual disregard for the feelings of those around her seemed to be dampened at the moment. Maybe she was still trying to decide if her parents gamed the system somehow. Or maybe she'd finally tapped into the empathy reserve she'd been hiding.

When the four teens stepped out into the open from the cryopod section, Suzanne met them. "I know you all are tired and need to clean up and get some rest, but is it okay if we just have a short, informal meeting before you do that?"

Matt looked at the others, and they all nodded. "Sure," he answered for the group.

Suzanne called the adults over, and they arranged the chairs in a circle so they could all see and hear each other.

"Well, first I want to welcome our new arrivals," Suzanne began. "Matt, Justin, Stacy, and Cody—the only survivors of the seventeen-year-olds' column."

The short, blond-haired man who'd greeted them spoke. "Yeah, welcome. We're all gonna starve, but welcome."

"Eric is our resident pessimist," Suzanne said.

Before Matt could even organize his thoughts into a response, Stacy jumped up, walked over to Eric, and stood in front of him as he wilted away from her in his chair.

CHAPTER 41

Stacy thrust her hands on her hips and raised an angry eyebrow. "Listen, jerk face! We've been through hell out there in the godforsaken apocalyptic *real* world while you've been inside this vault cowering in fear. If you're so worried about *starving*, maybe you should go out there and hunt down a few of the giant killer insects that dragged my Lance-Darin away and *ate him alive*!" She leaned closer to his face with each of her last three words, her voice rising in pitch.

Suzanne glanced at Matt, eyes a little wide. "You're right, Stacy. Eric is being insensitive." She cast Eric a scowl as Stacy whirled about and returned to her seat. "We are very happy you made your way here. And we have enough provisions to sustain us for a while."

"And we haven't even finished exploring this whole place. There could be more," Dave added.

"I agree with Miss Suzanne." Robby nodded in her direction. "Glad to have y'all here." He pointed at Cody and grinned. "Especially you, Tex. Now I ain't the only Southern boy here for them to make fun of."

Cody gave him a half-hearted smile.

"We do need to be conservative, however," Dave said, looking down at the floor. "I propose that we refrain from awakening anyone else for the time being so as to sustain the limited resources we have at this time. We can revisit this decision when we've been able to procure more food."

Eric straightened up like he was going to say something, but with a nervous glance at Stacy, he slumped back down.

"How do you kids feel about that?" Suzanne asked.

Cody, Justin, and Stacy looked at Matt to answer. He sighed, still the reluctant leader. "I agree. The good news is that we know a few places where we can get supplies, and one of those isn't too far from here. The bad news is that it'll be dangerous to get there and back."

"What kind of supplies?" Eric asked.

Matt, Cody, Justin, and Stacy took turns telling them about the hotel and the big storage building, the Sev, and the HZRD building. They outlined the dangers involved in getting to each place, and agreed with each other that the HZRD area should be considered off limits like a dangerous, condemned building, falling apart piece by enormous piece. Matt knew *he*, for one, would not be going back down into that underground death trap.

"I am relieved to hear about large stores of food nearby. We will have to work on finding a safer route back to the hotel than the one you took here," Dave said. "This seems like the safest place for us for the time being, and hopefully we can learn more about keeping the pods going and the inhabitants safe. We found a large supply of the nutritional substance being pumped through the feeding tubes, and the people in suspended animation need very little of it while their systems are sleeping—just enough to keep vital functions supported. Hopefully it will be enough to keep them safe in their cryogenic pods until the apocalypse stabilizes."

"But, like, *is* it safe here?" Stacy asked.

Dave looked at Suzanne and shrugged.

"That's a good question," Suzanne said. "I mean, I think it's safe for now. Our only threat is if we have to wake more people up when columns start to fail. We will run out of food and water."

"Yeah, but Westbrook said the vault was failing. That's why he piled our pods all up on a truck and took off," Justin said.

The adults all looked at each other, an air of confusion around them. Suzanne shook her head. "I don't know. I honestly don't know. He seemed so frantic when he woke Dave and me up. But we were both so dazed, and he rushed through his instructions to us. He spent a total of maybe five minutes telling us how to keep the pods going, then he rushed out of here, telling us he'd be back."

"Yes, Suzanne is correct," Dave added. "The pods that were inoperative at that time seem to have been that way for a while. They were not newly compromised."

Matt clenched his fists. "Darin was right about the whole thing. Westbrook was crazy and just wanted to be the savior of humanity. That's why he made Darin set off the explosion, and that's why he faked the vault failure."

Matt spent a few minutes putting the whole story together. West-brook faking a meteor strike, making Darin explode the outside, causing the columns to fail so he could continue the lie of saving people. Placing them in the HZRD building and becoming their leader.

The adults listened intently while Matt threaded it all together. When he mentioned they were on an island, it took a little convincing, but by the end, they all agreed that Westbrook's twisted plan was the whole reason they were in this mess.

"Some savior," Justin scoffed. "His stupid scheme just ended up killing him and most of our group."

"Okay," Matt said, "so we should be reasonably safe here. What do you all know about how to keep the pods going?"

"Not much, I'm afraid," Dave said. "We've been lucky so far. I've been able to figure out what some of the alarms mean and how to stave off disaster. There aren't any instructional manuals I've been able to find around here."

Matt nodded, making up his mind. "I'll take Westbrook's place for the time being, then. I've seen how he ran this place by watching the VHS tapes he stowed in my pod. It isn't as good as an instruction manual, but it will have to do for now. I'll take care of the pods until I can teach someone else."

"Great." Suzanne clasped her hands together. "Let me show you four where the shower is and where you can get some rest."

CHAPTER 42

"This is awesome!" Jake said with a mouthful of some sort of pasta dish he'd chosen from the box of MREs Matt and Cody had brought back from their latest trip to the hotel. The young boy's lips and half of his face was slathered in the red sauce. The months had passed, and everyone was happier and healthier.

Suzanne finished chewing and swallowed before she said, "Jake, don't talk with your mouth full. And I agree." She turned to Matt. "I'm so glad Cody got that big truck running and the two of you found a safer route back to the hotel. I was really getting tired of eating dried fruit and stale nuts."

"How much food did you say is stored there?" Dave laid out each package from the MRE he'd chosen in a neat line, starting with the main course and ending with the dessert.

"A crap ton," Cody answered.

"I noticed y'all brought back some guns and ammo this time." Robby licked gravy off his fingers. "Y'all still plannin' on trying to hunt some of those bugs?"

"Yeah," Matt said. "I think so. Even if they end up not being edible, killing them off will make this place a lot safer."

"Eww." Stacy screwed her face up in disgust. "Edible? Gag me with a spoon!"

"Whatever, Stace," Justin said. "You told me the other day that you've eaten *snails* before. Not that big of a difference, in my opinion."

"Uhh, like, escargot is a delicacy."

Suzanne laughed. "You know, people all over the world subsist on insects like grasshoppers and dragonflies, even tarantulas, during the lean months of the year."

"No thank you!" Stacy huffed. "I won't eat them, but I'll sure help you kill the evil demons."

They ate in silence for several minutes. Matt thought about how they'd all settled into a routine of sorts in the months since arriving at the vault. He'd been able to train a couple of the adults on how to take care of the cryopods and keep the people inside alive. Since finding a safer route to the hotel, they'd been able to bring back food and other supplies a couple of times.

Matt looked around the area they'd designated as the dining room. A couple of the most recently awakened people sat talking two tables over. Matt was anxious to wake his mom, but agreed with the lottery system Dave had come up with to make it fair. Every few weeks, after bringing in new supplies, a couple of the awake people were chosen in a drawing, and those people got to pick who to wake up next. Supplies weren't the only thing he'd brought from the hotel. He'd finally worked up the nerve to bring the tape recorder back. He desperately wanted to hear Catherine's voice again.

Robby and one of the newly awakened women strolled in from the warehouse. Robby wiped dirt from his hands onto his pants. Matt smiled, remembering the "yee haw!" the country-born man had hollered when Matt handed him a pair of jeans he'd brought back from the storage building at the hotel. Robby and the woman, Julie, had been working on nutrifying a large section of soil beds out in the warehouse in the hopes they would soon be able to grow some food. There were enough packets of seeds in the storage building to cover the entire island, and then some, with fruit and vegetables.

"How's it looking out there?" Matt asked.

Robby smiled at Julie, and they sat across from him. "Great! I think we'll be ready to plant our first experimental crops within the next week or two."

"What are you going to plant?" Matt was hoping for watermelon.

"We'll start with the vegetables we know are the easiest to grow," Julie said. "Carrots, green beans, squash, and tomatoes."

"No fruit?" Matt asked.

"If the veggies start growing, we'll try some fruit." Robby smiled. "Berries are pretty easy to grow, so we'll start with some strawberries, raspberries, and blueberries. How does that sound?"

Matt nodded. "Sounds great. To be honest with you, anything fresh sounds good, even green beans."

Robby laughed and gripped Matt's shoulder as he stood. "I'm

gonna go check out the MREs y'all brought back today. I'm starvin'."
He looked down at Julie. "Want me to bring you something?"

She shook her head and stood. "I'll come with you. I want to see what the choices are."

Matt finished his meal and gathered up the packages. After throwing his trash in the compactor, he entered the office.

"How's it going?" he asked.

Stacy swiveled in the chair. "Great! The alarms look good and the columns are stable for the time being."

"None have failed for a while."

"I know," she said. "It's a miracle."

"You're the miracle, Stacy." Matt put a hand on her shoulder. "Without you keeping an eye on all this tech on a constant basis, we would be SOL."

"Well, thanks, Matt. I truly love it. It's like my calling in life or something like that."

"It truly is." He turned to leave.

"Hey, Matt?" Stacy said.

"Yeah."

"One of these times you go back to the hotel, can you grab that computer from the lab?"

"Absolutely!"

"It'll be super helpful to monitor the columns. You know, make sure there's no glitches in the system."

"We will pick it up for you."

Matt left the area they deemed the office and stood in front of his mom's column, staring up at her pod. He missed her and wanted so badly to be able to wake her up. He wanted to tell her about Catherine—the others, too, but mostly Catherine. Matt sighed and continued on to the last column. A couple of the columns there had been having issues. He was worried they were going to completely fail before they had enough supplies to wake them all up. None of them wanted more people to die—not from either a failing pod or from starvation.

Matt clenched his jaw; his anger at Westbrook flared anew every time he thought about the intentional damage that had been done when he'd sent a young Darin out to set off explosions so the scientist could artificially save the world. Plus, who knew what other intentional sabotage he'd pulled when Darin was in cryosleep? The breach had been fixed, and the cave itself was a good enough shelter for the time being, but the damage had been done and the columns would fail sooner or later—especially these ones. Matt climbed up the ladder in front of him, carefully checking the tubes and wires keeping the inhabitants of the pods alive in frozen sleep.

As he climbed back down, footsteps echoed down the row toward him. "I figured you'd be down here checkin' on these columns," Cody said. "How are they doin'?"

"Okay for now." Matt stepped off the last rung onto the cement floor. "What's up? Is everything okay?"

"Everything's good. The others asked me to come get ya. Dave did the math on the supplies we brought back and gave the green light to do another drawing to wake a couple more people up. They're all waitin' for you to get started."

CHAPTER 43

Lily, the ten-year-old girl who had brought Matt and his friends food and drinks their first day there, stuck the tip of her tongue out in concentration as she reached into the large tin coffee can and stirred the small slips of paper inside. The can was held aloft by Suzanne, high enough that Lily couldn't see into it.

"Come on, Lily, just pick one," an exasperated Jake whined.

With an annoyed look in Jake's direction, Lily pulled a piece of paper out of the can. She unfolded it and looked at it, then smiled over at Matt where he stood off to the side of the crowd. "Matt Voorhees!" she shouted.

"Yes!" Matt pumped a fist in the air as Cody pounded him on the back in celebration. For the first time since finding the vault, Matt felt relief. He didn't expect the tears, but they came without warning. Then sadness struck. He was waking her up, only to tell her his dad was gone. He pushed that feeling aside for now. This was his first true win since being put into cryosleep decades ago.

* * *

The built-in lift for column forty-two moved Pat Voorhees's pod horizontally until it cleared the pods below it. Dave, standing on the column's ladder next to it, unplugged the wires connecting it to the power source running through the center of the pillar. He signaled a thumbs-up down to Cody, who toggled the switch that started the pod on its slow descent to the ground.

Matt shifted his weight back and forth from one foot to the other. His stomach fluttered, and he ran his hand over the short stubble of his fresh buzz cut. The closer the pod got to the floor, the faster his heart raced—he thought he might faint. He bent at the waist, resting his sweaty palms on his knees.

Justin stepped over to him and gripped both of Matt's shoulders in his hands, squeezing just enough to hurt a little. "Relax, chief. This is what you've been wanting since day one at Camp New Beginnings. It'd be a real bummer if your mom woke up to find you sprawled on the floor, passed out like a drunk who's been on a three-day bender."

Matt nodded. Justin was right. He took a slow, deep breath, then blew it out through pursed lips. He stood up and looked Justin in the eyes. "Thanks, man. I think I'm okay now."

With one more squeeze to his shoulders, Justin gave a quick head nod and moved to stand next to Stacy.

The pod now safely on the floor, Matt stepped up to it and slipped the chain with the spare key they found in Westbrooks's effects from around his neck. A solemn memory of Catherine and how she found the key on the first day entered his mind. He grasped the key in his shaky hand and fit it into the inconspicuous lock that was flush with the plastic. With a twist of his wrist, the airtight lid hissed, and Matt lifted it, smiling down at his mom.

Her eyes fluttered open. She blinked a few times before focusing in on her son. "Matt." Her voice cracked as it adjusted to being used after decades of lying dormant. She grabbed his hands and started to sit up. "Did we make it? Is it over?"

Matt gently urged her back down, gripping her hands as tears formed in his eyes. "Mom, lie back for a minute while we get the feeding tube out."

Suzanne stepped up next to him, removed the feeding tube, placed a piece of gauze over the site, and taped it down. She laid a plastic bag on his mom's lap, gave Matt's arm a squeeze, and stepped away from the long-awaited reunion of mother and son.

Oh yeah, Matt thought. *I almost forgot.* "Mom, you're probably going to throw up." He let go of her hands and gave her the bag—just in time—as her face turned ashen and she retched into it.

When she appeared to be done, Suzanne handed her a damp washcloth and a cup of water and took the bag of vomit from her.

Matt's mom wiped her face and rinsed her mouth out, then took his hands again and smiled up at him.

"Okay, Mom," Matt said, "when you're ready, I'll help you out of this thing." He turned his head to wipe tears away on his shoulder.

"I'm ready, sweetheart."

She swung her legs over the side and Matt helped her stand. As soon as her feet hit the floor, she pulled him in for a hug that lasted several minutes. She finally pulled away just enough to look at him.

"Matty, you look so good. How long have you been out? Where's your dad?" She craned her neck to look around him.

Matt took a breath; this was the moment he had been dreading. "There's a lot I need to tell you. Let's go sit down so we can talk." He didn't dare look at her face. He knew she'd see straight through to his sorrow, and he wanted to delay her grief for just a minute longer. He took her by the arm and led her out of the cryopod area to a corner of the common room, where he'd set up two chairs and had a wool blanket waiting for her.

As Pat Voorhees sat wrapped in the scratchy blanket, Matt sat across from her, knee to knee. "Mom." His guts twisted like he was just hearing the news again for the first time. "He . . . Dad . . . He didn't make it. I'm so sorry." The dam broke, and Matt's vision—his face, his throat, everything—flooded with tears. "His pod failed. He was gone when I got here . . . when I got back here." He shook his head. There was so much to tell her.

His mom lunged toward him and he opened his arms to accept her in his embrace. Matt's heart ached for her. It ached for him. Their shared grief seemed to multiply the sorrow, at least for a time. She sobbed in his arms as the tears silently slid down his face. He would be strong for her. She needed him to be strong.

"I loved your dad so much," she whispered in a quavering voice. "He was my knight in shining armor. My best friend. He was the best dad. The best husband."

Matt nodded, holding her tighter.

When her sobs subsided, she leaned into his chest for a few minutes longer before sitting back in her chair. She touched his face like she'd always done when he was younger. "You seem so much older, more mature. Tell me what you've been through."

So he told her everything.

"I'm confused." She shook her head. "This man—Westbrook—he knowingly put you in a deadly soundstage? A made-up simulation?"

"Yes." Matt nodded. "And if he hadn't wrecked and died, you'd all be there too."

Her face twisted with anger. "No, we wouldn't. Surely we'd be dead. At least half of us. Five thousand people with few resources, deadly weather, and a madman at the helm . . . Fully grown adults don't do as well under pressure as you four did. I hate that he did this to the four of you."

"I need to fess up, Mom. Camp New Beginnings was just the tip of the iceberg." Matt's eyes filled with tears. "There were eleven of us."

"Eleven?!" Pat's voice cracked. She pulled her son into a hug, and she cried. "Seven *kids* died?"

And here it was. Matt had the macabre task of retelling each and every death in detail. He smiled and choked back tears when talking about Catherine. Her loss still stung him to his core.

"You really liked her, didn't you, Matt?"

"I did. I loved her."

Pat cocked her head to the side, and a sad smile formed on her face. "For love to exist, utter heartbreak must, too, I'm afraid. I'm so sorry."

He'd never considered that before. "I guess that makes sense. Same as how you can't have good without evil. Westbrook was evil."

Matt continued pausing when he needed a break, and doing his Matt-itation when things were too overwhelming.

"I didn't know you still did that." Pat rested a hand on his knee. Her demeanor had softened—no longer furious with the circumstances Dr. Westbrook had put them in. "Does it still keep the scaries away?"

"Yeah!" Matt stifled a laugh. "But don't call it 'the scaries.' I'm almost eighteen—actually, I'm probably like forty years old or something in real time."

"Sorry, old man." She beamed.

"For real, Mom, I don't think I could have coped, let alone led, without it. You and Dad..."

"I know, honey, I know," she reassured him. "Tell me the rest."

Matt couldn't bring himself to look her in the eyes, and instead powered through the rest.

". . . So me, Cody, Justin, and Stacy have been going out to scavenge supplies. We've been cleaning out the hotel a little each time we go there. Even though it's only partially finished, I think it'll be a good place for some of us to stay when it gets too crowded here. And there's one more thing. Before we made our final push here, the six of us—including Darin and Catherine—made a recording. Do you want to hear it? A lot of it was what I've already told you, but I'm sure I've forgotten some things. Or we can skip to the end, and you can hear the best part."

"You pick, I trust your judgment."

Matt hesitated, then rewound until he found their final entry. Ghosts from the past, the speakers crackled to life. He knew what his friends, the six musketeers as Catherine had called them, were about to say. But still, he sat on the edge of his seat. Darin's voice haunted him, and it probably always would. He was a traumatized boy, and Matt had pushed him, maybe too hard, for the truth.

His mother stayed silent the duration of the tape until Catherine spoke.

"She had a lovely voice, Matt."

"Yeah, she did." He bit his lip. The tape finally stopped with a *click*. "Well, now you know everything. Do you have any questions?"

"Not right now. It's a lot to process," his mom said. "Matt, thank you."

"For what?"

"For waking me up. For being so brave, so grown up. For getting food for everyone and making sure the pods are safe. For everything. You amaze me."

"You're welcome, Mom. I just want you to know that my intentions are good."

EPILOGUE

The military cargo truck bounced along the terrain at a faster speed than they probably should have been going. The boombox in Justin's lap blared Bruce Springsteen's "Born in the USA." Deena, a sixteen-year-old newcomer, sang along, dancing on the seat between Matt and Justin. Matt had only been mildly surprised when Justin had won the lottery and picked the two girls to wake up instead of his parents. He'd just grinned at his friends and promised to pick his parents next time. Matt doubted it, though. Maybe this was Justin's payback for the neglect he'd endured growing up. Or maybe, he was just deeply determined to find a girlfriend. Either way, Justin seemed happier than ever.

"Maybe you should slow down a little," Brandi, also sixteen, shouted, flanked by Cody and Justin.

The five of them were crammed into the cab of the big truck, but none of them seemed to mind.

Matt reached across Deena and turned the music down. "I can't believe how many times we drove or walked past that entrance to the HZRD this morning."

"Yeah," Justin agreed. "It was hidden in plain sight behind that outcropping of lava rocks."

"I seriously can't believe the government built that place." Brandi shook her head. "It's just crazy."

"Yeah. It's like some insane parody of *Raiders of the Lost Ark*, but without the treasure." Deena held on to the dashboard as the truck bounced over a large rut.

Matt smiled at her comparison and slowed down just a little.

Maybe he and Deena had some things in common. He'd have to quiz her on her movie knowledge later.

"At least we'll be able to find it next time," Cody said. "I think we'll have the Sev cleared out with one or two more trips. This truck holds a crap ton of food and equipment."

"You guys really came all this way on foot before?" Brandi asked.

"Mostly," Justin said. "When we were underground, we traveled by tram some of the way, and we had a Wagoneer for a short time."

Matt pulled up to the vault and put the truck in Park. "How long do you think it took us to get back here today?"

"A couple of hours, maybe," Cody answered.

Matt shook his head and jumped down from the tall cab. He opened the overhead door, then got back in the truck and pulled it into the warehouse. He cranked on the wheel, turning the big truck around in the space between the partially framed-in rooms on either side of the warehouse. One of those rooms would be his and his mom's. It would be nice to have a private space for the two of them. The piles of construction material at the hotel had come in handy for this project.

Backing the truck up to the industrial garage door, Matt used the side mirrors to determine when to stop. He put the truck in Park and turned off the ignition. The five teens jumped down from the cab. He walked past the crops, which were full grown—they had been harvesting fresh vegetables for a couple of weeks now. Carrots lined rows that were sprouting mature, lacy stems off the sweet, plump orange root vegetable. It was in contrast to the nine-foot-tall soft, hairy-stemmed tomato plant. Its dark green odorous leaflets were holding on to ripe, bulbous red tomatoes.

Deena slapped his hand when he reached out to pluck a juicy red tomato from its stalk.

"You know the rules," she said.

"I know," Matt said. "I just love tomatoes. Thanks for being there in my weakness."

Deena blinked her big blue eyes and parted her lips to speak, but words didn't come out. She smiled and cocked her head to one side.

Matt cleared his throat. "Hey, have you seen *Attack of the Killer Tomatoe*s?"

"That cheesy movie? I did see it."

"Yeah, it was cheesy, wasn't it?"

"I loved it!"

"Oh good. Me too." Matt's hand brushed the back of hers, and for a fleeting second, he felt complete once more.

He pounded on the inner vault door. As it slowly opened, he

flipped up the canvas shell covering the back of the truck to reveal boxes of canned food and other items filling the cargo bed.

Matt retrieved a small cardboard box and put it under his arm.

"Did you get it?" Stacy asked.

"Yup," he replied. "More floppy disks for our resident IT supervisor."

Looking over their latest haul, he said to the gathering group of people, "There's more where that came from."

Stacy playfully elbowed Matt in the ribs. "I can't believe everything that's happened since we woke up in our pods. Now here we are, figuring everything out. Makes me wonder what will happen next."

"Next? Next, we live. We live for all the people we lost. We just live."

THE END

As a kid, Tyler H. Jolley always had a knack for storytelling. When he grew bored of old fables, he created his own exciting and unique worlds. Many years later, he still had so many new ideas and stories swirling in his head, but with nowhere to share them. That's when he put his pencil to paper and let the creative juices flow.

His breakthrough novel, EXTRACTED, came out in 2013 and swiftly became an Amazon Best Seller and Spencer Hill Press Best Seller. Since then, Tyler has been busy publishing over a dozen books.

He reexamined the publishing process and created an efficient way to get his countless ideas into print. Tyler definitely didn't like to work alone, so he restructured his writing methods into a team approach.

When he's not writing, you can find him at his orthodontic practice, mountain biking, or on the hunt for the perfect doughnut.

Twitter: @Docjolley
Facebook: https://www.facebook.com/tyler.jolley.319/
Instagram: https://www.instagram.com/tylerhjolley/